PASSION PATROL SERIES

CROWNS

Hot cops. Hot crime. Hot romance.

BY
EMMA CALIN

CONTENTS

CHAPTER 1

The first bullet hit an officer seated behind her in the personnel carrier. Something wet splashed her cheek and the exposed skin of her neck. The windscreen crazed into an opaque spider's web. She wound down the driver's door glass and pushed her head out into the cold London night. She slammed down the throttle, aiming the vehicle for the end of the street. Metropolitan Police radios were yelling, "Urgent assistance—live fire." She'd fucking well assessed that one already. Everything else was a complete bloody mystery.

The engine screeched and jammed. A bullet whined close by in the darkness. Twenty minutes earlier Sergeant Sophia Castellana had been working an overtime shift on routine crowd control at a football game between Crystal Palace and Tottenham Hotspur. The lives of her crew now depended on her judgment. Perhaps one or more were already dead. Just why the hell had she brought them here? They'd been on the way back to Streatham police station when she'd taken the call to a burglary in progress at some posh place in Dulwich. There was a frantic whimpering behind her mixed with a sound of machine gun fire further away.

"What's the score back there?" she yelled.

"Simon's lost half his head," came the response.

"Dead?"

"Yeah."

"Right—leave him and bail out. Keep low, spread out and use the parked cars as cover. We're all dead if we stay here."

"We could be dead out there," said a young female voice.

Sophia had never spoken to the kid but knew her as a new graduate entry straight out of the box.

"Do as you're fucking well told 'cos we won't be coming back to drag your corpse out of the bus. We'll try to regroup round the corner on the road ahead of us. Go now!"

The doors opened and twelve unarmed regular London bobbies scattered, diving into the shadows of parked vehicles. Bullets slammed into the stricken personnel carrier, shaking it on its springs. Sophia barged open the driver's door and rolled across the street to the gutter. At least now they weren't just one big white target in the night. The merciful shelter of an SUV gave her time to think. Just what the hell was happening?

She crawled out enough to look back down the street. The buildings were exclusive townhouses with railings and maybe basements. Her radio wasn't set to the area frequency but she guessed local units were also around her in the shadows. About fifty yards away on the other side of the street the front door of a house was. The interior was lit by an opulent chandelier. Outside was a light-colored BMW, engine running. A wave of realization that PC Simon Westcott, community cop and father of three kids, was dead in the back of the bus almost choked her. Think Sophia—get a grip and think. Some bastard had fired on them and the odds were that they were still at that house with the open door. If the BMW was the getaway car, the wreck of her bus was blocking the escape.

To Sophia's eyes the weapon in the hand of the hooded guy in the doorway was straight out of the BBC news. It might have been Paris, Brussels, Syria or some piece of sand with pick-up trucks, flags, and bandannas. He was yelling at a figure on the ground in the hallway of the house. She made her way along the far side of the parked cars, focusing on the gun with the curved horn-like shape hanging underneath. She had no firearms training but this had to be the machine gunner. The gunman turned his back to her. The same curved horn projected from the rear pocket of his jeans. She watched him calmly push his foot onto the neck of the guy on the floor as he reached behind. He flipped the other device from the gun. She got it. He was reloading and about to perform at least his second kill of the day.

She measured the distance. It was a straight 35-yard dash to the door. If she could hit the gunman at full speed with her 127 pounds before he could re-load there was a chance—just this one chance. About ten yards from impact she remembered she had set the timer for a curry in her oven. Well, what the fuck? She lived alone.

She heard the click of the magazine as she smashed into his back. He crashed forward into the base of a long case grandfather clock. She had no idea what to do next. She was sprawled partly on the legs of the gunman and partly on top of the guy on the floor. God, he was young, almost half her age, twenty-five at most. He scrambled up and looked at her.

"Jump on him—kick his fucking balls in," she screamed.

She swung her boot into the gunman's face as he tried to wriggle the gun from under his body. He was white, clean-shaven, about thirty and built like a commando. She stamped on his hands and wrists in a frenzy of fear and anger. The young man knelt on the killer's shoulders and held him by his gingery curly hair.

For a second their eyes met as he looked up into her face. Probably he was as afraid as her but he had a calmness almost as if he had already accepted death.

"What's your name?" he said.

"What's my name? Bloody 'ell...."

The banality and weirdness of the question stunned her as much as everything that had happened. What was all this?

"Tell me—please. I may not get the chance to find out."

The gunman was writhing under their weight. She could see that his face was swelling in the classic sign of a fractured jaw, the gun still trapped beneath him.

"Sophia. Sergeant Sophia Castellana."

The young man almost smiled. His eyes were dark, his skin slightly olive and smooth. She wondered if he'd ever shaved.

The muzzle of a Police Diplomatic Protection Group issue Glock 17 weapon stopped a few inches from the gunman's head. The hall had filled with cops.

"Put your hands behind your back," said a hard voice tinged with military steel. It was the kind of voice that didn't ask questions.

She looked around. A dozen weapons were trained on the back of the felled gunman. She heard the ratchet and snap of handcuffs. There was a smell of adrenalin-pumping fear which she knew as her own. She was fighting to hold back tears. Plain clothes Protection Squad type officers surrounded the young man as they ushered him away. He was tall enough to look over and catch her eyes one last time. He nodded calmly at her.

"I won't forget you. I'll never forget," he said.

CHAPTER 2

A hand was on her arm. There was a kind male voice.

"Sergeant, there's a lot to sort out here. You can relax now and come with me."

"Who are you?"

"I'm Chief Inspector Mel Kendrick."

She studied him. This guy was either gay or had a wife with the best coordinated fashion sense in the Met' Police. He had an air of urbane nonchalance like his expensive cologne and his Posh and Dandy cream silk tie. His thinning hair was impeccably cut and too long for a gutter monkey detective.

"There's statements to write and I've left a dead friend out there in the bus. Dead mates deserve a page or two, Guv'nor."

She was fighting to hold it together now. Christ! What bloody nightmare had she wandered into? She'd never thrown up outside of drunkenness or food poisoning. Nothing eighteen years in the police had shown her had caused her to vomit.

"I know. I know," he said. "Everything's in good hands. We need to clean you up and approach it in an organized way."

Clean up. Sure, she could feel dried blood cracking on her cheek. She put her hand to her white police shirt collar. There was soft tissue and blood between the fabric and her skin. She looked at it on her fingers. She knew what it was.

She let him lead her outside. The BMW she'd seen was now slewed across the road. She noted the bullet holes and the pale face of death on the driver. There must have been a shootout while she'd been inside. She had had no sense of time or reality. She flashed back to a childhood day going into the cinema in the sun and coming out in the rain. She felt ashamed of the thought. A driver opened the rear door of a maroon Range Rover and set off at once. The late November evening was cold and the vehicle was warm and luxurious. Nothing like cold death. They were heading north, away from her home territory.

"What? We goin' up west to see the Christmas lights?" she asked.

If she could just keep her tough shiny edge she would be able to cut through these next few days and hours.

"Somewhere up that way," said the Chief Inspector from the seat beside her.

She snapped back into sharp focus.

"Where's my crew? Did they make it?"

"Yes, except the officer in the personnel carrier."

She slumped forward. Christ she'd known the man for eight years.

"I should be telling his missus," she said.

"There's a team already on the job, Sophia," said the smooth senior detective.

"You checked out my shoulder number?"

She watched him nod. He was some weird kind of cop—somewhere between Jeeves and James Bond.

"I think you ought to know I've got a curry on fire in my oven, Guv."

"We're on top of it."

"You've called the fire brigade or what?"

"You need to check out your front door lock, Sophia," he replied with a raised eyebrow.

"Look, sir: none of this is making sense. Who's in my flat?"

Chief Inspector Mel Kendrick took a deep breath.

"You deserve an answer. You're one hell of a brave woman from a bus out of hell. Of all the jobs in all the world why did you have to walk into mine?"

"Are you on the level, mister? Show me a warrant card or I'll lock you up for impersonating a cop." she said, letting her voice convey real edge. An officer was dead and this lounge lizard was quoting lines from movies for Christ's sake.

He reached into his jacket pocket, giving her a glimpse of a police royalty protection issue Glock 26. He handed her his ID. It showed a regular Metropolitan Police photo and metal badge.

"Look, I took a call to a burglary. I had a couple of probationers on board and I thought it would get their blood pumping."

"You did the right thing. You did a fantastic thing," he replied.

"So what kind of burglary was that?"

He looked her in the eye and nodded slowly.

"I'm afraid you're not going to know much more than what you know now. It was a routine burglary except that the villain had a gun. A hero cop was shot."

She let out a long sigh. This stank of some stitch-up.

The Range Rover had stopped in a private car park behind a small red-brick block of flats. An armed cop was in the lobby nursing his Heckler and

Koch MP5 assault rifle. She'd caught a street sign telling her it was Ebury Street SW1. Buckingham Palace was just about two blocks away.

"So what's here?" she asked.

"You can change and clean up. It's a job place."

"Why can't we go to a police station?"

"Because we need to keep you away from unwanted eyes," he said. "Follow me and don't even think of being difficult."

She heard the Range Rover driver close behind her. The armed cop stepped out of the door as they approached. It wasn't like she felt threatened—just that she knew for sure not to be difficult.

They climbed plain concrete steps to the first floor. The Chief Inspector opened the dated 70s style pale yellow door with a heavy deadlock key. She heard serious metal bolts operate. The inside of the door was a single steel sheet. There was a smell of coffee and the sound of a Nespresso machine. A matronly woman in police civilian uniform was in a small kitchen.

"Jean will take you for a shower," he said.

"What about forensics? There's evidence of both those guys all over me and that's without police blood and brain tissue," she snapped.

"You're a real pro, Sophia, but I'm the senior detective officer here," he said with a cat's tail tweak of the eyebrow.

"So don't be difficult," she said.

"Jean will look after you." He nodded at the woman. "Milk, sugar?" he asked.

"Whisky," she said.

He smiled slowly.

"You got it."

Jean wasn't big on conversation. She had a black plastic sack, a white bath towel, and a white paper body suit.

"Give me your clothes," she said once the bathroom door was closed.

"You going to watch me?"

The woman shrugged.

"There's everything you need in the shower."

She was losing the will to resist. She should have parked up the bus and been at home with a curry. Her night shift as patrol sergeant in the south London area of Streatham started at ten o'clock. Simon Westcott was dead. She'd fought some lunatic with a machine gun and to round off a perfect day, she'd been kidnapped by the police.

She threw off her clothes and stepped into the shower. Her dark bobbed hair was stiff with blood. She watched the stained water circle the plughole. A growing bruise on her left breast hurt as she applied the soap. She didn't care anymore. The water took away her tears.

CHAPTER 3

A TV was on in the small lounge. Mel Kendrick handed her a generous scotch with ice. Even though she was there more or less without consent she smiled with a nod of gratitude. His eyes were pale with a flicker of kindness, still not completely burned out. She sat down on a brown leather armchair.

"You're in time for the news," he said.

The American president Ronald Grump was making a trip to Europe. The French president Martine La Plume was shaking his hand. Next up were the routine wars and riots. The bottom band was showing breaking news: "London police officer shot … police hunting suspect."

She did a double take. The Chief Inspector was watching her. The news crew had found a witness. The face of a young shaven-headed guy filled the screen.

"I was riding my bike. The gunman must have seen the police van coming. He had a gun and fired straight at 'em—bang, bang."

Sophia watched in amazement. She hadn't seen this guy.

"Did you see the gun?"

"Yeah. It was … like a real gun."

"What sort of gun?" demanded a reporter.

"Ya know—like a handgun—like a James Bond gun."

Sophia leaned forward shaking her head.

"What? Where did they find this idiot?"

"He's one of ours, Sophia."

"What? W.T.F., Chief Inspector?"

Her heart was racing. She took a gulp of the scotch. Dressed in only a one-piece paper body suit with no bra or underwear she felt exposed and ridiculous. Her hair was wet and turning to a ball of tangled frizz. The witness was telling his story.

"The killer ran off towards Pimlico and a couple of coppers ran after him but they were miles behind," he said.

"This is fantasy," she said.

"Absolutely, but it is the official story. And Sophia, that's the way we want you to tell it. The other officers on your crew didn't see anyone. All the other cops were on my squad."

"There was a dead man in the BMW. The personnel bus was shot full of holes."

"Did you see those vehicles on TV?

"No, and where's the stiff? And Christ, where's the machine gunner and the young bloke who was on the floor in the house?"

"What stiff? What machine gunner? What young bloke? What house? You acted alone Sergeant. You decided not to lead your crew to safety. You drove into a dangerous situation without a proper risk assessment. A discipline panel could lose you your rank or even your job."

She fixed her eyes on his, trying to read his mind. She was out of her depth and his suave pleasantness was ruthless.

"Bollocks!"

"Health and safety politically correct bollocks," he said firmly.

"OK. I'm a straight simple cop. There's going to be an inquest and an autopsy on a dead bobby. The system needs paper and I've got to make up a notebook and write a statement. If what I say is a lie and I get caught, I go to jail for perjury."

"You'll get crown immunity and you won't get caught."

Her mind was beginning to clear. She'd stumbled into something bigger than her little life. She was a divorced woman of thirty-eight years. She had a daughter who'd just started at university. If she wasn't a cop she'd be working the till at a gas station which is where she'd come from.

"So where do I write my statement? You got any blank forms?" she asked.

"It will be typed and delivered."

"What's this: Law and Order Deliveroo?" she said.

He smiled.

"You've got balls," he added.

"Glad I haven't, wearing this bloody thing, and what about my night shift?"

"It's covered," he began. "And Sophia, you don't work there any more, Inspector."

"Inspector? I've not even done the promotion exam."

"Did you ever hear me say we worked to the rules? I guess you won't mind a pay raise. It'll make up for the medal and Commissioner's commendation you deserve but you're not going to receive."

"So who do I work for and where?"

"You'll be working at Scotland Yard. That'll be after a short holiday," he said.

"How have you fixed all this up?"

"It's called power, Inspector."

"Like the bloody queen," she said.

Chief Inspector Mel Kendrick smiled and nodded. His look was appraising her.

"You're sharp and tough, Sophia. Just be honest and tell me what you make of me."

"You're gay and you're in some different league of cop to me."

"I was a Detective Sergeant at Streatham a few years ago. It's a long story but well, life's about who you meet and how the world turns. And yes, I'm gay."

"I shouldn't have said that, should I?"

"I'm glad you did. Otherwise you'd be an attractive woman trapped here wondering if I could resist."

She leaned back and laughed. The whisky had hit her brain. What sort of woman was she? A cop had died and the police were in on a cover-up. The TV news was in on it. She was in on it—with a glass of scotch smoother than anything she'd ever tasted in her hand. And she had to admit she didn't mind at all being told she was attractive. She'd forgotten that little novelty.

He refilled her glass and took a shot himself.

"Bottom line, we've had to clear up a mess. You shouldn't have been there, none of it should have happened. A lot of it didn't happen. We could have done without a dead cop, but the job needs heroes if only for PR so we'll take that one as an accidental positive."

She stared at him.

"You're fucking sick," she said.

He fixed her eyes in an equally hard stare.

"Watch that TV for a minute. A dozen or so died in riots in Germany last night. Shit happens and sometimes the stakes are higher than you can imagine. Now pin your ears back and listen. I'm going to tell you all you are ever going to know and it's far more than you should know. Relax and be grateful you're here."

His tone was cold and his face like granite. She was listening. Oh yes, he had her attention.

"Fact number one. There was an officer in that lobby who failed in his duty to kill you. Since I didn't have the balls you're here enjoying my scotch."

She blinked and nodded.

"Fact number two. Since you're alive we've got to take care of you. You will avoid your old mates and colleagues. You will have suffered a breakdown that will prevent you ever going over old memories."

"Why didn't you kill me?"

He took a deep breath.

"Respect for your courage, and—I shouldn't say this—it was your face, or maybe I'm just not a murderer."

"My face?"

"Yes. Yes, I'm a sucker for that aquiline nose noble look," he said.

"Fact number three. You're going to sign an additional copy of the official secrets act and your witness statement and this matter will be over."

"There'll be a funeral and an inquest," she said.

"Your statement will be served as uncontested evidence. You won't be at the funeral."

"Any more facts?"

"Number four. Sophia, I'm really sorry you landed in this shit particularly since we're going to be neighbors."

"Neighbors?"

"Yeah, you're on the floor above this flat."

"Look. You're taking over my life, turning me into a liar, making me turn my back on my friends."

"That's a pretty neat summary but you can only truly lie if you truly know the whole truth. When you took your oath to the queen did you think you were getting an office job with Amazon?"

She slumped back and glanced at the TV. She half watched some coppers in riot gear battling migrants pouring off a French ferry in Dover. Well, at least she was having an easier evening than those guys.

"Answer me one question and you've got a deal," she said.

"What's the question?"

"Who was the young man with the dark hair?"

He stood up, walked to the window and tapped it with his knuckle. The sound was dead and flat.

"Bullet proof," he commented. "And if you don't want to spend the rest of your life behind it I'd advise never telling people about someone who doesn't exist. People will think you're hearing voices. No one's offering you a deal, Inspector. No one."

She read the neat forms in front of her.

"Answer me a second question," she said.

He smiled and affected a weary sigh.

"How many bedrooms in that flat?"

"Two. One for you and one for Izzy," he replied.

The shock of hearing her daughter's name in a stranger's mouth froze her for a moment. These bastards were like burglars turning over her drawers.

He glanced up from a folder.

"I've been reading while you were going through your paperwork."

She signed and pushed the crisp official documents away to the far side of the low coffee table and threw down the black Biro as if it were Macbeth's knife. She didn't want to touch or see them again. She'd lied away a couple of dead bodies, an armed criminal who'd been taken away by police, a machine gun and some other young man who could have been a saint or the devil for all she knew. If they were as good as their word, it was over. And Izzy would have her own room in posh Belgravia when she came back from university for Christmas in December. At last she would have put something impressive in her life.

"So much for girl power," she said.

"Sophia, you don't mean that cliché shit. I saw what you did and you're a ruthless courageous woman. You wanted pure angry revenge for what that bastard had done. Fuck virtue. You can't eat it or spend it. Girl power is for college politics. If you'd been some hairy-arse ugly copper I'd have just blown your brains out and called the cleaners. You've got that look a straight guy would die to hold in his hands and a gay guy would die to wear on his face," he said.

The scotch was getting low. This was an intoxicating world where the gloves were off but lay like warm silk on the groin of her soul. The heat of blood and the noble sorrow of death played drunken music in her heart and filled her with terrifying shame and joy. She could never tell anyone how she felt at this moment. She would never admit to her craving for that jazzed up fix of lust and power that was pulsing in her gut. She'd lied. She'd signed. It was over.

CHAPTER 4

Jean appeared to be her jailer for the night. Sophia took the pill she offered and fell into a dreamless yet draining sleep. She awoke in a room with neither clock nor her phone. Clear winter light crept in around heavy soulless curtains. She was completely naked under a good quality Siberian goose duvet. Sections of her life started to slide-show across her mind. Somewhere in the flicker of consciousness there was a headache, sounds in other rooms and something being dragged across the floor in what must be the flat above. She needed the bathroom.

Jean was seated in the corner. She stood up and pulled the curtains. A stampeding herd of light particles trampled her head back to the pillow.

"This is for you," said Jean tossing her a new wrapped Adidas track suit.

"Don't you guys use underwear?"

"We don't get personal that's all," Jean replied with a shrug. "I'll leave you to get up and fix some coffee."

She dragged herself into the baggy black and white clothes and swung out her feet to find a new pair of trainers and sports socks. They must have thought she was the sporty type. The good news was she hadn't been sick but she wouldn't be cleaning her back teeth just yet. She stood in the kitchen with a mug of black coffee.

"Where's…?"

"There's only me here. You may not see Mel for a while," said Jean.

Sophia's thoughts were spinning in collisions. Simon Westcott was dead. It must be Sunday since she'd been at the Crystal Palace football match yesterday. There were no sounds from outside but she remembered all the windows were bulletproof.

"So what happens to me now?"

Jean smiled at her with a sudden warmth.

"Look, everyone's on your side Sophia," she began.

The kindness in the woman's face and voice ripped her open. She could fight an enemy but a friend was a harder battle.

"Where's my life, my home, my future?" she asked as tears soaked her cheeks.

"I'm only a civilian assistant so I don't know all the answers. They've

18

had to react quickly to the situation. No one was expecting you, Sophia."

"None of this was on my star chart in the Daily Mail either," she began. "What if I just walk away? Walk out this room now?"

"Did you see a cop downstairs?" said Jean.

Sophia nodded.

"They're always there. This is a high security block for police use."

"Why do I need to be here?"

"You don't need to be here but the bosses need to know how you are. You're lucky no one in that incident knows your identity."

She spluttered into her coffee. But someone did know exactly who she was. Just before the Chief Inspector arrived, the young guy had asked her for her name. An alarm bell was ringing in her head. It looked like she knew something they didn't know. For the first time she'd gained a little bit of the high ground a copper always wants. It was time to change the subject.

"So, you're a police civilian jailer, or what?" she asked.

"Something like that. They recruited me and gave me a Mickey Mouse uniform, a pay check, and a pension. Slowly they've brought me in. Once upon a time I was a soldier."

"Like the SAS or something?"

"I trained with them. Some prick tried to rape me so I played sexy and asked him to kiss me. When he went for his slobber I bit his lips off. Pity he didn't ask for a blow job. They said I was too extreme."

Sophia's eyes widened as she took in this stocky woman of about fifty years. Any thought of escape evaporated.

"You're not going to give me any information are you?" said Sophia.

"The first idea in my head is 'No' … but try me."

"What's this all about? Why do I have to be isolated and lie about what happened?"

The older woman studied her face.

"OK, they can't expect you not to ask those questions. I don't know any details. It's part of an operation that is beyond top secret. Something is going down that must *not* become known. And believe me, that is all I know except that the squad are authorized to do more or less anything they have to do to keep the lid on."

Sophia sighed.

"Is it legal?"

"Was it legal to kill Bin Laden? Was it legal for Pinupskin to march into Ukraine? Was it legal for Martine La Plume to seize power and deport half a million migrants from France? Was it legal for President McNichol to seize the oil rigs, to issue Scottish passports and close the border?" Jean replied.

"I really don't take any notice of politics," said Sophia with a weary shake of her head.

"Me neither. I just live in this world. You street cops are so close to the shit end that you don't see anyone swallowing the dinner."

Sophia smiled. The woman was right. Her work and her daughter were her life. She didn't watch TV news or study the papers. She had no news apps and all the hate stuff on Facebook was worse than the trash talk on the streets. A night shift with thugs on the streets of South London was nothing compared to a few minutes with brainy people on Twitter.

"Yeah, I've seen a lot of stuff going on I suppose, but none of that has got anything to do with me being here."

"No, because the story behind you being here hasn't happened yet. Look, Sophia. Respect to you 'cos you're a bloody hero. They don't tell me anything, I'm not even supposed to know it's called Operation Spaniel. Do as they tell you and you'll go back to your old life soon enough. I'm saying this to you as a woman looking out for a sister."

"I'm worried about my daughter. I've no idea where my phone is."

"I can give you a phone if I assess you're cool and we're singing off the same sheet."

"I'm OK. Nothing unusual's going on. I've got the chance to move to a better flat."

"Yup, but the news is pumping out the dead cop story so your daughter will find out about it. Did she know him?"

Her mind went into action. God … yes, of course she knew him. She babysat his kids. Izzy would be frantic and calling her if she'd seen the news. Color drained from her face.

"How can I lie to my own child about it? Where's my phone? She's bound to be calling me."

"She hasn't called yet. She was at a jazz bar last night and she's not touched her phone or laptop yet."

"What the fuck? How do you know that?"

"We needed to know in case you'd called her. Sometimes we have to join up dots if we don't have time for a portrait, Sophia."

"So, you'll give me my phone," she said.

"Look, I don't want to be a jailer. I want you to have it and get back to your life. I shouldn't say this but I like you. Mel likes you and that's why you're still alive."

"You're a well-informed kind of civilian police assistant."

Jean laughed with a wry nod.

"I'm fifty-one years old. I was never a looker. Old Ronald Grump would never have had me on his groping list. I'm a plain middle-aged woman so no one sees me. Try being invisible if you want to see things."

"I like you too," said Sophia, suddenly finding something of her default personality.

Jean went out and came back with an iPhone.

"That's not my phone."

"It is now. When would you normally call her?"

"I'm supposed to be on nights so around teatime."

Sophia looked at the time on the screen. It was three o'clock in the afternoon. The pill and the whisky had knocked her out.

"Call her now. She'll think it strange if you don't tell her about Simon. Tell her you washed your phone and had to change the SIM," ordered Jean.

Sophia didn't even bother to ask if she could be left alone.

"Izzy...."

"Mum. Hi! Oh my God! I didn't wake up and I've got an essay on French pre-modern neo-functionalist literature to get in."

"Better get writing sweetie. Look I've got some news," she began.

"Yeah ... Mum, yeah...."

"Simon Westcott got shot yesterday. He's dead."

"Fuck! What happened?"

"Some punk burglar had a gun. Simon showed up at the wrong time."

"Have they got him?" said Izzy.

Sophia could hear tears in her daughter's voice.

"No, he made off and there's no description."

"Were you there, Mum? Are you OK?"

"I was nearby but I didn't see anything. Yeah, I'm fine. That's the really bad news. I've got a bit of good news too."

Sophia watched Jean's face. She was nodding with a half smile.

"I've been offered another police flat in Belgravia of all places. It's got two bedrooms. I feel such a bitch for being made up with my own life when Simon's dead."

"The little one's only three," sobbed Izzy.

Now Sophia had started she couldn't stop. Thank God she wasn't doing a video call. She took a deep breath.

"We can't change things and the job will look after the family, you know that."

"He was a cool, kind guy," said her daughter.

"Yeah, he was the best. Sweetie, it's sad, but it can happen in this job. I want you to get on and do that essay. I'll get you on Whatsapp later to see how you're getting on."

"You're so strong, Mum. How can you just carry on?"

"Give me a list of other choices, sweet pea," said Sophia. Sometimes she wondered when her daughter would be ready for this world.

"Love you, Mum."

"Love you.... Oh, this is my new number. I washed the phone."

"Mum! You're losing the plot...."

"I'll lose the plot if you don't get on with your essay!"

She laid the phone down on the kitchen work surface and stared at it. She'd told her daughter a lie that she'd have to sustain for the rest of her life or be exposed as a woman unfit to be her mother.

"That really fucking hurt me and you're there smiling at me," she shouted at Jean.

The older woman nodded.

"I was smiling for me, not you. It looks like I can trust you and even if I can't, you've dug yourself so far into the shit that you're going to have to mix exclusively with people who smell the same."

There was an awful brutality in the way Jean had answered. Twenty-four hours ago Sophia had been chatting to Simon Westcott about the presents he was getting his kids for Christmas. Now she was promoted to Inspector and lived in a posh flat in Belgravia. She was dirty with lies and guilty of perjury before the law. Simon was in the drawer of a mortuary freezer, probably identified only by fingerprints on account of his head injury.

"So what the fuck department do you people work for?"

"SO1649," replied Jean at once.

"Never heard of it."

Jean shrugged.

"Go up and see your new flat. I won't stand over you."

Sophia remembered the sounds of scraping furniture from the floor above. There must be bare boards. Jean came with her to the door.

"Take a look inside. They tell me it's done."

Sophia stepped in. She was struck by the smell of new carpet. Looking down she saw a thick-pile autumn-gold luxury covering which spread through the whole place except the bathroom and kitchen where there were still floorboards. It looked like they were decorating the whole place. She walked through to the lounge. Something was wrong about this place. Very wrong. There was a bookcase and on it was a birthday card from her daughter from the week before. There were photos and books from her own flat in Streatham. There was a vase she'd inherited from an aunt.

"We brought over a few things to make you feel at home. I know you're worried about underwear," said Jean.

"You've been to my flat and gone through everything?"

"We're taking care of you," said Jean. "Relax and bed yourself in."

Sophia watched her go. The door closed heavily. The bulletproof glass and the thick carpet deadened all sound. It was good to be alone but she also felt afraid. It was useless to resist at least for now. She idled into the bathroom. There was soap, a toothbrush and toothpaste, all new and set out. Without thinking she decided to clean her teeth and carelessly dropped the brush on the bare floor. Her coordination was way off. She bent down to retrieve it. Pipes came up from below to feed the wash basin. In the deathly silence of the flat she could just hear the sound of a voice from the lower floor. She lay down flat to twist her ear to the openings where the plumbing was a loose fit. The voice was Jean's.

"Lieutenant Colonel Jean Bailey. Yup. You got it. OK, she's cool so far. Monitor all her outlets and her daughter's. We've got her old phone. For GCHQ the trigger words are SO1649 and *Operation Spaniel*. I just made them up to see if she leaks."

CHAPTER 5

Sophia flopped back on the bed. So, jailer Jean was a special-forces officer. She wasn't that surprised after all that had happened. If she ran she had nowhere to go and Izzy was on their radar. She had no choice but to lie back and think of England.

A huge flat-screen TV filled half the lounge wall. From what Jean was saying she needed to catch up on world affairs. Sky News was covering a big story from New York. The CEO of Sackman-Platinum Bank had been hit in a terrorist attack. Grainy mobile-phone footage showed guys in ski masks with machine guns like she'd seen only a few hours ago in London. So these were the famous AK-47 death machines. Manhattan was locked down and President Grump had condemned the attack. Migrants were rioting in Calais because the British authorities had flooded the tunnel to Dover. Jesus—why did people depress themselves with this stuff?

The death of Simon Westcott was well down the bulletin after some footage of armed Scottish border guards in kilts stopping trucks to check passports and collect taxes. It sure seemed that the last few months had boiled up a bit. Her own life had been getting Izzy off to university and getting used to being alone. And now what, or who, did she have? She'd been divorced for ten years and her handsome ex lived in Australia with a woman child of twenty-three who had hair extensions and a guitar. She'd never met her but Izzy had shown her the YouTube channel where she strummed to her own poetry and talked about her emotional counseling and eyebrow issues. Tens of thousands ticked her box and loved her.

A lot of the world had changed while she had just had her head down to her work on the streets, the processing of prisoners, browsing the catalogue of disappointment which added up to most people's lives from what she saw of it. Without warning she flashed back to the washing machine wet slop sound of the bullet hitting Simon's head. She wanted to panic. She held on. You're OK, Sophia. You're going to be OK.

An unfamiliar ringtone on her new mobile snapped her back to the moment.

"Sophia?" said a slightly accented female voice.

"Yes. Who's this?"

"My name's Anna, Anna La Salle."

Sophia's brain flipped into sheepdog mode, rounding up all the stray thoughts. She'd heard this name, somewhere she'd heard this name.

"Are you a cop?" Sophia asked.

"Yeah, almost. Assistant Director National Crime Agency," said the voice.

Sophia had seen her on TV talking about global slavery. She was about her own age, dark hair, voluptuous, and every serious criminal's pin-up girl.

"Have you got the right number?"

"I hope you're OK and being looked after. Do you need anything?"

"There's been an underwear drought, but it's raining knickers now."

The woman laughed.

"Only great cops make that sort of remark when they're in a fix like yours,"

"Fix?" echoed Sophia.

"For now yes. We'll talk tomorrow."

"I haven't got a thing to wear."

"Come as you are. A car will collect you at ten. Jean will give you a pill to help you sleep, Make sure you take it. Sophia, we're all so sorry and normally you'd be getting far more support. One day maybe you'll see what's at stake here. Now is there anything?"

"I had a lovely curry in my oven at home."

"I'll see you tomorrow," said Anna La Salle.

The mean day measured out self-pity onto the grey drizzling streets of London. Sophia settled into the black Jaguar XJF limousine. A plain-clothed guy sat in the front next to the uniformed driver. She still felt heavy from the effect of the sleeping medication. She had no makeup and looked a mess in the track suit.

"American prisoners get orange suits," she said.

The detective type looked her over.

"Not your color ma'am," he replied.

Ma'am indeed. The term shocked her. Of course she was an inspector now. She looked and felt like a dispossessed vagrant. She was tense, not least because she couldn't reach her daughter Izzy. She'd tried the phone, SMS, email and Whatsapp. Bloody students had no idea there was a life beyond booze and some ridiculous essay. For sure her phone would be out of charge, switched off or dropped in a bar. She sighed and glanced up at the view. No one had said she was going to Scotland Yard but she'd assumed it. She knew she wasn't thinking properly. Her mind had retreated to some low level inner core like a little creature hibernating in the Arctic. Watch and survive, Sophia, just watch, listen, and survive. To her left was Hyde Park and to her right, Mayfair. It looked like they were heading west. Sure enough they were on the Edgware Road and swinging left onto Westway. This route would take them out of London and at the speed they were doing they'd soon be in the countryside. She fought back a sense of panic. She'd never felt so alone. If she spoke she would seem nervous and edgy. The car took a slip road. A motorcycle cop was holding traffic at a roundabout. She glanced behind. There was a police outrider. She felt numb and helpless. Just what the fuck was going on? She knew better than to ask.

There was a blur of a soldier, a barrier, and the realization that she was on an airfield. She got it. This was RAF Northholt, made famous when the body of Princess Diana was flown back to England from Paris. Sophia remembered the TV coverage when she'd been just a teenager and dreaming a very secret dream of being a cop. She just had to break her silence but not look like she was trouble.

"Someone's got to tell me something," she said.

Her anonymous companion nodded.

"Sophia, we don't do all the ranks and title stuff now. You're going to see Anna La Salle, you know that. She's not in the UK. We couldn't risk you giving anyone any idea of your movements or even existence."

"I can't reach my daughter," she said, realizing her voice was raised and strained.

"There's a reason for that and there's nothing to worry about."

"Now you're going to add that I can trust you, I suppose."

"Trust me for sure, but I don't expect you to accept that at face value."

"My whole life's disappeared, my daughter's disappeared. I'm being bundled out of the country looking like a drug test failure deported from the Olympic Games."

The enigmatic escort half smiled.

"I'm Bastian Wolf I'll be flying with you. We're heading for France."

CHAPTER 6

They boarded a BAe 146 jet. Sophia noted the badges of 32 Squadron, the Queen's Flight. The plane was taxiing the minute the door closed. The engines screamed to full power and within seconds they were bursting into sunlight above the London clouds. They banked left and lost the sun pouring through the window. Sure looked like they were heading south.

A young RAF soldier poured her a coffee. Bastian Wolf motioned for her to sit opposite him on a cream leather armchair where he had his own coffee on a beautiful dark wooden table. The luxury and effortlessness that surrounded this level of power crushed her into a sense of helplessness.

"OK, this has been incredibly tough for you, Sophia. We've all been so impressed by the way you've done your duty. Anna's going to give you a briefing and you'll soon know a lot more. Once you do know, your life can never be the same. The truth is you barged into a situation that had already gone wrong. You arrived like a hurricane hitting an earthquake."

She didn't interrupt him. He was assured, calm, and coldly polite. She guessed he was about forty-two. His English was perfect but flavored with something like German. His eyes were a pale blue, his blonde hair cropped. Maybe he was a cop, but she had her doubts. She had checked out his police issue Glock 26 tailored into his Savile Row suit. A sudden thought bubbled out of her.

"I haven't got my passport," she said.

He reached down into a briefcase and handed her a new style dark blue English passport endorsed "Diplomatic." She flipped through the pages. There was a visa for France and other places she'd never been. The photo was the same as her police warrant card.

"You guys can just do anything can't you?" she said.

"If only that were true. Maybe we can, and everyone had better hope so."

His eyes were cold and suspicious. His manner towards her was androgynous, rather more earthworm than Bowie.

A calm professional female voice came over the speaker system.

"This is Captain Melody Salerno. Final approach into La Rochelle. Usual troubles with wind in this bloody place. On the deck in ten."

"Where the fuck is La Rochelle?" she said.

"Halfway down France on the Atlantic coast," said Bastian.

Sophia shrugged. When she got the chance, Google Maps would have to make up for all her missed geography classes. They walked to a silver Citroen C4 Grand Picasso parked on the tarmac. Two heavily armed paratroopers saluted.

"The local Gendarmerie are on our side," Bastian began. "The picture is patchy and not all police units support the Patriotic Front."

The French driver wore the uniform of a *brigadier de gendarmerie* and spoke good English. Bastian switched seamlessly in and out of French, chatting as if they were good friends. She knew they were only letting her hear what they chose.

"Welcome to beautiful France, Inspector," said the driver.

"I tried to come up with a chic little fashion number to show respect," she said.

The driver's eyes caught hers in the mirror and stayed there longer than was good for road safety. He glanced ahead and then back to her.

"It all looks like a chic model to me," he said with a smile in warm eyes.

She couldn't help but smile in return. She was still a woman.

"*Hervé, au travail. Elle ne cherche pas des histoires d'amour,*" said Bastian.

The driver smiled and shrugged raising his eyes once more to the mirror. She didn't speak French but she'd caught the drift.

"*Merde!*" exclaimed the driver.

Ahead of them on the auto route there were burning tires, tractors and big trucks. To their right was a slip road. The Citroen braked hard and swerved across the inside lane. They hurtled off the fast smooth strip and onto gravel-strewn country roads.

"It's nothing," said the driver. "There's a road block."

"What for?" she asked.

"Bread and circuses," said Bastian.

Small towns and villages flashed past in the deepening gloom of the afternoon. Here and there she saw armed police and even groups of rural type civilians with shotguns. French flags hung from most buildings. Time after time she called Izzy.

"I still can't reach my daughter."

"Another ten minutes and you'll get a signal," said the mysterious yet clearly powerful Bastian Wolf. She had no option but to trust him.

She'd heard the word *château*. Now its meaning defined itself against the twilight sky in a silhouette of brutal yet noble strength. English time, it was four o'clock and night was gathering up the last twigs of day to light the hearth of winter night. The powerful Citroen raced through high stone pillars with opened iron-railed gates. They had pulled off a road onto a wooded drive that led to something that looked like a Disney castle. Armed soldiers waved them through. Sophia watched from the window as if it were a film and somehow she were its star. Above the turrets and towers a chopper was lifting off into the night, its strobing colored navigation lights forcing its contemptuous counterpoint onto the music and canvas of history.

"Where are we?" she asked, careless that her voice betrayed her sense of awe.

"It's the Château of Roche Courbon. Everything about what is happening is bonded into every stone and every hand or soul that has touched this place. Sophia, you're part of this story. Both the past and the future are reaching out to all of us here. You've shown courage enough for us to let you live so far," said Bastian.

The night perfume of woodsmoke caught her senses as she stepped from the vehicle. Around her was the sound of voices and casual chatter of human life. Movie set lamps and microphones were mounted on high masts, and a circus of caravans seemed to constrain a world of vibrant showbiz.

She followed the men to a thick wooden door at the base of a tower. She noted that Hervé kept his hand on his sidearm pistol. The door opened as they arrived. Behind it was a saluting French gendarme. Dressed in a baggy and increasingly disgusting track suit Sophia doubted the worth of any acknowledgement. Odds were they thought she was a prisoner.

They entered a dark lounge lit by corner lamps and the flicker of a roaring log fire. A beautiful elegant woman was seated on a sofa. Her long hair was raven black and her skin a gorgeous rich cream. She stood and smiled.

"Sophia. God, you're far more than they told me. Please sit down."

Sophia slumped down on a brocade hunting-scene-pattern armchair, trying to hide what she saw as her plain unworthiness to be in such surroundings. She knew this woman as the famous smooth Anna La Salle.

"I can't reach my daughter," said Sophia, tears starting to burn in her eyes.

Anna got up and strode across the room. She spoke quickly in French to a figure in the shadows of the room. Then she knelt by Sophia's chair and took her hand.

"When you're a mother, are you weaker or stronger?" asked Anna

Sophia looked into her eyes. This woman knew the weight of her question.

"You're weaker because you're afraid and you're stronger because you're more afraid for someone outside yourself. The weaker one has thoughts. The stronger one has instincts and they hold hands," said Sophia.

A door opened at the far end of the room. A bewildered young woman blinked in the somber light.

"Izzy!" screamed Sophia.

CHAPTER 7

She held her child, standing in the center of the fabulous high-ceilinged room. Izzy had only been away from home nine weeks but already she felt different and a little unfamiliar. She also seemed about ten years older. Her skirt was far too short for winter and even modesty.

"They came for me in a helicopter. It was the Queen's Flight and landed on the rugby field."

"Sophia, we couldn't risk her as a possible loose cannon. She'll be with you until this thing is over," said Anna.

Sophia was somewhere between ecstasy and terror.

"Did you get that essay done?" she asked, stroking Izzy's long deep brown hair and assessing her look. She knew the question was dumb but it was an island in a deep sea.

"I did it but they scooped me on the way to my tutor."

Sophia turned to Anna.

"You can't just take her out of her education. What about her degree?"

"Look. She'll get whatever degree she needs believe me. She's doing French and that's a real bonus. Anyway, here she is in France. We've had a chat and her French is pretty good—far better than mine at her age."

Izzy smiled back at Anna with a genuine warmth. Sophia felt of stab of jealousy. These sophisticated people could steal her child, body and soul.

"It'll be cool, Mum. I'm fine."

Sophia sat down. She could tell her daughter was stressed but calm, and with all the innocent bravado of youth, she was up for the adventure, whatever it was. So far no one had had their head blown off in her presence.

"Everyone on this team has been hand-picked with deep, deep background checks," Anna began. "You guys selected yourselves and we've had to run with it. Everyone here is checking out everyone else all the time. No one outside of the team knows what's in hand, except for the kind folks who let us use their planes," she said with half a smile.

Sophia glanced at Izzy. The planes belonged to the British Crown, like the royal family of England. She could tell that Anna was letting her words sink in.

"There is no higher authority. All or any of us are completely dispensable," Anna finished.

Sophia stared silently into the fire.

"They're making a film, Mum," said Izzy. "I think I saw some old film star dressed up like a cavalier."

Sophia shook her head. As far as she knew she had no underwear once again. She was still dressed in the ill-fitting track suit and above all, despite everything that had happened, she was hungry.

"You've got him on DVD, Mum, old time Rom-Com stuff. He's got that floppy kinda posh look."

"Grant Hughes," said Sophia.

"Wow! You must be a film fan," said Anna.

"I've only got three DVDs and he's on two of them. I'm not quite dressed for Hollywood."

Anna stood up and spoke in French to a young soldier guarding the door. He nodded and spoke to Izzy.

"*Veuillez me suivre s'il vous plaît, mesdames,*" he said with a slight bow.

Sophia glanced at her daughter who was beaming at the young guy who obviously liked her attention.

"He wants us to go with him."

"You sure he wants old Mum as well?" she asked with a note of sarcasm. She felt like a torn sack. She knew nothing of the world, politics, or history. She sure didn't speak French. At least maybe she'd have some common ground with Grant Hughes. She doubted very much she was there to meet him.

They entered a large hallway with a beautiful tiled floor and followed the young officer up a magnificent wide curved marble stairway. He opened a door into a bedroom set with two double beds. A French window at the far end of the room led onto an outer balcony. The lieutenant went to draw the floor-to-ceiling deep blue curtains. Sophia put her hand to his arm to stop him. He stood back and smiled at her daughter. There were young guys and cops everywhere. Being a mother to this girl could be a nightmare. She looked out into the night. There were lights and small fires in old oil drums made into braziers. Groups of soldiers stood warming their hands while others patrolled among geometrically manicured trees and shrubs. She pulled the curtains and turned back to the room.

"*Je vous laisse, mesdames. Il y a tout-ce qu'il faut. On vous appellera pour manger. A bientôt,*" he said.

"*On a combien de temps?*" said Izzy.

"*Quarante minutes,*" he said.

Izzy dived fearlessly onto the bed.

"We've got forty minutes before dinner. Wow, Mum. This is like so cool."

"Aren't you frightened? Don't you see this is dangerous shit? I don't know what the fuck's going on and I don't know what we're ever going to know."

"Where did you get that track suit?"

"They gave it to me in London. I'm sick of it."

"Looks like it's sick of you too. Come on. Anna's shown me the stuff we can wear," said this confident wild child. This was not the kid she'd sent off to study at the University of Warwick. How could she tell her how Simon Westcott had died and what an AK-47 did to human flesh? How could she tell her that the mother she'd always known was a blood-soaked stranger? How could she tell her that all the smiling young men and beautiful people around her might kill her at the drop of the wrong word?

Izzy skipped to one of the enormous heavy oak French-style wardrobes. Every type of dress she could imagine was there and appeared to be her size. A series of drawers to one side contained packets of new underwear. The brand was French and unfamiliar. On the wardrobe floor was a rail of shoes. Izzy pulled out a black dress and an elegant cream bolero style cardigan.

"Anna said dinner's going to be pretty much everyday so it's not a big dress-up," she assured her mother. "That woman is just so cool. She's married to a millionaire business guy with a Champagne vineyard. He used to be a world champion boxer and he's like fit, like really sexy fit."

"Did she tell you that?"

"Nah. One of the French detectives told me."

"Anna La Salle is one of Britain's top cops. She's always on TV and meets up with the prime minister."

"She just told me she was a cop. She speaks French you know like perfect."

"Izzy, listen, aren't you wondering what's going on here?"

It seemed at last that Izzy had caught her mood. The girl just seemed over-excited and flippant.

"Mum, I simply feel it'll be OK. The world has gone out of control and there's all kinds of shit going down."

"Seems like the same old world shit to me."

"Mum, you really should watch a news show or check out a newspaper. The global liberal consensus around center ground elitism has crashed. There's a hole in the middle of politics and every saint or sinner is trying to fill it."

"What? Where did you get all that stuff?"

"We get lectures, Mum. The world was controlled by money and corporate business. Politicians kept pumping out the blah-blah words to keep everyone calm and hopeful. It started with Jeffrey Corbett, the socialist guy. The rank and file dumped all the toadies and went for someone who stood for something. People saw the elite power as a sham."

"He's the beardy with the old jacket?"

"Yeah. That led on to Brexit, Farouche, and Grump. In France we've got Martine La Plume. Everywhere races and religions are slogging it out. All the rest are waving flags and guns. And no one's getting a grip. Like no one, Mum. That's the scary shit."

"Do you think these guys are something to do with that?"

"What can a load of cops do? They're playing a spy game against some terrorists, that's all. We'll be fine if we stay cool. Everyone'll get bored with revolutions when Facebook and Instagram go down. Anna told me you'd seen something really secret and you're here for your own protection. She told me not to bother you 'cos you'd signed the official secrets stuff."

Sophia took a deep breath. Obviously they had reassured her and she'd swallowed it whole. She herself had lied to her about Simon's death and for now there was no easy way back to the truth.

"Let's get dressed for dinner. Do they really eat snails and rabbits?"

"Yeah. There's a big ears double shell burger at McDonald's. If you go large you get the bunny's tail as well." said Izzy with a giggle.

"I love you, Izzy."

"Love you too, Mum," she called back from the ensuite shower.

Sophia slid into a deep bath. The soaps and shampoos were luxurious and smooth. She took a razor to her legs. Her body and her being, warmed to the pulse of life. How much she wanted to live and grab the joys of this short span of time and even shorter span of youth. If she made it out of this she would never just tick off the days, waiting for the weekend, waiting for payday, waiting for another failed Internet date. Waiting, just waiting.

"Mum, these guys aren't politically correct metro sexual men. If you go out of the room like that there's going to be some too serious self-relief issues."

Sophia stared open-mouthed at her daughter's words.

"What? When did you start saying stuff like that?"

"So when did that stop being the truth? You're a complete stunner. I've never seen you dressed like that. You never make anything of yourself. You're so cool and aristo and so, well, sexy."

Sophia glanced down at herself. The black dress was simple with a lace yoke. She'd found a silver pendant and some matching earrings on the bedside table. The cream bolero cardigan buttoned beneath her full breasts.

The black half-heel shoes were light and elegant. She turned her eyes to her daughter. She had chosen a black leather short skirt, a red frilled long-sleeved blouse and pointed high-heel booties. Her full lips were a crimson red almost glowing like an ember against her flawless deep ivory skin. She just didn't know what she had! Or maybe she did.

"You can talk my dear child. That soldier boy was dribbling."

"He's just so want-able," said Izzy, adding the last touches to her mother's makeup. They were prepared for the knock on the door.

CHAPTER 8

The dining room was elegant and decorated with old paintings and wooden panels. Another huge fireplace roared out heat while flames leapt up into a broad chimney. Away from its direct blast it was cold. A chandelier lit the room, its light sprinkling sharp reflections on the polished wine glasses. Several carafes of red and white wine invited Sophia's attention. She sure could do with a drink. A smiling guy in an apron motioned them to sit, and offered wine. Both women took a red and saluted each other. They both downed it and poured another.

"Local stuff. *Vin de Pays de Saintonge*," said Mel Kendrick striding in and pouring himself a white. "Normally we do a posh aperitif, but hell, things aren't that normal. *Salut!*"

He had changed into a pink, long-sleeved shirt with old-fashioned, gold cufflinks. He wore black velvet trousers and a flamboyant broad pink and blue scarf around his neck.

Izzy was attacking a plate of sliced sausage and a bowl of stuffed olives.

Mel stepped forward and introduced himself by kissing Izzy on either cheek. The child seemed to expect it. He did the same to Sophia.

"I didn't know you would be here," she said.

"I choppered in just as you were arriving. I'm guessing you're a Catholic."

"We're an Anglo-Italian family. Is it important?"

"The bastards got the Pope. Suicide bomber dressed as a cardinal," said Mel.

Sophia looked at her daughter. She was equally stunned.

"Who was it?" asked Sophia.

"Does it matter? Pro-abortionists, Hindu fundamentalists, Islamists, Scottish nationalists, International Communist League, KKK, PKK, IRA— it's like an Amazon warehouse. Everything you can think of and instant delivery."

"The old bastard is dead, whatever. The main point is that the backlash could spark a world religious war," said cold-eyed Bastian as he wandered in. He didn't step forward with kisses. Sophia was relieved. Every woman vibe was joining up with every cop vibe in Sophia's soul to batter alarm bells about Bastian.

Hervé, the brigadier gendarme, entered quietly, still in his uniform. He shook hands around the table, yet kissed Sophia on both cheeks. She felt the slight pressure of his hand on her arm. There was a man smell to him.

"You are very beautiful," he said.

Anna La Salle was the last to appear. She looked a little tired, but fabulously elegant in a Max Mara grey pinstripe pantsuit.

"We've covered the news so far. His body double is already performing mass. My guess is we've bought no more than a couple of days," she said.

She did the round of handshakes and kisses. France was a strange place. There were armed mobs on the streets, but you still had to shake hands and serve the correct wine.

"And what are all us heroic tough guys going to do with those two days?" asked Bastian.

Anna poured a glass of wine with deliberate slowness and let a silence erode his pointed question. He didn't blink.

"We're going to make a fucking movie. That's what we're going to do, Bastian. What we're not going to do is launch air strikes on tower blocks in Paris or start public executions," said Anna.

"It'd better be a blockbuster movie," he retorted.

Sophia glanced across at her daughter. They met each other's eyes acknowledging the tension. She could see that the tone and the news had shaken the girl's tinsel bravado.

"You look so lovely, Sophia," said Anna.

"Thank you," she replied, uncertain of what to call her.

Hervé spoke to Anna in French. Sophia flicked her eyes to Izzy. Thank God she could understand. What kind of cops chatted about air strikes?

"I rather like your red wine of Saint John," said Sophia. She knew that wasn't the name of it but she was sure some French gentleman would love to puff out his chest and correct her. Hervé fell happily into the role. She was a bit drunk, but all women can play silly maiden. Why didn't guys ever see it?

"Oh yes. It is humble, but firm like the cutting arm of a peasant or the honest kiss of a good wife. The proper word is Saintonge—*Sahn-tonje, comme ça*," he said.

"Do you get honest kisses?" laughed Anna.

"First I need a good wife."

Sophia smiled inwardly. She had changed the mood.

Anna reached out and touched her hand.

"You are here by chance, but all of us here feel it was a lucky one."

Although she was bursting with questions, Sophia held her tongue. They would tell her what it was good for her to know. She was a little drunk and tired. She stuck to the red wine, The mood was buoyant and becoming more open. Dishes came and went, quite possibly rabbit. Hervé couldn't lift his eyes from her face. She was certain she had wiles enough to find out everything he knew. He was about her own rank, so perhaps that wouldn't be a lot.

"To Sophia," he said suddenly standing up and proposing a toast.

Everyone joined in.

"To Sophia," echoed the room.

A second later there was a sound of a struggle at the door. Sophia was getting used to the snap and click of machine guns. She froze in fear. Everyone but she and Izzy drew weapons. Hervé went to the door.

"*Quoi?*" he said.

A muffled reply in French seemed to reassure him.

The door opened slowly. Sophia's eyes shot to the face of a handsome young dark-haired man being held back by servants and soldiers. She knew that face.

"So who the hell are you?" she asked.

"I'm the king of France. I heard your name Sophia and I told you I'd never forget."

CHAPTER 9

"Jesus Christ you're a menace," said Bastian, stuffing his Glock 26 back into the holster.

The young man flicked a glance at him. He turned his attention back to Sophia.

"I'm sorry. I was on my way upstairs and suddenly your name was in the air."

"So you're the bloody king of France and that means you can just act without any sense or thought, I suppose. For the present you're the king on a bloody TV show, you idiot. If we change the script you're back studying your books of philosophy," said Bastian.

Anna interrupted. "Sophia, may I introduce King Charles the Eleventh of France."

"We've met," said Sophia, inwardly reeling at the surreal situation. Was France a monarchy? She didn't think so. She looked across to Izzy, whose eyes were fixed on the quite beautiful face of this unexpected guest. Oh no—he was a hot guy and her angel of teenage hormones was already folding in her wings to lie down.

The young guy smiled a full movie star sunburst all the way to his eyes.

"We met on the field of battle—a king and his beautiful warrior knight at his side," said Charles.

"I can't bear this shit," said Bastian. "I know you're a sensitive soul but you're starting to lose the real life plot here. There were four guns pointed at that door you stupid—"

"Bastian! That really is enough. You don't have to tell him the price and the risks," said Anna.

"I have the DNA of a king. What DNA do you have?"

"I've got the DNA of Cromwell and Robespierre. I was selectively bred to execute kings," replied Bastian in a flash.

Hervé laughed and Mel smiled.

"I think that's sorted out the genetic and political stuff," said Mel, raising his hand and clearly giving the round to Bastian.

Everyone else seemed to appreciate the interplay. Sophia would have to get a very quick history lesson from her daughter.

"Thank you for popping in, Charles. You know we usually keep the teams completely separate. I'm sure you'll not forget that again," said Anna.

The young man's expression changed. Either out of fear or respect he accepted her power.

"Good night to you all. It was wonderful to see you, Sophia."

She was completely out of her depth. His eyes were still on hers. Her mind flashed back to those seconds when they had both fought for their lives on the floor of that London house. She had attacked like a wild animal out of terror yet his eyes had calmed her. This boy and that moment were branded into her depths. Some destiny had welded them in a dreadful yet thrilling passion. He was nodding that appraising look at her again, the way he had as his minders had led him away. There was a visceral stir in her that was delicious and wickedly inappropriate. She didn't even try to hold it back.

"He's an inexperienced young man. You know what he's been through. You could be a bit kinder, Bastian," said Anna.

He pushed back his chair and looked at Sophia.

"How kind should we have been if our young king had gotten your guts blasted out on account of his selfish behavior?"

She wanted to dodge the question. Izzy knew nothing of this and the wine was blurring her internal vision.

"Kind enough to get the job finished here I guess. I wish I knew what the job is that's all. The more I learn, the less I know," she said.

"You should know everything. It's not my decision. If anyone can't be trusted we take them out, it's that simple," he said.

"Bastian has a very direct approach," Anna began. "All the same he's right, there's nothing to gain by not telling you the whole story and that means Izzy too."

"You would kill us?" said Izzy suddenly.

"I couldn't have put it better myself," replied Bastian. "Time for you to grow up too, young lady. You can't put an old head on young shoulders but you can easily take a head off. That's right isn't it, Sophia?"

"You're a brute," said Anna.

"And your team needs me and my people because *you* are not," he said, standing up from the table.

The dinner was over. Sophia shuddered as she looked at the serious face on her daughter. No kid could ever be ready to keep this sort of company. There was a round of handshakes and kisses. Bastian stayed aloof.

"Sophia, Izzy—stay in your room until someone comes for you. There's security everywhere and we don't want any accidents," said Mel.

After gendarmes had escorted them to their room, they both flopped onto the same bed. Sophia held the girl as if she were once again a baby. Izzy's lack of resistance signaled her need for that comfort.

"I'm so sorry I've gotten you into this."

"A load of guys with guns flying the queen's helicopter got me into this."

"I kind of gathered it's OK to give you the whole deal. I can't imagine this room's not on sound and vision so I hope I'm going to get it right."

"OK, Mum, tell me a bedtime story. I'm pretty sure I can stay awake."

Sophia took a breath and began.

"I was on nights but working an overtime shift at Crystal Palace football. We answered a call to a burglary...."

Izzy did *not* fall asleep.

"And here we are in a French château with a load of James Bond-on-acid-types, the king of France, Grant Hughes, and a film crew. Seems quite straightforward to me," said Izzy.

"Any questions then?"

"Yes, one very big one. When they don't need us any more, whatever it is they're up to, would they keep us alive? Life seems pretty cheap to that Bastian guy," said her daughter.

The question shook her. Out of the mouths of babes and sucklings indeed had come the question that was gnawing at Sophia.

"Anna's a different matter. She seems like the boss. We're alive and taking it one day at a time, OK. I'm guessing tomorrow morning we're going to get dealt the whole pack."

"The king of France is just too beautiful, Mum. He's hot, but he's only got eyes for you."

"Don't be daft. It's cliché but I truly am old enough to be his mother."

"Yuk! Incest. That means I can have him."

Sophia had to laugh at her child's careless flippancy. She was only too aware of something in the look of that boy. It was something she would never be able to set free. All the same as she lay at last in the soft bed turning over her thoughts, an awakened woman in her couldn't rule out an escape.

It was 4 a.m. when the door opened.

CHAPTER 10

Light flooded in around the silhouette of a broad gendarme or soldier.

"Will you please come with me," said a deep accented male voice.

Sophia snapped out of a shallow sleep. Her first thought was for her daughter who was sleeping next to her.

"You've got to be joking," she said.

"It's too early for jokes. We don't do comedy in France before midday. After lunch we are in a better mood."

"Who are you?"

"I am Major Stéphane Barrois de la Garde Républicaine. The king of France has asked for you."

"Has he? Well, whoopsy-do."

"I did English at your British Oxford but we don't do the whoopsy word."

"Look mate, I don't know what is film and what is terror in this place. Tell me straight. Is that young guy the king of France. From what I know, that Martine woman seized the presidency of France. Didn't you lot chop off the king's head with that guillotine?"

"Oh, yes. It was a big splash at the time," said the major.

Izzy was sitting up.

"*Putain*," she mumbled.

"Isn't that the Russian guy?" said Sophia, overwhelmed by the absurdity.

"No, Mum. It's French for fuckin'ell," she said. "*Stéphane, dites-moi. Ce jeune homme, il est le roi ou non. Ma mère ne parle pas du tout français. Le roi de France n'existe pas selon moi. Dîtes-moi la vérité s'il vous plaît. Je vous prie.*"

The stream of fluent French caught Sophia off guard. If Izzy had chosen to speak in French it must be because she wanted to keep her dumb cockney mother out of the loop.

"Don't mind me. I'm only being marched off in the night to be raped by the French army."

"She asked me for the truth and showing respect for our histories and tradition which is glued certainly to our language," said the major with patriotic pride in his voice. "Yes, he has the blood of the house of Stuart and the house of Bourbon. He has the love of the army and the police. He has the support of Martine La Plume—well, maybe she accepts forcefully."

"But he hasn't submitted a CV or made the interview short list for king," said Sophia.

"You Anglo Saxons always follow the rules," he said with a laugh.

"So he's not the king?" she said.

"He is a young man with a good heart, and Sophia, he needs you. He will do no damages to you. He is my king and my friend and I promise to you. I promise you too that if there is courage in this land he will soon be king. He has the guts of an emperor and the gentleness of saint," said the major.

"And if he doesn't make it?" asked Izzy.

"He will certainly die," said the major.

"Mum, he's too gorgeous to waste like that. We'll do anything, Stéphane."

"Oh yes, you will because if he die, most of us will die," he said.

Sophia felt the cold concrete ruthlessness of this man's certainty.

"Now or never then, I guess," she said.

The major nodded with a noticeable bow.

"This is the motto of Colonel Bastian."

"Really? Who and what is he?"

"He was in the Dutch Korps Commandotroepen. Now he's a consultant—you could say a mercenary."

"God, Mum, that's like Seals and SAS; those guys are just sooo fit."

"I'm not meeting the king of France without brushing my teeth. I feel like I've been spread with the cow dung on a garlic field."

"You have the heart and perfumes of a patriot, Sophia. You are feeling the first senses of a love affair with la France," he said.

"If ever I find out what's a joke in this country I'll apply to be a citizen."

"I can fix it with Madame La Plume today if you wish," he said.

A gendarme and a soldier stood guard outside the room. Izzy should be safe but she wasn't sure if they were. She had thrown on some tight-fitting jeans, a mauve angora sweater and the trainers she'd worn from London.

"Why does he want to see me now?"

"All day he is working. A king or queen is never alone just as it is for your Elizabeth."

"Elizabeth has palaces, the law, and the support of Parliament."

"Details. Time and destiny roll like tanks over the furrows of details," he said. "Blood that wrote the pages of history is always wet on the pen of the future. The blood of kings flows in the body of the nation. The patriots have a chapter to write. Vive la France."

Sophia was beginning to get the in-built poetry of France. This guy believed in his mission. You would never want him against you.

He punched a code into a security lock and swung open a heavy door that bore a large *fleur-de-lys* coat of arms. The king of France jumped up fully clothed from a very short four-poster bed and strode across the creaking uneven floor to greet her.

"Thank you so much for coming," he said. "It means a lot to me that you're here. It will change things won't it, Stéphane?"

"My Lord," said the soldier quietly behind her.

The boy kissed her quite tenderly on both cheeks. His eyes were searching hers for what Sophia took as approval, or support, or what? She had spent too long looking in return and couldn't pull back from the joy of warmth she found flowing out to him. This young man had never spent a night on a south London police patrol. How could he ever imagine her taint, the stink of what she learned from the gutter? Like her own child, he had a careless innocence wrapped in the cruelty of his capricious beauty.

"An officer died in that police bus. It was my fault," he said.

"I didn't see you shoot anyone."

"I shouldn't have been there. It was a trap. I got away from my guards and I walked into it."

"And what was the bait?"

He hesitated for a moment.

"It was my sister. They killed her."

She reached for him, stroking the back of his head as if to console him. He rested his chin on her shoulder. She both dreaded and expected tears. This poor boy, this poor boy. How much she had misjudged him.

The major broke the silence.

"The family are in hiding and he cannot see them. There was a mistake and the young sister phoned him with an address of a school friend where she would be."

Charles eased away and looked into her eyes.

"Somewhere there was a security leak. The killers were waiting for me."

"They panicked when the police showed up, his sister just got in the way," added the major.

Her cop instincts jangled for a second. How would he know if they'd panicked or not?

"Who were they?" she asked.

"The house belongs to a famous BBC intellectual journalist. He speaks often against Martine La Plume. We believe he was involved in the trap," said Major Barrois.

"You see, Sophia, not everyone wants to bring back a king or support the Patriotic Front. No one asked me if I'd like to apply for the job. All the same, I've got it."

Sophia studied his face and his eyes.

"You must be…," she began.

"It breaks my heart, yes. There will be a time to cry and mourn and live like humans again," he said.

"We are living like humans, there's whole problem," said the major.

"That's the cop's view of the world too. Who's ever going to tell me the whole story here?"

"I don't know what they've told you. What do you know? I didn't know when to expect you. I didn't know you'd arrived," said the young man.

"You expected me?"

"Yes. I asked for you. You will be with me now until it is over. Your courage and nobility is in your face. You would die for your king, I know."

Sophia took a step back. Street cops meet more mental health incidents than crime every day of the week. She'd met several Jesus Christs, an Elvis, and countless citizens of other planets. Most of them had issues with chemicals. This was her first full-blooded king, and noble death was not on her horoscope so far.

She glanced at the major, glad that he was still there. He seemed to pick up her thoughts.

"I know it seems crazy, but that is because you are still in the mystery. The truth is that everybody around him is French military or police. There is always diplomacy and power games. Martine La Plume won't have anyone foreign on the royal team."

"That's me off the hook then," said Sophia.

"Except for you. I have told her the story and because you are a woman and have no politics or connections, she will trust you. You were an accident and no one has planted you. All this seems like fantasy, but believe me, the bodies and the bullets are real."

She nodded. That much she did know.

"Please, tell me the score. Start somewhere sane and take it from there. And what the hell do I call you?" she said.

"For now I'm Charles, in French you say it like *Sharle*."

"And how old are you?" she asked.

"I'm twenty-four."

"I've got fourteen years on you."

"That's amazing—you're beautiful."

"We don't turn into dribbling prunes for a couple of years yet, but thanks anyway for the beautiful," she said with a smile. This lad was open and naive enough to cause a lot of trouble. For sure he was even more out of his depth than her. He took her hand as if he were the king of France and led her over to the tiny bed and motioned for her to climb on.

"In the old times of France they slept sitting up. They believed that lying down was for the dead," he said.

"I never thought I'd get into bed with a king."

"I'd never thought of being in bed with a woman. Anyway we are on the bed."

She blinked and stared at him, tilting her head to the side. Surely this beautiful dark-haired man had had his pick of girls. One never knew, but he didn't seem gay.

"You surprise me," she said.

"It didn't happen yet," he said with a simple innocence.

She smiled warmly at him.

"Tell me the story so far."

It was a day for story-telling. This time she would be listening and thinking. A stupid inappropriate thought kept bubbling up. Fourteen years was not that big a gap was it?

The major of La Garde Républicaine saluted and left the room. A couple days ago this young man had lost his sister. She hated herself for thinking about anything else.

"I'm so sorry about your sister."

"Yes, I can't think of it yet. It's in another room. Sorrow is a luxury in war. We eat and we do what we do, or what we are born to do."

"War?" she questioned.

"Make no mistake, war indeed. The news channels are playing it all down. The media types started it by encouraging the riots against Grump and Martine La Plume. Groups like the army and police all over the world have split into tribes and religions. Even Baptists are killing Quakers. Migrants are fighting border guards and migrants in camps are slaughtering migrants. Very soon food and water will be failing. You must have seen some of this carnage."

"I know about the Pope."

"They're keeping that secret for now, but it'll come out. They're afraid they'll blame it on the Moslems. When that news goes out we're in a bloodbath."

"Can I ask you a really, really stupid question?"

He looked at her with kind, sorrowful eyes. She raised her hand to his cheek. Sophia, Sophia, you should not be doing this. She really did know better. He nuzzled the warmth of her hand. In her life she had faked too many connections to fill a need. This time she caught the wave, docked with the space station, served the ace, took the hand of a human soul.

"I know your question because I feel you inside me. So, how can a lightweight young guy like me make the slightest difference? That day in London I'd never seen anyone so strong. You believed you could win and you did. You had no possibility of coming through that. Some of the time I believe...."

"I'm a mother. I have a child to bring through."

"And I have a continent and a rainbow of people and all their children."

Shit, this was for real wasn't it? Touching him she felt the still heaviness of duty and responsibility. His head—his beautiful cheek was resting on her hand. Her thoughts were jumping forward, beginning to get something of a picture.

"And only a king can pull it all back together," she said.

He nodded.

"I'm a puppet, no more than that; yet the power of one good king denies that power to a thousand despots. Soldiers could smash my way to the throne but I could only stay there if a world can find love for me in all their different hearts."

This was the blind leading the blind. Until two days ago she had never even truly known what politics was. At her side was a young man with even fewer years on this earth. She pulled him to her and gently kissed his lips. He seemed to melt into her, not like a girl, but without male threat. He drew back a little, gazing at her eyes.

"My God," he said.

"You wouldn't be a hard king to love, Charles."

CHAPTER 11

What had she done? The CCTV would report everything. She'd behaved shamefully but felt no shame. Well, it was a wartime thing if she needed an excuse. What comfort could she give to this poor lost lonely boy?

"We can never be alone until this is over, but thank you. Why would anyone dream of death and war when a woman's kiss is like that?"

"Because soldiers can seize a woman's lips, but her true kiss can only ever be given."

"Then I understand what you've shown me," he answered.

She'd overstepped the mark enough and she needed not to get any deeper.

"Then let's press on to your coronation. Why you?"

"Coronation—we're going to make it, aren't we?" he asked.

How the hell did she know?

"Why you?" she repeated.

"Charles the First of England married Henrietta Maria of France. She was the daughter of King Henry the Fourth and his wife Marie de Medici, Queen of France."

"Sounds like it was all a while ago."

"They married in 1625 and had many children. She was the mother of both King James the Second and Charles the Second of England. She had to escape to France during the English civil war," he said.

Sophia wished she'd had some education. She knew that whatever she said would sound dumb.

"Roundheads, cavaliers, cannonballs, swords, and horses," she said. A distant memory of a film or TV show was rattling around in her head. "And Charles the First—they cut off his head," she added.

"Now Sophia, we come to the story, the real story and the reason a mob of mega film stars are outside this castle getting paid more than the economy of Europe."

"Izzy told me she'd seen Grant Hughes dressed up as a cavalier," she said, merely trying to show some intelligence.

"They're telling the story of what really happened to Charles the First. The guy they executed was not the king of England. Charles escaped and made it to France where he had another child with Henrietta Maria. That child was my fourteenth great-grandmother."

"What was her name?"

"Her name was Sophia-Béatrice. Some called her the queen of Maryland."

"Was that why you wanted me?" she asked, inwardly shaken by some sense of the supernatural.

"No, but don't tell me there's no kismet or force of destiny in this world."

She shook her head. Was any of this for real?

"Maryland?" she echoed.

"Yes, by chance that's where I'm from. The state of Maryland is named after Henrietta Maria. She was always known as Queen Mary by the English."

"You're an American. I thought you had a strange accent."

"Her whole story is in a book by some guy called Oscar Sparrow. He's here writing scripts. I'll make sure you get a copy," he said.

"And they're making the film of the book?"

"Yup and far, far more."

"So who's playing the king?"

"I am of course."

"But you're the real king," she countered, still confused.

"And this is reality TV, Sophia. My face on Charles the First. My face in a boy band. My face on the billboards and cinemas. My face as an American soldier. My face, my face, my face. It's a show to captivate and unite the world. And it ends *maybe* on the throne of France. History is nothing but the boxed set of those stories that survive. And the stories that survive are the best stories. What we call history is the reality show before we had TV. Do you know what is true in any of it?"

"I just don't know any history," she said.

"All the better to fool you with my dear."

"Downstairs, there was some chat about DNA."

"Yup, I've got all that. They got bodies out of the Basilique Saint-Denis in Paris and from tombs and churches all over. I'm the real cookie."

"There must be other claims to the throne."

"No one who's got a reality TV show all about themselves. The throne is vacant if Martine La Plume goes for the scheme. You'd expect the best guy to seize it wouldn't you?" he asked.

"This does sound crazy. You've got to admit that."

"Your tough guy, Bastian, he's got a plan to wipe out all the heads of all the terrorist, religious and racial groups in Europe. He'd hang the prisoners and bring in firing squads for a bit of public entertainment. That's plan B Sophia."

"I like plan A," she said.

"With you here now I can do anything. Today I'm the old English king on a horse and doing some singing. Later there's a scene of me in the American army."

"Were you in the army?"

"I did a base camp summer training course. I had a uniform. Check out all those royal shows and weddings in Britain. Just look at their uniforms and medals."

"Did you see combat?"

"Far better than that. Far better than that, Sophia. You'll be with me today and you'll get the picture."

"Do you ever feel phony?"

He sighed before he answered slowly.

"Power is phony. If all the folks went out looting could the cops arrest them? A man can lead a bull happily as long as he thinks the man is stronger. If he stumbles, he's dead."

"You should sleep," she said.

Indeed he looked tired. She wanted to hug him, OK, to kiss him. There was something simple about his character, something other than his youth. He was intelligent and physically strong but there was something delicate. Had he never had a girl? What did that say of him? He had no big sense of self or ego.

"Neither of us planned for this did we? I look at you and I feel there is love, still love. Do you think so?" he asked.

"Real life love is loving the caterpillars and admiring the butterflies."

"You say some deep things. We will talk forever," he said.

More and more fragments of questions collided in her head. Did he say he was in a boy band? He had relaxed back onto the large bolster cushions behind him. She leaned over and kissed his forehead. He smiled and held her eyes softly as if she too were a butterfly.

CHAPTER 12

"I gather you had a chat with Charles," said Anna over breakfast. "You're a grown-up woman. What did you make of him?"

"In a couple of words, innocent yet wise."

"Matthew 10:16," said Anna.

"Can't say I've got faith, but you can't escape the power of the Bible," said Sophia.

"He wants you as his, as his ... look, God knows what. Are you up for it? Maybe I can save you. The French want control of him and we've had to agree. The Patriotic Front don't want any kind of authority beyond their own. They're letting this roll only as a way of getting all the patriots marching under one flag."

"He knows he's only a puppet."

"Yeah, I saw the highlights of your meeting. You were good with him. Any woman would want to cuddle him. That's what we need to come across."

"Can he save the bloody world from itself?" asked Sophia.

Yes, with half of Hollywood, the best writers and directors, prime time slots on all media channels, wall-to-wall Internet, the written press and about half the world's politicians. Yes, he has a chance. If not the world he'll get to number one with his single and sell a bunch of boy band dolls at Christmas."

"What *is* this boy band stuff? Does he sing?"

"Who knows? Who cares? He's dubbed in every language. There's an Asian, an African, an Arab, and Charles the beautiful white guy."

"That'll be my boys, the Four Skins," boomed an enormous guy in a kaftan as he shuffled into the kitchen.

"They are *not* the Four Skins, Vandervell—they're Boymondo," Anna said with half a laugh.

"You've heard that Brittany has raised the black flag and declared independence. Belgium has split between French and Flemish overnight.

The anarchists took a shot at Martine La Plume yesterday but one of her heavies stopped the bullet. She is not a happy lady. Fuck me, Anna, we've got the first episode of *Born to be King* going out tonight and the new *Rex Factor* show on straight after—let's fucking hope," said the big guy.

"What's *Rex Factor*?" mumbled Izzy looking up from a plate of porridge.

"It's a talent show to select a bride for the new reality TV King of France. The boy band hero born to be king gets a beautiful bride. Tonight they get to see him singing a solo love ballad dressed as Charles the First, the three other skins sing the backup as cavaliers. It's shit but what else have we got?" he said.

"Let me introduce our film and media director, the absolute genius Vandervell O'Brien," said Anna.

"Wow! You did *Red Flag of the Grimethorpe Zombies*," said Izzy, wide eyed.

"How the hell would a beautiful child like you know that?" asked a stunned Vandervell.

"It's a cult. We did it in media studies. It's an icon of proto-dystopian neo-liberal hypo-realism."

"Ha! The child's a genius. Who is she?" boomed Vandervell.

"She's my daughter," said Sophia.

"Don't either of you comrades go away. I'll get you screen tested later. Is there any bread?"

"There's no bread. We've had to feed the movie guys to keep them sweet. There's big problems out there, Vandervell," said Anna.

"No bread—Jesus, the fucking circus had better work."

The vibration of a chopper shook the room.

"That's Bastian coming back," commented Anna.

"Back from where?" asked Sophia.

"An editor in Paris was going to press, blowing the whole show. He's hanging by the neck from the Eiffel tower as we speak."

"You just can't afford to be scooped in the TV business," said Vandervell.

"Can Selena look after Izzy today? Show her around, make her feel at home? Sophia's going to be sticking with Charles. He's asked for her," said Anna.

"Sod me! A woman. Perhaps you can get him up a bit. I guess you're not a nun," said Vandervell.

"I'm not a nun!" said Sophia.

"Thank Christ for that. It's bad enough with him being a soddin' priest," he said.

Sophia wondered if her mouth was open.

"The Pope set him free last week, you know that," said Anna.

"I've got some porn and Viagra if he needs a bump start," said Vandervell.

"Thanks, we'll keep that in mind," said Anna. "For now he's got Sophia and the prospect of a gorgeous sexy bride selected by the public."

"Could I be a contestant?" asked Izzy.

"No!" snapped Sophia.

"I was only joking, Mum."

Sophia was beginning to wonder about her sense of humor.

"All the beautiful Hollywood gods will be out of here by tonight. Everything's in the can and anything that's not can be faked up with body doubles and impressionists. Once the stars are gone we've got location and studio days," said Vandervell. "What's the response to the trailers?"

"Bit mixed. A lot of Europe had power cuts last night," Anna replied. "The good news is that Boymondo is number one on iTunes with *Queen of my Dreams*. There was a small riot in Amiens last night when crowds of girls attacked the power workers for being on strike."

"We go out with episode one tonight and that song is on the show," said Vandervell.

"That's why the girls attacked. No one wants to miss it. We've got the lookie-likie bands out all over France today miming at free concerts. We're pushing all the buttons and pulling all the levers," said Anna.

"Will you be OK without me today?" Sophia asked her daughter.

"It'll be cool. Selena is Selena Fontesse. She used to do *Kitten's Kitchens*— you know football wife celeb-chef stuff, and she's just done *Fortress of Fans*."

"Do tell me more," said Sophia.

"Well, there's like a big castle filled with celebrities and their fans get to attempt a load of ordeals to break in to meet their heroes and eat a prison meal cooked by Oliver James."

"You know, getting a boy band king on the throne of France suddenly sounds much more possible," said Sophia.

"There's a brave family man hanging by the neck in Paris to help us along and keep us focused," said Anna.

Chapter 13

"You know, don't you." said Charles as Sophia joined him at the foot of the stairs.

"Know what?"

"That I was studying for the priesthood."

"Yes, I didn't know."

"Or you would never have kissed me."

"I think you're right, but I'm not sure why," she answered.

"It's beautiful to God that a kiss comes to a man in innocence," he said. "I saw in your eyes as you looked at me that they'd told you."

"I can't promise I'll never give you a guilty kiss."

"I wouldn't want a promise it would trouble you to keep," he said.

Major Stéphane Barrois joined them and saluted.

"It's a big day. The show goes live tonight and just before, Martine La Plume will address the nation and the world. I will be travelling to Paris myself to handle the English interviews," he said.

"Is it a stupid question to ask what she'll say?" asked Sophia.

"It's not stupid, but we have no answer. She will speak as she feels to the patriots of France. All patriots share the one heart," he said.

"So if she'd stopped the bullet yesterday, France would have no heart," said Sophia.

"Sophia, I fear you are right. The old-style politics tried to manage the people but in any big business there are many managers. Martine leads the people and there's only one leader. Our prize is as fragile as it is big," said Charles.

"With His Majesty we cannot fail," added the major.

Sophia glanced at Charles. He was innocent, wise, and brave. If he'd arrived that morning on her shift as a probationer cop to police the streets of London she'd have taken him to a main street pharmacy to watch the junkies. Maybe she'd have fitted in a suicide or a trip to the morgue to see an autopsy on a body from the river Thames. As it was this beautiful boy who'd been aiming to be a priest, knew the dreadful brick wall of death separating grief from touch, and had fought for his life alongside her. All the things that defined their difference had crumbled to nothing as she had kissed him. Something had to be true in this blood-soaked circus of deception.

They made their way out onto the film set. The Château of Roche Courbon was the backdrop to a tale of seventeenth-century action drama. Roberto Nero clattered past on a horse. Teddy Friedman raised his sword to the camera. Armies of technicians and serious types with clipboards seemed to make some sense of the chaos. Vandervell O'Brien called them over.

"Charles the scene where you rescue the baby rabbit for the little Chinese girl has changed. I just can't believe the French."

"What's gone wrong?" asked Charles.

"The bloody frogs ate the rabbit and the kid's gone emotional. What we've got now is a scene where you rescue a baby pig for a little black boy."

"Sounds a great storyline," said Sophia.

"It's based on a true story. I reached up and got a cat out of a tree when I was on my summer army camp," said Charles. "Cats are hard to organize anyway. The scriptwriters added a quicksand and tornado that's all."

The eight fighter Alphajets screamed across the clear blue winter sky. Several technicians and actors dived for cover. As they soared up into a loop, trails of red, white, and blue smoke proclaimed the French national flag. Major Barrois saluted.

"*Patrouille de France.* Martine La Plume has ordered a show over every region of France today to unite the patriots. The display over Paris will roll on TV before her speech," he said.

Sophia watched the majesty of power in the overhead ballet. It was a job not to feel its emotion. If only the grey of politics had had some noise and color, she thought.

They followed a technician to a huge motorhome where Charles had to change into an American army uniform complete with helmet. Major Barrois supervised the transformation behind a closed door. Sophia would not have objected to a sight of a young fit male body. She sat watching the French news on CNN. The Russians had moved an aircraft carrier and two destroyers into the English Channel. A Russian girl had been trampled in Bordeaux queuing for a *Rex Factor* audition. President Pinupskin had claimed the right under international law to protect all people of Russian blood wherever they may be. She watched the footage of the hopeful queens and princesses. Hundreds of winners would get VIP wedding tickets and first class air travel. Some would be maids of honor and bridesmaids. Journalists reported in from all over the world as the frenzy grew. Girls with eyes swollen from crying held up pictures of Charles and the other guys of the Boymondo band. Girls stood in line in the sleet and slush of Stockholm, the heat of Lagos, the smog of Tokyo.

"This is my one chance, my one chance," wailed a South American girl with severe acne.

"How's it going to be if you end up TV queen of France?" asked a bleached anorexic reporter.

"I want Charles, but queen is good," replied the girl.

They cut to an interview with Mason Trowel, the owner and director of the *Rex Factor* franchise.

"All these beautiful girls are winners. They're sharing the same dream. They're building the dream of the world," he said from behind dark glasses. Behind him dancers twerked to Boymondo remixed music tracks. A solitary boy dancer wore a crown.

"What are you looking for in a bride-queen?" asked a serious news anchor guy.

"That quality of magic—that princess in every girl in the world," he said.

"And how can these girls display these qualities?"

"Any way they have in their talent, soul, or character. We've got tap dancers, singers, and rope walkers. Some of 'em bring just their beauty and minds," replied Mason Trowel.

"Is it true you're testing for venereal diseases and fertility?"

"*Rex Factor* is for every girl in the world," said Trowel with a dismissive wave of his hand. The show was over.

Charles reappeared in American army combat clothing. He was beautiful with his dark questioning eyes searching at once for Sophia's smile.

"OK, ma'am. Let's go save a pig."

A paratrooper checked them all with a metal and explosive detector. They more or less strolled through the gardens of the château with a troop of soldiers, a camera crew, Major Barrois, and Vandervell. A breathless middle-aged French guy holding a squealing cardboard box caught up with them.

"We've used a body double for the quicksand shots. All we need is for you to run across the open ground towards the cottage holding the piglet. We'll CGI the tornado coming in behind you. You can hand the pig over to the black kid in a studio shot," said Vandervell as they stopped at the edge of a field.

Sophia watched the guy with the box. Detectors only developed by street cops were jangling. She'd had the same feelings many times when stopping a car or a suspect. He began to open the box but his actions were too slow. He was focusing in a pre-strike moment. She knew, she just knew. Hand in pockets of her jeans she moved to his side as if to see the piglet. He didn't pick up her suspicion or intent. His eyes were closed in that last silence before action. She knew. She just bloody well knew. Her spinning karate kick landed to the side of his head. The man staggered and the box fell to the ground. A piglet squealed and ran. Sophia kicked the box out of range and folded the guy's wrist in a swan neck arrest hold.

"What are you doing?" yelled Vandervell.

Major Barrois recovered the box and pulled out a revolver. He quickly checked it over.

"Loaded. It's an old Russian communist army revolver," he said.

Soldiers with weapons had surrounded them. Sophia still had him in a police hold.

"Get clear, he's got a suicide vest," shouted the major.

The troops formed a circle, guns aimed.

"Step away, Sophia," repeated Major Barrois, his own gun in hand.

She let go and moved back. Soldiers were shouting instructions for the guy to lie down and spread his arms and legs. She was walking away as there was a single crack of gunfire. Charles was in front of her. He folded her into his arms, holding her head to his chest.

"I guess he was going to detonate himself," he said. "How did you know—how did you know?"

"Cops are best when they don't know. They pay us to suspect."

"It should be me rescuing the maiden."

"I'm hoping you'll never need to," she answered.

And then he gently kissed her cheek, holding her tightly. What sort of a human being was she? Even in the middle of this surreal horror show, a sensual woman inside her was responding to the embrace of this man. She was too old and every girl on Earth wanted him.

"We'll get back to a world of love, Sophia. We'll meet properly there," he said.

She softened into him. Most probably he was going to die before either of them got to such a place. The word "love" on those lips that she had kissed warmed her even so.

"Did anyone catch the bloody pig?" she asked.

He laughed and exchanged his embrace for a boyish cuddle.

"Yes, to work," he said, looking on as the soldiers dragged away the limp body.

CHAPTER 14

"So who was the piglet assassin?" she asked the major over lunch in the motorhome.

"He's from a loose group of terrorists. We just call them the Intellos. They will accept no king and no gods. They are intellectuals, scientists, and media types like TV people and journalists. They despise the common people as stupid. Their god is science and their king is their own snob class of opinion makers and experts. Martine La Plume has suppressed them."

"Does Martine La Plume believe in God and the Republic?" she asked.

"She believes in the people of France. The shoe of politics must fit the foot of the people and walk with them. The old politics forced the foot into the shoe," he replied.

"So if they want a king and a reality show monarchy complete with fairy tale princess she's OK with that?"

"She is OK if it works and the people follow. I must advise you I cannot discuss with you these affairs too much. There is treason all around and many spies. I am with the king not as a monarchist but as believer in peace. Charles can bring everyone under his umbrella. Vive la France," he said.

Charles had changed from US army to English cavalry clothing. He looked perfect as Charles the First of England complete with beard.

"This afternoon I sing to my wife, Henrietta Maria of France. It is when she flees to France from the English under Cromwell, maybe never to see me again," he said.

"Some lucky girl gets to play your queen then," she said with just a little tease in her voice.

"They have someone very famous I think," he said.

"Don't you know who? Aren't you at least curious?"

"I suppose it doesn't matter to me. Since I've been here I've seen and met so many of them. They are very ordinary and a lot of it is makeup and created image. You are my star, Sophia."

She stared at him, taking in a deep breath and letting the air release in a sigh. He had no guile or deception in his body. Couldn't he understand that however inappropriate her feelings were, his words drilled right to her thrilling spot? She could tell the major was fidgeting awkwardly.

"If it's live tonight you guys are running it tight," she said.

"It's my fault. I escaped to London as you know. The shoot was scheduled for that day."

Vandervell burst in and slumped down.

"First the bloody rabbit, now the bloody queen. The script makes it clear that the fucking queen of France can speak at least ten words of fucking French. They recruit the biggest name in Hollywood and she speaks French like a mad cow and she's got a less organized brain."

"Who is she?" asked Sophia

"Tinka Swallow, Jesus, someone help me here," he added, pulling his mobile from under his kaftan.

"Yes Selena."

"Fuck it! Get her made up. We're going to have to roll with it," he declared. "That woman is a pain-in-the-arse fucking genius."

It was three o'clock in the afternoon of a late November day. They had to complete the main element of a TV show due to air in five hours' time on all world channels. In the courtyard of the château the three other lads of Boymondo in cavalier costume waited idly by their horses. The building imposed its pressure on the human heart, the dying day catching the mood of a doomed cavalier king saying goodbye to his beautiful noble wife and lover. Sophia sat behind the cameras with Major Barrois. Charles had mounted a horse and was entering the courtyard. The Boymondo patrol seemed ready to roll. Huge movie lamps snapped on. Sophia could feel the heat. Steam rose from the nostrils of horses as they circled.

"Action!" called Vandervell.

The horses cantered up to the chalk line and stopped, one pawing the ground. The cavaliers dismounted, Charles with a guitar. A door in the castle opened and the desperate queen ran out for a final moment with her king. Sophia watched from a distance, tears in her eyes. The song *Queen of my Dreams* started to play as the Boymondo guys mimed. The queen had fallen sobbing to the ground while Charles raised her up for that one last kiss. Without permission Sophia crept up closer to see the action on the camera monitor. The song was fading.

"*Je t'aime*," said King Charles.

"*Je t'aimerai pour toujours mon amour. Dieu réunit ceux qui s'aiment,*" said Izzy.

Izzy, for God's sake! Sophia watched as their lips met, a terrible jealousy in her heart. The kiss went on, as her own child had no intention of letting go.

"It's a wrap," cried a joyful Vandervell, "Can someone pull that queen off the fucking king."

"What do those words mean?" she demanded of Major Barrois.

"That I will love you forever and that God reunites those who love each other."

"Bollocks!" said Sophia.

By the time she got to her daughter, they had peeled her off the king. Izzy was standing in her long queen of England robe. She looked stunning in full Cleopatra-style makeup. Charles had been led away like a stud bull who had done his work for the day.

"Mum, I can die now. Life could show me no more," said Izzy.

"You stupid girl. How the hell did you get involved in this? Don't you know there are terrorists who know that Charles could claim the throne and that the government are letting it roll at least for now?"

"Tinka Swallow can't speak French, Mum. Mum, he kissed me, like really wet-snogged me. I was trying to go for tongues but I guess the royals can't really let go."

"I had to karate kick another gunman today, Izzy. There's killers who want to stop any chance of a return to monarchy, not just in France. You're in the crosshairs now, baby."

"The crosshairs of Cupid's bow," said a white blonde woman with some strange tattooed eyebrows as she wrapped herself around Izzy.

"Mum. This is Selena Fontesse. She swung it with Vandervell for me."

"Well, thanks. I don't suppose you thought it was any of my business," said Sophia.

"She's nineteen. How d'ya think she'd feel if you'd stopped her?" said Selena.

"This ain't some celebrity jerk off in my pastry show. This is like yeah wet-snog my AK-47 bloodbath show," said Sophia.

"Mum, you can't talk like that."

"Christ, child, you've no bloody idea what we're into here."

"I know how it felt, Mum, and I know he felt it too."

"Did you grab his dick?"

"Mum, you're disgusting sometimes. Charles respected my safe space and I respected his. You're so incorrect, Mum. The university offers counseling and therapy to anyone who wants to change themselves to a more inclusive being."

"I hope the next murderer we meet has respect for my safe space," said Sophia.

She'd begun to calm down. Sure she was jealous and in a way she was thrilled for her child. At her age she would have jumped in even deeper.

"I love you angel. You were a star."

"It didn't feel like acting, the words just came to me from an Edith Piaf song we studied."

"It's nice you're getting some use out of your education."

"Could I marry him, Mum? Could I win *Rex Factor*?"

"Are you brainless? You don't just marry a man because he's a king or a pop star or incredibly handsome or rich, or kind, or sensitive, or needs you," said Sophia with a smile.

"I know, Mum. But it would be a place to start and maybe get him into bed, wouldn't it."

"Is bed a safe space?" asked Sophia.

"Depends on my ovulation cycle," she answered.

CHAPTER 15

The mood over dinner swung from joyous to anxious. Vandervell had insisted on a special meal of English steak and kidney pie with pints of draught bitter beer from a wooden barrel. Infinite quantities of gravy and chips completed the feast. Somehow he had coerced the RAF into bringing in the supplies by helicopter. He gave a small speech.

"Comrades, you will know my politics. Tonight we taste the honest working man's socialist banquet. The show goes out tonight to an audience of at least two billion viewers. I've seen the edit and we've captured something very special this afternoon. A toast to Charles and Izzy. Vive la France."

"*Vive la France, Vive l'amour, et Vive le roi!*" cried Selena Fontesse.

The whole room repeated the words. As the voices trailed away, Sophia could feel the tension. No one knew how the show would play to the world and more importantly no one knew the response of Martine La Plume.

"We have come a long way along a bloody road," began Anna La Salle. "The world has fragmented into groups. Great Britain is now a mob of tribes. France is going the same way. Civilization is fragmenting."

"Can a reality TV show change any of this?" asked Sophia.

"Can a reality show star get elected president of the United States?" replied Anna. "The fact that terrorists attack this project again and again shows we *are* on the right track. They fear that the power of the screen is greater than the power of the scream. Every country these days has an extra political force. It's called the Kalashnikov party."

"So the plan is just to distract the mob and defeat terrorism with a media circus," said Mel Kendrick.

Bastian Wolf stood up and spoke with an edge of anger. Sophia had no doubt as to his merciless character.

"You all know what I think privately, but I'm following orders. Showbiz types have created the Boymondo phenomenon. They've also created a media entertainment series to prepare the French for the return of a powerless soap opera monarchy like we have in England. If Martine La Plume plays along maybe we can subdue the masses. When it comes to the killers, I'm not expecting to get put out of business for a while."

"Well said, my brave soldier. You're completely right. We will win, and as king I'll be above and removed from politics. All good people of all beliefs will unite around me," said Charles.

Bastian sat down and shook his head.

"The *Rex Factor* show is beating all records. Girls are queuing for days to get an audition. Viktor Pinupskin insists that the winner will be a Russian girl and that's going to be a political problem," said Anna.

"Particularly if he launches an airstrike from his carrier which is fifty miles from here," commented Bastian.

"He can't really believe the winner hasn't already been selected can he?" said Vandervell with a chortle.

Sophia's jaw dropped.

"So all those kids have no chance? And all the people paying to phone in are wasting their money," she said.

"It's not that bad. There's all the VIP and bridesmaid stuff. Anyway all the phone call cash will pay for the show," said Selena.

"So, who'll be the winner?" asked Sophia.

"Now that, my dear, is the question. For sure it will be decided well above our heads," said Anna.

"Do you know what worries me?" asked Sophia.

"What?" said Bastian with a glance, indicating his respect for her.

"If you get the people excited and hyped, you've got to know how they'll behave. The old British government never thought the despised mob would vote for Brexit. Cops don't like asking questions if they don't know the answer."

"You're a brave and sensible woman. It's pure arrogance of these elite airy-fairies to think they can just herd the mob at will. That was a marvelous job you did today by the way, even though no one here decided to drink a toast to you. If you hadn't taken out that terrorist there'd be no show and no leftie-luvvies mincing up red carpets and getting Golden Turd awards," said Bastian.

Sophia winced at his harshness. At a deeper level it almost thrilled her to feel his respect for her.

"Well said again, Colonel. You saved me again today, Sophia. You're as brave as you are beautiful," said Charles.

There was a murmur of agreement around the table. The stillness was broken by a soldier who entered carrying a mobile phone.

"It is a top priority call for Mademoiselle Izzy," he said, handing it to her.

All eyes fixed on the girl. Sophia felt for her. This hadn't better be some lovesick student lover threatening suicide by lager and masturbation in a Coventry bed-sit.

"*Oui, bien sûr, merci, merci madame. Ouais, je n'ai jamais attendu un tel moment dans ma vie. Franchement je ne le crois pas, je serais ravie de parler avec vous madame. A bientôt madame.*"

Izzy looked shaken to her size 8 core. Her hand was trembling as she handed the phone to Major Barrois. He listened intently for what seemed like ten minutes.

"*Je comprends, Madame Présidente. Vive la France,*" he said at last.

Sophia stared at her daughter. Evidently she had been chatting to Martine La Plume who held more or less power of life and death over everyone in the room.

"That was Martine," began Major Barrois. "She phoned to say she is so, so happy with the show and the addition of the beautiful English queen. She is honored that the girl has spoken French with the heart of a patriot. She has honored la France by repeating the words of Edith Piaf. She knows that with her beauty and charming accent she will win the heart of every French boy and male patriot who still has the power in him to love a woman. She assures us all of her joy and support for our project. She tells me that no one must miss her speech. *Vive la France.*"

Sophia's mind drifted to those happy old days when a trip to Walmart and a fight with a drunk was an exciting day.

"Bloody hell, Izzy," she muttered.

"Well, we'd better not miss it then," said Mel Kendrick.

Everyone bundled into the draughty drawing room. The huge fire spat and roared up the chimney into the cold clear night of rural France. A soldier handed out glasses of cognac from a tray. Sophia downed it in a single gulp.

"Every moment that passes is history. When the moment seems to stop, it's historic," said Mel at her side.

"Where are we all going?" she said.

"To the very end," he answered.

CHAPTER 16

Sophia sat holding Izzy's trembling hand. A big screen had been erected. A blue sky filled the picture. The display jet fighters screamed and climbed above the roofs of Paris, trailing their plumes of red, white, and blue smoke. The French national anthem started to play. Many in the room joined in. The major saluted. French flags hung elegantly from golden poles behind a lectern. Martine La Plume came into view in a blue suit, white blouse, and an extravagant red scarf. She was either president of France or an airline stewardess. She smiled into the camera with kind pale blue almost wistful eyes. Her blonde hair was a little undisciplined but gave out the air of a genuine working woman. She was calm and very relaxed. Sophia was grateful for the subtitles.

"My friends, fellow citizens and patriots, I salute you. I will not give a long speech. All our French channels are about to show you a film documentary concerning the patrimony and history of our beautiful country. You will learn that King Charles the First of England did not die on the cruel chopping block. He escaped to France into the loving arms of his beautiful wife, Henrietta Maria, the daughter of the Bourbon King Henri the Fourth. A secret baby girl was born and smuggled to America to escape the English murderers. The blood of the Bourbon, Stuart and de' Medici families were bonded to the soul of this child of a French queen.

Many generations followed, carrying the noble and national genes of a patriot. Blessed with beauty and artistic talent, Charles Gonin became a singer in the world phenomenon known and adored by billions as Boymondo.

Citizens and patriots I can reveal to you that if la France were to have a king, this man would be Charles the Eleventh of France. My friends, France no longer has a king or queen. Instead we look longingly at the affairs of the British royal family. We follow every business of the house of Monaco. We read in magazines of the royal affairs of Lichtenstein. These are monarchies without power that unite the blood and passion of their nations. And my dear, dear patriots, these are inferior nations unworthy of our admiring gaze.

My dear people of French heart and guts. My blood mixes with your pure blood of courage and loyalty to the name of France. This night I am telling you that as president of the world's greatest people, that after you have shared in the sadness and beauty of our true story, I will be putting a question to all patriots.

Do you want to restore a constitutional monarchy to France?

Could a young and beautiful king and his bride fill the hearts of all Frenchmen and women? Is there a nation more valiant and proud of its own soul? Do we have to grovel to the golden carriages of the British marching bands? Would not a French royal child bring ecstasy to the world's press at its birth and every stage of its life? A public referendum will be held and if the greatest and purest nation of thought and philosophy desires it, the Patriotic Front will create a new republic to include the office of king or queen. They will have no political power. They will be above corruption. The Palace of Versailles would become their home and all the other tin pot nations would crave their splendor.

People of France, it is time to unite, whatever our politics or religion. Put aside all regional pride and share this new truth of our patrimony. It is a story of noble courage and of love. I join you my friends on the side of love. Yes; love my patriots; that eternal wedding ring worn with honor and valor on the battle hand of France. Vive la France. Vive la France!"

Once again the jets screamed and looped across the sights of Paris. French soldiers marched in full dress uniform the length of the Champs Elysées to the music of *La Marseillaise*. A French warship entered port with saluting sailors lining the decks.

"*Vive la France. Vive la France!*" echoed the major and several other soldiers.

"Looks like she's very much on our side," said Anna.

"I believe it was Izzy who convinced her," said Selena.

"You're right. We'll double your guard. You must never be alone or unguarded from now on," said Mel Kendrick.

Sophia closed her eyes and tried to contain her emotions. Youth was a precious moment and her child had just lost hers.

She squeezed Izzy's hand. Could her child ever go back to a normal student life?

"Wow! Mum, that's so cool. I'll always have a hot guy with me," she said.

Was she just being flippant to disguise her terror? For now there was nothing she could say to change a single thing. Boymondo music was playing and the *Born to be King* show was beginning. A mosaic featured prime shots to come. Over and over Charles and Izzy kissed in close-up with an awful longing tenderness, like a beautiful queen saying farewell to her handsome lover-king. Sophia motioned to the soldier for another brandy.

The story unfolded on the screen. Battles with swords and cannons gave way to a chase and a desperate attempt to escape by the charismatic king. He has one last meeting with his passionate and beautiful French Queen Henrietta Maria. Charles sings a farewell with the other Boymondo cavaliers. Finally he throws himself from a castle wall into a raging sea with treacherous currents and rocks. The English assume he is dead since no one had ever survived in these waters. A Roundhead general is terrified to tell the cruel and merciless Cromwell that the king has escaped. He finds a royalist prisoner already sentenced to death. He promises him that if he pretends to be the king he will care for his beautiful wife and child. The noble prisoner agrees and is taken to London for trial as the episode ends.

"How's it playing on Twitter?" asked Anna.

Vandervell looked up from his iPad, shaking his head in disbelief and with tears in his eyes.

"It's a masterpiece. Ninety percent positive and here's the big deal— forty-four percent male. That's the first sign of a mantrap."

"What's a mantrap?" asked Mel.

"All these shows and reality stuff pull seventy to eighty percent female followers and voters. Just at this moment Izzy is the hottest thing there's ever been on social media. She's grabbed the guys by the gonads with that kiss and the French speak. There's hashtags #Frenchkissing and #snogulike. YouTube servers are struggling to handle the kiss scene replays. There's fabulous death threats coming in from jealous girls. Wow, that's passion out there guys," said Vandervell.

Sophia checked out her phone screen. Martine La Plume was hot with wall-to-wall approval.

"Charles isn't doing quite so great," said Vandervell. "First signs are that he's too pretty and nice."

"He respects a girl and her safe space," said Izzy.

"That's lovely up close, sugar; at an unreachable distance girls want some threat of hard action," said Selena Fontesse.

Sophia glanced at her. It sure looked like she knew what she was talking about. More important was how her naïve child was going to cope with being the celebrity fantasy object in a social media sex frenzy.

"I've just had an email from Mason Trowel. He wants Izzy in Paris tomorrow for a photo shoot. They can just catch the Christmas calendar market. He's fixing *Queen of my Dreams* T-shirts with Izzy pictures and all the usual lonely boy bedroom posters. There'll be a studio album and dance re-mix DVD. This is big, guys. This is massive," said Vandervell.

"Please tell me this is all a dream," said Sophia.

"It's just a dream, Sophia, and it could save civilization," said Anna.

"No pressure then," she replied.

Vandervell kept up his social media commentary.

"*Born to be King* and Boymondo are just about everything on the planet. Charles is trending with Mumsnet. His fans are under fifteen and over forty. Kids are phoning Childline to report their mothers as pervs. Facebook is trending with a demonstration at the Elysée Palace tomorrow to demand the referendum. Someone has thrown a brick at the English Embassy for what they tried to do to King Charles in 1649."

Sophia swigged back the brandy and wondered if she could possibly risk another. As the soldier-waiter passed she took two. The first episode of *Rex Factor* was already rolling. Girls sang, danced, back-flipped, yodeled, begged and cried. Judges smiled, sneered, allowed the touching of hems, adored, dismissed, and blessed the hopefuls. Beautiful winners were segregated from the ugly losers. Celebs in sparkling jackets interviewed breathless kids and smiled to the camera. The fact that Sophia didn't grasp a word didn't affect her understanding. She knew that in nearly every country in the world the same game was being played out.

"This is so, so sad," she said. "I feel dirty and ashamed."

"Better muppets than bullets I suppose," said Bastian.

"I know, I know. I'm just saying how I feel."

The brandy had blurred her awareness. A hand pressed over hers as it rested on the arm of the chair. Charles had crossed the room to come to her and she hadn't even noticed.

"I share that with you Sophia. Every day I have to ask myself if what I'm doing is good in the eyes of God."

"Can't God just let you know to save all the bloody worry?" said Bastian.

"Maybe he *has* told me. Maybe he's sent me Sophia to share my question."

"Not sure I want God as a third party in this business," said Sophia.

"God is always in the business of good and love whether we want him or not."

She looked up into his sad brown eyes. He was searching into her, begging her not to reject his seriousness and beyond that, his soul. How easy it would be to destroy him now, to slap down his faith as superstition or wishful thinking, to play the tough cop card to please the crowd.

"Then you should tell me more of God," she said.

He pressed harder on her hand.

"I would love to do that."

"And where there is God there is love," she said, hoping she wasn't slurring.

His eyes didn't move from hers. She drew him in with her breath and cradled him in her heart. In her half-drunk mind she longed for a candle that burned in the stillness and the gorgeous warmth of tears in a cathedral-sung Ave Maria. She could easily find in her heart a blind faith in love.

"We will come through this together," he said.

She didn't reply but gently placed her other hand on his. Around her the room was filled with chatter and noise.

"I know nothing of you," she said.

"Soon we'll have time to do our adult coloring books together," he said.

She smiled. It could have been worse. He could have said a train set.

EMMA CALIN

CHAPTER 17

At last she slumped onto the bed, Izzy at her side.

"If I knew where to start, I'd start."

"Mum, I've got to trust that these guys know what they're doing. If I stay grounded I can make enough to pay off the student loans and maybe get a life free of debt and some good contacts. All these guys who like the way I kiss only like it 'cos they don't kiss anybody, 'cos their life is on a screen."

"They love you 'cos you're beautiful and special."

"Yeah, just like all those *Rex Factor* girls. Come on Mum—this is a chance out of nowhere. I'll ride the wave and play the game, but I ain't stupid. The main deal in town is that he's just soooo in love with you."

"Who?" said Sophia.

"Don't give me that."

"Love is something abstract to him, like something spiritual. You seem to have grown up all of a sudden to be lecturing me."

"I've had a day with Selena Fontesse. She's like Wiki wisdom. She's sussed out the whole show with you and Charles. She's sussed out the way I've got to play to the crowd and suck out the max while the lights are on me 'cos the darkness can be the rest of my life."

"The rest of your life isn't darkness just because you're not rich and famous."

"Being in debt with a shit job on a zero hours contract that only just pays the rent ain't what you call social mobility Mum."

"Honey, I know you're right and I'm proud of you. As long as you can see through the glitz to your true self. Promise me you won't let the hype run off with your soul," said Sophia, studying her daughter's eyes to measure the penetration of her words.

"Of course I won't," sighed Izzy.

"If that Selena's your role model I'm not sure if I want you like that," said Sophia. "I'm pretty sure she's had a coke issue or maybe she still has."

"Sure—she told me about that. When she met Vandervell she was off her head. He truly, truly loves her. She's really tough and wise, Mum."

"How's her karate?"

"She's not tough like you, Mum. I know that," said Izzy. "I love you, Mum. I can use Selena to help me face things folks like us just don't know about, that's all."

"Folks like us?" echoed Sophia.

"Yeah, basically we're people who can't go anywhere different from where we are. We've not got the inside track, we can't whisper in the right ears. Come on, Mum. You know that!"

Sophia nodded. From where her daughter stood, she was right.

"Life's different at your age. To be honest I don't want to go anywhere much different. I'm a mum and a cop and no matter what kind of juice you soaked me in I'd still come out that flavor. Your DNA has started you, but life hasn't finished you yet," said Sophia.

"I don't want you to worry while I'm away. It'll spoil things for me if I think you're in a state," said Izzy.

Sophia blinked.

"Where are you going to be away at?"

"Paris of course, with Mason Trowel."

"Well, I'll be going, won't I," said Sophia.

"I don't think so. Anna told me you were staying with Charles and it looks like he's headed for England in a couple of days."

"No one's spoken to me," said Sophia.

"You were talking to Charles. It's so intense and lovely to watch that no one wants to interrupt. Wow, Mum. He's much younger and nearly a priest. That's like gross out sexy naughty. You gotta go for it!"

"I can't just let you swan off," said Sophia, only too aware that she had little power. She decided to leave the sexy naughty gross out sealed in a box for later.

"Kids younger than me went off to fight in Vietnam. I'll be with Selena, Major Mustard, and all his paratroopers. I'll be at Mason Trowel's studios so there'd be nothing for you to do anyway."

"Major Mustard? You mean Stéphane Barrois," laughed Sophia.

"Selena calls him that. You know, like Colonel Mustard in Cluedo. He's so sort of keen if you know what I mean."

"He salutes a lot," Sophia agreed.

"He's a patriot, Mum. He wears tricolor underpants."

"He seems to loves Charles," said Sophia.

"Well, from what I know he's leaving the loving of kings to you in the morning. He's defo coming with me to Paris and is doing all the security for the meet with Martine La Plume."

Sophia lay back exhausted on the bed. Izzy was getting ready to sleep. If

Anna La Salle ordered her to stay at Roche Courbon there was nothing she could do. An escort platoon of heavily armed paratroopers should keep her daughter safe. A dreadful shameful thought played in her mind. Charles would be doing no more kissing with Izzy and the Major would no longer be their constant companion. A king must know his subjects and their lives. He had a lot to learn and Sophia knew a few places to start.

As the day fell away and fragmented into a jumble of moments and words, one question would not subside. How did the piglet assassin get to be where he was? Everyone around her had been searched but the piglet arrived late. An ex-army guy might have come home from war with a revolver, but they said he had a suicide vest. That's a different league of weapon and they're not on Amazon. They'd killed him with a single shot, more like an execution and dragged the body away. Who was that guy and who was the guy she'd fought in London? She'd been so close to her own situation that until now she hadn't stood back to take in the view. When she'd arrived at the house in London, Charles had escaped from his guards in France and crossed the Channel. How had a soft lad like him evaded hardened paratroopers, police, gendarmes and legionnaires? She could start by asking him. It might be a good idea to know, just in case they had to do it again.

CHAPTER 18

Every morning began with the French BFM rolling news channel which played constantly in the kitchen. Izzy's eyes were fixed on the screen. Warplanes and warships mixed with pictures of Ronald Grump and Viktor Pinupskin.

"The Americans have put a two-carrier battle group off the coast of France to shadow the Russian carrier and escorts. The English have moved a frigate and a nuclear submarine to watch them. The Scots have asked for a non-aggression pact with America and Russia. Ronald Grump says an American girl should win *Rex Factor* but he wants to check her out physically in his penthouse."

"Really?" asked Anna La Salle.

"I lied about checking her out. He wants her to be his daughter Esmeralda," said Izzy.

All the other news was *Rex Factor* and *Born to be King*. An online petition had seven million signatures demanding the royalty referendum at once. Bootleg *I heart Izzy* T-shirts were already on sale. Tharindu, the Boymondo singer from Sri Lanka was the choice heartthrob of world girls.

"I can see why. He's just got man musk," said Izzy.

"You can't get his pheromones on TV can you?" asked Anna.

"It's just in him. He's got a look you know and I've been close to him."

"Charles is doing OK," said Sophia.

"Yeah, it's early for the mums to get online. He'll be trending once the school runs are over," said Anna. "In any case he's got to ease away from the boy band angle. He's got to get more gravitas and regal confidence. Boymondo was only ever a booster rocket to get him into orbit. We needed the teenies and the weenies to give him a fan-base for life."

"What will you do with the other boys?" asked Izzy.

"Their orbit will decay and they'll burn up in the atmosphere," replied Anna.

"Do they know?" asked Sophia.

"Who cares?" said Bastian, looking up from his coffee. "If any of them make it back to Earth, Mason Trowel will put them up for adoption. They'll waste the rest of their lives on *Fortress of Fans*."

"Selena was a star on that," said Izzy.

"Need I say more," Bastian mumbled.

Sophia poured herself a cup of tea, realizing just how little she knew.

"Whatever happened to the Pope situation?" she asked.

"News came out overnight. Two hours later there was a puff of smoke up the Vatican chimney and it's business as usual. Dead popes are buried in fairy tale princess and palace stories," said Bastian.

"And the Moslem-Christian war is cancelled," said Anna.

"Yup, death was by heart attack. Pretty much true since the blast got his heart and lungs in one piece."

"Will the truth come out?" asked Sophia.

"Of course, one day. There's a couple of bodies on ropes just to spread a bit of PR and guidance to any would-be gossips," said Bastian.

Sophia took a deep breath. She felt an appalling admiration for him. His ruthlessness was at her service and she had to admit, filled her with courage beyond her own. So far she hadn't asked exactly who authorized any of these guys to run this show. Anna La Salle was from the English National Crime Agency. She seemed part cop, part politico, part theatre manager. Bastian was a mercenary and seemed to work globally and not for Anna La Salle.

"Vandervell wants Izzy for some kissing shots with Charles. Then most of us'll be heading for Paris and I'm hitching a ride. My eldest boy has a birthday and I'll be at my home in Champagne for a couple of days. I'll be seeing you at Scotland Yard next week I expect, Sophia," said Anna.

"Who's going to be staying?"

"Bastian, Mel, Vandervell with a film crew, Charles, and you. You'll be filming the life of Charles before Boymondo. Half the French soldiers are coming to Paris and the other half will be in Charles's bedroom to keep you two apart," said Anna with a warm smile.

"Looks like a quickie somewhere then," said Sophia, returning the smile.

What the hell, she thought. Deep down she still expected to die.

A studio with a green screen had been improvised in an old stable in the inner courtyard of the château.

"Plonk yourselves in front of the screen and just give me some full-bore snogging. Give me tender, give me splendor. Give me cavernous, give me ravenous, give me tongues, give me slobber, give me punk, give me drunk, give me guts, give me sluts, give me cow-eyed moos, give me the howling blues. Don't give me holy fucking communion, Charles, OK!" ordered Vandervell.

"I feel I'm at a moment of cinema history," said Bastian.

"Let the girl express herself. Yeah, that's right, Charles. Think flesh. Think juice. She's warm and sexy," said Vandervell as the action developed.

Sophia watched with fascinated horror. Her child was eating the poor boy alive. Time after time they changed costumes and positions. After two hours of more or less constant lip work, Izzy came back to her mother's side, apparently unharmed. Sophia took advantage of a private moment to ask a question.

"Did that feel like work or...?"

"It's a little bit of a turn-on, yeah, but not like desperate. Mum, whatever you think or fear, Charles is *not* the one. He's with someone else in his mind, geddit?" said Izzy.

"How the hell d'you know so much from a kiss?"

"Ain't you heard? You gotta kiss a load of frogs to find your prince and I'm still working my way through the frogspawn and tadpoles," she said with a laugh.

"I'm just happy you weren't enjoying yourself then," said Sophia.

"That's a wrap, comrades," boomed Vandervell. "We've got enough footage to put some snogmondo chutzpah in front of every tourist spot and capital in the world."

Major Barrois accompanied Charles back to the château, holding a deep conversation in French. Sophia could see Izzy had got herself close behind them and was eavesdropping. She glanced back as if a little troubled. Once in the house she motioned with her head for her mother to follow her back outside. No one came with them.

"Mum, I couldn't quite catch all of it, but basically Major Mustard was saying that you couldn't be trusted and not to be influenced by you. He told him that no one but Major Mustard himself could be relied on and that Charles must NOT, NOT, NOT open up to you or believe you."

"There's no surprise there, Izzy. Martine La Plume only wants French officials and soldiers around him."

"It's a bit gross but he's in love with you, Mum. It's wrong to block his chance of love."

"You're a lonely naïve romantic innocent my global sex superstar," said Sophia.

"I just wanted you to know that he's against you."

"Have faith in your old mum. I've done the frogspawn, the tadpoles and the Internet dating croaking frogs. I know a prince when I see one. I've got a bunch of stuff to outdo Major Mustard, unless he's in final stage transition to the vaginal side of the lily pad."

"Mum! You're not allowed to say that. You're so incorrect. You really can get therapy!"

"If we all make it through this I'll hand myself in as an undereducated

Brexit voting MILF," said Sophia.

"MILF is like the N word. You could end up in jail."

"OK, I'll never say never again," said Sophia.

They hugged tearfully, maybe for a last time.

"You're as much of a woman as me. I still know more than you but I know it in another world. I love you," said Sophia, knowing that her little ballet dancing, jelly party, Christmas Day, photo album girl, was crossing an ocean to another continent of love, from which a mother on higher ground could see her waving, yet could do nothing but wave back.

Mason Trowel had sent his own helicopter, fabulously presented in glittering gold. The young crew wore *Je t'aime* T-shirts covered with heart-shaped pictures of the Izzy kiss. As the door opened, Boymondo music blared out from the fur-lined cabin. Major Barrois, Anna, Selena, Izzy, and half a dozen paratroopers boarded. Sophia watched as her daughter strapped in and sang along with Selena to the *Queen of my Dreams* track. God, she was sick of Europop drivel and the boastful bling of showbiz.

"I'd like to say all that gold is tasteless, but I think they got the idea from the Vatican," said Charles.

He had approached her from behind as she stood in the early dusk mistiness of the geometric manicured grounds. The chopper rose above the fairy tale turrets of the Château Roche Courbon. The navigation lights strobed out an eerie artificiality onto the face of nature, in the bare trees and the white cold indifference of the coming night.

"She'll make it through, won't she?" said Sophia looking into his face as if this boy could know the answer.

"Yes, I know it," he said.

His response surprised her. It was only a nuance but she'd expected him to say that God would care for her. She had penciled in his answer already and would have taken comfort from it.

"How can you know?" she asked.

"I trust those around her and she has the spirit of her mother. Come here," he said, opening his arms to her.

He was strong and muscular. She sighed out her soul into his as he held her. She heard the sound of the boots of soldiers stiffening their stance and moving closer. Beyond Charles she saw Bastian motioning them to stay back.

"Stéphane Barrois has gone now. We'll find some space," he said in a whisper.

"And you want me in your space?"

"Yes, yes."

"And will God be there?" she asked.

"God is everywhere but sometimes he sends you out alone," he said.

She looked up into his face, longing for him to kiss her in the way he had spent the morning kissing her daughter. She had closed her eyes. His lips came to hers, searching for her response. His longing was shy but as she softened her lips to his, some dam of warmth and need broke inside him. She felt them flowing in the current, turning or drowning to live or die but never end the kiss. If the single creature born from the two of them in this moment were ever torn apart, she would hold the wound open rather than reseal herself into the woman she'd been a minute before.

Around them soldiers were fidgeting with machine guns. He sighed and studied her face.

"I can't believe I dared to do that," he said.

"Because of my age?"

"Because you're so beautiful, so much everything."

"I don't want to mother you or patronize your youth with years of wisdom blah-blah-blah."

"Then you'll have to be a woman and loved, as simple as that."

"Love?"

"Yes, love—unless you know of anything stronger," he said.

She stared at him. In a whole marriage her man had hardly spoken of love. Yet, here the word was on his lips.

"Charles, love is many things including the pain and loss of it. You should never tease a smiling person before you know their sadness."

"You promised me no wisdom of your years," he said.

"I didn't promise."

"I wasn't teasing you, Sophia. Maybe you'll have to fall to see if I hold you. I know in my heart you would hold me."

"A woman it is then Charles," she said, meeting his lips and falling, falling, falling.

CHAPTER 19

"Christ Almighty. Like daughter, like mother. At least it'll all be family germs," said Vandervell. "Come on, we've got five hours' work yet."

Sophia smiled as the big guy winked at her with a warm smile on his bearded face. Charles shrugged and walked away, the French soldiers folding around them.

"I'm sorry. That wasn't so professional was it," she said to Bastian.

"I don't know your orders. I'm very happy to keep you as close to him as you can get."

"I haven't got any orders. I haven't got a plan, or a life anymore," she said.

He nodded, apparently uninterested in such trivia.

"A couple more days and we'll be out of here. The bosses want you at the boy's side until the end," he said.

"The end? When and where is the end? And who are the bosses for that matter?" she asked.

"Who knows? If he survives there'll be the wedding to some breeding bitch. They'll be freezing the cute little prince and princess embryos quite soon to ensure the succession if he can't find his tool under his cassock," said Bastian.

"Have you ever thought of being a diplomat or poet?"

Bastian gave a grunt.

"And the bosses? You didn't tell me about them," she said.

"There's the French government. Your government are on board but waiting to see what happens."

"And who exactly do you work for?" she asked, well aware he was ducking and diving.

"I work with Martine's team same as your Mel and Anna."

She had one last try.

"But who do you answer to? Who recruited you or pays your wages?"

Bastian fixed her with a hard stare.

"The world needs fixing, Sophia. A bunch of powerful guys favor monarchy as the best means of clear decisive government. They offered Martine La Plume this scheme and the resources to achieve it. She's giving it her best shot and for now I'm here to help," said Bastian.

"And you're not going to tell me who your masters are."

"No, but there are many of them."

Sophia smiled.

"One last question. What if this crazy idea doesn't work?"

"Then my bosses will press on to achieve their aim. This approach is a soft luxury option and you'll understand I'm sure that we could use other more direct tactics," he said.

Sophia could fairly much imagine the possibilities. She decided to return to the present.

"I'm glad we can talk. I've been thinking about the piglet assassin and how he managed to get through the security."

"I'm listening. You're a good cop."

"Well, we were all searched but the guy with the box caught us up on the way to the field to do the shoot."

"These frogs are amateurs, to be frank, Sophia. It's all saluting and anthems. My guess is they just figured he was from the local farm and waved him through," he said.

"Do you know where the body is?" she asked.

"No, I wasn't involved. Why do you ask?"

The guy was spread-eagled on the ground. They said he had a suicide vest but I only heard one shot and they dragged him away. If he was going to detonate the vest wouldn't soldiers just hit him with a burst of bullets?"

"You would expect that but with foreigners you just don't know, but you've got my full attention."

"I'd like to know who the guy was and where he'd come from. Who'd arranged for the piglet and if the gunman took his place, how did that happen?"

"So if there's not a dead pig farmer in a ditch somewhere, we've got a mystery and more than likely a rotten apple in the French barrel," said Bastian.

"And if that's true, we could just be standing here waiting for the bullet," said Sophia.

"Hmm ... we do need to know and quick. Who was there when the guy was shot?"

"Major Barrois, a few of his soldiers, Charles, Vandervell, and me," answered Sophia.

"I noticed he hand-selected the men who went with him to Paris," he said, nodding thoughtfully to himself.

"Look, I'm a plain cop, but if I have a suspicion it's that just maybe, just maybe...."

"That it was a set up."

"The piglet guy would have to have known he was on a suicide mission unless....

"The soldiers were in on it," finished Bastian.

"Sophia, I'm going to find out or rather you're going to find out. Do you remember Hervé, the brigadier gendarme who drove us here?"

"Yes, I think he liked me," she said, recalling his eyes in the rear-view mirror.

"Exactly. He's patriot through and through, and a serial womanizer. I've tried to recruit him as an agent and he's on the edge of coming over. You can push him over the cliff. He can get us to that body, the gun, and that suicide vest. You're not stupid, Sophia. You know what the implications are," said Bastian.

"Yeah, my child's flown off to Paris with a gang of guys who very possibly aren't on our side."

"But we have to be sure before we act, you understand that," he said.

"Where am I going to find Brigadier Hervé?" she asked.

"More than likely loafing about in the kitchen. He's sniffing around one of the cooks."

"Are you coming with me?"

"No, he'll prefer you to be alone. I've got a sudden taste for a bacon sandwich," said Bastian.

Bastian had been right. The brigadier was relaxing with a bottle of wine at the big farmhouse style table in the kitchen. A pretty French girl was chopping onions and sharing a glass of the red Saintonge with him. From her smile as Hervé gently stroked the inside of her thigh under her dress she was very receptive to his charm and relaxed manner.

He stood as Sophia walked in.

"Madame, it's so good to see you again," he said.

"And you, Hervé."

The girl almost sprang into the air and busied herself with her work.

"Too many soldiers for me in this place. I'm just so glad there's a fellow cop like you to talk to," said Sophia. "Only cops can really talk together, Hervé."

The brigadier drew himself up and pushed out his chin and chest.

"I am your strong shoulder, madame. You are so right. When we are police professionals we are brothers. We are sharing freely the same passions with each other."

"It's so good to know there's someone who understands me, Hervé. I've been very lonely here."

"Madame, I will be as close to you as you wish. Sometimes I too am lonely and need to share the concerns of my police life with someone who feels my insides."

Hervé flashed a smile and a nod at the young cook. It seemed she didn't understand English.

"There's a couple of police things you might be able to help me with," said Sophia.

He spoke in French to the girl who flicked an angry glance at him and left the room.

"As many things as you wish of course. I do not boast but I am of some importance here," he said once she had gone.

"I know. Bastian told me how much respect he has for you."

"He is a top man. We respect each other as men and warriors. He has told me that I am an inspiration to him. He needs a woman in his life and I have tried to offer some little guidance."

Sophia couldn't help but smile broadly.

"I can imagine," she said. "Hervé, Scotland Yard want to know a bit more about that guy who turned up with the pig and the gun."

"Scotland Yard, oh yes. I am the level of man to help them."

"Where did they put his body, his gun, and suicide vest?"

"They don't tell me and honestly, I am not happy because the judge has to know of anyone dead and I have to write a report. That Major Barrois tells me forget it. He says his men will see the judge."

"And have they?"

"They must have," said Hervé.

"Can you check?"

He looked into her eyes. She held his gaze. He was a handsome man in a ruddy-faced, thinning dark hair, practical, outdoor kind of way. His eyes were deep set under dark hedgerow eyebrows.

"I know a girl in the office of the judge. For you I will call her at her home," he said.

He pulled out a mobile and obviously hit a familiar number.

"*Monique, bien sûr—ouais—je t'aime….*"

Sophia watched him as he spoke in high speed French. At last he ended the call.

"*Merde!* No body, no report," he said.

"And the gun and the suicide vest?"

"Nothing!" said Hervé.

"The piglet guy looked like a local farmer, maybe he was fifty plus. Major Barrois said the gun was an old Russian army revolver."

"I don't trust this major. He is Parisian, one of Martine La Plume's personal bodyguards."

"Do you know some terrorists called Intellos?" she asked, trying to repeat what Barrois had said.

"It is a French word for the clever experts. They are guys like professors, journalists and communist intellectuals. They fear the Patriotic Front will set up a king again and give more powers to the priests and bishops. They are influential on TV and in the papers. They despise the police and working people as stupid."

Sophia sighed. The man she'd karate kicked might have been an intellectual professor but she doubted it.

"They only used a piglet because someone ate the rabbit," she said.

"No, no, this is wrong. It was always the pig. The rabbit is in the stables. The film crew said they don't need it," said Hervé. "I saw it this morning."

"Vandervell said the soldiers had eaten it," she said.

"This is stupid. I am thinking someone lied to him because they had another plan."

"But who and what did they want to achieve?"

"To shoot Charles. It must be that," said Hervé.

"Maybe, but if the army want to kill him they could just have shot him and covered it up in a hundred ways."

Sophia's mind was racing through an index of motives and scenarios. There were factions in the police and the army. There were militias and a myriad of militant or outright terrorist groups. Half her mind was working as a cop, the other half as a mother.

"God, Hervé, how the hell did society stay glued together before it all got like this?"

"We had kings, bishops, and cinema," he said with a note of sadness in his voice.

"How did that work?"

"Everyone followed the same stories, sang the same songs, waved the same flags and walked the same road. We tried to use money as the new glue, but the money stuck to rich pockets and the shoes un-stick themselves. Then, no one walks," he said.

Sophia looked at him with a little admiration. He was a womanizer for sure but he had the poetry of a cop.

"We just need to know more," she said.

"Madame, the gendarmes of France have the strategy for these times. We take prisoners."

"Anyone in particular?"

"You have to start somewhere. It is like the bonbons. You bite straight away on the soft centers and you soften the hard ones with your tongue,"

"OK—we're a team," she said to him with a smile. In her mind a clock was ticking. Deep down she hoped and feared that Bastian's ruthless approach would solve it.

Vandervell was directing a scene with Charles gorgeous in a dinner jacket and Great Gatsby hair. Hervé approached a young technician girl at the edge of the crew who was clutching a clipboard. He put his finger to his lips.

"You are under arrest. You will come with me," he said

The girl's face paled with trembling lips and just let herself be led away to a vacant stable.

"I'm an American citizen," she said tearfully in terror.

Sophia took a deep breath. She had no authority to operate as a cop outside of England.

"Who told Vandervell the soldiers had eaten the rabbit?" she said.

"Not me," whispered the girl, now crying helplessly.

"That is not the question. I never think it was you. Who? Who?"

"A soldier came over," said the girl.

"Do you know which one?" asked Sophia.

The girl nodded as if too terrified to speak.

"Which one?" repeated Sophia.

"They call him André."

"Thanks. What's your name?" Sophia asked.

"Diana," said the girl. "I saw him getting in Mason Trowel's helicopter."

Sophia glanced at Hervé. He'd already caught up with the implications.

"Thanks, Diana, It's important and we had to find out. You're not in any trouble. I'm sorry if we shocked you," said Sophia.

The girl had recovered.

"I'm not very brave. He was with another soldier and he's still here. I don't know his name but he's got a big scar under one eye."

They all walked back to the film set together. The scene had ended. Sophia scanned the faces of the soldiers guarding the perimeter. She spotted the scarred suspect.

"So we've bitten the soft center bonbon. No problem to soften up a hard centered heavily armed paratrooper eh?" said Sophia, shaking her head. On another level her mind was in Paris wondering how close Izzy was to soldier André.

CHAPTER 20

She strolled out of the courtyard with Hervé. A Jeep Cherokee with French plates was pulling up. Bastian Wolf got out of the driver's seat. Sophia saw another man, maybe Mel Kendrick slide across to take his place. Bastian called them over.

"Great, this saves me finding you. Take a quick look in here," said Bastian

He opened the back door of the Jeep. The pale dead face of the piglet assassin stared up at her.

"Just wanted to be sure," he said.

"What the fuck?" said Sophia.

"Ex-Colonel Anton DuMaurier of the French Foreign Legion. Leading member of the Napoleon Brotherhood, local farmer, failed would-be assassin of Vandervell O'Brien, uncle of Major Stéphane Barrois of La Garde Républicaine *and* personal bodyguard to Martine La Plume," said Bastian

"What's this Brotherhood," asked Hervé.

"It's a group inside the French army who are planning a military coup. It was their guys you interrupted in London, Sophia. GCHQ picked up some traffic last night and it didn't add up until I heard about the rabbit. We had no idea that Major Barrois was in on it, said Mel.

"Did this guy tell you all this?"

"He did when Mel dragged his wife outside for raping," said Bastian.

"He didn't do that?" gasped Sophia.

"Nah, but she could sure yell as if."

"But you killed him," she said.

"Did you want him to call Major Barrois to tell him we'd twigged the piggy pantomime and the plan to blame the Intellos?" asked Mel.

Hervé nodded. Sophia could see his point.

"And the wife?" she said.

"There's a few of my guys watching over her. She'll be OK."

"And why hit Vandervell?" asked Hervé.

"Because Martine believes he can bring peace and stability with his TV show. She seems to love the guy. It's like Hitler with Wagner. She's in raptures about last night's episode. If Major Barrois could have convinced Martine that the Intellos had killed Vandervell she'd order a massive purge. You were there as an independent witness after all if they needed extra proof. Maybe that's why they went for it. The army hate and fear the Intellos. They want Martine to get the blame for locking them up so that the brave liberty-loving generals can seize power in the name of democracy and press freedom.

"And what about Charles and *Rex Factor*?" asked Sophia.

"Intelligence tells us that no one wants to stop the show just yet. It might still be useful to a lot of different groups. The army is comfortable with the idea of a royal family in uniform. All the English princes are regimental commanders with medals to match," said Bastian.

"So who can we trust? How many soldiers are in this Napoleon Brotherhood?" asked Hervé.

"Who knows? I can tell you for sure that every French military man here except one is a suspected sympathizer. The main question is how we get to Martine and convince her before they decide to pull her plug," said Bastian.

"But do we want her to win?" said Sophia.

"My dear, dear lady. Above our heads in palaces and parliaments, people with real power are double- and triple-guessing the same questions and answers. I'm following the last order," said Bastian.

He walked to the driver's window.

"Chuck him in the pig field. There's two hundred sows. He'll be bacon fat by morning. Onwards to Paris."

"How?" she asked.

"No problem, there's a bus every two hours to Saintes," said Hervé.

Bastian ignored what she assumed was humor.

"I've got orders to get Charles and Vandervell out. Once the soldiers get wind we're onto Major Barrois they're dead or even worse," he said.

"Worse?" said Sophia.

"Hostages," he answered.

"Might a lady enquire as to her fate?" said Sophia, conscious that her own sense of humor was approaching doomed-king level.

"The boy'll kick off if you don't come and I want you guys close. You might be critical in convincing Martine. I've got a coach coming in for the film crew at first light and the troopers will be told the filming is over. While we're here they'll be happy. I'm going to get Vandervell to put on a big screen porno and set out some barrels of wine and beer as an end-of-shoot party tonight. Get any women or pretty-looking boys out of sight," said Bastian.

"And if they suspect something?" said Hervé.

"I've got six of my guys dug into the woods. An Apache chopper came in under the radar from a Royal Navy frigate an hour ago."

"And who is in command of the French soldiers here tonight?" asked Hervé.

"Captain Gaston Côté. He's a double agent inside the Brotherhood. That's how we knew they'd laid a trap for Charles in London and allowed him to escape so he could run into it. Major Barrois wasn't on the team then. He turned up after Charles came back," said Bastian.

Sophia was beginning to see what she'd barged into.

"So, it was the Napoleon Brotherhood who shot up my crew," said Sophia.

"Yes, the plan was to take him prisoner simply to hold up the filming and make shit for the Intellos. That house belongs to a well-known Intello journalist in the BBC. Since it all happened outside of France, Martine would have little power over the police. It all went wrong when a nosey neighbor phoned Scotland Yard and a bloody van load of cops turned up. You just can't cover all the angles," said Bastian.

"When Charles escaped we quickly got on his trail. We realized that the army had allowed him to escape. We were letting it run to identify who was in the Napoleon Brotherhood. When your van came down the street and the soldier panicked I couldn't believe it. No one had any idea about Major Barrois," said Mel.

"That guy in London didn't have a French army machine gun from what I've seen here," said Sophia shaking her head.

Bastian smiled, almost with some human warmth.

"You're a good cop Sophia. They used AK-47s to look like terrorists. If they'd used regular French army weapons any chance photo would have betrayed them," he said.

"Maybe I'll give all the kitchen girls a lift home in my humble Citroën Berlingo," said Hervé.

"You're a true gentlemen," said Sophia as she hugged him.

His incorrect passion for women and wine warmed her. He wanted no more than to live, to taste, to touch, to pleasure, and also to reflect. His heart was the flag of France, gentle in the warm summer scent of companionship and a promise of love. Surely, one day, such a life would be possible again.

CHAPTER 21

The wine and beer had relaxed the soldiers. Sophia, Charles, Bastian, Mel, Vandervell, and the stand-in French military commander, Gaston Côté, gathered in the lounge to watch the second episode of *Born to be King*.

"First signs are that it's a world viewing record. The *Rex Factor* show might go higher," said Vandervell.

The opening scene was Charles the First struggling in impossible seas after diving from his castle prison. The night was dark and only the thunder of the storm gave any light. He appeared close to death. With closed eyes he dreamed one last time of his Bourbon lover wife and Queen Henrietta Maria. The farewell kiss scene replayed.

Sophia heard a gasp and looked up to see Captain Côté wiping away a tear.

"It is so tragic and so beautiful," he said.

Then, in the wildness of the storm a small boat appeared. Two brave French smugglers were on a brandy run to the English coast. Charles saw their outline against the sky as lightning flashed and called to them with his last breath. One of the sailors heard a sound but saw nothing in the boiling white spray. Suddenly through a gap in the black clouds shone a full moon, like a searchlight beam picking out the drowning king. The sea folded around him, transforming into an angel holding him in its hands. The brave smugglers steered towards the apparition and dragged him on board as the seas calmed. The angel of the tempest subsided back into the waters and the smugglers turned their boat for France.

Sophia felt Charles's hand take hers as they sat together on the sofa.

"What do you think of it?" he asked, turning to her.

"You're just too good looking."

He smiled and lightly traced a finger down the bridge of her nose.

"You have the noble face of a queen."

"You'll be getting your queen from a talent show."

He sighed and nodded, turning his head back to the TV. She knew her comment had stung him. She had meant it to.

The scene had moved to London. The imposter-king is chained to a prison wall. The Roundhead general tells him to refuse to speak or to attend or acknowledge the power of Cromwell's court. Finally Cromwell signs the death warrant and Charles is led to the chopping block. He asks for an extra shirt because of the cold. In truth the imposter has a scarred arm which could reveal him and which his one shirt did not fully cover. He addresses the crowd and says to a bishop. "I have a good cause, and a gracious God on my side." He tells the executioner that he will pray and then spreads his arms wide to signal that he is ready. The blow falls and the executioner holds up the head to the crowd. Everyone believes that the Stuart King Charles the First is dead.

Vandervell was already busy on his tablet.

"The stats are great and Twitter's more like a bloody gull colony. The guys are still drooling over Izzy and they don't get the bed scene until tomorrow," he said.

"Bed scene?" said Sophia.

"Yeah, when Charles gets back to his queen and makes the baby," said Charles.

"I never knew you'd shot a bed scene," she said.

"Izzy didn't want to mention it," said Vandervell.

"I'm not surprised," said Sophia.

"There was a film crew there. It was acting, it was only the top half. We both kept our jeans on."

"So only her breasts were pressed against your bare flesh as you were gum sucking then," she said.

"That's showbiz—didn't even have to ice her nipples," added Vandervell.

"Well, she's a well brought up girl and she's always done her best to please," said Sophia, standing up. "I really can't bear this. I'm sorry but I don't want to think about it. I'm going to bed."

She walked directly to the door without looking back. Two gendarmes accompanied her to her room. They searched the whole interior before taking up guard outside her door. She turned her face into the pillow, angry with herself, with Charles, with death and deception. Her shame at her own jealousy overwhelmed her horror at the blood and violence which was framing her life. She was disgusting for wanting him. If she were twenty-four and he were thirty-eight the world would applaud her youth and his maturity. She wouldn't have let herself feel for him if he hadn't been begging her in his eyes every time they were close. This whole scheme had to be crazy. Could a soap opera melodrama capture and unite a nation? Was it even true that Charles the First had escaped? Could a queen be chosen by telephone voters and breed photo-call babies to complete a synthetic monarchy? And just who the hell was behind this show? Martine La Plume had reasons to try something wild, but England was stable and already had a monarchy. And they even had their own planes like Ronald Grump used to have on his own reality show. Oh Sophia; what's real?

She let her thoughts float, fly, and tangle as she lay in the bath. OK, OK, she wanted to. Her hand ran along the edge of her triangle, just creeping down to touch. So what if she was on camera? She was kissing Charles. Her thoughts jumped to his bed scene with her daughter. She wanted to, she wanted to, but the scene playing in her head blocked the flow. Christ, she hadn't understood theft and violation until her own child had stolen her fantasies.

In bed she tried to reach her. The mobile wasn't responding. She lay back, noticing the book on the table. She opened it and began to read *The Queen of Maryland*. She was still reading when Charles came in. With only the light from the bedside lamp his head and shoulders were in shadow. She studied his large hands and the flatness of his stomach. Shamelessly and secretly beneath the duvet she moved her hand to a comforting aroused self-caress and set aside the book. It wouldn't hurt to add a little secret tingle to his voice and presence. Wordlessly he lowered his lips to hers and she couldn't stop, couldn't stop, OMG, just couldn't stop. The kiss was breathless, wet and pulsed out into his hair as her free hand held the back of his head.

"Now I *have* been kissed," he said.

She was trying to recover her senses. She was guessing he didn't know what had just happened. He had one knee on the bed and was leaning over her. She moved her hands to his lips, like an animal wanting him to sense her. Some instinct in him made him clasp her fingers there and let the warmth of his tongue push between them. She knew where she wanted that hot tongue but not recorded on the bosses' CCTV.

He took off his shoes and sat upright on the bed beside her.

"You know I can't stay, Sophia. Captain Côte is outside and I promised him I'd only be a minute. He has guard me and he's a good man. His soldiers are a bit rowdy after Vandervell's film show and the wine. I don't want to make things any harder for him."

"Did you just come to kiss me goodnight?"

"Of course and to say I understand how you feel about the stuff I had to do for the show."

"The kissing and the bed scene," she said.

"I felt nothing. I just did what I'd seen on movies."

She smiled, again letting her hand trail along his lips, gently parting them and feeling the warmth and wetness of his mouth. This time he kissed her fingertips.

She brought her lips to his and ran her hand along the fabric of his thigh. He gasped as she continued over his hard shaft. She paused at the head and pressed as she kissed him again, this time with her tongue.

"Do you know how you made me feel just now?" she asked.

"I don't think so exactly," he whispered.

"You know I want you to let go too, don't you?"

She pressed on his shaft, gently stroking him. He nodded and looked down.

"I just want you to think of me and say my name and I'll be saying yours, Charles," she whispered.

He sighed and looked at her. She could feel the tight spring of his desire in every muscle of his body and chamber of his mind.

"I love you," he said in an awkward rush.

"And desire me as a woman?"

"Yes, Yes. It's impossible not to...."

"Then imagine me and say my name as you come. Hold me, only me, in that moment."

"I must go," he said.

"I'm thinking of kissing you, Charles. I'm not ashamed or shy about that," she said as she slipped her hand back to her hot wet hood. She knew he was watching her face even through her closed eyelids. He was breathing hard as he watched her from the door.

"Charles, Charles, think of me, oh God say my name, say my name too," she pulsed out in a groan.

CHAPTER 22

"We're going to be getting out in the chopper. We don't know who to trust so we trust no one," said Mel Kendrick.

"The soldiers are still pretty bleary and Captain Côté is letting them come to in their own time. The bus has turned up for the film crew but the driver's gone on strike about all the equipment," said Bastian.

"Isn't that a big problem?" asked Sophia into her morning coffee.

"Any bloody monkey can drive a bus. That Sparrow guy, the scriptwriter; he used to drive buses when he was a starving poet. I've got him on the job," said Bastian.

"And where are they all going?" asked Mel.

"Bordeaux Airport. The kit will be air-freighted to London. If the French driver doesn't want to cooperate he'll be tied up in the bus so he can drive it home when he comes off strike. I always wanted to work in industrial relations," said Bastian.

The comedy distracted Sophia from the fear of what lay ahead. At least thirty armed paratroopers remained at the château. Some, if not all of them, were part of the Napoleon Brotherhood, waiting for their moment to seize control of France. Any hint that they had been uncovered would almost certainly end in a hail of bullets.

"At all costs I must protect Captain Côté. He is my one agent inside the Brotherhood. I've got our own guys in the woods as a last resort. A shoot-up with the French would *not* be ideal politics. The bosses have authorized me to use any means, absolutely any means, to save Charles," said Bastian.

"Just who the hell are these bosses and why is a boy band soap opera king so important?" asked Sophia, aware that Mel was studying her.

"He's a boy band soap opera king who carries the blood of the great royal houses of Europe. Have you seen the news?"

Sophia shook her head.

"The petition for the return of the monarchy has reached fourteen million signatures. Martine La Plume has granted the referendum. Petitions have started in Germany, Italy, and Holland. It looks like all the old European Union countries will soon be demanding their own *Rex Factor* shows," said Mel.

"We avoided the Christian war with Islam by burying the death of the Pope under the *Born to be King* show. People are putting away their guns and buying celebrity magazines. Brittany has taken down the black flag of independence on condition that Breton lace is used on the wedding dress. There's a royal wedding cheese. There's a new Citroen Amour in red, white, and blue. Unemployment is falling, restaurants are full serving Versailles swan dinners. Bookies are taking bets on royal baby names. It's working, Sophia. It's bloody well working," said Bastian.

"And that means that not only is Charles the most beautiful boy band royal idol, he's also hot commercial property like Elvis meets Apple," added Mel.

"And he's not even aware of what he's got," said Sophia.

Mel smiled and reached across the kitchen table to touch her shoulder.

"But he knows what you've got, Sophia. Christ, I remember first love—it was a boy very much like Charles."

Bastian raised his eyebrows, pulled an earlobe and twisted his mouth.

"Is it so disgusting that I could feel for him too? A man can love a man, a woman can love a woman. A man who used to be a woman can love a woman. A woman who used to be a man can love a man. But a woman can't love a younger man, can she?" she said.

"No, because Charles is going to get his woman from the *Rex Factor* show. There's some stunners. They've got perfect dental specimens playing guitar and singing to the camera in sexy French. They're maxing out at size ten and twenty-three years, Sophia. Looks like he may get something ethnic depending on what the bosses want," said Bastian.

"God, I used to think police were racist and sexist," she sighed.

"We need you for now, Sophia. Keep him clean and calm and let the pros go on with the show. You've saved his life twice but yours is the new incorrect love that dare not speak its name. Gay is old hat now," said Mel with kind eyes.

"Shag him if you want to, or if you have to. Get him de-frocked and up to breeding speed. You're a pro, Sophia. Don't even imagine a female love drama," said Bastian with a hard stare. "None of us are worth a penny if we don't do our jobs and that's what this is. Once we're out of here you're his close bodyguard. You've more than proved yourself. When the time comes to disappear and forget, I'll tell you. You'll be out of this and back in London well before his wedding."

She knew it was useless to say or think more. She didn't even know if she was still on the Metropolitan Police payroll.

"Any news of Izzy and Selena in Paris?" she asked.

"No bad news. Izzy's a dance sensation on all the music channels and there's a social media campaign to make her the queen. She's doing a daytime TV slot talking about what it was like to kiss Charles. Mason Trowel's signing up every show in town. She's doing a lip gloss commercial and driving the new 'Citroen Amour' up the aisle of Notre Dame. A fake king and queen in wedding dress step out from the back. '*C'est la voiture d'amour*' is the tag line," said Mel.

Sophia shook her head

"So what's the plan?" she said, anxious to focus on the immediate problems.

"OK. The Apache is about two miles away. The idea is that no one knows that's how we've escaped. We're heading for Paris under the French radar, no one's going to be expecting us to pop up. Once the bus has pulled out and the crew are all safely away, we're going to create a diversion. Sophia, you're sticking with Charles whatever happens. About midday every day the yellow post office van comes in. That's your way out. The driver will be one of ours," said Bastian.

"Yeah, and just how?"

"You're going to get Charles to your room and convince the soldier boys that out of respect for love they should step outside. Captain Côté will choose the best prospects but the female wiles are over to you, Sophia. Just get him to that room and get the soldiers the wrong side of the door. The rest is down to us," he said.

"And the CCTV," she asked.

"The guy watching it was so pissed he can't open his eyes to the light," said Mel.

"I've got to get the bus away and sort out the French driver. We've got a couple of hours so let's relax and get prepared. Good luck, Sophia. We're relying on you. I'll see you at the chopper," said Bastian.

"You're a top player, Sophia, and you're playing the game of your life today. The bosses already know the contribution you've made and won't forget you. Your daughter will always be OK. History turns on moments," said Mel.

She knew what he was saying.

"Moments and escaping kings," she replied.

CHAPTER 23

She showered, selected a blue dress, stockings, and heeled shoes. On the chair she laid out the track suit and trainers she'd worn from London. Remembering her last encounter with it, she stuffed every pocket with underwear and her mobile. There was no way she was going to flee from the French army with no knickers. She brushed her black hair and painted her nails and lips a fresh blood red. Finally she checked the operation of the window. The gendarme outside her door stiffened and let out an involuntary sigh.

"Madame," he said, looking into her eyes. "You are looking so lovely."

She smiled. She really was beginning to like inappropriate, sexist, chauvinist France.

"I'm going to see Charles. He might come back with me with his own guards. You could get a coffee and bring one back for me at about twelve fifteen. I'd love to chat with a colleague cop."

The gendarme smiled back.

"That would be a great honor, madame."

He seemed to be so stunned that he let her walk unescorted to Charles's room. Two soldiers saluted as she arrived at his door.

"*Bonjour*," she said, downloading her French dictionary folder in one go.

A soldier tapped the door and another opened it from inside. Charles was seated at a writing table looking out into the courtyard. She walked across to him. He stood and politely kissed her on both cheeks. Through the window she watched a scruffy tramp-like guy climb up into the bus and begin to drive away.

"Looks like they got the driver to work after all," she said.

Charles laughed. "Oh, you heard about the strike. That guy is Oscar Sparrow, the scriptwriter. He published that book himself and no one had ever heard of him. When they found him he was working as a bus driver."

"Oh dear, I stopped by to talk to you about his book, *The Queen of Maryland* but I've left it in my room. Shall I go and get it?"

His eyes were searching into hers. She flicked a glance towards the door, conscious that the soldier was watching them.

"I'll come with you. It would be nice to get a change of scene," he said.

Captain Côté stood up from the corner of the room, bowed a little and spoke quickly to the soldier in French. Sophia's eyes took in the ugly scar under his eye. At once he opened the door. She turned to look at the Captain as she followed Charles out of the room. She guessed he was putting a lot on the line for them, just as royalist cavaliers had done for another King Charles. He nodded and silently mouthed, "Good Luck."

The two soldiers came with them, one in front, one behind. At her door, one took up position outside, the other strode ahead of them into the room and commenced a search. This was a real stroke of luck. This was the guy who had shown her and Izzy to the room.

"Do you speak English?" she asked.

"A little."

"We met when we arrived. My daughter keeps talking about you."

"Pretty girl, yes," he said with a shy smile.

She took off her shoes and put one foot on the bed. His gaze flashed to her panties as her dress rode up her thigh.

"She will be back later today and I know she would like to see you again. Young people need to be alone together sometimes."

"Yes, yes," he said.

"Maybe Charles and I can have a moment together. I know Izzy would like me to give her some space later on."

The soldier watched as her hand drifted up to the lace edge of her panties.

"You'll only be just outside, you'll be able to hear anything that happens."

"You mean—madame, you mean I am here with her later?" said the young soldier.

"I can see you'd like that. She has been asking me to get a message to you."

From the corner of her eye she could see Charles frowning, almost on the point of interrupting.

"I can finish three hours of the afternoon," he said.

"I'll see if I can tell her. Maybe you can give the king and me a few minutes together. Then I would be very grateful," she said, letting her finger tease inside the hem of her panties as his eyes followed her movements. "Very grateful."

She could tell that the poor lad was bursting. He had positioned his machine gun to hide his arousal.

"OK," he said. "Not tell, big problem, please understand."

The lad stepped outside. As the door closed she tip-toed to the chair and silently wedged it under the door handle. She put her finger to her lips and motioned for Charles to sit on the bed.

"Bounce," she whispered, indicating she wanted him to make the bed creak. She let out an audible orgasmic cry as she stripped and scrabbled into the track suit and trainers.

"They're going to kill us. We're getting out," she whispered between cries of sexual abandon.

"What?"

"Fuck yeah, fuck me," she screeched as she got to the window. A grappling iron clattered the balcony of the room above. A plain rope led down to a waiting yellow post office van. She motioned for Charles to come over as she opened the window. She got on the bed to take his place and continued.

"Yes! Yes! Yes—fuck yeah aaaaahhhh."

Charles seemed to be hesitating.

"Fuck yeah—go for it now," she screamed.

He seemed to get the message and took hold of the rope.

"Yeah, that's it. I'm coming, I'm coming," she called to him.

He was obviously strong and lowered himself to the ground. She gave one last burst of ecstasy.

"Come in my pussy. Fuck. Fuck, do it inside me. Yes! Yes!"

She covered her retreat to the window with a continuous howl of lust. He took her waist as she reached the ground.

"Just trust me," she said.

They clambered into the back of the van on top of parcels and bags of letter. A Brit dressed in the uniform of a mailman of *La Poste* was at the wheel. He drove away calmly up the long tree-lined drive and turned left onto a road.

"We're heading for a little place called Crazannes. The chopper is in an old quarry. By the way, I'm not Postman Pat, I'm Sergeant Shawn Henning at your service," he said.

"Are you coming with us?" asked Charles.

"No, sir. I've got my men in the woods. We're getting out overnight to the coast. There's a submarine off Tremblade. We'll move out once we get the all clear from Colonel Wolf. We're not anxious for the French government to know we've been here. A local gendarme is giving us a lift in the company minibus.

"That'll be Hervé! We'll have to make sure he gets acknowledged," said Charles. "You'll have to fill in quite a few gaps for me about today."

Sophia leaned back against a sack of Super U hypermarket junk mail flyers. Where to start? Guns, kings, rebels, planes, helicopters, submarines whirled in her head. Then there was her daughter, her job, her flat and a world of politics and showbiz. And her stupid, longing, bloody heart. Ah well, the whole thing seemed more or less kamikaze anyway.

Charles put an arm around her.

"There will be a space for us. I promise you," he said.

"You can't imagine how much I want to believe that and how much I don't believe that," she said.

The van swung off the road onto a gravel track signposted "*Chemin de la Pierre.*" In an open quarry an Apache attack helicopter sat silently covered in camouflage netting. The driver picked up a walkie-talkie style radio from the passenger seat.

"Affirmative," he said.

Military crew started to pull away the ropes.

"Right Charles, listen and listen good. There's a group inside the military called the Napoleon Brotherhood. They're going to seize power. We've got to keep you out of their hands and keep all of us alive for that matter. They'll take out anyone who can tell Martine La Plume that the Brotherhood are plotting against her and prove it. Their scheme is to blame all the trouble on a group they call the Intellos. They're intellectuals and media types who hate the army and also hate Martine and any idea of God or monarchy. They wanted to kill Vandervell and kidnap you in London and blame it on these intellectuals. Once Martine La Plume starts purging them, the army will move in to rescue them from the Patriotic Front and seize power themselves. The media will then have to love the generals publicly for saving them. What happens to you is anyone's guess but you may or may not end up being a useful circus."

"Sophia, that was quite a download," said Charles.

"At least a download is better than a dump. I didn't realize what I understood until I tried to put it together," she said.

"I believe you were sent to me," he said.

"I was kidnapped by the police and brought to France in the queen of England's plane with no knickers," she said.

"The Lord moves in curious ways," said Sergeant Henning from the driver's seat. They all laughed as the Jeep Cherokee hurtled into the quarry. The chopper blades started to turn and the jet turbine to whine.

"Time to go," said the Sergeant.

Mel and Bastian were ducking down to miss the blades. Charles and Sophia scrambled out of the van.

"Charles, fuck knows what love is but I'll match you two to one if you mean it," she said, as they ran bent double, hand in hand, towards the chopper.

CHAPTER 24

"I meant it," he said as he sat beside her.

She took his hand and squeezed her happiness into him. She smiled at the men opposite. Mel was dressed in a very British dark blue pinstripe suit with a pink hanky in the breast pocket. An elegant pink scarf was tied lavishly around his neck. He caught her interested look.

"Darling you just can't look a fright in Paris can you?" he said.

"Well, thanks again for my ball gown," she said.

"Regulation issue, sweetie. How could I outshine your beauty otherwise? Anyway you chose your outfit," said Mel.

Sophia laughed. Only the day before he'd fed a body to the pigs without a shudder. He knew the value and the cheapness of life. She'd learned in the château that an open fire to warm the flesh magnified the cold of the air. He lived in the immortal smell of death, in the red velvet of requiem and the fading note of mortal pleasure. He had the wisdom of devils and the foolishness of saints.

Charles leaned forward and spoke firmly as if he had snatched her own, private thoughts.

"Beauty is ruthless, Mel, to those it denies from the start and even more to those it first blesses and then ignores. You don't need gowns or robes. Ruthlessness is always crowded by admirers long after beauty has faded. Think of Castro or even Hitler. You are beautiful to your king," he said.

Sophia stared at the floor, wondering what she would see if she turned her eyes to his. Would it be a madman? Would it be a deluded boy? Would it be her king?"

"That fucking scriptwriter Sparrow's got a lot to answer for," said Bastian.

Charles sat back quietly. At last she lifted her eyes to look at him. Whatever he knew in his mind, she felt it in her heart and it soared like music. She loved him. Dear God, she loved him. And she had no definable idea as to why.

They flew low, briefly following a river at treetop height. Sophia watched in awe as they swooped past châteaux, farms, and distant cities. In an hour the landscape began to change to tower blocks and houses.

"We're landing at Versailles near King Charles's back garden. You can get a look at your new place," said Bastian.

"Where do we go from there?" she asked.

"There's no one looking for us so we're going to hop on a train and head into town like a family of tourists," said Mel.

"Three tourists and a dispossessed bag lady without a bag," Sophia commented.

As soon as they were clear, the chopper turned and headed off, hugging the rooftops. In the relative silence she looked around. They had landed in a small park close to an ornamental lake, astonishing a couple of dog walkers with a blizzard of fallen leaves. A few strides took them to a main road which led past a cathedral to a comfortingly normal area of shops and even a McDonald's, the international sign bright in the darkening winter afternoon. Suddenly she felt homesick for the familiar companionship of a Big Mac and a ride on a red London bus. The rail station Gare de Versailles Château Rive Gauche seemed foreign, the alien loudspeaker voice echoing her feeling of homelessness. Charles and Bastian got tickets from a machine and they boarded a train to head in to Paris.

They rattled along the bank of the Seine, Charles pointing out the sights like an excited native. As they skirted the great river, the Eiffel Tower criss-crossed itself like scribbled kisses onto her blurred postcard of images. Her first ever sight of this great iron icon should have thrilled her, yet it seemed no more than a tick on a tourist list she had never even written. The city was cold and infinite with unknowns. She knew and loathed the limping identical twin in the DNA of herself. Her name was Fear.

They left the train at Saint-Michel–Notre-Dame and walked the Pont Neuf to re-cross the Seine. Mel led the way to La Rue de Rivoli. They stopped at a bland-looking doorway near the corner of La Rue du Louvre. He punched in a security code and gestured them inside a grand hallway. A small lift took them up three floors to a landing with a single door which he opened with two separate very serious keys.

"Home sweet home," he declared as they followed him inside.

The woman in her awoke to wonder just what she was going to see. There was a scent of jasmine, a boarded floor scattered with oriental rugs, walls crammed with modern art, a white upright piano, a golden Buddha on an engraved brass table, a statue of two men either wrestling or making love, a giant photographic portrait of Bowie, a framed music score, shelves of books in French and English and a mini kitchen which was a white marble worktop, a three-burner gas hob, and a microwave. A bedroom led off. She glanced in to see a buttermilk deep pile carpet, a midnight blue four-poster bed hung with cream drapes. The walls displayed classical scenes of male-on-male appreciation. Charles was running his hand around the contours of the statue.

"This is quarter-size Epstein's Jacob and the Angel isn't it. I saw it in the Tate Britain when I was in London. It's gorgeous and ambiguous," he said.

"It's two blokes at it," said Bastian.

"If angels are male it's two blokes and so what? It's a story from Genesis. Jacob wrestles an angel or God. In nakedness they stare into each other face to face. Can you define love otherwise? Whom could we hate if we were to meet them free of rank, celebrity, or wealth?" said Charles.

"You've read too many books," said Bastian.

"What is the ideal number?" asked Charles.

"One. It's the army manual on getting the enemy before he gets you," said Bastian.

"And what would I read in my freedom if I were to defeat my enemy?"

"The army manual on not being a clever dick," he replied with an almost affectionate hand on Charles shoulder.

"You'd better stop there, guys, or Epstein will have to come back and use you as models. I can offer tea without milk, coffee, or whisky," said Mel.

"Whisky!" was the joint response.

He served a doubly-generous single malt with ice. Sophia loved the hit. She knew nothing of art or philosophy. Her wisdom was of the street and the wound spring of a blow in the heart of every angry man. Cops wait at the terminus of every frustrated journey. Even Bastian didn't sense that moment when the rat trap was about to snap. She knew her limitations and her talent.

"Martine La Plume should be at a meeting with the Italian prime minister and the president of the World Bank right now. Next up is a far more important encounter," said Bastian.

Mel had switched on the TV. Images of men and women being led from schools, universities, and office blocks to police vans and army trucks looped and repeated behind the newsreaders.

"Fuck!" said Bastian.

"Looks as though someone like Major Barrois has convinced her that the elites and the intellectuals have to go, maybe because Charles is missing," said Mel.

"Sophia, call your daughter. I need her to fix a meet with the president of France," said Bastian.

"She's a kid, a student," said Sophia, ignoring the global sex superstar development.

"And what was Joan of Arc?" said Bastian.

"A visionary Christian martyr who died aged nineteen at the hands of the English," said Sophia.

"And put Charles the Seventh on the throne of France," added Mel.

"And is loved by France and worshipped by her king," said Charles.

"Get Izzy on the phone, tell her the score, and hand the fucking thing to me. There's no way Her Majesty's government is going to let her slip out of student debt that easily," said Bastian.

CHAPTER 25

She hit the call button. On a normal day she'd be out of battery.

"Mum! I've just met Jason Barber. He knows it's my sex scene with Charles tonight and he wanted to watch it with me! I blew him out 'cos he's not my type."

"That's great, honey. I've just escaped out of a castle window by making porno noises, got a secret army helicopter ride to Paris and I'm in hiding, so I'm doing OK, thanks."

"Wow! That sounds a bit unusual."

"I'm with Bastian Wolf. He's going to talk to you and I want you to do what he says. Is there anyone who can overhear you?"

"No, we're OK. I'm having a break from pelvic pulsing."

She decided not to add more, put the call on speaker and handed the phone to Bastian.

"Izzy, you know who I am, don't you? You are about the only person I can use for a very important job. We can't trust any police or army personnel. No one must know we're in Paris. Now, do you have any access to Martine La Plume?"

"She's called me to say a few things. She's a like massive fan of the show."

"I need you to call her and I need you to convince her not to mention anything to any of her guards including Major Barrois."

"That's the Major Mustard guy. He's got the hots for Selena," said Izzy.

Sophia shook her head at her daughter's natural sense of gravitas.

"She's in great danger. Some of her guards will kill her if they find out we're in Paris. It's too difficult to explain why now. I need you to contact Martine and just make it seem like a girly chat. You've heard that some showbiz type has got the hots for her and wants a meet and has asked you to fix it."

"I kind of get the picture. She's quite sexy really if she dressed better," said Izzy with a hesitation in her voice.

"Now, this is the critical point and you must get this right. The guy's name is Caesar Roboris. The message is that Caesar Roboris wants to see her alone and he just can't wait. She must be alone. Tell her you can fix it up and it must be at once. It must be at once."

"Is he an actor?"

"He's a celebrity; I'll bet he'll be on *Fortress of Fans*. He's done a lot of historical stuff over the years," said Bastian with a wry smile.

"Caesar Roboris has got the hots for her and wants to see her alone immediately. He sounds kind of passionate," said Izzy.

"OK, so far so good. You must tell her that you can take her to him and that she needs to come with you alone if she can. No one is going to suspect you or worry if she takes a break from the presidency to have a chat with you. You don't have to explain to her what is going on. Once she hears the code name she will know the score. Repeat it back to me."

"Carlos Fandango," said Izzy with a giggle.

"Don't be a stupid fucking brat! Your mother's in this too and there's bullets lined up for all of us, geddit?"

"Caesar Roboris," she said in a chastened tone.

I've no idea where she's going to be when she takes your call or when or where you will get to meet her. Once you know call me and we'll be there too. Remember you're just about the most famous actress on the planet at this moment, so act the part my dear," said Bastian.

"Sounds like real method acting," she said.

Sophia sighed. Maybe her naïve lightweight approach was their best hope. She took back the phone.

"Izzy, focus on this at the expense of everything else. This is your priority. Contact Martine and then get straight back to us. Minutes matter. I love you," said Sophia.

She glanced at Bastian who had crossed his fingers. Mel had opened a beautiful wooden trunk hand painted with Japanese scenes. He pulled out bullet vests, firearms, and familiar police-style belts with handcuffs and gas canisters.

"It's surprise party time for Caesar Roboris," he said in a boxing ring announcer's style.

"Is there any bloody point in asking who Caesar Roboris may be?" said Sophia.

"Nope, but if we pull this off you might get a hot date yourself," said Mel.

"Caesar Roboris contacted me. It was him who told me about my family and who I am. He sent people for me and fixed up my audience with the Pope. I never got to meet him. He told me never to say his name unless I was with others who knew it. He told me to forget about him until I took the throne of France."

"So Martine La Plume is in the club?" said Sophia.

"I didn't know that until now," said Charles.

"Sophia, Martine La Plume seized power using discontented police units and the civil service. Police were rioting and civil servants were being sacked in thousands. The electoral system in France would always have defeated her party, the Patriotic Front. Her power is fragile and she needs to create something permanent and ally herself to it. Her mission is...." Mel hesitated as Sophia's eyes widened.

"To recreate the monarchy and get generations of kids, mums and dads waving the flags and guessing the royal baby names," she said.

"The good bit is that no one else in the Patriotic Front knows it. She has to box clever. She does need to slap down the liberal media and the intellectuals and it plays well to her close supporters. She is a brave but lonely woman but you may not agree with her. Sophia, the boss is Caesar Roboris and everyone you've met is a cavalier, including Martine and Captain Côté. A thread that runs through history binds us in the same truth and belief but for now no one knows all the others. That's one of the reasons you were kidnapped," said Mel intently studying her face. "I want you to know that Charles pleaded for your life because he saw in you the courage of Joan of Arc and felt the fold of an angel's wings in the nobility of your face. He loved you at once as a chosen queen. You're alive because he told Caesar Roboris that he would kill himself if we killed you. Believe me, you don't try and do deals with these guys."

She looked at Charles who sighed and reached his hands out to her. They stood in the room in a silent embrace.

"You wouldn't have told me would you?" she said.

"There's a time for everything," he answered.

"And still as yet, we've had no time. No time for us," she almost implored.

Her phone was ringing. Bastian picked up.

"She's still in a meeting with the Italian prime minister and the president of the World Bank. She's determined to watch *Born to be King* at her apartment in the Elysée Palace. She's at the World Bank HQ in Avenue d'Iéna.

"Yeah, I know it," said Bastian

"Major Barrois is always with her. She's going home in a government limo at seven o'clock. She will do everything possible to be exactly on time. That's all I know. She understands about Caesar Roboris and says she's ready to meet him whenever he shows up."

"Good girl, we can't ask any more of you except to tell you that you never say that name again unless someone says it to you. Where are you going to be this evening?" asked Bastian.

"Selena and I are about to head out to Anna La Salle's vineyard near

Troyes. Vandervell turned up and he's hired a car," said Izzy.

Sophia took the phone.

"You'll be safe there. Anna will take care of you I know," she said.

"Mum, it's cool. There's loads of police and soldiers everywhere in the studios. They're arresting producers and beardy brainy types. I saw that guy Sparrow who wrote the scripts being dragged off. He was waving his driving license shouting in English that he only drove the bus. They grabbed Vandervell but he told them he was an orthodox bishop. He was saved by his kaftan."

"It's the purge of the Intellos, Izzy. Just play dumb. They'll never realize you've got any sense," said Sophia.

"OK, Mum, I won't wear my porn star librarian specs or stroke my chin," she said.

"I didn't know you knew about libraries, angel. Love you. See you soon," said Sophia.

She sat down and looked at the three men.

"Do either of you gentlemen feel in any sense that I've done enough to learn just something about Caesar Roboris?" she said with an air of exasperation. "For how long do I have to be kept as a second class sacrificial lamb waiting for slaughter?"

"Caesar Roboris is my boss. It's a big number of people," said Bastian.

"Like who?"

"Like world leaders, like CEOs, like religious leaders, like central bankers, like members of the English royal family," said Mel. "They're working with simple cops like you and me because we're walking the same road for now at least."

"And the English government know what's going on?"

"Yes, that's how come we use their planes," said Bastian.

"Well guys, I reckon we've got about two hours to come up with a plan," she said.

"Any female or cop intuition?" said Bastian.

"If I were Major Barrois I'd be stepping in now to rescue the Intellos. They know we're on the loose and that we probably know about the Napoleon Brotherhood. They have to act now and so do we. Sometimes it's nice not to have too many choices," she said.

"There's only three of us and we're not in a position to phone Manpower for a few extra guys. The good news is that there's nothing the fire department loves more than rescuing a maiden," said Bastian.

CHAPTER 26

Sophia strapped on her equipment belt. She checked the canisters of tear gas and adjusted the unfamiliar holster holding the Glock 9mm pistol. The dagger was definitely not a police issue. Charles tooled up with the same kit and made practice cowboy pulls of the gun.

"Good job you've got blanks in there," said Bastian as he issued high-energy glucose gels. "Get these inside you even if you feel sick. Political violence is a full contact sport."

Mel produced a range of coats and anoraks to hide the weapons. Charles received an elegant blue overcoat, Sophia a grubby ski jacket from the 1980s. Everyone had a scarf to discreetly hide the face. Well, at least she had underwear. Bastian made the final statement.

"We have courage, we have a king, we have a plan and we have the angel of the bold. Surprise! *Vive la France. Vive le roi!*"

The street outside was cold. Shops glittered with Christmas decorations. Briefly glanced magazines in a corner *tabac* carried nothing but pictures of Charles, Martine, Izzy, *Rex Factor* girls and Boymondo. They descended into the metro and rattled the few stops on line-1 to Charles de Gaulle Étoile. It was 6:40 p.m. and they needed luck.

As they came out of the Métro, the Arc de Triomphe above them seemed to stamp the authority of the state onto the tiny beings who scuttled at its feet. Far ahead down the Avenue d'Iéna, the view was of the Eiffel Tower, in its night costume of sequin brilliance. A few hundred meters down that road stood the incongruously plain and functionalist headquarters of the World Bank. Her heart was pounding as she walked hand in hand with Charles. He had wordlessly taken it as if they were no more than strolling lovers in the romance of the Paris night. She knew what she had to do. Generally a cop's courage is in reaction. This time she was setting the pace and pushing the button.

Mel pulled a cheap mobile from his pocket. He spoke in a panicked breathless voice.

"*Vite! C'est la Banque Mondiale, Avenue d'Iéna. Y a des flammes Vite! Vite!*"

He dropped the phone down a drain. A few yards ahead of them the limousines were lined up with their escort vehicles stuffed with armed police. Heavy retractable bollards blocked both ends of the service road. It was 6:55 p.m. Distant sirens peeped through the closed blinds of a cold Parisian night. Nearly everything that was about to happen would have to be an improvisation. One chance, Sophia. She knew what she had to do.

They stopped in the shadows as a heavy fire appliance began to swerve and bludgeon its way towards them through the traffic. From behind them more sirens were approaching from the direction of the Arc de Triomphe. Still all the guards and drivers stayed in their cars. It was 6:59 p.m.

Sophia and Charles began their stroll along the line of waiting cars. The first fire truck was pulling up. Firemen in silver helmets swarmed onto the pavement. A guy was running out a hose. It was 7 p.m. Now police were opening car doors. Another two fire trucks pulled up. More silver helmets more hoses. Charles stopped and took out his mobile, taking tourist pictures of the drama. And there she was, Martine La Plume at the doors, Major Barrois half a pace behind. They stepped out into the street as firemen ran past them into the building. He was hesitating, aware of danger, almost seeming to pull her back inside. She kept walking. Mel and Bastian had moved close, blending with security staff and firemen. At a range of twenty feet, Charles pulled his gun and opened fire on Martine. As the major tried to react, Sophia hit him with the tear gas directly into his eyes. They had only a couple of seconds to exploit the advantage of surprise. Charles turned and walked with a fireman back towards a truck, discarding his overcoat and pulling out a bright red woolly hat. Bastian and Mel folded round Martine and led her away as if they were her bodyguards. Sophia walked on calmly into the building as Major Barrois staggered blindly back.

The entrance hall was filling with people. Sophia carried on along a corridor waiting for a hand on her shoulder or a bullet in her back. She pulled off the ski jacket and wrapped the belt inside. She was beginning to like the track suit. Still nothing. Still nothing. She turned and looked back. There was a crowd of bank personnel at the doors. Uniformed police had arrived, bodyguards had guns drawn surrounding their VIP banker masters. She dropped the jacket casually and ambled to the edge of the bustle. Major Barrois was on the floor being treated by medics. She edged closer, pleased that he was still completely blind. She got into earshot.

"That poor woman was dead.... It was terrible. So much blood. She was torn apart. It was Martine!" she said.

People turned to stare at her. Many of them understood English.

"*Martine La Plume est morte,*" cried a young guy.

"*Oui, je l'ai vu moi même,*" said a woman.

Major Barrois was getting the message. Sophia made a step towards the door. A vice-like hand gripped her arm from behind.

"Who are you and what are you doing here?" said a uniformed Parisian police officer.

"She's my girlfriend. We work for the Bank of England, she went out jogging and came back to find all this," said Charles.

Her brain went into overload. What the hell was he doing here? He was supposed to have fired turned and gone.

The officer let go his grip and smiled.

"That explains the clothes. OK *Monsieur*, carry on. *Bonsoir.*"

Charles held out an elbow for her to take as they walked calmly to the door. Police and firemen were still swarming outside. He put an arm round her as they ambled back towards the Arc de Triomphe.

"What the hell are you doing? You were supposed to fire the blanks at Martine, turn away towards the fire trucks, change your appearance and walk down to the Metro at Iéna. My job was to hit Barrois with gas and spread the story that she was dead. Bastian and Mel were going to look like her bodyguards and get her away either in a limo, metro, taxi or bus depending on how it went.

"Exactly, did you hear any mention of you ending up inside the World Bank?" he said.

"No, but no one expected Major Barrois to end up back inside," she said.

"And did you expect me to just leave you in there?"

"Yes, because I'm a pawn and you're a king."

"Yes and the most powerful piece on the chess board is the queen."

"Things aren't always that black and white."

He laughed, paused, turned her to him and kissed her lips.

"And I love you," he said.

She looked into his dark eyes. They had somehow cheated death three times together.

"That's one life I owe you and two lives you owe me," she said.

"I only write checks in lifetimes. Would you take it?"

CHAPTER 27

The police had closed the road ahead, blocking their way back to Étoile and the anonymous safety of the Metro. He guided her across the road and walked to Rue Jean Giraudoux. A right turn and a cut through to Avenue Kléber brought them to a station where they slipped unnoticed onto a line-6 train. One change in the swirling hordes at Étoile put them huddled together on a train back to Louvre Rivoli. There was a smell of food from a corner restaurant. Everywhere there were sirens, and army trucks seemed to be at every junction.

"Looks like a war," she said.

"My guess is that Major Barrois has launched the Napoleon Brotherhood missile," said Charles.

He punched in the security code and took the lift back to Mel's flat. He felt for the keys under the mat. The door swung open.

"Saw you on the CCTV. Come in and have a drink," said Mel.

Bastian was seated talking to a French woman, eating pizzas from their takeaway boxes and drinking red wine.

"Got you both a *grande Quatre Saisons*, hope that suits?"

Sophia stared at the scene and at the woman.

"May I introduce Martine La Plume, president of France," said Mel.

The woman stood and smiled warmly, still holding a wedge of pizza. She extended the other hand to shake.

"You are in time to see tonight's show," she said in beautiful English.

"My daughter does her bed scene tonight with Charles," said Sophia, more or less blurting out anything rather than remain staring at her.

"This I know. This all of France knows and is waiting."

She seated herself with Charles on a sofa. He poured two glasses of wine.

"So the king is turned cavalier to expose the Roundhead plot," she said.

"That's a neat way of putting it," said Charles.

"You are even more handsome up close, but I must say it's Sophia who

109

catches my eye. What is your family name?"

"Castellana."

"It has a good sound. You are a *Jeanne d'Arc* for your king."

"Excuse me for asking but are you just here watching the TV show and having a takeout pizza?"

"Yes, and also chatting as '*amis.*' I don't get these times so much."

"There's soldiers on the streets and probably a military coup going on," said Sophia.

Martine looked back at her calmly with kind light blue eyes that carried her smile to the crow's feet lines at the corners. Her blonde hair was quite grey at the roots. She was dressed in a business style blue trouser suit and wore flat-heeled dark grey shoes.

"A coup, yes I hope so. I am enjoying one of your Anglo Saxon meat feast pizza with chilies to set my mood. Generals will tell you in close fighting the hardest thing to see is your enemy. Now they jump out from their holes and our snipers can see them. It's a good thing to relax while they get into range," she said.

Sophia hesitated, unsure whether to probe further.

"Martine knew about the Napoleon Brotherhood but not about Major Barrois and his bosses. When he believed Martine was dead he made some calls. GCHQ and the French DCRI were set up to monitor and trace them. We have their network," said Mel.

"And where does everyone think Martine is exactly?" asked Sophia.

"The army doesn't know. The others think she is where I've told them she is; that the so-called Intellos have her as a hostage. I gave their codeword to Ruyters News Agency. They are sitting on the story because all these Intellos are friends. We have an agent in there who's leaked it to Fox News and RT, the Russian news guys. They're pushing it out now and it'll be a house of cards," said Bastian.

"I think you should have been Machiavelli's ghostwriter," said Charles.

Bastian grinned.

"After the *Born to be King* show, they will release me unharmed when they see the social media storm is against them and that only the patriots of France will decide my fate. I will praise their good sense and forgive them on condition they understand that the people will tear them apart if I give the word. For now all patriots should unite around Charles and his *Rex Factor* bride."

Sophia let out a long breath.

"And the Napoleon Brotherhood will soon see they've been tricked."

"You have a cunning mind, Sophia. Yes, of course I will forgive many and again of course a few will commit suicide as military men of honor. Bastian and some patriots can make sure they do not suffer. We cannot have a public shooting war with our own army. Caesar Roboris would not accept that," said Martine.

Sophia's mobile was in the bureau drawer where she had left it when she had set out on her mission.

The muffled ringtone snapped her back to her humble reality. She retrieved it and headed for the bedroom, closing the door.

"Izzy, are you OK?"

"Course I am. Mum, Anna's husband is just so gorgeous, He's like those tall dark triangle shoulder guys in those books you read,"

"Did you call me to tell me that?"

"No, don't miss the show, Mum. This is my big break. Anna says there's two and a half billion viewers."

"That's one and a quarter billion for each nipple."

"Love you, Mum!"

For a moment Sophia sat on the edge of the bed. In truth she would have preferred to crawl away now to the burrow of her old life. She was tired, had no makeup and was ugly in a ridiculous track suit. Charles probably did love her in his own way but the mob would howl the name of his bride. She was looking at the floor when a hand stroked the top of her head and the bed moved beside her. She felt a gentle kiss on her cheek. She turned to look into kind blue eyes.

"We should stay close," said Martine La Plume.

CHAPTER 28

Kindness always unlocked her tears. Martine held her to her breast. Sophia let herself accept the warmth and power of this remarkable and magnificent woman.

"I've heard a lot of your story. You feel alone and far from friends. Your tears are the sun that follows the storm. Let yourself feel it on your face. This is how I explain my own tears to me," she said.

Sophia regained some control of herself. She couldn't ignore the fact that this woman was one of the most powerful on the planet.

"It can't be real that you're talking to me like this," said Sophia.

"Because I'm not an ordinary woman and I can't see another woman's heart?"

"No, not that or maybe I just can't see you as a woman like me."

"Maybe I can't see myself as a woman like you either. You have raw courage and some rare beauty," said Martine.

"You've more courage than me. You've such weight on your shoulders."

"To carry a big weight you must have a big heart too. It is beautiful to me that I've held you a little in this moment."

"I love the way you speak English," said Sophia with a smile, trying to deny Martine's emotional attractiveness by deflecting the mood.

"We must watch the show, finish the wine and the pizza, and then I must be president," said Martine.

Sophia stood up, sensing a hesitation in this other woman. Then she stood and kissed her, half lips, half cheek. Martine had taken her hand.

"Thank you for the voice in your eyes. I can hear you," said Martine holding her gaze.

Sophia briefly looked away and then back to her, softening again her mind to this woman. This woman! This woman who knew her! Who could pull her. Like feeling the passion of cathedrals without religious faith, she felt a connection with the essence of her, surely not stained with sexual desire. She returned the kiss maybe only imagining a stir of faith and a flight of spirit that brushed her sensual core with its wing.

"Before we go back, let me call your number so you have mine," said Martine.

Sophia gave her the number and waited for the connection. She stored it at once and smiled.

"Now we have a hand to hold. That will be a wonderful feeling," said Martine.

The show was just starting. Sophia sat back with Charles and poured a glass of wine. For now she put away the moments she had just lived. King Charles the First of England had made it back to France. He was travelling in disguise to see again his beautiful wife and lover Henrietta Maria. She had set up a court in exile of royalist cavaliers at the beautiful Château Saint-Germain-en-Laye, close to Paris. The desperate king walks alone through rain, stumbling with exhaustion. At last he nears the château, knowing that there are sure to be spies. He cannot risk revealing he is still alive. He puts his fingers to his lips and forces out a high-pitched sound before he falls to the ground. Wind whips the trees into the form of an angel and celestial music builds.

Sophia glanced up to see Martine make the sign of the cross. For sure there was a tear in her eye.

In the château, a King Charles spaniel pricks up its ears and whimpers, making its way through the legs and feet of courtiers. Outside the dog sniffs the wind and sets off into the trees. Swimming torrents and jumping ravines the dog arrives at the semi-conscious form of his master. It licks his face and dries him with its floppy ears. King Charles reaches out his hand and the dog offers its paw. A Boymondo ballad track, *Lover girl, faithful friend of my heart* fades in for a few seconds.

Bastian was smiling but making sick-bucket faces at Mel.

The king rips out a lock of his own hair, folds it in a leaf and places it into the dog's mouth He tells it to go to Henrietta Maria and bring back help. The spaniel stands up on its hind legs and raises a paw salute to his king who then falls back in exhaustion, close to death.

Martine La Plume was in full flow of tears.

"I love dogs," she said.

The dog reaches the bed chamber of Henrietta Maria who is sleeping fitfully tormented by dreams of King Charles being led to the chopping block. The dog whines, jumps on the bed and lays the leaf into her mobile and pneumatic cleavage. The queen senses it and is forced to push up and caress her breasts many times, sighing with parted lips in order eventually to retrieve it.

Sophia imagined a world of fly zips hurtling south in millions of boys' bedrooms.

"She is beautiful like her mother," said Martine.

At once she draws the lock of hair to her lips and knows that it is a sign from Charles. The dog whines and gestures with its paw for her to follow. They go to the stables where Henrietta Maria saddles up a horse and rides into the night behind the dog. They reach the king who seems to have died. She breathes life back into him with kisses. Again the wind whips the trees into angels. With strength beyond anything seen on WWF wrestling, she hauls him up onto the horse and heads back to the castle.

"She's got to get some Hollywood offers?" said Charles.

"As long as they don't want a double-act, Charles. I can't see your talent-show bride wanting that," said Sophia.

He didn't respond, but stroked the back of her hand. She knew well that he had no taste for what was his destiny.

The scene had flipped to England. The Roundhead general who had promised to care for the family of the substitute king, had gone to their country house with a platoon of coarse unshaven soldiers. The beautiful aristocratic woman is thrown to the troops for their pleasure and then murdered with her children. Finally they burn the house.

"I could have told him that would happen," said Bastian.

"Really?" said Charles.

"Never trust a murderer without a horse and a big feather in his hat," said Bastian.

The scene had moved back to the Château Saint-Germain-en-Laye. Charles hides in the stable straw while Henrietta goes off to find him food. She returns with cheese, wine, snails, and dry clothes. They kiss passionately. She tells him that a trusted cavalier will come for him in the morning. She goes to the castle chapel and prays for guidance. A track from *Boymondo does Sacred Christmas* plays. A beam shines through a stained-glass window and makes a blurred shape on her breasts. She pushes herself up and closes her cleavage with a sigh. As she calls out ecstatically to God, the shape of a baby and crown snap into focus. She knows what she must do.

"Christ, that was method acting," said Mel.

Sophia held her head in her hands. This was overload. She wished she had shares in fly zips.

The next day the trusted cavalier leads Charles to Henrietta Maria's bed chamber. His rock-star flowing hair has been cut and he is clean shaven. He looks like Gaspard Ulliel from the film *Jacquou le Croquant*. He strips, tight firm-buttocked teases, back to camera, slides into bed. Henrietta emerges from a side room. Naked. Yes, Mum. Yes, Sophia. Naked.

"I'm not sure I can watch this," said Sophia.

"It's not real," said Charles.

She puts her hand on hips, squats, hands on knees, wrists out, and twerks. Then she slides in beside him. The rest is adult-channel soundtrack, remixed Boymondo dance-edit, strobe flash of nipples, buttocks, bellies and then explosion into sunrise over planet Earth, parted Izzy lips and groans of cracking ice, swerving ball soccer goals, knockout punches and whales blowing plumes in perfect blue seas. The scene resolves into fireworks, Beethoven's *Ode to Joy*, and *La Marseillaise*. A scientific-style video of sperm penetrating an egg plays for a second. Izzy turns naked to camera caressing her fertilized belly as a beam of light from the window creates an angel in the motes of dust. A misty future shot in modern times shows a coronation cavalcade through the streets of Paris with Charles waving regally from an open-top Citroen limousine, followed by magnificent cavalry. Joyful citizens wave the French flag, the red, white, and blue now with a center band of *fleurs-de-lys*.

"Bit understated," said Mel with a chuckle.

"I love it," said Martine.

"If it works I love it," said Bastian.

"Just tell me the truth, Charles," said Sophia.

"You know the truth," he said.

"I wasn't there," she said.

"And neither was I. I got into bed in my jeans and we did one kiss. The rest is CGI,"

"Fantastic butt," said Mel.

Martine La Plume laughed.

"Love is an any-gendered thing," she said with her kind eyes turned to Mel. "We have our lives, our hearts, and la France. We must make of them our happiness. God will never give us more," she said.

"*Vive la France!*" said Charles.

Sophia took his hand.

"*Vive la France!*" she echoed.

CHAPTER 29

The *Rex Factor* show began with a thirty-language subtitle menu. Sophia watched a gorgeous South American teenager slinking along the catwalk in a ball gown. Then she had to give a small speech in French and perform a specialty act of her own choice. The child was beautiful enough to have gotten away with anything. Almost anything. She had chosen to juggle oranges badly while whistling out of tune to a samba rhythm. Mason Trowel stepped in and put an end to her misery.

"Can you sing my dear?" he asked.

The child stood crying with oranges at her feet.

"Well my dear, I suggest you take those oranges home and get some Vitamin C to stop your sniveling," he said.

Minders led her away while the audience booed at Mason Trowel.

Charles sat resigned and sad, shaking his head.

"Poor kid," he said.

"She'll get some decent cash and a VIP wedding ticket. One of the Patriotic Front ministers has got her lined up as a mistress. She's set for life," said Mel.

Martine and Bastian were leaving. She made a short phone call.

"Have a car at La Place du Carrousel in fifteen minutes," she said.

"Time to go clean up a few details," said Bastian.

Sophia studied him. She knew that the details meant human lives, guys who had chosen the wrong side of history and maybe had as much right on their side.

"*Au revoir*, Sophia. I'll see you again soon," she said, kissing her on both cheeks. "You've had very little calm. Find some moments to explore what you feel. It is a joy to know yourself."

Sophia looked down, afraid of what might connect in her if those kind eyes were to hold her again.

"Thank you, madame."

"Martine!"

"We've finished the pizza. You're president again."

"Then I know what to bring if I visit," said Martine with a smile.

Mel and Sophia slumped down. Charles had remained silent, half watching the *Rex Factor* girls.

"Anyone you fancy?" asked Sophia.

He seemed to snap.

"Do you think I want this shit any more than you?"

"As a matter of fact, yes. I want a straightforward life with a partner who wants me. I'm just a simple girl."

"Do you think kings and royals have ever married for love or choice? Just look at your Prince Charles."

"He always loved Camilla and at last he's with her."

"Exactly. The marriage of a king is not the heart of a king."

"Anyone in mind for your Camilla?"

Charles looked at her. She could see the pain of his situation in his eyes. No way was she going to offer to be a royal mistress while he bred children with some young fertility certified virgin selected by Mason Trowel.

"They need the show to engage the people, Sophia. This *Rex Factor* crap is necessary. The riots have stopped, the militias have gone home, the trains are running, the farmers aren't burning tires on the motorways."

"And we've closed down the Napoleon Brotherhood. We're a long way from home but we're lining up for final approach on this project," said Mel.

"Do I get pushed out of a van with my old uniform and told to walk home?" asked Sophia.

"We'll get you a new uniform. You're with us right through to end and you'll be recognized for what you've done. You're a pro cop, Sophia," said Mel.

"So what's next?" she said.

"The *Born to be King* show will run over the next few weeks. Charles has a final Boymondo farewell concert and a farewell limited edition album to cut. He'll be at the concert but all the Boymondo tracks are done by session guys," said Mel.

"We've got to phase in the swing from showbiz to royalty. It's a PR job of maintaining one fan base and building the next. Serious journalists from all over the world are jockeying to get my thoughts on world events. It's a career game changer to be a chosen toady or a court jester."

"Sometimes, Charles, you sound as cynical and manipulative as Mason Trowel," she said.

He sighed and nodded.

"You're right and I'm not proud of it. When I was studying for the priesthood I had to confront all sides of the human condition. I'm a man like any other except for my genes and my relationship with God."

"Are there 'special ones' other than football managers?" she asked.

"There are kings."

"And...."

"Men believe in God. God believes in kings."

Sophia stared at him. A couple of times she had wondered about the underlying stability of his mind.

"He means that the king is the natural officer of God. All systems in nature and politics lead to kings. Democracy leads to elected yet castrated kings. Straightforward dictators rule as kings. Revolutions revolve until the man strong enough to be king stops them. In a pack of dogs, one of them is king," said Mel.

"How does God inform the dogs of his choice?" she said.

"The top dog knows it, not from God but from the truth of the universe that God has put into him," said Charles.

"Like Pedigree Chum instead of bread at communion," she said.

Both men laughed. Mel went to a cupboard, took out a bottle of cognac and distributed three glasses.

"To the divine right of kings," he said.

Sophia sipped the brandy as the *Rex Factor* show rolled on with yodeling blondes and roller skating redheads. The audience howled, chanted and held up homemade banners proclaiming their girl. She had to acknowledge that it was great TV.

"Charles, where do you really, really stand on the divine right of kings? Your show told us that Charles the First truly believed that God had appointed him and that no ordinary man could challenge him," she said.

"Yes, that's a fair appraisal of his attitude," said Charles.

"So?"

"So he was a king in those times."

"And God now chooses kings with TV shows and boy bands?" she said.

Mel leaned forward and looked into her eyes.

"The goal is human happiness, Sophia. Men are at their best under kings. They are at their holiest under bishops. Look at the history of art and valor, of architecture and music. Kings make artists and poets, republics make toilet cleaners and secret police. Kings build palaces and cathedrals, republics build shopping malls and industrial estates."

"I'm out of my depth here," she said.

"The system has denied you an education. That's not your fault. There are those who believe in restoring the truth of God and the glory of man. The beheading axe and the guillotine may as well chop the air as try to behead a truth," said Charles.

"And you guys believe that?"

"This is the first time we've spoken openly without guards and surveillance, Sophia," said Charles.

"So just what the fuck is this?" she asked.

"It's a quest for the natural order of things. We're using the tools at hand," he said.

"And the boy band soap opera show is a bloodless way to get us there. Once you possess a throne you possess its people and we can bring them happiness," said Mel.

"Who is we?" she asked.

"Soon you'll know more. I'm only junior management," said Mel.

"And Martine La Plume?"

"Martine is an awesome woman. Caesar Roboris saw her as a chance to create a monarchy," said Mel.

"But she thinks she's also using them to secure *her* power," said Sophia.

"And she is! My guess is the moment of truth will come when Caesar Roboris starts to dictate the style of monarchy they want, or rather demand. They're using her and she's using them and for now there's no conflict."

"But there will be, won't there? Martine wants a politically powerless ornament. This Caesar Roboris wants kings with balls and horns by divine right. How do you see it Charles?" she asked.

He let out a long sigh.

"I define my role as a man above politics, a man who can be of his people and speak for them."

"Does that put you above or under Martine La Plume and the Patriotic Front?" asked Mel.

"It puts me at her side, seeking happiness for the people. She is their president. God called me to be king. My power is that of loving my people. I would never harm Martine."

She needed to sleep and simply not be anyone or anything. For sure, she was still something, but it would take the best cop in her to assemble the clues into a joined up woman. Maybe this night there could be something between her and Charles. Mel had his own room, and there would be no police or soldiers. The mood was wrong. Charles was part of something wider—wilder than anything she could have imagined. She had taken him, maybe patronized him, as a serious young man, a beautiful man who desired her. She had known when to hold his eyes and what spin to put on her smile. His awkward love was pure in a compelling way but could never be expressed. He could never be hers. At best she'd be the educating mistress watching him cavort with his beautiful young soap opera queen and their royal children. And then there was the issue of his ambition. Did these guys along with Caesar Roboris' plan to seize the full power of king? She'd gained that impression, but Charles was vague. She'd opted to play dumb, sensing that too many questions might stir suspicions. She was a Metropolitan police officer from South London. Her oath was to the queen of England. And exactly what were the feelings of Her Majesty?

Mel folded out a clic-clac bed from a sofa.

"A lady needs her privacy. Please take the bedroom, Sophia. I'm pleased to share my space with a gorgeous young man if only for the view."

"Viewing is harmless," said Charles with a chuckle.

"Well, make sure I get a good sight then and, if you need a friend in the night...," said Mel.

She didn't argue. It resolved her situation. She showered and slid into the glorious perfumed magenta silk of Mel's bed. Sounds of the great city crept into her consciousness. Whatever the affairs of states, there was always the unloading of fruit into restaurants, the engine notes of buses, the struggle of pigeons for a ledge. Who was she? What was inside her, coiled, hidden, stuffed into the corners? Could a hand just reach in to her and stretch out the coil? Could a light unravel her slovenly debris? She'd learned from addicts that the monster never stops its whisper once you know its voice. The path of flowers and perfume led steeply down to the cliff edge in her dream. She couldn't say the name of the half kiss on her lips that called her there.

CHAPTER 30

In the morning Bastian had returned. From her window Sophia could see that the police and soldiers had melted away. She shuddered at the idea of asking him about his night shift. He was cleaning a gun on the coffee table.

"Everything OK out there?" she asked.

"Yeah, pretty good. Napoleon's met his Waterloo I think."

"And Major Barrois?"

Bastian sighed and drew back his lips tight against his teeth.

"He was a good man. We couldn't risk a military government."

"But he's dead?" she said.

"Yeah, he did his duty," said Bastian.

"I can see this hurts you, Sophia. You have a tender heart," said Charles.

"And your heart?"

"A king must accept honor, duty, and pragmatic sacrifice."

"Did the Pope explain that to you?" she asked.

"The Pope kind of relies on a story of sacrifice," said Charles.

"I'll have to check out the Bible and read up on Saint Bastian," she said.

"There's plenty of Bastians in the Bible. Most of 'em worked for Caesar or Herod," said Bastian.

Sophia let the subject drop and made coffee. The mood was edgy. She knew she'd said too much.

"What a splendid day to get out and about," said Mel with synthetic jollity.

"Not in this poxy track suit."

"Ah, vanity thy name is woma—"

"Vanity thy name is not fucking Adidas!" she interrupted.

"Darling, you'd look gorgeous in anything," said Mel.

"Exactly. I'll settle for *anything*, but not this fucking track suit, geddit?"

"We understand. We're going to Anna's place. A wardrobe has been carefully selected for madame and awaits you," Mel said with a beaming smile.

Her mood lifted. Izzy would be there with Vandervell. Anna La Salle was so far above her in the police structure that she could never approach her as a friend. Her presence in this team reassured Sophia that at least everything must be authorized and legal.

They walked the Rue de Rivoli, cut through the Louvre courtyard, past the Pyramides to the Place du Carrousel. A black Citroen C4 Grand Picasso was waiting with a smartly dressed driver. Sophia sank back into the black leather. The vehicle moved off smoothly, leaving behind the sights of Paris like crumbs fallen from a feast of visual gluttony. Her eyes caught billboards of Charles in cavalier costume with the tagline *Born to be King*. Further on she spotted a bus stop plastered with *Rex Factor* front runners. One girl looked like the youngest of President Ronald Grump's daughters. The words read *The Tiara Spangled Banner*.

"Can we speak openly here?" she asked.

"The driver's on the team," said Mel.

"Is that Esmeralda Grump?" she said to no one in particular and not wanting to accuse Charles.

"Sure is, sister, two nations divided by an uncommon dentistry," said Bastian in a deep drawl.

Charles chuckled.

"She smiles with her back teeth," he said.

"But not her eyes," added Sophia.

"Eyes cost an extra million, sister," said Bastian.

"You've got American teeth," she said to Charles.

"I was born perfect."

"Fucking hell, this is surreal. Are you going to marry Esmeralda Grump?"

"They've not had a stars and stripes princess since Grace Kelly. They're due for one," said Bastian.

Charles looked at her seriously.

"A royal marriage is about alliance and power," he said.

"Not if it's just an up-market TV reality show. Who gives a shit?"

"Ronald Grump gives a shit. He doesn't believe in losers," said Bastian.

"I just know it's going to be her, isn't it?" she said.

No one answered. She knew. She knew.

"The reality show is for now, Sophia. It's our way to achieve what's important for all the peoples of the world. An alliance with the USA would be a beautiful thing," said Charles.

"Have you fertilized her eggs yet?" asked Sophia.

"Not yet."

"I'd get on with it if I were you. You could have dozens frozen up ready for transplanting into surrogates. Esmeralda doesn't look like a stretch-mark babe to me."

"Stretch-mark?" he queried.

"Ah, something the Pope didn't cover I guess. If you ask me nicely I might show you some one day."

"Sophia, I understand your point. I do. I do," he said, reaching out for her hand. She accepted it but didn't return his grip. The landscape either side of the A6 Autoroute du Soleil was flat and dressed in its winter skeleton costume. She watched it roll past. It fell away just as everything in her life was falling away. She owed him nothing, yet she had accepted his awkward stupid love and it had empowered her to be wanted by such a man. She had shamelessly signaled her open intimacy to him. His pride and arrogance were not about himself but about his position and his destiny. Inside there was a person she could love desperately in return for his need for her. She knew little of him, but he knew nothing of her. Did he even know she was divorced and why? He had said that there would be a time for them to talk. It would have to come soon or the blowing sand of history would choke the voice of her soul.

CHAPTER 31

Anna La Salle's farmhouse and Champagne vineyard estate were beautiful beyond chocolate box or calendar kitsch. The drive led through acres of bare vines and opened out into a grand courtyard of cobbles and even a water well. The building was stone with tall ornamental brick chimneys and dormer windows. Vandervell had improvised a film set around a number of outbuildings and an entourage of motor homes completed his travelling circus. The big man almost scampered to the car as they arrived.

"Charles, get your snogging kit ready, could do with bit of extra lust in the dust for the croak scene," he said.

"The man's an artistic genius," said Mel.

"So where did Charles the First die?" asked Sophia.

"In France, about two years after he'd escaped," said Charles.

"So he saw the secret baby Sophia-Béatrice," she said.

"Yes, it was his wish that she should go to Maryland with the Jesuits. A famous guy called George Calvert was a friend of King Charles and it was he who set up the Catholic colony," said Charles.

"So she made it and that's why you're here," she said, imagining the trauma and heartbreak of that period.

"The Catholics had a hard time in struggle with the Protestants but the child survived. You really should finish Oscar Sparrow's book," he said.

"He was arrested in the purge of the Intellos," she said.

"Most of them will be out soon," said Bastian. "Martine's going to do a peace and reconciliation speech tonight in between *Born to be King* and *Rex Factor.*"

"Three billion viewers last night. Three billion!" said Vandervell.

Sophia looked around for Izzy. What could it have been like for that exiled queen of England to hand over her little daughter to priests in the slim hope that their dynasty just might survive? Maybe kings and queens did fate and destiny rather than love and sorrow?

Charles had been led away to prepare his snogging kit for death in Izzy's arms. Sophia imagined that another blockbusting collision of human lip tissue would propel her child to even greater galactic fame.

"Mum!"

Sophia spread her arms as her daughter ran at her. She was dressed in 17th century court clothing with enough cleavage liftoff to get a space crew to the moon.

"You didn't need to dress up for old Mum."

"It's been wild, Mum! Mason Trowel's signed me for two films and two more albums. I'm at number one on iTunes with my first song."

"What song? You can't sing."

"They do stuff with the sound, but it *is* me underneath. It's called *Hey Boy! Got your selfie in my heart,* said Izzy, breaking into a tuneless rendition.

Sophia held her away, looking into her eyes.

"Tell me now, are you OK with this? Are you coping with this?"

"Yeah, I'm fine. Selena knows all the angles. She's like been there, Mum, you know with Mason Trowel and politicians like Baloney Flair and Neil Farouche. It's like an inside club, Mum."

"You mean they breathe in each other's farts and suffocate in the air outside."

"Like I mean, Mum, I've already got two million in the bank offshore, like no tax," said Izzy.

"Two million what?"

"Dollars, yeah dollars I think."

Mel died instantly.

From the corner of her eye, Sophia had seen the Peugeot 308 approaching along the drive at speed. Mel had signaled urgently to Bastian who drew his pistol and hit the ground taking careful aim. Mel walked on to investigate the driver, raising his hand with a gesture to stop. Sophia was pushing Izzy down as Bastian fired three rounds into the car. The heat seared Sophia's back. Metallic shreds and glass screeched over their heads. The shock wave of sound punched the breath from lungs. She lay on top of her child, feeling her move, feeling her life.

Bastian was the first to react.

"Fuck! Fuck! Fuck!" he said.

In the clearing smoke she saw the burning remains of the car, now in a crater three feet deep.

"Fucking suicide bomber driving a fucking car bomb," said Bastian.

Izzy was scrambling up, sobbing incoherently. Sophia checked her over.

"Instant fame. Instant death," said Sophia with a harshness that surprised herself.

Bastian walked back to them as a shard of human flesh burned in the gravel a hundred yards away. Between them Mel and Bastian had saved their lives.

"Who?" Sophia demanded.

"The worst of enemies—the man with nothing to lose," said Bastian, blood running down his face from an ugly gash in his scalp. "Mel was always too bloody polite. Why the fuck didn't he just open fire?"

"'Cos he was a cop, Bastian. We don't just kill."

Her ears were ringing from the blast. There was a pain in her arm. People were surrounding them. Charles was holding her to him.

"Sophia, oh my God, you're OK, thank God," he said.

Her mind was adjusting to her new reality. Mel had led her away from the shooting in London where Simon Westcott had died. He was a Metropolitan police officer and was her link to some kind of structure. He'd become her friend. Could she go home now? She knew the answer to that one.

"So much death, so much senseless death," she said.

"Mel was a gentleman, a true and brave man in the cavalier tradition," said Charles.

"He didn't have a bloody horse. This isn't the Three Musketeers. I guess you believe this stuff," she said.

"I believe that terrorists once used to cut the heads off kings, their queens, their children. I believe that all good men seek a better way to live. Mel believed that too. I'm a humble and inadequate man in myself, in the tradition of kings. Sacrifice and valor is the steel of monarchy, Sophia. If we don't press on, all this death will have been wasted."

"And monarchy will put an end to terrorism?"

"Monarchy will give the people themselves the pride and self-confidence to defeat it. You can manage terrorism with police and politics. Only a king can lead a united people away from it."

She sighed into his chest as he held her. He had lost his own sister in this carnage and yet he stood firm.

"You guys have got balls and daring, I'll give you that."

"I hope we have compassion too. A king is first a protector of his people," he said.

"Did Mel have anybody?" she asked.

"Yes, a corporate chic designer guy called Tim. The Paris flat is his, in case you wondered how a London cop could afford it."

"I don't ask cop questions any more. I just wonder if I'll live until my next meal."

"One day soon we'll be able to talk."

"I just hope I'll be able to listen," she said.

Selena was comforting Izzy. Her leopard skin trouser suit and shiny silver booties looked obscenely out of place. Some gendarmes had arrived as Bastian was organizing the collection of body parts. Whatever you could say of him, he was ruthlessly professional. The cop in her made her feel guilty for not joining in. Half a blackened hand lay not far from her. She imagined Mel the night before handing out pizza and pouring brandy with those fingers. Tears forced out from inside her. She tensed herself against the urgent need to vomit. She had to turn her eyes from the scene and hold her breath. The smell was of petrol, burning plastic and an element she knew from house fires in London: human flesh.

CHAPTER 32

A French army medic dug a small piece of shrapnel from the back of her upper arm and put in a stitch.

"Your hair is burned and you have a heat blister on your neck. It is a miracle you know. If you had been standing up.... You can guess the story," he said.

"Who was the bomber?" she asked.

"I think it is religious. Yes, the same people who did the Pope. This is what they are saying."

She was seated on a stool in a tiled bathroom. She heard the door open behind her. A woman spoke in French to the medic as he left.

"Sophia, my poor Sophia," said Anna La Salle hugging her from behind. Sophia swung round to face her.

"Anna, this place is your home. All this at your own private home."

"Yes, it's not ideal. Luckily we'd sent the children away because the filming is hard to hide and it provides a juicy target."

"Where are your children?"

Anna seemed to be posing a question to herself.

"They're not in France, maybe I'll leave it there. I'd hate you to have to suffer to keep the secret," she said at last.

Sophia understood. If she were to fall into the hands of terrorists it would be better not to know.

"Mel is gone. He was a good man. He worked well with Bastian, but he's not a cop. He doesn't know discretion or mercy. He is completely fearless and ruthless. We need him so, so much," said Anna.

"How does that affect me?"

"Mel acted as an advisor and moderator. Maybe he just took the sting out of Bastian a little. You and I are police officers. We answer to the law and Her Majesty's citizens. Bastian carries out orders and we're not always in the same loop."

"Yeah, so how can I...?"

"Mel kept an eye on Bastian's work if he could. He was our way of keeping up to speed sometimes. Keep me informed of everything you can about him, that's all," said Anna.

"Like note times and dates, when and where."

"You're not alone. You won't know everything and that's the intelligence game."

"And your job is intelligence gathering," said Sophia.

"Exactly, just in case you were wondering why I'm here, I'm hiding in plain sight and so far I'm alive," said Anna.

"He's very close to Martine La Plume," said Sophia.

"Yes, she respects him very much. He's not French army so he's not going to be connected to any cells or cliques. That's her take on him."

"And what *does* Martine want?"

Anna gave her a sideways look before speaking.

"I'm guessing you're getting a crash course on politics."

"Well, I started at zero," said Sophia.

"Martine grabbed power but even within her Patriotic Front there are enemies. Two of her own close civilian aides were part of the Napoleon Brotherhood and she didn't know Major Barrois was earmarked to kill her. The old European Union has collapsed and it's a free-for-all for power and dominance. Martine needs some potent glue to pull the gaps together," said Anna.

"So did she dream up this monarchy idea?"

"No, I can see in your eyes that you've figured that out," said Anna.

"There's a name...?"

"Caesar," said Anna. "Now tell me the next word."

"Roboris."

Anna nodded.

"I didn't know what you knew Sophia."

"Not much. They discovered Charles in America and organized a chat with the Pope. Charles had believed himself called by God and assumed it was to be a priest. Caesar Roboris fixed it for the Pope to tell Charles that God had called him to be King Charles the Eleventh of France," said Sophia.

"Well, I guess if you're going to get that kind of news the Pope would be the best messenger," said Anna with a smile. "Are you a Catholic?"

"Yes," said Sophia.

"I'm Church of England so I don't have to worry about the existence of God—unless he arranges flowers and makes jam," said Anna.

"We can still get on. I promise not to burn you at the stake if you promise not to cut off my head."

Anna laughed.

"Yup, you've obviously mastered theology, history, and politics."

"So how did Boymondo, the *Rex Factor* show, and Vandervell's film come into existence?"

"They hired Mason Trowel and Vandervell to fix it. Trowel's on a knighthood in January and Vandervell's getting to be Lord Grimethorpe," said Anna.

Sophia smiled, relieved at last to be learning something of this woman's thoughts.

"Anna, you know the question I'm not asking you don't you?"

"Who is Caesar Roboris?"

"Yes."

"Caesar Roboris is not one man or one woman. It's a group of people and entities who seek prosperity and well-being for mankind. At least that's the mission statement on the side of the box. They believe that the experiment of democracy has failed and that kings are the natural pattern of the universe. They don't always agree and doubtless, some of them have undisclosed personal ambitions. We're trying to figure out who and what. Her Majesty's government likes to back winners. Her Majesty just likes to race horses," said Anna.

"Same horses, same race, different perspective," said Sophia.

Anna nodded.

"And what do you make of Martine La Plume?" she said.

Sophia sighed and looked to the ceiling.

"She's complex and brave."

"And attractive isn't she? A woman can feel it," said Anna in a matter of fact voice.

"Yes, she has kind eyes. You don't expect that, do you?"

"She likes you very much, Sophia. It's a lonely place where she is. If you can get close to her it would be of great service to us. We can't be certain of her intentions."

"And you'd like to know more? How do you know she likes me?"

"She told me and I told her I'd pass on her sentiments. Any insights into her or the Patriotic Front would be quite wonderful," said Anna.

Sophia shook her head.

"Bastian wants me to snuggle up to Charles and I think Charles also wants me to educate him for his role as stud king of France. The lady president just likes me as a woman. Could be quite a threesome."

"Just remember you're an Inspector from the Metropolitan Police South London. The streets of Streatham prepare a girl for anything. I was on L District at Brixton myself," said Anna with a smile.

Sophia returned it. She liked this woman and would trust her. She opted to deal with more practical issues.

"My prison issue track suit is completely useless. Mel told me...."

On saying his name she was ambushed by tears. That morning he had cared about her as a person and had promised her a new wardrobe. Now he was dead and ripped to shreds in the dirt as if his kindness, his humor, generosity, and his courage had never existed.

"I'm sorry," she said.

"I understand. He'd phoned me last night to say how well you were doing and that he thought you were beautiful. He listed the clothes he thought you'd like. He'd studied your style and coloring. Many of us loved him. Shannon will be heartbroken." Anna broke off with her own tears.

"Shannon?" queried Sophia.

"She's a Met' cop. Mel was her best friend and idol. Someone's got to tell her and I want you to do it, Sophia."

She knew well enough the police job of breaking bad news to loved ones after sudden death and accident. She dreaded this one but she wouldn't pull back from her duty or show weakness in front of Anna. Some other officer had had to notify Simon Westcott's family.

"Sure, where is she?"

"In England. There'll be a plane on the tarmac at Vatry Airport. It's a few minutes away."

She showered. Bomb debris and crumbs of flesh circled the plughole in a banal horror show. She brushed and conditioned her hair to smooth away the singed areas. Her burnt neck was stinging. How many days had she been lost in this maze? About a week separated her from her old life. She knew she could never go back even if her physical body was transplanted there. She chose a sleeved blue dress, a deeper blue tasseled poncho and medium heels, yet talons all the same. She made up her face. That any vanity remained in her appalled her.

She joined Charles and Izzy in the warm vibrancy of the farmhouse living room. Beams, wooden supports, and stonework blended with chairs and sofas in deep green and red patterns of vines, grapes, and rural scenes. A roaring log fire focused the eye on a huge fireplace. Charles stood and kissed her on both cheeks.

"You do look stunning," he said.

She wanted to snap back at him for mistaking her mood. She wanted to feel clean and ignorant of death, not praised for selfish narcissism of which she had already accused herself. This stupid boy knew nothing of her.

"Thanks," she said plainly.

She looked at Izzy. Dear God, she hadn't even reflected on her own daughter's situation. Was she safe here?

"I'm flying to Los Angeles, Mum. I told you I had a film deal and Vandervell has all he needs from me now. My flight is out of Charles de Gaulle and they're waiting for me."

"Just like that, like it was a trip to Walmart?" said Sophia.

"Just like I've signed a two-movie deal and it'll make me for life even if I never do another thing."

"Who else is going?"

"Selena and Tharindu," answered Izzy.

"Who?"

"Tharindu, the Boymondo guy."

"Is he the male musk musketeer?" said Sophia.

"Yes, he was kind of on the Bollywood fringes when Mason Trowel picked him up. Mum, we have a bit of a thing and he's part of the movie deal."

What could she say or do? What would she have done at Izzy's age? She'd have killed anyone who'd tried to stop her.

"Izzy, I should be there. I should be advising you and caring for you. These aren't normal times. I want you to grow up twenty years to see where it is that I'm waving from and then try to wave back. I'm glad you're getting out of France for now."

"We'll get together as soon as things are normal, Mum."

"Superstar global sex icon is normal for you," said Sophia.

"No, it's not, Mum. It's trash and it's hype. I'll ride the wave, but I'll keep my wet suit on. You can take the girl out of South London but you can't get Crystal Palace football club out of the girl."

"You know I'm going to England?" asked Sophia.

"Yeah, Charles told me."

"I'm coming too. They're glad to be getting me out for a couple of days. It's safe where we're going. We'll get some time," said Charles.

"Ahh, that's so sweet," said Izzy.

"Are you patronizing your dear mother?"

"As if, Mama mia."

Over her daughter's shoulder she could see Anna and a gendarme.

"I think your driver is there," she said, hugging her child, not saying a million things that could be said and re-said and be of no account to the gods.

"Love you, Mum."

"A mother's love is always ahead of you Izzy, guessing the rocks and the currents. It's the inherited greasy pole none of us can grip but none of us can release either. Love you."

CHAPTER 33

She heard the car drive away. She didn't wave, she didn't cling or embarrass herself or her child. She thought of Henrietta Maria handing over her daughter to priests to take a chance on life in a distant unreachable world. Her own anguish was nothing in comparison.

"You're not just going to England to see Shannon. There'll be a meeting the day after tomorrow with some government guys and a representative of Caesar Roboris. We didn't choose you Sophia but you've turned out to be a star. I'll see you there," said Anna.

Sophia nodded. Her voice would have broken if she'd tried to speak. Maybe Mel would be a star in the sky by now.

A French armored car in camouflage livery took her and Charles to the airport at Vatry. They drove onto the tarmac and took a few paces to a BAe146 of the Queen's Flight. On board was a team of three men and a woman.

"I'm Commander Sandys, SO6 Diplomatic Protection," said a smooth-voiced man in his late thirties.

"Not sure where I fit in exactly," said Sophia aware of this guy's high rank. "But my companion is King Charles the Eleventh of France."

"It's an honor to meet you both," said the commander.

Already the plane was taxiing. In seconds they were airborne and soon the English Channel was doing its imitation of a Google map beneath them. She took Charles's hand and looked into his face.

"Let's leave everything bad that's happened back there if we can," she said.

"Yes, maybe we can," he replied.

She noticed that away from Bastian and Mel he'd become the much more uncertain young man she'd first met. Maybe now she could know him without the carnival of kings and gods. Ahead of her lay the job of informing a woman called Shannon that Mel was dead. It was a regular police job but this time, she'd have to be controlling her own emotions.

"Landing into Northolt," came the clipped RAF voice of the pilot.

It was a revelation to travel on private jets and not be troubled by customs or passport controls. Power could seduce a girl. Soon the Protection Squad convoy of BMW X5s was at 100 mph on the M25 orbital motorway around London. Commander Sandys turned to them from the front passenger seat.

"We're heading for Fleetworth-Green. It's a village right on the edge of London. The Earl of Bloxington has his estate there. His wife is Shannon," he said.

"She's a Met' cop?" questioned Sophia, seeking confirmation.

"And the countess," said Commander Sandys.

From the moment she'd collided with this situation she'd been out of her depth and the water just kept getting deeper. She tried to think of Mel Kendrick as just a name, not a man she'd liked and respected. And who had probably saved her life and maybe the whole show. They swept onto an opulence of gravel drive that led through a straight avenue of bare oak trees. Pasture land either side was dotted with fine chestnut horses. Bloxington Manor filled the windscreen view. The entrance was framed by stone pillars and imposing steps. A large man and a smaller woman were standing at the door. He exuded the strength and confidence of a bear, she guessed he was early forties. She was slim and beautifully coffee-skinned, maybe thirty-two. She came to the car door as Sophia stepped out.

"Blimey, you didn't have to come mob-handed, we ain't that rough," she said sweeping her arm to indicate the convoy.

Sophia blinked. Was this the Countess? Her accent was pure South London, even more pronounced than her own.

"I'm Sophia Castellana."

"I'm Shannon Chamberlain-Knightsmith," she said.

"Countess of Bloxington?" said Sophia.

"Well, I had to take him on for better or for worse so I went along with the bollocks," she said.

"And I'm Spencer," said the big guy in a deep posh voice. This guy growled babies.

"The Earl?" said Sophia.

"He's got more titles than Harper Collins. Just relax and come in. Anna's told us a lot about you. Bloxington Manor is a great place for conferences and all the stuff you're going to be doing," said Shannon.

Charles had taken her hand. She liked that. He was in some sense a king and in any event had noble blood. In taking her hand he'd seen or sensed her loneliness in this alien world and he was giving her his own status. She smiled a thanks to him. He seemed to catch the meaning. He squeezed. She squeezed back.

"What we need is a proper brew," said Shannon.

Sophia smiled in understanding.

"Yorkshire Tea! My God, France is a tea desert."

They walked through a grand gallery of large oil paintings. Spencer pointed to a man on horseback in military clothing.

"Charles, that's the first earl of Bloxington. He rode with Charles the Second to restore the Stuart monarchy to England in 1660. Of course Charles was the older brother of your ancestor Sophia-Béatrice who ended up in Maryland, poor little mite."

Charles stopped in front of the picture. He tightened his grip on Sophia's hand.

"History is far more than a subject on the school curriculum isn't it?" he said.

"That it is. Most modern plants, trees, and vines are grafted onto roots from pre-history. The root of a plant is the truth of a plant. The blooms, the crowns, the glory only display the strength of the root. A leader first loves his people, Charles," said Spencer.

"That's good advice, sir."

"I'm a pompous old bear according to Shannon, but you know what I'm saying, Charles. The old European management class took the people as crude and stupid. They saw themselves as the natural class of leaders. Point is, Your Majesty, they were smug and plain wrong."

"You speak from the heart."

"I speak from history, Charles. And history is the cardiac trace of kings."

"Spencer, the zip of your noble genes is undone. Put it away!" said Shannon.

"You agree with me, Shannon," he said putting his arm around her slender waist.

"You know I do. The poor guy's only just arrived and you're giving him the blueblood hard sell."

"I don't need to sell it. He has it," said Spencer Chamberlain-Knightsmith, Eleventh Earl of Bloxington.

They entered a magnificent high-ceilinged room with sideboards, candelabras, embroidered chairs, and chaises longues.

"He always gets this way with other aristos. He's quite normal with me," said Shannon.

"What is the truth of happiness? Are people better led by unelected kings or managed by unelected bureaucrats?" said Sophia.

"It depends on who surrounds the king, Sophia. Few bad men were well loved. Few good men were badly loved. The problem is not in the office of monarchy but in the officers of monarchs. It's easier to provide a stupid king or queen with a white stick than it is to convince an intellectual political class of its blindness," said Spencer.

"Bloody hell, Spencer, give the girl a break. Sophia, here's my politics.

Everyone blames everything on the police. That's it," said Shannon.

Sophia laughed. These two certainly had a rare chemistry. This woman was shiny bright and cockney cheerful, but she sensed a sympathetic intelligent soul. Sophia knew she had a job to do and put behind her before she could develop any genuine rapport. When everyone was seated, Shannon poured tea. Sophia calmed her breathing and watched her almost as if she were a deer in the crosshairs of her rifle sight, still innocent of that void the other side of moments. She watched her take Spencer's hand, almost as if....

"You're in sad-faced serious cop mode, Sophia. We've all been there haven't we?" said Shannon.

"I can't deny that. I do have some news about Mel. There was an incident and he was killed."

"I thought there was something in the air today," she said with a slight tremble.

"He was a hero. He spotted a suicide bomber and went towards him. He saved a lot of lives."

"He always had to show off. I hope he had his silk hankie in his breast pocket."

Spencer was biting his lip. Shannon was staring at that merciless wall separating before and after.

"You want to beg don't you? You always think that if you begged enough you could change something, make things different. You can't imagine that stone, that lack of pity," she said.

Sophia could see she was struggling to hold back her emotions.

"One of the finest men I ever knew," said Spencer,

Sophia nodded, keeping her professional manner.

"Were you there?" asked Shannon.

"Yes, he certainly saved me," she replied.

Shannon took a deep breath. This woman was tough.

"When I was first a cop, he saved me too. I had a dead body, a real stinker. He caught the radio traffic and turned up in case I needed a mate. I was a gobby cow and there were a few who'd have liked to see me fail. I was about to turn and run from that job and he was the only one who ever knew that. Both of us were gagging at the stench."

"You'd never forget a friend like that," said Sophia.

"He took me out for a curry after...."

And then the poor woman couldn't stop. Sophia knew she wanted to scream at the wretched waste and stupidity of it, at the cold shrug of the infinite universe and at her own emotional powerlessness. Spencer held her as she sobbed.

"There's his partner Tim, I'm assuming he doesn't know," said Spencer.

"No, the Met' Police bureaucracy haven't been informed. I'm here to find him too."

"Leave it to me. He's working for one of our companies in London. I'll go to his home tonight myself."

"You don't have to, sir," she said.

"I do. He's a long-standing friend. He met Mel here at a cricket match."

"Ours was a bizarre relationship, a sophisticated middle-aged gay guy and a junk-munching dance freak," said Shannon.

"You're both cops," said Sophia.

Shannon stood up and took an endlessly deep breath.

"I've got so much of that guy inside me. He was an endless free download machine. He's gone, but he's still in here," she said tapping her heart and tearing up a little. "On shit-days we did beer and take-away curry and that's what we're going to eat today 'cos this is a big-shit-day. Some bastards have killed the Mel out there, but they ain't ever gonna kill the Mel in me."

Sophia looked at this beautiful mixed race blue-eyed woman. Inside herself she was stitching together a pouring wound. She guessed that she'd never lost parents or loved ones until now and that this was the first scar tissue on her soul. Maybe she wanted to talk about him or maybe not.

"He told me he'd worked at Streatham," said Sophia.

"I'm kinda keeping him private inside me, safe from the world for now. Does that make sense?" said Shannon.

"Of course, keep him there until you can share."

"You worked with him?"

"Yes, we had some adventures."

"And you were there when he died too. I should be hugging you shouldn't I?"

"When you're ready we'll both get him out from inside and hug him together," said Sophia.

"Thanks, I appreciate that you've come to tell me. I hope we're gonna be friends."

"Of course," said Sophia.

"Thanks from me too. No one understands even half of what cops do. Please help yourself to tea. We need to arrange some things. Please excuse us for a little while," said Spencer as he took Shannon's hand and led her out of the room.

Sophia, relaxed her chin onto her chest. She felt Charles's arm around her shoulders.

"Oh, my lovely Sophia. That was a tough job for you. Dear God how strong you guys are. Who cares for *you* at the end of the day? What can someone like me offer in words that can approach your kind of, I don't know, maybe ache?" said Charles.

"Ache?" she questioned.

"Well, yes, ache. I was aching on your behalf. Cops must carry some sort of pain at what life is. Shannon makes things funny or a bit cynical to deflect it, but who actually cares about you?"

"She has Spencer. You can see he adores her," she said.

"But does adoration help her in itself. Where do you guys offload?"

"To be honest, the truth is with other cops and more often not at all. Once I broke a rib in a fight and I was really pissed off, 'cos it was agony and I didn't get a word of sympathy. I'd have done anything for a black eye. Life's a body puncher for everyone, not just cops. You learn to really milk the black eyes if you get lucky. It's self-harm with applause," she said with a chuckle.

"You know I care don't you?" he said.

"I think you do. I know you do. Police work can hurt you, but you deserve as much care as me. You're one man, maybe soon a king of a people. That's a really lonely place," said Sophia.

"I've got you," he said.

Sophia sighed. She didn't want to change the mood, but she wouldn't duck the issue.

"You can never *have* me. You're headed for a life with Esmeralda Grump. I don't want to beat you over the head with that fact because it seems that's the inescapable game plan. Anyway I'm far too old, we don't know each other and you've only known me for a week," she said.

"Time is relative to intensity I think. Two people may contemplate a candle flame for eternity and go their separate ways. An instant in a furnace and they're welded as one."

"You're a philosopher, Your Majesty."

Charles looked down and shook his head.

"You know I can't believe people will call me that. I know how ordinary I am."

"Rule by extraordinary elite people led the ordinary man to vote not for democracy but against politics itself. The elites make everything complex to exclude the ordinary man. They told a hungry man that his bread was politically incorrect," she said.

"Let them eat words indeed. Who's the philosopher now?"

"If I keep hanging around you guys I'm going to end up having a brain. If the police had meant officers to have brains they would have issued them."

"That's an old priesthood joke too," said Charles with a laugh.

"If God had wanted priests to have what? Lovers?"

"Lovers, miracles, angels, virgins, all the things that would be very useful in the toolbox."

"A priest's toolbox is a great image for a girl. That Pandora woman just couldn't resist."

"She didn't have a priest's toolbox."

"Whose was it then?"

"God, in pagan terms."

"God's toolbox would be even naughtier."

Charles leaned back and sighed.

"Wow! An improper conversation not involving murder, death, or politics."

"Yes, I feel better and naughtier already," she said. "You don't know me, Charles. I've survived years in police canteens and vans full of hairy-arsed coppers. Politicians always want the common touch. Well, Your Majesty, your quest is over."

He tightened his arm around her and pressed a kiss to her cheek.

"I need you, Sophia. Please."

She turned her head to face him.

"Need for what?"

"I need to know you'll be there, to ask, to talk."

His large dark eyes were shy but unafraid of her. He was a beautiful male. His lips were full and firm.

"You told me...."

"I love you, yes I kind of spilled that on you. I frightened myself because I wasn't expecting it," he said.

"Neither was I," she lied. "Incontinence can strike at any minute."

He laughed.

"I shouldn't have said it. I've been hiding from you a bit because it was such a stupid schoolboy thing to do."

"It was a wonderful innocent thing to do. Not all words of love are innocent or from the heart."

"You didn't laugh at me or want to avoid me?"

"No, Charles. No. I took your words away and wondered what I could do with them. If you tell someone you love them and they say it straight back, it's like words in a mirror, a reflection with no sense."

"Maybe next time I'll shout at a wall and at least fool myself with the echo," he said.

He moved forward and she met his kiss halfway. His lips probed for hers in that searching blindness of a finger tracing Braille. She closed her eyes to let herself be read.

CHAPTER 34

True to her word, Shannon had ordered curry from the Masala Magician, the Indian take-away restaurant of Fleetworth-Green. Sophia's mind flashed back to the homemade curry she'd never returned to remove from her oven in Streatham. Bottles of ice cold Cobra beer were generously supplied to the sumptuous dining room table.

"To absent friends and to success in our endeavors," said Spencer, raising a bottle of beer.

Unexpectedly Charles stood up.

"I simply want to thank our hosts for their hospitality and record my absolute admiration for the courage and character of everyone who is working with us for a better way. May our peoples be loved by their leaders and may leaders love and protect their peoples."

"Well said, Charles. Like a king, if I may say," said Spencer.

Shannon smiled, a halo of sadness almost visible around her. Sophia hugged her from a distance.

Charles sat down. Sophia touched his arm.

"I'm proud of you for that," she said quietly.

"It's easy when you're by my side."

"Martine La Plume is speaking on French TV tonight. We'll have to watch. She intends to show mercy and forgiveness to all these bloody media clever-clog types who sneer at the common people. She's locked up most of them. Shame we don't do it here," said Spencer.

"It's a balancing act, isn't it? The media can be corrosive of trust in everything. They hammer the police day and night. Most of them have got the squawk of crows and the courage of social media. On the other hand they can create a good image," said Charles.

"You're right. The buggers can never decide about English royalty. One minute it's cooing at babies and the next it's hacking phones to reveal Prince Henry's gay and cavorting with a transsexual zookeeper."

"Christ, Spencer, get me the editor. A story like that could put a new roof on this place," said Shannon.

"I made up the transsexual zookeeper and everyone already knows he's gay."

"Talking of Martine, what do you make of her, Spencer?" asked Charles.

"In the context of gay? Yes, I've heard she has swung both ways."

"I think she's beautiful as a mature woman," said Sophia.

"I was forgetting that you'd met. Yes, I'd agree," said Spencer.

"I met her when she was at the last meeting here. She didn't put a blip on my 'gaydar.' Did you sense anything Sophia?" said Shannon.

Sophia was pleased that the subject was away from Mel and involved Shannon.

"Not really but I'm not going to say I didn't find her attractive. She's very much a woman and is warm with need for human love I think. Maybe these things are fluid. A man or woman can cross a line if no one has drawn the line for them. Many women have had a close friend and dreamed of more perhaps or even soothed a loneliness within another woman, out of love, respect or admiration. The touch is mental and the sex its expression."

She knew Shannon was watching her. She'd also noticed how quickly Shannon had passed the ball.

Sophia was happy to get the poor woman open again in a neutral context.

"You do sound a bit of a fan," said Shannon with a broad smile.

"A woman like Martine doesn't turn me on. She turns me up."

"Turns up your volume?" said Shannon.

"Yes, because she wants to hear me too as a woman."

"What you're saying interests me."

"Look I'm not a guru on Martine but I'm not shy to talk about my impressions," said Sophia, at last throwing off her status as an accidental kidnap victim with no life or history. These guys were listening. She could see Shannon was very much alive to her own beauty and sexuality. She was completely straight but thirsty for knowledge. This chat would put life rather than death into the front of her mind and she would not deny her that warm wind. She decided not to hold back. She could also signal her openness to Charles. "Men and women talk about sex like it was one thing, like everyone understands what it is and what they are. A good man wants to give pleasure to a woman sexually as if he were the artist and she his canvas. He stands back from it and can kind of admire his work before he goes off to wash his brushes or whatever. He might say to himself, 'Hey, I did some good strokes today.' A woman might say to you, 'I need you to make a picture together.' Actually making that picture is what a woman always does. Her life deepens her and folds her in to hold the warmth of love, to keep it in. All the strokes of men or even another woman make her and stay on that canvas. There's no washing out. A man can create a beautiful canvas and walk away but only a woman can hand you a brush and say 'Let's paint the love of ourselves.'"

Sophia had let herself be carried away. Shannon's eyes were big and almost excited.

"I think that's poetic. Did you get that buzz from Martine?"

Sophia knew by the woman to woman look in Shannon's eye that she had indeed felt that buzz. If not she wouldn't have used the expression.

"It's not a blockbuster buzz. She's got a way of humming a tune that's so natural you believe you can sing and want to join in," said Sophia.

"These ladies are deep and profoundly different beings, don't you think?" said Spencer to Charles.

"Yes, makes you wonder what you're involved in," he replied with a smile.

"It's an ovarian conspiracy theory," said Shannon.

"I think the guys are washing their brushes together," said Sophia.

Shannon smiled as the mood swung to the moment.

"We ought to catch the end of today's *Born to be King*," said Spencer.

They trooped through to the lounge. What a joy it was not to be guarded and saluted. The Met' Police Diplomatic Protection guys were there in the shadows, but not on top of them. The show was already running. An infant Sophia-Béatrice was walking and beginning to talk. King Charles the First of England was pale and clearly dying. He performs a last kiss only just stopping short of tongues with his pneumatic self-caressing pouting queen. Finally she hands him the child.

"A truth cannot be untold my little one. No lies or violence that pervert weak humble men can keep the will of God secret from men's hearts forever. Go on my angel. Go on to your destiny," says Charles as he slumps back and dies.

A huge chorus of choirs builds as nuns hand the child to Jesuit priests who will convey her to Maryland in America. Newsreel style footage rolls of Henrietta Maria returning to England in 1660 to restore the monarchy in the form of her son Charles the Second to a grateful people. The scene changes to a space shuttle view of Earth. As the sun rises a semi-transparent angel folds the continents of Europe and America in its wings. A modern-day teenage Charles is seen boarding a yellow school bus as a beam from the sunburst picks him out. In the clouds Henrietta Maria blows him a kiss. Charles looks to heaven, raises a hand, and draws the kiss back to his lips. A deep voice says, "So it is written."

"Old Vandervell doesn't hold back does he?" said Spencer.

"It's so far over the top that the top is too far below to see," said Charles.

"That poor little baby," said Shannon.

"It's a masterpiece with beautiful actors," said Sophia with a smile at Charles.

"But isn't it just too much?"

"Yes, it's far too much like champagne, *foie gras* and Wagner's operas. Come to think of it, the crown jewels, the golden coronation coach, and soldiers in dress uniform are completely over the top. No one is going to judge this show on taste, they're going to judge it on its color and emotion," said Spencer.

"I bet all the intellectuals are sneering at it," said Shannon.

"Luckily the braver ones are in prison and the sheep are huddled in a corner grumbling that the nasty mob have turned into beastly collie dogs," said Spencer.

"I'm a bit worried about the Intellos. Some of them are decent guys and we can't keep 'em locked up forever," said Charles.

"Seems like a good idea to me," said Spencer. "There was some clever clogs professor on CNN this morning saying that Charles the First didn't escape at all and that the writer Oscar Sparrow is an ex-communist working for Viktor Pinupskin."

"Anything's possible, but he's dead anyway. I saw it on the BBC earlier," said Shannon.

"What happened?" asked Charles.

"Murdered in prison by some agent of the intellectuals."

"He was only locked up by accident," said Charles.

"Sorts out a problem if he did make it all up. Now he's a martyr and a cavalier and can't be questioned," said Spencer.

Sophia listened to the conversation. She'd worked as a detective before she'd come back to uniform on promotion. So, someone had murdered the guy who'd written the book about the escape of King Charles the First. Apparently an Intello was guilty. If the story was a fake it would have been better to let the writer live and allow the media types to sneer at him. Maybe leading intellectuals weren't so bright? For sure it was something for a humble cop to think about in quiet moments.

La Marseillaise was playing on the TV. Martine La Plume stood at a lectern against a tricolor background. She was dressed in a white blouse, a dark jacket, and a white scarf around her neck. She smiles warmly to camera.

"My friends and fellow citizens you are the fearless patriots of France, a new France, a courageous France which has re-found its identity as French. An identity that the world is recognizing and respecting. I lived with you through the grey days of socialist conformity when patriots were afraid to breathe the pride which is born in the heart of every son and daughter of la France. Now again your pride is worn on the chest as your medal and in

your voice as the anthem of the world's most glorious people.

Briefly the picture fades to a French warship flying the flag from its stern as it opens fire.

Like you I am following the history of Charles, a young man born to be king. The story unites us in tears and pride. It finds the true love that lives in French hearts. It rejoices in human beauty so much known to patriots of France and our admirers in the world. My friends, we are the nation of life, of love, of perfume and the sensual joy of a shared meal. For so long the intellectuals despised the people who longed for these passions. Communists and global businessmen tried to rob you of your souls and even of your sweat as it fell in sacrifice on the sacred furrows of our soil. They fed you lies that you were lazy and backward because you were not slaves like the Chinese poor or robots like the mechanistic Germans who have so often raped and tortured our ancestors. My beautiful patriots, even a year ago you were not free to say such things.

Picture fades to Adolf Hitler giving Nazi salute at the Eiffel Tower.

Fellow citizens, the demand for the referendum on the re-creation of a new modern monarchy in France has been profound. As your president I declare that this vote will be held next week. I will be voting with you my friends for a new type of society, united by our love for a young family forging a life with their babies in the traditions of France. A royal showcase for the traditions of France my friends! Now, we all know there are enemies of the true people. There are those who hold themselves above the honest man or woman who toils at the desk, the machine, or the plough. These Intellos brewed the failed grey soup of the old Europe and tried to make you believe it was a meal. We have vomited their global swill. We have seen their deceptions, my friends. We have counted the money they have printed for themselves. Patriots, even these individuals are French although they try to deny it to themselves. The peasant sauce of France anoints the sausage of their entrails.

Picture fades to Chinese master whipping French peasant in beret as he tends his grapes.

The Patriotic Front has had to sweep these destructive selfish elements from our path. But my dear friends, if the referendum allows me to proceed with our new way, I will set them free—every one of them. If then, these Intellos sneer at you who are of my own blood, in their papers and snob media shows, I will leave it to you to assert your pride with the anger I know you will feel as patriots. To all those who would deny the beauty of our honest bread, may they gorge on the cakes of our hatred.

Finally, I will add the fleur-de-lys to the tricolor of France and I will alter our national motto. The old Liberty, Equality, Fraternity has served us well. The word Equality has been trodden in the dirt by the elite class of Intellos who saw themselves as superior and used the word to smear you with foreign filth who took your jobs, your partners, and your menus. The new words will be Liberty, Identity, Fraternity. Those who identify with France are patriots and all patriots are equal in their love for our home and our history. Vive le Peuple. Vive Le roi. Vive la France, Vive la France."

The display jets scream along the Champs Elysées trailing their red, white, and blue plumes. Marching soldiers play the anthem, Martine La Plume places a red, white, and blue sash on a wheelchair-bound army veteran with the Arc de Triomphe as background. Picture fades to Pope marrying royal couple, the girl's face in digital disguise.

Sophia let out a long sigh and looked up at the beautiful high ceiling.

"It's shit but it has the smell of Andouillette," said Spencer.

Charles chuckled.

"And you know what that smells of?" he said.

"Bastian believes the SAS motto of who dares wins—and she's daring, isn't she?" said Sophia.

"Yes, total respect to her," said Spencer. "The old politics said 'who spins, wins' and the woman is going for the lump in the throat. We mustn't forget that she in herself might fail. She has enemies within her own party. A king can still be put on the throne of France, but for now she's cutting our path through the field of sunflowers. Let her slash on until she hits an ambush or merely falls."

"She's a caring woman leading her people, her children if you like," said Sophia.

"Yes, yes, but let's not forget we're Brits. The old euro elite slammed the door on England when we left their selfish club. Martine's an ally, not a friend," said Spencer.

"She's a good woman and I just believe in her," said Sophia.

"Good for you. Politics is for turncoat bastards. Follow what you believe," said Shannon.

"Forget the French. Why and who in England supports this project?" said Sophia.

"Now that's an ever-changing landscape. We may know a bit more after tomorrow's meeting," said Spencer.

"I'll show you your room," said Shannon. "We're cops, not robber barons."

She stood and kissed Spencer on the lips.

"You know I'm not a robber."

"Pity, I might fancy a bit of a chase later," she said with a complicit smile.

Sophia smiled as Charles took her hand.

"I'll see you later, I hope."

"As you wish, Your Majesty," said Sophia with a smile.

CHAPTER 35

Shannon led her to the kitchen, collected a couple more Cobra beers and climbed the central staircase to the landing. There must have been a dozen bedrooms to Sophia's eyes. Shannon opened a deep brown paneled door and stepped in to a huge room with ensuite bathroom. The bed was broad with cream sheets turned down to reveal an embroidered crest.

She threw off her shoes and flopped back on the bed, motioning for Sophia to do the same.

"So, what do you do when the virgin king of bloody France adores you?" she said.

"Dunno, I just thought he adored *me*," said Sophia.

Shannon squealed with laughter.

"You're a cute cookie. You know that boy's looking to you to see how he's playing every minute of his life."

Sophia swung up onto the bed beside her and studied this cop countess.

"I'm a divorced thirty-eight-year-old woman with a grown-up child. He's a twenty-four-year-old ex-priest virgin. He's also a boy band star and would-be king of France with ten million would-be groupies."

"Well, sister he's only going to be a virgin once, although I must say I played that fiddle a few times."

Sophia chuckled and nodded her head at Shannon. It seemed you could ride bareback with the Countess of Bloxington.

"Shannon, I'm out of my depth. There's been killings and horrible things. I'm a cop like you. I didn't plan to meet this guy or get into any of this."

Shannon sat up and took a long swig of beer. Sophia did the same.

"These guys are for real. You and me might talk about changing something in the world. Just imagine Martine La Plume and all the Caesar Roboris guys. They've got balls. They're do or die makers of history. The old game left the ordinary guy grubbing about in the ruins of the industrial revolution, Sophia. There had to be a new game. Spencer is pure blueblood and a wonderful, kind man. He believes in loving the people in order to lead them," said Shannon.

"So, history awaits my walk-on part," said Sophia.

"Nah, history ain't scripted with parts. Someone like you can write the play. Charles needs to grow into the figure of a complete man and destiny has put you ahead of him on that road. To submit to him would be an act of surrender. To lead is an act of power. He's a king and you're a Cinderella without a glass slipper."

"So how do I play it?"

"Open an exclusive shoe shop and get him to buy you a pair."

"He's a sexy guy if only he knew what sexy was."

"That door over there joins your room with where I'm putting Charles. I won't lock it unless you ask. It's up to you how history gets written."

"So essentially I'm offering myself as a stepping stone so that he's in decent shape to mate with Esmeralda Grump."

"I can see that and it wouldn't suit me."

"What is the age difference between you and Spencer?"

"I'm thirty-three and he's forty-five."

"So that's twelve years. Charles is fourteen years younger than me."

"Yeah, so what? The rules are different for women but that's 'cos we don't make a fuss. If you want him, you know you can get him don't you?"

"And if he has some mad idea like Edward the Eighth of giving up everything for the woman he loves, my guess is that the woman he loves might fall under a bus," said Sophia.

"You mean that all those interested parties who want a fairy tale princess from that *Rex Factor* show and a political alliance between France and the USA if Ms. Grump happens to win, would wipe out some little commoner like you?"

"Exactly, my dear Holmes."

Shannon smiled and gave her a long appraising look.

"So you've met Bastian Wolf?" she said.

"Yes, he's ruthless and devious. He has total confidence in himself and fears no one. In France I only felt a tiny bit brave because he was there. I know he'd kill me if I got in the way."

"Yes, he would. I'd advise you to keep him in sight but the truth is, you wouldn't see him coming."

"He works for these Caesar Roboris guys. What *is* their agenda?" asked Sophia.

"I'm guessing, like you. They're helping Martine with her little scheme. They're using it as a wedge in the door. Once Charles is actually on the throne we'll see their teeth. Martine wants a soap opera show. Those guys want hard-core kings with full political power. She's using them because they've got the resources and the cash. The truth is, she's deep in hock to loan sharks."

"That's my suspicion too. They'll force Charles to declare himself king by divine right and then assassinate Martine, probably making sure that the Intellos get the blame," said Sophia.

"I want you to know that Spencer is part of the Caesar Roboris gang, but only as a spy for Anna La Salle. The queen of England is OK with Martine's monarchy-lite but nothing more. Prince Richard and Princess Caroline are in the hard-core camp."

"Now that's what I call a soap opera storyline," said Sophia. "How the hell did some little nobody like me end up in this situation?"

"Good question. Can I read your palm?" asked Shannon with a laugh, obviously wanting to shift the mood.

Sophia offered her hand and Shannon traced the lines, looking up into her face. Her touch was light but conveyed competence and interest. Sophia relaxed and enjoyed the sham of offering herself to the gods of superstition.

"You have some noble blood in your past. It's not in the lines, I can feel it. You have a conflicted path to this point, I'd say a marriage and a love story that destroyed it."

Sophia stared at Shannon. This was gold-plated bollocks, but actually true.

"Go on," she said, enjoying the attention.

"One child, one love and that was lost. There is pain and longing in your heart. You love Charles because at last a man loves you as a woman, not as an extension of himself, not as the desired object of his gaze. He wants you as the greater part of himself and you know you can fill him."

Sophia fixed her eyes on Shannon's face as she continued to trace the lines of her palm. She wanted to pull back from the ecstasy of being with this woman.

"You loved a girl once didn't you?" said Shannon warmly tracing the lines of her hand.

She knew that Shannon had sussed her out when she was talking about Martine La Plume. She hesitated for a moment and then dived in.

"Yes, yes I did. I fell in love and it destroyed my whole life."

"Do you want to talk about it?"

Sophia sighed. Yes she did want to talk, maybe in order to explain things to herself.

"I was a young cop. I married a cop I'd met at training school. He was good looking and strong. Look, he was a good man. A lot of the attraction was that loads of other girls wanted him. I had a good relationship with him, a sexy relationship. The truth is I like sex. I'd had feelings, you know but I was mainstream and a girl does boys."

"But?"

"But, but, but I fucked up. I wasn't looking for a situation with a woman. It wasn't that I had overwhelming sexual feelings for a girl. It was more that I just didn't reject the feelings I had. I liked them, but it didn't drag me into gay clubs or change my life. I could kind of feel warm for a woman and go home and express my sexiness with my husband, maybe look at an adult film. You know.... I was under control...."

"I'm a loner and a man's woman. I'd never loved anyone before Spencer. Maybe some women end up living what they deny rather than what they embrace."

"I met a woman who was involved in a local youth group. She was clever and strong and I was like the cop who went along to tell the kids that cops were just born to this world like them and were trying to make a difference out of a cliché."

"You liked her?"

"I liked her and I admired her. These were tough kids and she showed them love and respect. One day she told me I was beautiful to her and I kissed her for saying that."

"Did you think she was gay?"

"She didn't have frontiers of love. She crossed into the no man's land of adult and child, of race and class, man and woman, and just spoke humanity. The great people in your life don't give you instructions, they give you permissions. They tell you—you're OK, explore it, go with it. I let go."

"And you feel that with Martine don't you?" said Shannon,

Sophia sighed and looked up. She was saying too much to this woman.

"Yes, yes I do. God, Shannon I don't want to be saying this to you but I'm crying inside for her loneliness and I want to...."

"You want to hold her."

"I want to absorb her, distract her, let her kind eyes release the love in me," said Sophia.

"It's one hell of a privilege to be sharing this with you. I can feel the pull in Martine and I'll admit to you that it's not something I'm about to share with Spencer. She kind of disturbs me, like I'm not powerful enough to pull back so I just have to blank it."

"It's been good to talk."

"I've loved it. Can I ask you what happened with that woman?"

"She was married and so was I. She was Indian and they took her back there on a holiday. I believe she was murdered because of the shame. Her family made sure my husband found out. The rest is hatred and pain. My husband has never told my daughter and neither have I. Now, you have that power over me if ever you want to use it."

"You say that even as I'm holding your hand. Life's battered the trust inside you, Sophia. Love in all its joy and passion is the puppy dog scampering ahead. The master is trust who plods behind. If ever I betray you, have me put to sleep," said Shannon.

"I'll hold you to that, but I feel very safe with you. You must have one hell of a story to your own life."

"Yeah, but this game now dwarfs everything. Spencer's a blueblood, but we're all in the same boat. All our stories now as cops and as citizens are in the hands of our government and they're sitting so much on the fence that the crack of their ass has reached their neck. Look, the biggest players are Viktor Pinupskin and Ronald Grump, that much I do know."

"Surely the Americans don't want a monarchy."

"No, but they want Europe to be weaker, individual states, and Grump wants Esmeralda as queen of France. He's one hell of a vain man."

"Why would the Russians want a monarchy in France?" asked Sophia.

"So that it would be respectable and fashionable to have a tsar in Russia. The new French king would recognize the new tsar and the dominoes would start to fall. Bingo! A new world order," said Shannon.

"Is any of this legal?"

"Christ knows. There's still a lot more to this than we know. Winners write the rules so you don't lose if you want to stay legal. Bottom line is that you can be ruled by bankers and bureaucrats or by kings and queens," said Shannon.

"And bankers just manage the show for bankers. Those guys rip off millions and laugh at the police."

"And where's the pride and unity in rich man's money for the average guy?" said Shannon.

"Do you have doubts about any of this?" asked Sophia?

"Sure, I doubt we can stay out of the fight. Martine's plan has to work or we're in for a riot of kings and their barons looting the booty of the world. Foot soldiers like you and me are likely to be early casualties.

CHAPTER 36

It was getting late when Shannon left. Sophia showered and went to the door that linked Charles's room and her own. She left it half open and slid into bed. She left the curtains open to see the sky. The crescent blade of a half moon cut and shared the clouds as random slices of chance. So, in this moment, was her own little life, and no more predictable. There was a mumble of voices on the landing, an opening of a door to Charles's room and the sound of him moving. There was running water, the click on of a lamp, and then darkness. He would come to her now or she would leave this whole show behind whatever the cost. She knew too much and she knew what that cost would be.

She saw his tight slim body silhouetted against the moon in the window. He had come to her naked as she awaited him, naked.

"Sophia?" came his whispered voice.

"Is that the king of France?"

She felt the weight of his body on the other side of the bed as he slid in. Now she turned to face him. His arm folded around her shoulders.

"My God, you're like silk. You're soft, oh my God," he said.

She teased her hand down to feel his hard cock against her belly. His tip was wet and bursting. She pushed him away a little so he lay on his back. She kissed his lips and for a moment stroked her hand back through his hair.

"So you came to me. I wanted that."

"So, you *do* want me too?"

"I would want you for mine, mine, mine, nothing less."

She didn't expect an answer. She lay back and brought his hand to her pubis.

He groaned as he slid his fingers into the silky hot mystery of her.

"Do you remember when we were in France and I asked you to say my name when you let go," she said.

"Yes, of course,"

"Did you do that for me? It was very sexy to think of you doing that for me."

"Yes, I did."

She pressed her hand over his to curl his fingers into the deep wetness of her. She groaned at the pleasure of the semi self-touch.

"Women come too you know. I like to come with my pussy."

She heard him swallow as he fought for control. She pressed his hand against her clitoris, holding herself tight to build her need. She clasped his hot cock and pulled him to her. She was starting her early tremors. His instinct drove him now as she opened herself to him. His taut, sinewy body was above her, probing her entrance. His longing cock driving in to her flowing hot channel. She groaned and pulled his hard butt to feel the man of him inside her. He was breathing hard and almost lost in joy.

"That's so good," she said as she drew his lips down to hers. She teased him with her tongue until he tuned to the rhythm of her. She moved under him, keeping his butt tight into her. She knew that he was so close that once he was free to move he would come. Her own desire was screaming. She released him to let him plunge in and out in helpless need to let go. In the half light of the moon she could see his beautiful face almost in pain as his first shudder trembled at the edge of ecstasy. Her own hand moved to her button and shamelessly added to the thrill of his driving need. As he groaned and shot his seed deep into her, her body pulsed in waves of abandoned orgasm.

"Do it in me, fucking do it in my pussy," she said as she felt the spasms of his cum pouring into her hot belly.

His spent body rested on hers. Her aftershocks squeezed the last twitches of convulsing pleasure from his hot cock. Her juices had poured out with his. She wetted her hand from her thigh and ran her hand along his lips and through his hair. She kissed the flavor of their union and breathed the musk of his semen and her juice. The act brought her a last shudder of carnal passion.

"Sophia, Sophia, Sophia."

"I like it when you say my name."

"I've wanted you so much. I love you."

She sighed. This was *not* the moment to talk about their future or *Rex Factor* brides.

"That was so good," she said.

"I can't live without you."

"You're saying that because you've not been with a woman before and you don't know any others."

He lay back and sighed. His face was silhouetted in the moonlight from the window.

"You know my story. I believed God was calling me to be a priest. Now

I know he was calling me to me to be a king. I believe you have come to me with the joy of heaven. I will never see it any other way."

"Maybe God will send you other things," she said.

"What could God send me that was more than you?"

Her instinct screamed Esmeralda Grump. She played a longer game.

"A younger woman?"

"No, you came to me when I was about to die in London. I was afraid and you gave me courage. We've been through a lot together and no man or woman could step into the prints you have left on time."

He turned towards her and propped himself on an elbow. He reached for her breast and savored its texture. "You fill me, you're my mind Sophia. I love you."

She closed her eyes as he brought his lips to her nipple. Some instinct was driving him now, as the thrill screamed down to her groin. She rested her hand on his head, stroking and gripping his hair. His touch was almost making her come. She'd never been so wet for a man and she didn't care.

"And if I loved you too?" she half groaned.

"Do you, would you?"

His hand was caressing her belly. She pushed it down into her nest and awkwardly found her spot. His lips had returned to her nipple and her juice softened his clumsy pressure. She was on the edge, and at one with him. She wanted to say she loved him as she let go. She held back.

"If I said that, if I gave you that, and you went with another woman you would break my heart."

"I won't, I love you."

She couldn't hold the torrent of her feeling for him or the pulse of her orgasm. She pulled his lips to hers. His tongue responded as she grunted out the spasms of her release.

"I love you, my king," she groaned.

As she still bucked in pleasure he was above her again, driving his hard hot cock into the silky wetness of her. He was hitting her cum spot and bringing her off again.

"Sophia, Sophia, I'm doing it. I love you."

"Fucking love me Charles, fucking say my name and come in me."

She felt the push and pulse of his release as her own spasms joined his. She wanted to keep him inside her. She pushed him away so that he lay on his back, her above him. His young body was firm and hard, his cock still firm.

"I'll love you, Charles. I'll love you like this forever if you love me. I'll show everything of love with a woman and I'll die for you. I want to love you as my king. Would that be enough?"

"I'll never love another woman."

She smiled at him. The moonlight bathed his serene beautiful face. In this moment she knew he loved her, yet a universe was spinning on with changing orbits and gravities that would pull at both of them. Weight was relative to mass, and time was relative to speed. He was a world and she a chance asteroid heading for collision. Although the impact could destroy them both, she would return his love with the same force.

CHAPTER 37

"So who was your father?" she asked over breakfast in the grand dining room of Bloxington Manor.

"He was a French aristocrat, Jean-Pierre de Gonin, Baron of Saint Savinien. As you know, the French aristos were displaced by the revolution. Both his parents were descended from the royal house of Bourbon. He has a small château and farm in the Loire but he had a regular job when he was young."

"And how did he meet your mother?"

"He was an officer on the Cunard liner Queen Elizabeth the Second. My mother was travelling from Southampton to New York and my father hosted her table for dinner. Apparently I was conceived during a stormy night in mid-Atlantic."

"Wow, what a start to life! Why was your mother on the ship?"

"She was accompanying Lady Baverstock-Malbourne, the cousin of the queen. She never flies and my mother was her personal assistant. The British royals knew of my mother's background and ensured she was properly employed. Seemingly the royals arranged with Cunard for the Baron to host that particular table."

Sophia chuckled.

"You guys can just kind of get what you want and do what you want."

"Yes, that's true, but a modern monarch has to live with constant intrusion by everyone who wants a slice of the media action."

"So where were you born?"

"My father wanted me to have French citizenship so my mother came to France. I was born at the American hospital of Paris in Boulevard Victor Hugo. I have joint citizenship of France and the USA."

"But you grew up in Maryland?"

"Sure did, ma'am. I had French lessons nearly every day. *Je suis circonflexe.*"

"I'm going to learn French the best way possible," said Sophia with a broad smile.

"How's that?"

"In bed."

He laughed.

"We didn't cover a lot of that vocabulary."

"And for sure not at the seminary."

He sighed and pushed his hands back through his hair.

"How could I have been so wrong about that? How can a man deny himself the joy of a woman?"

"We're not total joy, Your Majesty," she said with a tilt of her chin.

"You are to me," he said with irresistible loved up brown eyes. He had it bad. How little he knew.

"I like calling you Your Majesty. It makes me feel it's OK to submit to your desires. If you were just a Joe I'd have to analyze my pathetic girlie attitudes."

"I'm just a Joe to you and I'll always be that. You're the one I look up to Sophia."

"That'll be our secret then."

The unmistakable sound of chopper blades snapped her back to the moment.

"Dear Lord, we've got this meeting now. We've only had a few hours away from it all." He sighed.

"Yeah, what's it going to be about?"

"The whole program from now on. Which way are HM government going? What's the score with Martine's referendum? Who are our enemies? Blah, blah, blah," he said.

"I'd better pay attention then."

She chose a charcoal business suit, a cream blouse and very much heeled shoes. Charles wore a double-breasted pinstripe suit which was too old-fashioned for his age. He looked very much the squire on market day, too confident and important to be troubled by modern fads. For all that he looked gorgeous. Before they went downstairs to the meeting, he took her in his arms and kissed her.

"You're beautiful. Are you mine, are you?"

"If you're truly, truly mine."

He smiled and caressed her cheek. She looked him in the eyes, knowing that her unspoken question lay heavily on his innocent soul.

"C'mon, let's see what the gods have to hand down from the mountain," she said.

The meeting was in the library. Immediately she saw Bastian and Captain Côté, the French soldier who had aided her escape from Roche Courbon. Anna La Salle called her over to meet a tall thin large-nosed man of about fifty.

"Sophia, meet Gerard Derlet. He's the French ambassador in London and of course, Martine La Plume's husband," said Anna.

"I have heard a lot about you," he said with a slight bow of his head.

Charles had stopped to chat with an awkward-framed guy in his sixties whose trousers looked too baggy. He wore a military style blazer with patched elbows, a paisley patterned bow tie and sandals with woolly red socks.

"Prince Richard, do meet the French ambassador," said Anna.

"Honored," said the prince, squinting at Sophia. "And who else do we have?"

"Your Royal Highness, this is Inspector Sophia Castellana of Scotland Yard," said Anna.

"I rather thought so from the descriptions I've heard. Jolly fine woman I hear. Well done. Hope she's looking after you, Charles," said Prince Richard with a tight-lipped sideways grin.

"Yes, sir, she's a marvel."

"Marvel, eh? Captain Marvel, he was a favorite when I was a boy you know. Then they re-made him as a bloody American police girl. Ghastly thing; was never the same...." said Prince Richard.

Sophia smiled. It was her first encounter with a British royal. Was this guy really sensible enough?

"I never got into comics, Your Highness," said Anna.

"Shame, but things progress. A lot of this new stuff troubles me. There's even hormones getting into pheasant and partridge meat, turning us all into cross-dressers or something like that. Never mind, must move on," said Prince Richard as he strode away to wrap his arms around Shannon and Spencer.

The French ambassador was the first to speak.

"You can always be sure to learn something new from His Royal Highness," he said with a grin.

"It's all put on you know. He's as sharp as a pin but he plays the duffer to put you off the scent," said Anna.

"He does a bloody good job," said Sophia, almost giggling.

"OK, I'm going to kick off the show," said Anna La Salle.

Sophia watched her as she went to a lectern and looked up at the room. She was a gorgeous full-bodied woman with long dark hair. Her skin was creamy and flawless. She wore a navy blue trouser suit and a vermilion blouse. She had total poise in front of these people.

"Thank you everyone for being here today. Probably we won't meet again until this is all over. We all know that this project has one aim; to restore a constitutional monarchy to France. If other states surf that same wave we will support them. We know that traditional politics failed and we ended up with Scots fighting Welsh and Bretons fighting French. Civil wars in the Middle East and in the old Yugoslavia scarred both this and the previous centuries. Africa is in constant tribal conflict. The British are involved because France is a critical ally and trading partner. The British royal family support the move to non-political monarchies throughout Europe and the world. We have here today representatives of the World Bank, the International Monetary fund, the world combine of corporate businesses, the World Trade Organization and the French, British, American, and Russian governments. Need our project do more to prove its rightfulness? What other body could assemble such a consensus? I applaud you all and you should applaud yourselves."

The delegates all stood and applauded. Sophia watched a guy near the door who didn't clap and wasn't one of the SO16 protection squad. She looked for Bastian but couldn't see him. Years of squalid street work had honed an instinct in her. Her target was about forty, bearded, slightly shabby in a sports jacket, shirt, and crooked red tie. She'd done countless training courses telling her not to stereotype people. To her this guy was a stereotypical intellectual. He was edgy and alert. She wouldn't be able to approach him easily. The danger would come as everyone sat back down.

"Charles, do just what I say," she whispered to him.

"What?"

"I think we have an enemy in the room. Cry out and fall over," she said. "Like do it fucking now!"

Charles gave her a last look. He had total trust in her. She would love him for that.

"*Je suis circonflexe!*" he cried out and fell theatrically to the ground. People scattered or came towards him.

"Bastian! The guy in the red tie," called Sophia as she lunged towards him.

The target turned to get through the door as Bastian appeared from the hallway. His side-handed blow to the guy's face floored him at once. In an instant Bastian retrieved a handgun. Sophia helped to turn him over as protection officers arrived with handcuffs. She pulled off his ID badge, "Professor Miles Rutland, Faculty of Politics, University of Chipping Sodbury."

"How the fuck did he get in here with a gun?" asked Sophia.

"We're about to find out, aren't we, professor?" said Bastian.

"He's under arrest. He has rights," said one of the police protection officers.

"Fuck off, you soft cunt," growled Bastian.

The officer looked perplexed and backed off. Sophia understood the dilemma. The police had to work by rules, the suspect couldn't be required to answer questions and had the right to a lawyer.

Sophia realized she was on UK soil and her career was over if she didn't respect her duties.

"Get up!" she said to the suspect.

Bastian pulled him up by the hair.

"Let's do our nasty cop, nasty cop routine," he said with a smile.

Sophia nodded and took the suspect's arm. Anna had resumed at the front of the room.

"Deal with him Bastian, It's on my authority," she said. "We'll take a thirty-minute break ladies and gentlemen. There will be additional security checks."

She assisted Bastian in moving the professor to a small back kitchen pantry. Shelves of pickles and jams in jars lined the walls.

"Talk!" said Bastian.

The professor swallowed.

"You're going to talk 'cos you're about to shit yourself. You can talk before you mess your pants or after."

The professor was weeping.

Bastian slammed the handle of the gun into his groin. The guy let out a wail.

"You'll never succeed," he gasped.

"Tell me why not," said Bastian.

"Because you're wrong. People fought for democracy and science. We won't accept kings, bishops and popes."

"You're not a killer. How the hell did you get talked into this?" asked Sophia.

"We have no choice. Men of truth and science have to defeat the ignorant mob."

"You mean Her Majesty's loyal citizens," said Bastian.

"I mean the single brain cell mob, the Grump, Brexit and La Plume brigade."

"I'll tell Her Majesty, Mr. President, and the French government how you feel about their hardworking honest supporters," said Bastian.

"A talent show to select a bride princess and a boy band king with some fabricated royal history. It's laughable."

"Why aren't you sitting at home laughing then?" asked Sophia.

"Because you may well win in the short term."

"Who sent you?" asked Bastian.

"I was invited. I'm an expert on political propaganda. My wife is a friend of Princess Caroline. She knows nothing of this. I beg you not to harm her."

Sophia watched his trembling lips and hands. His eyes were pleading."

"You got kids?" asked Bastian.

"Two little girls."

"Ha! They're fucking dead once they've been raped," said Bastian.

"Please, please."

"Where did you get the gun?" asked Sophia.

"A friend, he's in a gun club."

"We'll string him up by the fucking neck," said Bastian.

"Miles, who did you come to kill?"

"Your fake king of course. I'm a professor, I've written fourteen papers on social demographic trends behind the rise of populism. I care about what's happening."

"Have you ever fired a gun?" she asked.

"No."

"You're a serious fucking idiot and you're telling me that I've got one brain cell," said Bastian.

Sophia looked at Bastian. Probably the next step was summary execution.

"D'you want to keep your wife and kids alive, Miles?" she said.

"Please, yes."

"You're going to work for us. One slip and we'll execute your family. No mercy, no second chances. Just fuck off out of here and go and write some more papers, tweet you bleeding heart shit about freedom and refugees just as if nothing has happened. We'll be in touch to tell you what we want. We'll let you go if you name everyone else you know in your poxy little clique," said Bastian.

The professor stared at Bastian as if he were seeing the devil. Suddenly Bastian drove a punch into his stomach.

"That's how I'll start on your missus before she's raped by my men."

The professor was crying in pain.

"The dean of the university, he's the organizer. There's a post grad guy called Ben someone and a Special Branch cop called Dave from Bristol. That's all I know. Once I'd killed the fake king, the decent educated folk were going to rise up and seize control."

"You've saved your family for now, professor. Now fuck off and when I want something you just do it. *Capiche?*" said Bastian.

Sophia stepped aside as the guy staggered to the door and out into the driveway.

"He's a liberal weakling. He'll blab sooner or later. He's too pathetic to turn into an agent."

"He's a small guy, an idealist with a bit of a fantasy life," said Sophia.

"So were the guys who shot Kennedy, Lennon, Reagan, Lincoln, Pope Paul, and Archduke Ferdinand. None of them were big tough trained assassins," he said with a shrug.

"So why did you let him go?"

"His wife's a mate of Princess Caroline. We can't alienate all of the intellectual class 'cos their mates run the BBC and the rest of the media.

Then we'll need their groveling royal baby specials. All these Intellos are up the arse of the royals. Even Comrade Vandervell is going to be a lord of the toadies."

"What will you be?"

"They've promised me Prince of Fucking Darkness. That's if we win," he said with a chuckle.

"And will we win?"

"Sophia, the roller coaster is just a fraction over the top of the big slope. The only way we can avoid the ride is if we crash."

CHAPTER 38

"So what's this 'je swee circus flex'?" said Sophia as she re-joined the delegates in the library.

"It's a French grammar-guerilla organization. The circonflexe is a little hat that sits on the head of some letters in some words," said Charles.

"There's traitors who want to do away with accents on French words," said the French ambassador.

"I'm afraid the rot started with tele-printers in the Sixties. Texting has finished off the job," said Charles.

"So who was the would-be assassin?" asked the ambassador.

"An Intello. A complete dolt. I doubt he would actually have done anything."

"Martine wants to let them all out if the people call for the monarchy in the referendum. I'm not so sure. I'd like to keep all these snob globalist parasites in prison," said the ambassador.

"How are the polls calling the vote?" asked Charles.

"Eighty to twenty, in favor. The only problem is this Esmeralda Grump. Patriots want a French girl. Our own Nathalie Collobert is a lovely Gallic beauty."

"Mason Trowel runs the *Rex Factor* show. He could trip up Esmeralda even though it's been fixed for her to win," said Sophia.

"Mason Trowel is a Grump toady," said Charles.

"And how do you feel about getting to grips with Esmeralda under the duvet?" asked the ambassador.

"You're the first person to ask me!" said Charles, glancing at Sophia. "If I'm honest I don't want to think about it."

"A girl with so many teeth would be dangerous in the love department," said the ambassador with a wink.

"A girl with so many teeth could do with losing a few," said Sophia.

Charles looked embarrassed as the ambassador raised an eyebrow. Anna La Salle saved them from further conversation. She re-started her talk.

"OK guys, we had a bit of an incident as you know. The old ruling class of Intellos and experts are always going to be a lone wolf terrorist threat. They are used to setting the agendas in society and measuring everyone against their narrow standards. Our French cousins have locked them up as have the Turks. As far as I know President Edamame won't be letting them out until he's sultan," said Anna pausing to smile. "Please forgive my flippancy but this may be the only time in history that a bean will turn into a grape." Prince Richard and Spencer chortled.

"The French referendum is in four days. Once the new monarchy is declared Martine La Plume will create the new constitution and proceed at once to a coronation. The British made the mistake of not hitting the Brexit button immediately. It gave their globalist elite enemies time to re-group. Martine has noted this lesson. In six days' time France will have King Charles the Eleventh on her throne. The *Rex Factor* show to select a royal bride will have its finale as the referendum result is released. Audiences are at nearly three billion. The *Born to be King* show will have its final episode on the night before the referendum. Charles will do a BBC World News slot this afternoon and be back in France tonight for a series of TV interviews and celebrity chat shows. His approval ratings are at ninety percent. Church attendances have doubled and a third of people believe God has anointed Charles as king. Schools have got counselors ready to comfort Boymondo fan girls if the referendum goes against him. Safe zone cry-ins have been added to university timetables just in case. Martine is advancing emergency legislation to bring the voting age down to fifteen. Vandervell is already in Paris planning the staging of the coronation and the royal wedding. Ladies and gentlemen we are committed and we will bring a better way to the peoples of the world."

The delegates stood to applaud and cheer. Anna made a calming hand gesture.

"My guess is that not all of us will make it to the end. Opposition will be fierce. Charles must survive at all costs. Sophia will be with him all the way to victory. Once again today she has proved her courage and skill. I'll give the mic now to the specialists who will brief you all with their own areas of expertise. *Vive la France* and long live the king."

An executive of the World Bank began a discussion on world economics in a world of peoples and monarchies.

"I don't think this is for us," whispered Charles.

"Let's get a coffee and talk about what you're going to say to the BBC this afternoon," she said.

Shannon was in the kitchen.

"Hi guys. You're a star act, Charles, and Sophia, you're amazing."

Spontaneously Charles folded her into his arms.

"This is all I would ever want in life."

She resisted a little then softened into the natural fit with his body that had come from the same mould as her soul. A slight flick of pleasure rippled through her as he held her against him.

Shannon was smiling.

"You'll get me hot and I'll have to find Spencer if you don't stop it."

"It's not too professional I guess," said Sophia, pulling away.

"Looks like you've kinda James-bonded."

Shannon laughed at Charles's bemused face.

"English humor—stuck on an agent, geddit?"

Charles smiled and looked upwards.

"Oh love, love, love, love, love. You guys might die anyway but for Christ sake die on the same road together where love takes you," said Shannon.

"And where does love take you?" asked Charles.

"Love can only ever take us back to love, like a beast always coming to the river to drink. Predators know that path too. To love is to risk. Not to love is to die of thirst." Shannon's voice tailed off into sobs. Sophia held her.

"I'm sorry, I was thinking of Mel and how full of love he was."

"I knew him as brave, kind, and cultured," said Sophia, not wanting to take love out of Shannon's basket of personal grief.

"I'm OK now. You guys fucking go for it. Mel gave me that advice once so I'm passing on the boot-print he left on my butt," said Shannon with a brave smile.

"If I go for it I could bring down the tent on the whole bloody circus," said Sophia.

"Nah, a circus ain't the jugglers or the elephants. The great common crowd makes the circus and they know the roof's going to fall in 'cos it always does on the poor. The Intellos despise them but they are real life. Let the roof fall and let the force of humanity pull you out. It *is* there and a king who knows love and passion knows the way to his people's heart," said Shannon.

"Thanks, Shannon. Your words mean a lot to me. A king or queen has no right to rule a people unless he shares their loves and wishes. He's not the leader by right, he's their focus and Sophia will be with me."

"You're an innocent Charles. I'm a throwaway if the whole Caesar Roboris machine sees it that way."

"I'm going to be the restored king of France Sophia. You were at my side when I should have died. I'll be at your side when we should live. Now, let me find my strength and face the weight of what destiny has called me to do. Just be there and know that I love you."

CHAPTER 39

"Who've the BBC got to do the interview? Can't bear most of 'em. Slimy little drivellers. That Mareck Kibosh should be chopped up and fed to my hunting hounds," said Prince Richard.

"I believe it's Crispin Satchel," said Anna.

"Ah, ghastly man, mind you not too bright and a complete ass sniffer. Take my advice and don't get drawn into all that squalid politics. We're above all that backstabbing, hand in the till and up skirts goings-on. Lower the voice, talk about love for and duty to the people. Tell 'em how you respect the traditions of the Christian Church, whilst embracing the joy of diversity. They gobble all that up without chewing. Do you hunt with hounds in France?"

"No, sir," said Charles.

"Good, best not to mention it anyway. Tell him you love cats and dogs and how much you look up to women, refugees and the BBC. And another thing, mention the LGQTB community or whatever they are. Do they all live in one place? They love that, you always have to fit that in. Chap I knew at Eton used to wear a frock. Think he was in Thatcher's government. Don't think Maggie would have appreciated rival handbags at Number Ten, eh?" said Prince Richard.

"We've got the questions in advance. Mainly they're interested in Boymondo and how you feel about going from boy band to king. There is a question about choice of bride," said Anna.

"What do you think I should say, Your Royal Highness?" asked Charles.

"Nod, then look grave and thoughtful. Tell 'em you'll accept the wisdom and desire of your people. They'll suck that up and actually it's pretty meaningless. Too many startling teeth on that Grump girl. Any scandal wouldn't be Watergate, it would be Colgate," said Prince Richard, silently convulsing his shoulders in amusement at his own joke.

Sophia stared at him. He was from some other planet, but she couldn't help liking him.

"Lovely to see you all. Got a bit of a shoot this afternoon. Prince Fiscal Hessian's coming over. Got to sell him a brace of jet fighters but the Foreign Office-type's doing all that. The prince is one of us you know. Rules with an iron fist inside a steel glove. His people love him you know. Good luck Charles, I'll see you at Versailles end of next week," said Prince Richard, calling over a couple of his valets and heading for the door.

"The Intellos in the press have given him a terrible time over the years. Good advice though to keep to cats and dogs. I bet your mother gave you a rescue puppy one Christmas," said Anna with a smile.

"Don't think so," said Charles.

"Oh yes she did. Your mother called it 'Brianmay' after the Queen guitarist 'cos he was so curly. The press love it when you mention another celeb. Anyway, the Obamas had a rescue dog," said Sophia.

"You mean I should lie."

"It's called PR, Your Majesty," said Sophia.

"I'll get the boys to get a curly dog and Brian May photo montage together as a chat show trail," said Anna.

"Dear Lord, you know I'm just going to take the questions on the chin and tell them I define a king as the champion of his people, talking with their voice with the privilege of knowing that politicos have to listen."

"You go for it Charles, but if you get backed up on the ropes hit 'em with the dog story," said Sophia.

Charles went to makeup with three SO16 guards while Sophia put in a Facebook call to Izzy.

"Mum! It's early," said a puffy undecorated face from a small gap in a duvet.

"It's 8:30 out in Hollywood. How are you?"

"Yeah, good."

"What have you been doing?"

"Making films with all these big stars and stuff. Yeah, and Mason Trowel got me in his studio for some new songs."

"Have you got to get up?"

"Yeah, I suppose like you know I'm doing some charity Christmas orphans gig where I go and meet people with no hope in their lives or something. Mason wants some dental work on me 'cos one of my teeth is a bit off tone on camera."

"I won't keep you then."

"OK, Mum. Love you."

"Love you too. Call me any time if you need me."

The picture died. She let out a sigh. All in all she didn't feel like much of a parent.

She half watched the interview on a small monitor with Shannon and Spencer. Charles was confident and expressing his views on modern monarchy. Then Crispin Satchel hit him with the low punch.

"So it looks like you're going to be marrying Esmeralda Grump?"

Charles smiled slowly.

"I'm putting that in the hands of the people of France whom I love and respect. Their wisdom and labor have created the finest society in the world."

"But if that's their choice...."

Charles smiled again.

"When I was a child I had a rescue dog which my mother called 'Brianmay' because he was so bubbly with curls and she was a big Queen fan. She chose it at random and brought it home. That was destiny and neither king nor mutt can escape it. The dog loved us and we sure loved him," said Charles.

"That's a fantastic story, Your Majesty, I can't wait to hear what Brian May will make of it," said Crispin Satchel.

"I'm not quite Your Majesty yet. That matter rests with my fellow citizens of France."

"Quite so, sir," said Satchel in full grovel. "Now, tell me how you see the future of the world."

"Brilliant!" said Shannon. "He ducked right out of it with a virtue advertisement and spun a celeb angle all in one go."

Sophia nodded. In just a few days the question would be unavoidable.

"He handles these treacherous journalists very well. Good for him. Destiny is the code of the aristocrat. Leadership brings its troubles but we are destined from birth to do our duty," said Spencer.

"Gorblimey my Lord, could it be your duty to get me a cup of Yorkshire Gold tea?" said Shannon.

"Yes, milady," said Spencer with a smile.

Charles came in with a box of wet wipes, removing his makeup.

"We've got a bit over an hour before we're flying out to Paris. I need to get cleaned up."

Sophia took his hand and gave him the slightest wink.

"Me too. See you guys in the Palace of Versailles."

She flopped down onto the bed. Charles went straight to the shower. She slipped off her suit and blouse. He'd never seen her body in the light. Her skin was light olive and her belly flat. A few stretch marks were proud scars of battle in the maternity trenches. Her nipples still angled up in the beckoning posture which she'd read were perfect and a shared design with the Duchess of Cambridge. She unhooked her bra to liberate them. She retained her crimson panties, just in case he would like her to remove them or do the job himself. He came out of the bathroom, toweling his wavy dark hair. He had wrapped a towel around his waist to preserve his modesty. Then he saw her and stopped.

"Oh God," he sighed.

She could see at once that the view was sending unstoppable signals to his cock.

"Stay there and drop the towel."

He gave a nervous cough.

"When you get stiff I get wet Charles and I'm getting wet looking at you," she said.

He let it fall to the floor. His cock sprang up from his dark bed of pubic hair.

"I like making you so hard, it makes me want you inside me."

He swallowed as her finger lightly trailed her groove. She could feel her wetness through the fabric. She could tell he was bursting to touch his cock.

"You're so lovely," he said, swallowing.

"I'm making my panties so wet."

His eyes were fixed on her stroking hand. He moved closer and stood at the end of the bed.

She wriggled out of her underwear and opened her legs to his gaze.

"This is a woman's spot. This is how a woman touches herself and how a lover can touch her," she said, slowly rolling her inner folds over her clitoris. She watched a bead of pre-cum ooze from the head of his cock.

"Can you see how a woman does it?" she said softly.

He groaned and came to the side of the bed. Suddenly he knelt beside her and kissed her lips. The thrill of the kiss almost made her let go. He kissed down to her breasts and then down her belly to her stroking hand. His lips sought her inner flesh and some force of nature brought his tongue to her button.

"Oh my sweet man, my lover."

Her mind drifted to some timeless unconnected place. She was nothing but that one part of her body. She was coming and had no care as to what or where she was in the universe. She gripped his hair as the spasm convulsed her belly and pulsated inside her. She knew she was making a sound but she had no conscious voice. He was moving as she opened her eyes. He was kneeling between her legs preparing to plunge his hot cock into her. His hand stroked her soaking inner lips. His erection was ruthlessly hard. He grunted as his seed shot and pulsed from his tip. She felt the hot juice drench her belly.

"Sophia, Sophia," he said as he grasped himself and shot the last spasms of his cum onto her breasts.

The sight brought her to orgasm as she pushed her breasts together. His lips came to hers in an abandoned heat of tongues.

"That was so sexy," she said.

"I just couldn't stop."

"You made me cum and I made you cum. That's so, so good. I love you, Your Majesty."

"Even though I did that to you."

"What? I loved it, that's going to be my sexy dream fantasy, seeing all that helpless man juice pulsing out on me."

"I love you Sophia."

"Back to the office and back to reality," she said, heading for the shower.

CHAPTER 40

The BAe146 of the Queen's Flight banked left over Paris. Sophia could see the Eiffel Tower in its evening robe of golden light.

"Landing into Villacoublay to the southwest of Paris. Should be a breeze. It's more or less the president's strip," said the RAF captain.

They had travelled with Captain Côté and Bastian. A black armored Mercedes limo was waiting at the foot of the steps. Police National officers filled two vans and motorcycle outriders moved ahead.

"You're on the seven o'clock BFM show with Beth Le Boeuf and then TF1 are going to do an interview at the Elysée Palace," said Bastian.

Charles nodded. He was calm and seemed confident. For sure his boy band career had gotten him used to the press and interviews, but all the same being grilled by top political pundits was a tough call for a young man who had nearly become a priest. Sophia knew that there would be those who would sneer at him as a lightweight or imposter. She was beginning to sense the steel certainty within him and that in itself commanded her love.

The studios of the French 24-hour station were just off the outer Boulevard Périphérique of Paris. The limo slowed as the police motorcycle outriders began to run into a crowd. To Sophia's eyes they were young and the majority female. They were chanting, "*Charles mon roi, Charles mon roi.*"

"They like you Charles," said Bastian.

All of them were wearing French flag T-shirts with the additional royal emblem of the *fleur-de-lys*. The chant had changed.

"Esmeralda pas ma reine! Esmeralda pas ma reine!"

"What are they saying?" asked Sophia.

"Esmeralda not my queen," said Charles.

"I think I'd go along with that," said Sophia.

"Mason Trowel sold the T-shirt franchise to the Chinese for two million Euros. They've sold eight million at twelve Euros a pop. Mason's pig sick," said Bastian.

"What's wrong with Esmeralda?" asked Sophia.

"She's foreign and she's Ronald Grump's brat," said Bastian.

"The wisdom of my people is paramount," said Charles with a smile.

Suddenly the French driver spoke.

"And her smile—it is like a manhole cover with teeth."

"Isn't she the reigning Miss Florida Aquarium?" asked Bastian.

"Poor girl. That sounds like fake news," said Sophia. "She was so much better before the beauty queen surgery."

The crowd had realized Charles himself could be in the limo. Police officers surrounded them as the car crept forward. Crying girls struggled and pushed, yelling out, *"Charles, je t'aime."* They bundled into the lobby of the BFM TV studios. A sophisticated dark-haired woman in her mid-fifties was waiting, raising a superior intellectual eyebrow and performing a cold smile.

"La racaille," she said.

"Mon peuple," said Charles

The woman winced.

"You like the mob of scum?" she said.

"Your words not mine. I love my people. They are young girls enjoying a shared passion. That is all. I'm still young enough to know the young heart. I can see it would be far harder for you," he said with a smile.

Bastian shot a glance at Sophia. The interview with Beth Le Boeuf was going to be interesting. She waited with Bastian and Captain Côté while Charles performed. Most of the time Charles was smiling. His interrogator held her manicured hand to her forehead and shook her head as if the subject was too crude for such a refined mind to contemplate. Several technicians were laughing.

"He's taking her to the cleaners," said Bastian.

"Every time she spits on the ordinary working people it is blowing back in her face," said the captain.

The monitor screens went blank.

"Electrical problem," said a technical guy with a shrug. "The show is nearly over."

Bastian pulled his Glock 26 handgun from his shoulder holster as he stood and jabbed the butt into the guy's head.

"Get me into that fucking studio now."

"It's locked. *Vive la France! Vive La Science!* No kings, no popes, no gods!" shouted the guy, giving a raised fist salute.

Sophia tried the door. The guy was telling the truth.

"Key or death," said Bastian.

A single bullet finished the conversation. Captain Côté crashed his foot into the door lock. The frame began to splinter as Bastian joined in.

"Get into that studio and get Charles. Focus only on that. We'll neutralize any opposition," said the captain to Sophia.

The door gave way. A wide corridor led to the double doors of the soundproofed studio. A screen was displaying the current broadcast. There was no sign of Charles. Beth Le Boeuf was speaking to camera. Captain Côté translated.

"We have been left with no choice. The French nation can only be managed with intelligence and science. People of France, you have been tricked. You are under-informed. You do not understand enough of difficult ideas to make political choices for yourselves. I call upon all educated people to rebel against this disgusting low-class populism. Take to the streets. Seize your town halls, march on the Élysée palace. Your proper leaders have deposed Martine La Plume and your tin-pot king. There will be no referendum or talent-show bride. Proper government is now in place."

"These fucking liberals won't have the balls to kill Charles or Martine. It's not over," said Bastian.

All three of them charged at the doors. There was a crack but they stayed shut. They charged again.

As they hurtled into the studio, Beth LeBoeuf was still talking. Bastian leveled the barrel of the gun.

She stopped. Bastian motioned for her to move aside. Captain Côté took her place. He spoke in French to the TV audience.

Sophia grabbed the presenter as Bastian jabbed the gun into the soft tissue of her throat under her chin.

"Where is he?"

Sophia looked around at the technicians. They were young and frightened. She spotted a young guy almost whimpering.

"Speak English?" she said.

"Yes," he replied

"Where is Charles? Speak or that woman's dead."

He pointed up at the roof.

"Heli-pad."

"Show me."

The guy hesitated.

"Take her," gurgled the presenter, clearly less certain of victory.

Captain Côté was still talking. Bastian was making sure the broadcast went on with his gun.

"Hurry," she said, hearing the sound of chopper blades.

The young guy swung open a door and set off up a flight of steps. A door led out onto the roof. A chopper was on the pad. Charles was struggling for his life as two heavy security guards were wrestling him on board. If he refused to duck they couldn't get him under the revolving blades. One was trying to grab his legs. These guys were big but they weren't pros. Hendon Metropolitan Police College, day one. Legs are stronger than arms. She assessed her options. Where was her advantage? These guys wouldn't know if she was friend or foe, so she could get close.

She strolled over, trying to recall all the French words she knew from her sink south London secondary school.

"*Bonjour, fromage. La maison de mon oncle,*" she shouted against the noise of the chopper

"*Quoi?*" shouted back one of the guys.

She stepped back and waved them to come closer, pointing to her ears.

"*Fromage. Le poulet est dans mon lit,*" she shrieked.

Charles spotted her and stopped struggling.

She motioned them further back from the blades.

"*Mon oncle maison fromage poulet,*" she shouted motioning her hands urgently.

"*Quoi?*"

They were clear of the blades. She motioned the guy a bit closer to shout into his ear. The side of her hand chopped viciously up under his nose. She felt the crack and the instant torrent of blood. Charles drove his forehead into the other guy's face and pulled away. Suddenly the chopper motor roared. The pilot was panicking. She guessed he was getting news that the TV coup d'état had failed. Charles spoke to the heavies in French as the machine lifted off and fled into the night sky.

"*Mes amis. Du calme. C'est fini,*" he said.

Sophia understood. Everyone understood.

"I've got to get out a tweet," said Charles, already tapping on his phone.

"What are you saying?"

"I'm saying that I love the people and their love has saved me," he said. "We need a live selfie-video for Facebook to show I am happy and alive."

Charles held up his phone and slung an arm around Sophia's shoulder.

"Still alive. *Vive la France, et Vive l'amour,*" he said.

He pressed the screen and sent a moment of history out into space.

Bastian and Captain Côté arrived on the roof with Paris police and gendarmes.

"Where's Martine La Plume?" asked Sophia.

"You're the cop. You tell me," said Bastian.

CHAPTER 41

"I have her private number," said Sophia.

"There's nothing to lose by calling her," said Bastian.

"She pressed the screen. The alien French ringtone blared out on the speaker,"

"*Oui, Sophia?*" said Martine.

"You're alive?"

"Of course. I saw this stupid TV stunt. Captain Côté saved us with his speech. I'm seeing your tweet and Facebook stuff now. All channels are putting up your video as breaking news."

"Did they try to grab you?"

"I was tipped off. The Russians have hacked the emails at BFM and they picked up a couple of clues. Viktor Pinupskin called me. I was on the way to the Élysée so we diverted to the Russian Embassy. I'm guessing they had an ambush somewhere or they've infiltrated my press staff. The Intellos have tentacles everywhere."

"So do the bloody Russians," muttered Bastian.

"But you're OK?" said Sophia.

"I'm enjoying a very large vodka and celebrating. The Intellos have done themselves more harm than anything we could do. I'll see you at the Élysée Palace. Charles has an interview there tonight with Françoise Hauton. She's Intello but old-school royalist underneath. Can you pass me to Captain Côté?"

Sophia handed him the phone.

"*Bravo! Mon capitaine. Je vous salue,*" she said.

"*Ce n'est que mon devoir,*" said Captain Côté.

Bastian was organizing the two heavies with gestures of his gun barrel. They were in no mind to argue. Parisian police handcuffed them and headed down the steps from the roof.

"They'll tell us exactly who gave them their orders and where they were going. Air traffic radar will have logged the chopper. This time we're going to stamp on the head of the snake," said Bastian.

Sophia took in the view from the roof. The lights of Paris glittered into the distance. They'd been lucky yet again. No one's luck held forever.

Charles folded her into his arms and kissed her. He studied her face.

"Angels have many forms," he said.

She smiled as she looked up at him.

"And so do devils. Are you sure you know what you're holding?"

"I'm holding the woman I love. Love makes angels of all devils."

"And its loss makes devils of everyone."

She caught sight of a female police officer with a mobile phone snapping a couple of pictures of their embrace. Nothing could be private in the life of a king.

They made their way back to the limo. The driver was watching TV on his tablet.

"Wow! You should get this! They're playing it over and over."

They watched themselves as they performed their selfie to the camera. Their video kiss played continuously on a rolling news loop. The police girl must have streamed it live to a news channel. The presenter cut in. "*Les yeux d'amour—impossible de se tromper.*" His female co-host added, "*Qui est-elle? Téléphonez à France 24 si vous avez des informations.*"

Charles translated. "The look of love. You can't mistake it. Who is she? Call us if you have information."

"That's put a new twist to the story," said Bastian.

Cameramen were beginning to run at the car. Flash photos were firing from all sides. A police outrider started his siren and blue lights. They moved off with a following car of gendarmes. They picked up the road that ran along the right bank of the river Seine, running red lights with sirens blaring. Once again the Eiffel tower, the Grand Palais, Place de la Concorde flashed by the windows. Soldiers were on every corner. Crowds of young people were wearing the French flag with the added royal emblem. A huge Christmas market stretched up the Champs Élysées toward the Arc de Triomphe. Concrete and police-operated barriers blocked the entrance to the Élysée Palace. They wove their way through into the outer and then inner courtyard. The building was magnificent with steps leading up to enormous doors framed by stone pillars. They climbed the long wide red-carpeted staircase to the first floor accompanied by a host of staff.

"Please take seats in the waiting room. May I serve you drinks?" said a tail-coated butler.

"I'd love a Rhône red," said Charles.

"Bring a bottle and a couple of glasses and we'll share," said Sophia.

The butler gave a weak smile and a twitch of his eyebrow.

"Big, big scotch and ice. Don't suppose you could bring the bottle," said

Bastian.

The butler looked to heaven and bowed.

"For this interview I'm going to be in the room," said Bastian.

The drinks arrived. The wine was a delicious Crozes-Hermitage. The waiter poured Bastian a whisky and left the bottle of Old Pulteney single malt on the table.

"Well, we're worth it aren't we?" he said.

Charles and Sophia warmed up on the wine.

"It's the last episode of *'Born to be King'* tonight," said Sophia.

"And the final of *'Rex Factor'* in two days," said Charles.

She looked at his face. This was the first time he'd raised the subject himself.

"Well, it's sure not going to be Esmeralda Grump. The crowd has turned against her. That leaves Nathalie Collobert from France and Anita Szymborska from Poland. I'd go for the dark passionate mademoiselle myself," said Bastian.

"You know, I'd always hoped all this would go away. They're just kids trying to get a break at the end of the day. How could you just turn up and marry someone?"

"You're not anyone. You're going to be Charles the Eleventh of France. It's a ready-meal womb. Most kings dine out when they fancy some proper home cooking," said Sophia.

"Not sure that Nathalie Collobert is that kind of gal. She comes across as a bit jealous and fiery," said Bastian.

"I've not even looked at the show," sighed Charles.

"You'll be looking at one of 'em for the next fifty odd years."

Bastian was studying his tablet.

"Your rooftop moment is totally viral," he said.

"What are the comments?" asked Charles.

"All sorts, mainly who is the older woman?"

"Anyone asking if I'm his granny?"

"No, quite a few mothers but no grannies. There's a new hashtag *#YearsMeanTears* for feminists to support women fighting age-related prejudice. It's red hot with traffic. There's talk of sisters' protest marches in London and Paris."

"Protests about what?" asked Sophia,

"About the institutional prejudice against older women. A few wrinkles and they're locked in the closet. If we use it, that's my angle," said Bastian.

"This bloody instant world. It can make you or destroy you either way in seconds. As king I will try to balance these ideas a little. Loudest is not the truest."

"There'll be time for principles when you've spun yourself to the throne," said Bastian.

"But can we control it? An idea goes out there and we can't control it."

"Oh, ye of little faith. The dark arts of manipulation are darker than you can imagine. Consider then the lily-livered of the tweeting field. They toil not, neither do they spin. But we do, Charles. And the camera only tells you the truth it's pointed at," said Bastian.

Charles nodded.

"Matthew 6:28, somewhat mangled," he said.

"Not mangled, Your Majesty, but spun," replied Bastian.

Something of a mob was approaching. Martine La Plume had arrived with Françoise Hauton and the TF1 camera crew.

"Sophia, you're a total sensation and fluent in French I hear," said Martine as she embraced her and kissed both cheeks.

"Charles, this is truly an honor," said Françoise Hauton, offering a handshake.

"Madame La Plume, you speak English it seems. It is part of your public persona that as a patriot you only ever speak French," said Françoise.

"It is part of your public persona that you will be rewarded very well for your loyalty to la France," said Martine with an icy smile.

Françoise seemed to understand the message.

"This interview will go out live. We have only twenty minutes to prepare. Since your moments on the rooftop people only want me to ask you about your beautiful companion. How will she fit in with your *Rex Factor* bride?"

"Love fits with the heart. I love and trust my people. Their heart is my heart. I am in their hands."

"But you have to marry the winner," said Françoise Hauton.

"Yes, and my people know this. I will be their king and they will be by my side. The old elite wouldn't trust or involve their people. They looked down on them. The hand that tends the soil to grow food for his fellow citizens or toils to mend a road for others to use is blessed with great wisdom. A king speaks with all their wisdom but from a single voice."

"Where do you get these ideas?" said Françoise.

"From my soul which was given to me by God and blessed by the Pope."

"You understand that many distinguished men and women of science would *not* agree."

"Tell me who is more distinguished than the man who grows or delivers my food or assembles my stove to cook it? Who?" said Charles.

"OK, we'll powder you up and do the show. We're at a rare moment of history, Charles, and it really is an honor to be here with you as it happens," said Françoise Hauton.

"For me too. Destiny isn't the familiar friend who shakes your hand. It's the lonely stranger who reaches back for company in the darkness and among all those reaching out, finds your special hand."

CHAPTER 42

The TV crew set themselves up in the president's magnificent office furnished with Louis Sixteenth style chairs in gold and cream. Bastian and Captain Côté took places in the deep shadows, guns drawn, safety catches off. Sophia remained in the outer room with Martine and the half full bottle of scotch.

"Quite a day," said Martine glugging out two huge doses of whisky.

"Yeah," said Sophia, almost averting her eyes from the seductive contact with this woman.

"You're creating quite a stir on all the chattering wires," said Martine.

"Help me. I'm a victim of modern life," said Sophia with a smile. She just could not fucking well help smiling and relaxing with this bloody woman. What the fuck was wrong with her?

"He loves you helplessly."

"I know. And I love him as a good man and king-to-be."

"I love my husband, Gerard. You met him in England I think."

"He was charming and handsome."

She looked across the room to Martine who was leaning against the back of the sofa, softening into the hit of the whisky.

"You love your child and you love a man who loves you. These are things I know myself as a woman," said Martine.

"Do I need to say the words about how I've loved in my life? Can you trace the scar of it?" said Sophia.

"Maybe. Maybe we should compare our wounds. Your life, my life— these are not normal lives. It is a moment when you fall in love isn't it? It happens and it fills you and then you live each season exclusively with that other person from the joy of spring through to the melancholy of autumn. And every song is their name and you say it or sing it until it has no sense. It is a stupid sentimental madness," said Martine.

"It is a stupid sentimental madness, Martine," said Sophia, enjoying her name and the feeling of the same words on her tongue.

"A stupid, stupid sentimental madness, Sophia."

She left her eyes on Martine's face, just enjoying it, just enjoying the pull of her kind eyes. She stood up and moved behind Martine's chair lowering her hands onto her shoulders and gently massaging her. Martine groaned and let her head tilt back. Sophia watched her closed eyes as her hands stroked up across her cheeks and drew back through her hair.

"Does this help?" asked Sophia.

"It doesn't help me with not being in love with you."

Sophia sighed. She *did* love Charles and he loved her. And yet, and yet....

"You can't and I can't."

"But that feeling of possibility is delicious isn't it," said Martine.

Sophia nodded.

"Yes it is, you know it is."

Her hands drifted lightly onto Martine's closed eyelids and forehead. She gave a long sigh.

"Your touch is sublime," said Martine.

Sophia had closed her own eyes as she stroked this other woman's cheeks and ran her finger along her lower lip, feeling the slight reflex of the kiss. Her own belly enjoyed a low, heavy warmth.

"Are you lonely in your life?" asked Sophia.

"Yes, of course, I'm the boss if you like. That's what I always wanted to be, to have some power I suppose."

"I admire you so much."

"Thank you."

"And the feeling of possibility is delicious and I don't want ever not to feel it," said Sophia.

"You just said that helplessly didn't you," said Martine. "You didn't want to admit it, but it got out through the wire didn't it."

"Yes, you pull me and you know that."

Martine raised her hand, took her arm and drew her round to face her. She leaned forward as Sophia knelt in front of her. She felt the softness of her lips on hers and caught the scent of her perfume. She just had to stop this now. She stood up, disturbed by her arousal and her intense emotional connection with her.

"Everyone will be coming back soon. What is your perfume?"

"Shalini."

"It's lovely, it will always mean Martine for me."

"Sophia, I think that was flirtatious," said Martine with a warm smile.

"Well, it's a delicious possibility I guess," said Sophia smiling back from her own chair.

Voices were approaching from the president's office where the interview had been held.

"Grab a scotch," said Martine to Françoise Hauton.

The interviewer smiled and took a shot.

"That was fantastic," said Françoise.

"Your questions were very kind," said Charles.

"I gave you the freedom to express yourself that is all. You define your role in a very new way—you know, king as champion of the nation. It is playing very well to the people."

"Francoise, you have been around politics all your life. Are we going to pull this off and will it unite our society?" asked Martine.

The veteran interviewer sat down. Martine smiled and topped up her whisky. She took a sip and rubbed her chin.

"You'll never convince the Intellos. They are the current class of kings who assume the right to rule the ignorant mass if you like. Essentially you are fighting an enormous rival royal family. They have a weakness in that they are not ruthless. Tonight they should have killed Charles—just killed him. But the liberal elite can't do that and retain their high ground."

"Yes, that same weakness in Cromwell allowed Charles the First of England time to escape," said Charles. Françoise shook her head slightly.

"Not everyone accepts that he did escape."

"Only the Intellos."

"No, many people doubt it, but it doesn't matter. They have factored it in. People are beginning to love you in a way, they don't care if you're a fake or not. The elite have never handled this aspect of the mob. The modern Internet keeps you in your echo chamber. You hear repeated only what you already believe," said Françoise.

Sophia watched this poised, intellectual woman with some admiration. She could tell that Charles had recruited her as a fan.

"So how do we unite all these disparate groups in their separate echo chambers?" asked Martine.

Françoise smiled.

"You give them a beautiful, kind and wise boy-king. Who could wish to harm him? You give him a beautiful French bride, weddings, coronation, ceremonies, babies. You close the lid of the glass box and you watch them suffocate as a national sport. It is a game the English have perfected," said Françoise.

Martine topped up the whisky and passed the bottle around.

"Old-style kings married foreign royals," said Charles.

"Yes and your apparent ancestor Henrietta Maria of France was hated by the English for being French and a Catholic. Probably she caused the failure of the monarchy," said Françoise.

Inside Sophia could feel herself shrinking. The woman was right. Charles had a mission to be king, albeit as a powerless plastic monarch of the mantelpiece. The British King Edward the Eighth had had to abandon his throne to love his American bride. She couldn't be such a woman in the history of another country where she didn't even speak the language. The ceiling wasn't glass, it was granite. Very soon now it would be time to pick up the threads of her old life as a London cop.

Françoise continued.

"But your question was whether you would succeed in re-creating the French monarchy. My answer is yes, you will achieve that. The people want that buzz to live in a situation their will, maybe also in a sense their love, has created. Politics either involves the people or politics becomes the game of the elite where the unexpected consequence is the guillotine," said Françoise.

"Thanks for your views. I respect your experience," said Martine.

"Good luck to you all," said Françoise as she left.

"There's a lot to think about over the next twenty-four hours," said Martine.

"It's the *Rex Factor* semi-final tonight. Maybe it's time you took a look at your missus," said Bastian.

Charles sighed.

"I can't just ignore it can I?"

"No," said Martine.

"This is when reality TV becomes TV reality," said Sophia.

"I'm meeting that Mason Trowel bastard tomorrow," said Martine.

"He still wants Esmeralda because she can sell more merchandise worldwide. The Polish girl is big in Europe with her Catholic Christmas Dance Hits album although the new Pope's thrown a wobbler about getting her breasts out at the manger on the YouTube video," said Bastian.

"I expect Holy Mary got hers out," said Sophia.

"Not holding a crucifix to her groin," said Bastian.

Sophia laughed. She had to accept the madness of it all. Her own daughter was rich, starring in blockbuster films and hopefully made for life because the chance hook of fame had lifted her out of the morass. She gave interviews to cuisine mags about how she prepared her pot noodles. She'd worn odd trainers on her feet and made a fortune endorsing a new yin yang craze with Taoist twerking courses. She'd received ten thousand dollars for 46 seconds of suggestive branded banana eating. If, on behalf of her child she was prepared to take the gain, she would have to accept the pain.

CHAPTER 43

"Let's go through to my private apartments. I'll get some food brought up," said Martine.

The salon was gorgeous, a mix of modern pale blue and gold set against walls of cream and salmon. A luxurious sofa which would have seated ten, faced a huge TV screen. The regal intro music was fading. The broadcast was live from the ice rink of the Grand Palais only a couple of blocks away on the other side of the Champs Élysées. Mason Trowel is hosting the show himself dressed in reindeer antlers. He skates up to his mark, turns to best profile and exposes his perfect teeth. His French was subtitled for the international audience. The French anthem played to a hand-clapped dance beat. Mason Trowel encourages the excited audience to join in. The first theme of the evening is the chance to see each girl ice dance with a pro skater. A panel of celebrity judges would award points but Mason Trowel declares every few minutes, "The only vote that counts is the democracy of you folks at home on the phone." The girls all skate out hand in hand as great friends in mini-skirted Santa Claus outfits. First to go is the Polish girl Anita Szymborska. She's beautiful and elegant. Next up is Esmeralda Grump. The crowd jeered and whistled. She performs her huge smile and raises her arm in a circus ta-dah flourish. The crowd hiss and whistle. She skates beautifully until the pro skater throws her with such force that she couldn't quite manage the landing and sits on her butt. The crowd laugh and applaud. Esmeralda dances on. She's no quitter and something of a trouper. The third girl is the outsider from Martinique, Solène Charlone She's a gorgeous dark-skinned girl with a proper womanly body. It's evident that there's very little chance to ice skate in the Caribbean but she stays upright. The final dancer is Nathalie Collobert the French favorite from Cannes. Her eyes and hair are dark. She has something of a disdainful pout in her expression. She remains slightly apart from the other girls. She survives the dance but is underwhelmed by the occasion. The crowd stamp, clap, and cheer but she does *not* acknowledge them.

The commercial break features Izzy wheel-spinning her Renault Amour up the nave of Notre Dame Cathedral and a bunch of folks talking about Brittany oysters.

The next round was for each girl to sing a classic French song of their choice. Anita does a fair job on the Madeleine Peyroux song, "*J'ai deux amours.*" Esmeralda does "*Je ne regrette rien*" with real passion. Even the hostile audience applauds. Solène Charlone sings a lullaby "*Dodo Ti pitit Manman*" in Créole to massive applause. Nathalie Collobert sings another Piaf song "*Les Amants d'un Jour,*" about a tragic young couple who commit suicide in a squalid hotel room after one last moment of love. There were tears in Martine's eyes.

"Only the French make beautiful songs like this."

The crowd stamp and scream for an encore. Nathalie repeats the verse about finding of the dead bodies.

"Nathalie, you owned that song. We all died in that damp discolored room with you," declared Mason Trowel.

Of the bunch any sensible guy would go for Solène from Martinique. Sophia held her thoughts.

The final round was a simple catwalk in evening gown with a Miss World style interview at the end.

The Martinique girl was a bit short in stature and too bouncy. She wanted a better world for baby turtles and for her sick cousin to recover. The Polish girl wanted a university degree in classical philosophy and a world of love and travel. Esmeralda wanted nothing other than to keep goats for cheese making and a world united by dance music. Nathalie wanted an iPhone 7 and to find a real cigarette that didn't cause cancer.

On the night, Nathalie Collobert was the runaway winner with the French judges. "You, the people will decide," said Mason Trowel over and over as the show ended. Charles looked dismayed.

"Does anyone think Nathalie is a bit miserable?" asked Charles.

"She's beautifully miserably French," said Martine.

"She has the Mediterranean summer fruitfulness of a lemon," said Captain Côté.

"She's a fair looker. I'd get in there," said Bastian.

"I wish you would," said Charles.

"I'm in love with the dark Solène," said the captain.

"Let's love some food," said Martine.

They went through to a sumptuous dining room with an oval walnut table. A waiter served *foie gras* and a sweet white wine. Sophia was feeling drunk but also hungry. This was no longer her show, she knew that. Very soon this life of clinging to the slipstream of the powerful would be over. She was with them, but she was not of them. And never ever would be. She looked at Charles. She must set him free to fulfill a greater destiny than just loving her. She had made love with the virgin king of France and had kissed the female president. It seemed that both of them were in love with her and in different senses she was in love with both of them. She was a street cop. She knew love mainly by the forensic post mortem report on the dissected body of its absence. You do what you have to do. You're a cop. You go home, you peel the potatoes, you change your wallpaper. A fist in a woman's face and a rape report on your desk. You do your shift. You're a cop, you go home, you peel the potatoes....

"Your thoughts are far away, Sophia," said Charles.

"No, they're wrapped up in me."

"A woman's thoughts are always in a different universe to a man's," said Martine.

"Do women ever wish they were a man?" asked Charles.

"I just couldn't afford all the new underwear, but I love your question. A man may freely love a woman and that I envy, because I know how much love a woman has to give him in return," said Martine.

"I would be a woman to feel the whole thing of growing the baby inside me. What can a man truly know of life without that?" said Charles.

"It is better not to know especially when you get older. Viktor Pinupskin poses for bare chest photos, not a stretch mark in sight and he's sixty-six," said Martine.

"I wonder if he'll still do his pin-up calendar when he's tsar?" said Bastian.

Martine was examining her tablet.

"The French girl stormed it with the suicide song in France, but Esmeralda is still huge out there in the world. Mason's going to be sick when I tell him she's got to go."

"The male skater just threw her," said Sophia.

"His father's a Patriotic Front deputy. He was told to sabotage her," said Captain Côté.

"The Americans and Brits love her more because she got up, smiled and fought for it," said Bastian.

"The fact is she's foreign. It was worth a try because we don't want Grump as an enemy and she would have sold worldwide merchandise. But it's got to be Nathalie 'cos that's what the patriots want," said Martine.

"I don't feel there's an elephant in the room here. I feel I *am* the elephant in the room," said Sophia.

No one answered.

"It's OK, guys. These are spinning world events and I got caught up in the hurricane," she added.

"Leadership, politics, call it what you like, is pragmatism, Sophia. Charles doesn't have to like Nathalie," said Martine.

"No, he just has to put his erect penis in her vagina and ejaculate now and then. In the meantime she travels around the world, meets the great and the good, waves from limos and gets adored and pampered by fawning grovellers," said Sophia.

"You could still get the penis and ejaculation treatment," said Bastian. "Prince Richard did his stud duty and had a better one just to love. A few of the guys who've lived in this place have kept the real woman off the books."

"Does anyone ask how that would seem to Nathalie? Where's her pride and esteem?"

"It's in the fucking bank, the palaces, and the fame," said Bastian.

"You know so little of women. I don't think I could ever conspire in cold blood to mock another woman," said Sophia.

Bastian chuckled.

"I know enough of women never to have got tied up with one," he said.

"Look, just stop it guys. Please just leave it. At first sight I don't take to Nathalie but she's a human being worth no less than anyone here. You all know Sophia is very special to me," said Charles.

"But she's too old and off the scale for not being French," said Sophia.

"And you're not a stupid greedy trollop wanting instant wealth and fame on a talent show," said Martine.

"Now *you're* looking down on the people, Martine. The hem of your elite slip just fell down. These girls are just like all of us, snatching any chance at success 'cos you don't get many. I respect her. These kids are no different from anyone buying a lotto ticket. My chance came fighting for my fucking life against a guy with a machine gun," said Sophia.

She took a deep breath and let it calm her. She was out of her league and for sure it wasn't her place to tell the president of France how to run her country. She shot a smile of resignation at Martine who responded with a nod and a long appraisal with her kind eyes.

"She's right guys. Caesar Roboris and the Patriotic Front dreamed all this up. Mason Trowel and Vandervell O'Brien have delivered the spectacle we wanted. No one cared who got caught up," said Martine.

"So where's the problem?" said Bastian.

"The problem is that love is the currency of the human world. You can print more paper, but you can't print love. In the end you can't fake it. The people found out the management elites and now they look to kings. Let's hope we avoid inflation," said Charles.

"Christ, economics *and* philosophy," said Bastian.

"He's a king," said Sophia.

"And I control the money supply and the printing presses," said Martine with a laugh.

"I have a farewell Boymondo concert tomorrow evening and then I'm live at the *Rex Factor* final to kiss my bride."

"Don't look to rehearse the final scene with me," said Sophia.

Charles sighed and hung his head a little.

"You guys need some space to talk. Come on the rest of you, let's enjoy a small cognac in my office. Come through when you're ready," said Martine.

Sophia acknowledged the sheer presence of this woman. She controlled things with complete confidence. She had seized power, she had faced assassination attempts, a military coup, and only a few hours ago, the TV studio Intellos had tried to depose her. Yet, here she was, relaxed and offering her guests a cognac. Dealing with the king and his future was just a small affair of state.

As the door closed, Charles stood and opened his arms to invite her into his embrace. She didn't move. This was her Lady Macbeth moment, she knew that.

"Charles, not one of those guys is going to let you do anything but follow this through. You and I both know that. This conversation is only to be polite and civilized about moving on to our own destinies."

He let his arms fall to his side.

"But I love you."

"You'd have loved any woman who came to you in this moment, to make love and set you on your way."

"I believe you were sent to me. You've saved my life for Christ sake."

"OK then here's the deal. You walk out of here tomorrow morning with me. We catch the Eurostar to London and get a tube train to my flat in Streatham. I go back to work as a street cop and you sign on at the job center. I'll cook us a curry and we'll watch world affairs on my TV. We'll put up pics of our cat on Facebook. You'll get a job flipping burgers and we'll make love every night. Everyone will forget us and leave us alone. Then you'll meet a suitable girl who comes in for a big whopper and come home to realize you're tied up with a woman of fifty with gynecological issues," she said.

"I'm OK with the curry, the burger flipping, and the lovemaking."

"Charles, you're a good, good man. I believe in your wisdom, gentleness and courage. You will be king and your people will love you. I'm setting aside my own feelings here and I just don't want to talk about them even to myself because if I do, I'm going to break down bawling like a stupid pathetic cow."

"Please let me hold you. Please."

"It won't help you or me. Alcoholics and junkies only ever want one last shot."

"Would you deny an addict?"

She looked into his eyes. He'd changed, become aware of his own persuasiveness and beauty. He was developing the tone of the politician.

How much she wanted him to hold her, not to withdraw his love for her. His love was still naïve and open. God, how the wrong woman could destroy him. She did love him, but she couldn't love uninjured by the blows and slaps of life. No Sophia, suck it up. You weren't born to win.

"Denying addicts is the only hope you've got of keeping them alive."

"What if I haven't got the courage to live without you? What if I'd rather die than go without a fix?"

"In that case you'll die with the fix or without the fix," she said.

"Then why deny me?"

"Because my dear sweet Charles, you won't die of a broken heart, but you will with a 9-millimeter bullet wedged in it."

"I don't know if I can do what's in front of me without you."

"No one ever knows that. OK, second deal. Marry Nathalie or whichever bride. Keep me as a whore on the side and general purpose counselor. Live a life of deception and smear your wife and me with shame. When you have a row about the kids come and cry on my perfumed wrinkled shoulder."

"No, I couldn't accept that."

"That's because you're a good and caring guy I could love with all my heart, and now you're making me cry."

He came to her and took her in his arms.

"I love you," he said.

"I won't say I love you straight back 'cos it's not genuine to return the word like it was the same tennis ball. I'm keeping this ball and taking it home. No one else is ever going to hit this one back," she said.

CHAPTER 44

Bastian said goodnight with a cold smile.

"I'm working the night shift as a cleaner around the TV studios."

Sophia had no doubt that some suicides by hanging would greet the Paris dawn. An official led them through to another grand building. Two uniformed valets carried their luggage. How she would miss power!

"This is the Hotel de Marigny, where visiting heads of state stay," he said. They had walked through a courtyard busy with soldiers. Inside were gendarmes and Parisian police lavishly equipped with machine guns. She hadn't spoken further with Charles because she'd said it all. The wound of separation was still wet and fluid. She knew from her life that it wasn't until the scar tissue formed that you knew what stiffness had found its way into your soul. Mad young love could be a prison and even its unwanted loss a joyous escape. Up until now only one love had left a knot of tissue to map and comprehend at leisure. This latest had been a short affair, but in war the guy who killed you in a second didn't wait for your consumer feedback. Oh Sophia, what now?

A bunch of soldiers split them up and escorted Charles and Captain Côté to their room. Until it was over, Charles would be under ruthless close guard. Sophia was shown to another room on an upper floor. Two gendarmes guarded her door. She looked out of the window to see soldiers patrolling the courtyard. No chance of just slipping away into the night physically. Mentally now she had a distance from events and a space to think. She showered and lay naked in the huge grand bed. Her hands gauged the condition of her body. Her fingers traced her aquiline nose. For sure she could be a lot fitter but night shifts in south London held temptations of fried chicken at 2 a.m. and a whisky or two at 8 a.m. bedtime. Her life was a cigarette end burning itself out in an ashtray or a kebab turning to cold fat in the gutter for a pigeon or rat feast. She herself, this woman, this flesh, had shared love with a king as his equal, a king who loved her. She had opened the soul of the lady president of France and had shared her lips. OK, she was pansexual but she didn't love a man less because she felt the pull of a woman. She could love a man more because another woman's love expanded her being as a woman. A woman who could love another woman understood that longing in a man to drink that hot flow of love. All those guys who wore women's clothes were worshipping at the temple of woman, not wanting to attract a man. She wanted to sleep, sleep, sleep. OK, a little comfort would be a kindness. If you want to know kindness, firstly be kind to yourself. She turned and pressed her face into the pillow.

"You know I need to stop this now, Martine," she whispered.

A young female soldier brought her breakfast at 8 a.m.

"Madame, I have a message from Anna La Salle. She would like to come at nine o'clock to see you."

"Where?"

"In your room, please," said the girl.

"Fine, thank you."

The coffee was strong and she needed it. She dressed in a black trouser suit and cream ruffled blouse. Anna would not be coming to her room just to check on her health, but it was something when the deputy director of the UK National Crime Agency came to see you. At nine o'clock precisely there was a knock at the door. Anna came in smiling with a glossy magazine and new pot of coffee which she set down in order to embrace Sophia.

"Brilliant job at the TV studios. Well done yet again," said Anna.

"Wrong place, right time," said Sophia, her eyes drifting to the front cover of Paris Match magazine.

"Yes, Houston, we have a problem."

Sophia studied the image. It was a still from the video the young French police officer had made on the roof of the TV studio building. It showed a close up of her and Charles in a kiss.

"The headline says '*Les Yeux d'Amour*,' the look of love," said Anna.

"Is there an article to go with it?"

"There sure is. There's body language experts analyzing the depth of your love which they pronounce as profound and passionate. There's features with leading feminists demanding that the stigma of the older woman, younger guy relationship be regarded as criminal sexism. There's features about who you are or might be. There's a double-page spread on the government minister Manuel Macaroni. His wife was his thirty eight year old teacher when he was a schoolboy of fifteen. There's an astrology guide to what star sign you must be to be so close to the king. The only thing that isn't about you is the crossword and a recipe for rabbit ear soup."

"Oh dear," said Sophia.

"As we speak Mason Trowel has got the *Rex Factor* girls in hiding because a mob of press want to interview the girls about how they feel towards Charles seeing him clearly already in love with another woman."

"And an old hag," Sophia commented.

"If the magazine said that it would partially solve it. They describe you as supremely beautiful and clearly of noble blood. Their top staff reporter claims an inside source has named you as an Italian principessa descended from an illegitimate daughter of Carlos the Third, King of Sicily. He goes on to say that you are a warrior maiden in an undercover network of bluebloods seeking to restore monarchy as the principle type of world government," said Anna.

"Does he know about Caesar Roboris?"

"We think not but obviously he's got hold of a whisper and made a Mona Lisa by joining up three dots. We've asked Bastian to interview him."

Sophia sighed.

"I'm so sorry Anna. I feared something like this and I've finished any romance with Charles. I was going to contact you today to see if I could just go home."

Anna gave a wry smile and nodded.

"What do you think the answer would be?" she said.

"So what can I do?"

"That's why I'm here with you. Look, none of this is your fault and we all accept that. We encouraged you to get close. The boy needed to grow up for Christ sake. We can play it three ways. We could reveal you as the passionate principessa and you play the role of the predatory femme fatale who simply overwhelmed the poor lad. We can hide you away saying that you were a maverick bodyguard who's now out of work. Or we can rubbish the whole feature as fake news put up by the Intellos," said Anna.

"I'll go for the unemployed bodyguard option and go home," said Sophia.

"That'd be my choice. The one problem is that Martine won't hear of you disappearing. She told me this morning that if we remove you, she'll take you on as her personal assistant."

"But I wouldn't have to take the job," said Sophia.

"The Met' police would order you to do it, on the instructions of Her Majesty's government. Apart from that the project needs you. Charles could still get a fit of the wobbles."

"And I would rush in, hold him to my sagging maternal breasts to keep him calm and rush back to my cell."

"It's not quite as cold-blooded as that," said Anna.

"They're not that sagging but I wanted a compliment," said Sophia with a laugh.

Anna laughed.

"You're a bloody trouper, Sophia."

"OK, I disguise myself as a French maid, hide in Martine's wine cellar until she calls me to her office."

"That's not as silly as it sounds. Martine wants you to learn French. We're sending you back to the flat in London for a few days. A language teacher from the French embassy will come every day to give you intensive tuition. You'll only speak in French, you'll watch TV in French and you'll dream in French," said Anna.

"How many days is a few?" asked Sophia.

"My guess, no more than five," said Anna.

"And then?"

"Then there'll be a king of France, a fabulous coronation followed by a huge state wedding performed by the Pope."

"And then?"

"You'll come back to Paris. Then we'll see how things shake down, what the Caesar Roboris guys want and what the English government wants," said Anna.

"It could be worse. *Je suis votre fille,*" said Sophia

"Your plane is on the tarmac at Villacoublay. Thanks for everything you've done so far. I'll see you again soon," said Anna. "Oh yes, I was forgetting, Martine gave me this box for you."

Anna dug into her overcoat pocket and produced a beautifully wrapped box about the size of the palm of her hand.

"Thank you," said Sophia, obviously looking perplexed.

"Martine thinks a lot of you and thinks about you."

A black Citroen C5 government car with three armed soldiers and a driver sped her to the airport. The BAe146 of the Queen's Flight banked left over Paris. If Charles looked up he would see her, a vapor trail in the cold clear winter sky. Below her a young man went on to face a life without her, a life few men with ten times his experience would be able to handle. Some destiny had put them together on the same track and destiny would do its work whichever way it was written. Carefully she opened the package. It was a beautiful bottle of Shalini perfume in a Lalique crystal bottle with a butterfly wing stopper. A small card was folded inside.

My darling Sophia, it is so egoist of me to let you go with my own perfume with which to recall me. Maybe your breath will carry a trace of me close to your heart. Maybe you will hold it there for just a little while and think of me as I will be thinking of you. Nothing will defeat me if I fight knowing that one day I will feel your lips on mine once again. With love, Martine.

"Oh God. Martine, Martine," she sighed, holding the letter to her breast.

She smoothed a drop of the intense floral perfume onto the back of her hand. She breathed it in, reading the card again, imagining her hand writing it, imagining the kindness in her eyes as the words were born on the paper.

A love letter. She would not have to leave this earth without a love letter. This woman was smashing a post into the hard virgin soil of history with her will and strength. And yet she had a moment to express her beautiful vulnerable love. If Martine wanted her to learn French she would do it for her and reply. She was a woman and she was free. And a woman in love, loves.

CHAPTER 45

It hadn't even been two weeks since she'd first arrived at the flats in Belgravia when Mel had more or less kidnapped her at the scene of the shooting in Dulwich. The whole area was closely guarded by armed police. This time she'd arrived in an SO16 Protection Squad red Range Rover. Her ex-jailer Jean greeted her in the first floor flat, still furnished as if Mel were alive. Sophia hugged her.

"I'm guessing you know about Mel."

"Yeah, he was a cool guy. I think he knew somehow he wasn't coming back. He told me to take Fortnum and Mason home with me to look after them."

"Who are they?"

"His bonsai trees. He used to say they were his children because if ever he had any, he'd keep them small so they wouldn't drink his wine or borrow his car."

Sophia smiled at the thought of him saying it.

"Have you been here ever since I left?"

"No, I got a call this morning. I'm here to deal with anything you need."

"And to handcuff me if I try to escape?"

"No one specified handcuffs, just whatever I had to do."

"Jean, I won't give you a hard time I promise. To be honest it's good to be out of the front line for a few days."

"They've installed satellite TV upstairs in your flat for you. You can get all the French channels," said Jean.

They went up to the top flat and made coffee. A pile of French grammar books and a dictionary were already on the table. There was something important on Sophia's mind.

"I need a card, plain on the inside for my own message, some tape, a small gift box and gift wrapping paper."

Jean finished her coffee and left her alone. Sophia clicked on the TV to watch the news. Her schoolgirl French enabled her to pick out a few words in the running tape of breaking stories. The pictures spoke for themselves. The *Rex Factor* finalists had been announced as Nathalie Collobert and Esmeralda Grump. Both girls were in VIP seats at the Stade de France football arena to see the farewell Boymondo concert. From there they would be travelling on to the final showdown at the grand Hall of Mirrors at the Palace of Versailles. The final contest would be based on relationship science and some kind of expert analysis. The result would be announced immediately after the show on the basis of the phone-in vote. If Charles was to be king then the winner would be queen. TV shows would be made about their lives and pets. If the people rejected the monarchy they would marry and become boy band and bride celebrities with recording contracts, film and TV deals. There would be a weekly show called *Regals and Beagles* about their lives and pets as if they were royals.

She found some sliced bread and a tin of baked beans in the kitchen and fixed a meal. How she'd missed her poor banal life. There was a knock at the door. She opened it to a serious looking guy of maybe fifty-five years.

"I'm Jean-Claude Godineau, your French professor."

"*Ahntray muss yer.*"

"Excellent. You are fluent," he said with a warm smile.

"*Mare see.*"

She knew she was going to like this guy. They were in mid-nasal sound exercises when Jean arrived back with her shopping.

"I want to get a small gift to Martine."

"Martine La Plume?"

"Yes, she's a friend."

"That explains everything. She is a wonderful woman bringing back the pride and prestige of France," said Jean-Claude.

"I need to write her a small message in French."

"OK, what is it?"

"I want to say 'I have worn this cross and it has kept me safe through all the life of a street-cop. Keep it to guard you whenever you are alone. It will not fail you. Love Sophia.'"

"OK, I will help you," he said.

He dictated the letters and words while Sophia wrote them in the card. She found her crucifix where she'd left it on her bedside table, wrapped it in tissue and placed it in the box. Finally she wrapped the parcel.

"I need to get this to Martine."

"It's OK. I'm going to the embassy this evening. It will be in the diplomatic bag overnight to Paris. She will have it in the morning."

Her head was spinning with R-sound tongue positions and lists of vocabulary. Mixed in were Charles and his brides, Martine, and all those who would take them down given half a chance. And she was in London, unable to save them. Only now with the evening did her numbness begin to lift as if from an anesthetic. Charles needed her and yet she had allowed herself to be pushed away from him. She'd kept herself busy, but now in this lonely flat she ached to be involved in the action. She'd sent a token of herself to Martine, but had left Charles to face his issues without a word of love or care. He was in the wings and the lights were going down in the auditorium. He needed her, but she could never be at his side. Was she was flirting with Martine only as a way to deflect the hopelessness of her feelings for Charles? Could she allow herself to fall in love with Martine and never go beyond those couple of kisses? Her heart could beat just to the thrill of such a woman's desire for her. With Charles she was the leader and the bringer of joy to his door. She could pull him apart or in any direction she chose. But Martine could just push through the door and take her. She had never asked if she could love a woman. She had opened her book and let those kind eyes find that page of her, just find it and read it.

Jean brought in some good old-fashioned fish and chips. They drank strong tea and watched the *Rex Factor* final on the French TV. Sophia cheated with English subtitles despite the instructions of her teacher. The setting in the Versailles palace was superb. Both girls had filled in detailed psychological assessments. Celebrity love-experts discussed their reports. Documentary films had been made about the background lives of the would-be queens. Esmeralda travelled the world working as an assistant to her father. She handed gifts and sweets to poor children. She saved baby orangutans in rainforests as globalist logging barons raped the planet. She surfed, made cookies, and went to shopping malls. She read hot romance novels. She had many smiley teeth. Her shallow life fizzed on the outside of her.

Nathalie rode a motor scooter in bare feet sometimes while smoking a cigarette. She wore torn jeans and listened to music on headphones. She handled life via her cell phone. She bronzed on the beach at Cannes, played beach volleyball, and drank only Coca Cola from the bottle. She met her friends in the college canteen and stood smoking outside in the rain. She liked a Big Mac and fries. She read surrealist poetry at college. She never smiled. Her moody life scowled and pouted on the inside of her.

Charles chatted to the experts about the films and the psychological profiles, praising both girls in what was clearly a contrived and scripted piece.

"But which one would you choose?" asked Mason Trowel, dressed in 18th century Versailles courtier costume with his trademark sunglasses.

"My heart is that of the people of France."

"You heard it folks. It's the democracy of the telephone vote that'll choose the bride. We'll know this time tomorrow if tonight's winner will be queen and Charles will be king. So get ready to call," said Mason Trowell.

For the final lap each girl had to read out a love tweet in no more than 140 characters to Charles explaining why she was his ideal bride. Esmeralda went first.

I would love you as my king and share the duties of your life. I loved you from the moment I heard you sing. I offer you my life and heart.

The crowd stamped and applauded. Nathalie had the last word.

You're a hot guy and you turn me on. Your music's not my style but we can work on it. Queen's cool but we could just make out anyway.

The crowd cheered even more.

"Bloody hell," said Jean, that little madam wants a boot up the ass.

"She's honest, I'll give her that."

"She's not queen of France material, is she?" said Jean.

"Would you go for Esmeralda?"

"Anyone looking for someone to help Charles would choose her."

"But she's foreign."

"So was Marie Antoinette."

"And that didn't end too well," said Sophia.

The show morphed into a Boymondo concert while the telephone votes came in. Behind the scenes cameras tracked the girls. Nathalie smoked and worked on her cell phone screen. Esmeralda called home and then tried on some tiaras. Both girls changed into evening gowns. Clocks counted down, digital counters flashed the millions of votes coming in.

"How does all this play with the French people? Do they take this show seriously?" asked Jean.

"That's the whole thing, it's not supposed to be serious. The idea is to present it as a celebrity soap opera monarchy without political power. They dress up and do photo shoots. In a multi-religion, multi-tribe society it provides at least some kind of focal point or that's the hope."

"The Caesar Roboris guys don't see it that way," said Jean.

"No, and plenty of people have died because they realize that. If the mass of people thought this was a serious return to absolute monarchy and the divine right of kings you'd be looking at civil war."

"And what does Charles think?"

"He thinks he's been chosen by God. He thinks he can expand the role a little and become the steadfast champion of the people to balance the fickle and corrupt politicos. People like Prince Richard and President Edamame see this as a step towards a serious power grab."

"And what does that Martine La Plume think?"

"I think she just doesn't know. I don't know what she makes of the Caesar Roboris guys or what she knows of their plans. She's an absolute patriot of France. She believes the monarchy can bring pageantry and color to the public life of the country and involve all the people. She's a brave and daring woman," said Sophia.

Jean smiled.

"I like her. I did hear ... I did hear, she had a bit of a thing for you."

"Really?"

"Martine talked a lot to Mel. She's an attractive woman."

Obviously Jean knew more than she was saying. Maybe she had been briefed to do a bit of fishing. Sophia let it slide. On the TV it was nearly time for the result. Behind the scenes Nathalie stubbed out a final cigarette. Esmeralda brushed her hair. Mason Trowel had changed into a formal dinner jacket with red, white, and blue bow tie. Rock music blared, lasers flashed, endlessly he teased the audience with a gold envelope containing the result. Nathalie and Esmeralda walked out hand in hand and stood at either side of him. He pulled out the card inside, then pushed it back in.

"There can only be one winner, and the result is in this envelope," he said.

Music blasted and a troupe of dancers came on waving French flags. Curtains opened to reveal wide stairs carpeted in red. At the top stood Charles in a dark suit. He extended his arms in a Jesus pose.

Mason Trowel looked at the card.

"Who could choose between these two wonderful girls?" he said, pushing the card back into the envelope.

The crowd was screeching. Rock guitar orgasms were pulsing, drums were pounding. He pulled out the card.

"And the *Rex Factor* bride of France will be...."

A whole brass section played a deafening fanfare.

"And the *Rex Factor* bride of France will be, will be, will be ... Nathalie Collobert!!!!"

Heavies moved in and ushered Esmeralda away, seemingly never to appear again. Nathalie shrugged and gave half a wave to the audience.

"Wow, Nathalie, how does it feel?"

"Well, the polls said I was ahead so I figured it would be me," she said.

Mason Trowel hovered between a smile and a grimace.

"You nailed it with that love tweet."

"Yeah, me and my best mate Céline thought it up."

"Charles, get down here and kiss your bride," boomed Mason Trowel.

Sophia watched his face. He didn't take a step. She could see he'd frozen. He just had to go through with it.

"Don't be shy, she's waiting and we're waiting aren't we folks?"

The crowd were stamping and chanting.

Charles had his eyes closed in concentration like a diver about to plunge. He opened them, took a deep breath, smiled and gave a wave to the crowd before scampering down the stairs in a La La Land dance step.

The crowd screamed for the kiss. Nathalie remained cool and unmoved, facing the audience. Charles arrived behind her.

"Nathalie, turn and kiss your man," said Trowel.

She shrugged and offered her face to him. Charles opened his arms to embrace her and placed his lips on hers. Sophia guessed he wouldn't like the cigarette flavor. He winced and raised his eyebrows.

"At least she's not fucking well sucking his tongue," commented Sophia.

"Wow, how was that?" Mason Trowel screeched.

"He's not as tall as I thought," she said.

Charles shrugged, smiled, gave a ta-dah wave and stood on tiptoe. The crowd went wild.

"Jean, can you check out all the twitter on this?" said Sophia.

"They love Charles. The tiptoe joke's really playing well. The general tone in English is that he's sweet and gorgeous and she's a miserable little cow. There's a hashtag #FagAshPrincess," said Jean.

Sophia tried to make sense of the French comments. She spotted *miserable* and a phrase *sale moutarde* which she translated as dirty mustard. A lot of comments just seemed relief that a French girl had won.

"A lot of people are saying they want him to marry the woman he's in love with from the rooftop kiss. They've blown up the picture so that you can see who she is and the Eiffel tower lit up in the background. It's totally viral. It's you isn't it?" said Jean.

"Afraid so," said Sophia.

Mason Trowel was winding up the show.

"The referendum poll opens at seven o'clock in the morning people. Will Nathalie be marrying the new King Charles the Eleventh of France? It's up to you now. Do we love Charles?"

The crowd burst into applause and wild screams.

The cameras panned to Nathalie who was texting on her phone. Mason Trowel put his arm around her.

"Is it sinking in yet?"

"Yeah."

"This must be the proudest and happiest day of your life," enthused Mason Trowel.

"Yeah, sort of. I went out with Louis Zongalero for a bit, but I was only thirteen," she said.

"The famous international footballer?"

"Yeah, he was cool," she said.

"Well, with your beauty you'd attract any man, even a king," said Mason, with a nervous sideways glance.

"I know, and now I'm famous too," she said.

"That's it folks. Nathalie Collobert, the *Rex Factor* bride of France."

The crowd applauded, maybe a little less wildly. Sophia clicked off the screen.

"I like her. She's a straight kid, gorgeous gamine face and lovely size-ten figure," said Sophia.

"Queen of France? I don't think so," said Jean.

"She represents the information age youth of Europe. The big stuff is going on someplace else on the screen."

"But she just didn't care a shit," said Jean.

"She probably doesn't understand the history of monarchy or the world. Why would she?"

"She could have pretended to be excited. She'd obviously prefer a footballer."

"Well, her autobiography launches in the morning, her song album will make her a fortune, and with luck Charles will just do what he has to do and find a true life for himself."

Jean was grinning.

"Twitter is hot with denials from Louis Zongalero. He says he never touched her."

"Well, he would say that, wouldn't he," said Sophia with a laugh.

Her cell phone was ringing, but she didn't recognize the number. She picked up.

"Sophia, it's Charles."

"These phones are monitored," she said.

"Yes, they would be. Did you see that horrible show?"

"Yes."

"I can't do it, I just can't."

"I can see why you feel that, but keep it together. The referendum is tomorrow and you won't have to marry her until after your coronation. Anything can happen yet. Just hold in there."

"She's a decent kid I think, but one hell of a storm is brewing up about this footballer. Apparently her book covers at least a team."

"I was amazed she said that."

"She's a decent honest kid. In many ways her generation aren't buying into all this hyped shit. They are disparate and get their info from a hundred sources. She's going to be a cult hero, the 'sister of shrug,'" said Charles.

"You know Charles, you'll be a great king."

"You can't imagine how it feels to me to hear you say that."

"We can never be together, but I'll always believe in you and be at your side in my head."

"I love you," he said.

"I love you too," she replied.

"I feel stronger now. I was fighting to keep it together after the show."

"The tiptoe thing was great. Who's with you?"

"Captain Côté and some soldiers."

"Where's Bastian?"

"You know, on a mission in London I think."

A slap of suspicion jolted her. Bastian was like a submarine in inky water or a crocodile at the calm watering hole. She kept her shudder to herself.

"Keep smiling, sugar."

"Sophia."

"Charles."

"I'm touring on an open bus around Paris tomorrow as the referendum takes place," he said.

Her mind shot to John F Kennedy in his limo smiling and waving to the crowds in Dallas.

"Be careful."

"There's bulletproof glass. No one's going to get a head shot."

"They'd better not, I might need those lips on me one more time."

CHAPTER 46

Monsieur Jean-Claude Godineau, her French teacher, arrived at 9:30 a.m. In the cold he wore a red, white, and blue bobble hat and a heavy blue overcoat with a collar that converted into a hood. She'd seen the early news in French. Poor Nathalie was now plunged into an under-aged sex scandal involving more than one footballer. Ronald Grump had withdrawn the American ambassador in Paris and flown F18 Super Hornet jets off the carrier USS Roosevelt up and down the English Channel. He'd tweeted, *"Never piss on my family you stinking crooked-toothed Frenchies."*

Referendum voters were queuing at the polling booths. Anti-ageism feminists were blockading the Faubourg Saint Honoré close to the Élysée in a protest against chauvinistic attitudes to older women. Riot police were tooled up with shields and tear gas. Earnest breakfast show experts were asking how Mason Trowel didn't know about Nathalie's sporting past. Louis Zongalero and four other footballers had been arrested.

He sat down while Sophia made him some coffee. He seemed very quiet and serious. He opened a book and left it open on the table. He flicked his eyes to signal she should read it.

"I have a small grammar exercise to start with," he said. Sophia studied the text.

We have intercepted traffic to suggest that the agent Bastian is in London. We believe you may be his target in order to bring pressure on Martine. We believe the woman here called Jean could act against you if ordered. There are members of the Patriotic Front who oppose Martine over the monarchy and are siding with the Intellos. We do not know who to trust so we cannot use anyone. We believe that Caesar Roboris has ordered the death of Martine and her close supporters so that they can declare a full executive monarchy once the referendum gives Charles the green light. We believe that Martine's death may be staged as an accident of some kind. France will then acknowledge the other leaders in the Caesar Roboris group who seize power as legitimate governments. You are in danger here and our intelligence service in Paris needs you to spot Bastian if he surfaces and maybe deal with him. Your phone is bugged. You need to get out of here.

Sophia let the implication sink in for a moment.

"I don't think I'm going to enjoy grammar too much," she said as she began to write. She handed her notepad to Jean-Claude.

I am a lawful officer of the Metropolitan Police. I'm not a hit man or any kind of killer. I don't know what you want me to do.

"That's not too bad, I'll write it out and you can study the gender agreements," said Jean-Claude.

She read his response.

Anna La Salle is with us. She has always had a watching brief on behalf of the English government. The English cabinet met this morning and at last finally a policy is now fixed. They will support a politically powerless constitutional monarchy in France but withdraw all support for the Caesar Roboris group. The queen of England is in agreement although members of her family believe in the divine right of kings and are ready to seize power. You are authorized to take any necessary steps to support Martine and her vision of the future. Anna will confirm this.

Sophia sighed.

"Yeah, I think I can see my way through this gender agenda. I think it's a game of finding the lady and chasing the male ace."

"Bravo, Sophia. We're going to master this together in no time." said Jean-Claude.

He was writing again.

"Try this exercise," he said.

She read the note.

My clothes will fit you and the hood will cover most of your face. The scarf will just leave your eyes. We just don't know who is with us and who is not. You will leave in my clothes. Tuck your hair in the hat. My car is a black Peugeot with diplomatic registration plates outside the door. The driver has a change of clothes and a French diplomatic passport. He knows what is happening. He is a good man. You will drive to St. Pancras station. You will join a party of language students as a teacher and catch the 12:24 Eurostar to Paris Gare du Nord. You will get a taxi to the hotel Opéra Migny Montmartre in Rue Victor Massé in Pigalle. The concierge is one of ours. He will brief and equip you. No one must know you are there. I don't have to tell you that agent Bastian is ruthless. Bonne chance, ma belle Sophia.

"Grammar is just so complicated. Do you know what you're going to do with your future tense?" she said.

"Ah, often it's best to use a conditional. Look, I'll show you." he said as he began to write.

I am wearing two pairs of trousers more or less the same. Once you are away I will wait for a change of the guards and hope they don't realize the teacher has already gone. I will wear the jacket and you wear my overcoat to hide your shape. You wear my shoes and I will take my chances in whatever there is. Trainers? It's improvised and it's risky I know. This is a turning moment of history and there is no going back. If I get caught I've got diplomatic immunity and I used to be French tutor to Her Majesty. I've got a number to call as a last resort.

He pulled off his trousers, socks, shoes and jumper. Underneath he had a shirt tie and second pair of trousers. He replaced the jacket. Sophia went to the bedroom and folded her hair into the bobble hat. She wriggled into the trousers and jumper. The overcoat hid her curves. In the pocket she found the scarf. The shoes were two sizes too big but she could cope. She dug out a pair of plain trainers that possibly would work as shoes for Jean-Claude if his feet would fit. This whole thing was a long shot. What other options were there and what was there to lose? She tried not to dwell on the possible answers. Once she had got away, Jean-Claude only had until Jean came up from the lower flat which she did at least once an hour.

She kissed him on both cheeks. She doubted he would make it. They wouldn't hesitate to deal with a small fish like a language teacher. Anna La Salle might save him and the guards were regular Scotland Yard officers but the loyalty of individual soldiers was anyone's guess. She was on her own and if no one knew where she was, that was the safest place to be.

She pulled up her hood, opened the flat door and stepped out.

"Bonjour," she said gruffly, avoiding eye contact with officers. She took the stairs to the first floor landing. The officers there glanced at her, one of them looking her up and down. She kept moving.

"Bonjour," she said.

There was no reply. She kept moving. Two officers guarded the door to the outside. One of the cops from the upper floor was right behind her on the stairs. She was guessing he suspected something. In Ebury Street outside she could see the black Peugeot 407 with the distinctive plates with the D in the middle of the number. She focused on that vehicle, each step taking her closer. She went through the doors. The officers stood aside. The officer from the landing was still behind her. Ten strides would get her to the car. She didn't turn, she heard him click off the safety catch of his Heckler and Koch MP5 automatic rifle. Seven strides.

"Stop there, ID check," said a voice.

Three strides.

The driver was looking in his mirror. He had started his engine. If she went for the door the cop would grab her. Met police wouldn't open fire. She took a jump and lay face-down on the roof, grabbing the radio aerial.

"Go!" she shouted.

The driver floored the throttle. The road was straight for 200 yards. She could hold on at least until the end of the street. Cops were running behind them. If she could retrieve the clothes and papers she could bail out of the car. No one knew she was headed for the Eurostar. The guy at the wheel was an ace. He slowed, crept around the corner into the main Pimlico Road. He booted it for another 200 yards and stopped. She scrambled into the back of the car.

"I need the clothes, passport, and ticket," she said.

"The hold all," said the driver.

This guy could handle a car. He made an extra lane up the outside of traffic in Buckingham Palace Road and shot by the palace at a speed of at least 80 miles per hour. Sophia had begun to change into jeans, T-shirt, black leather motorcycle jacket, and flat-soled boots. She liked the look. He squealed left into Constitution Hill and pulled over.

"Dress and go, make your way across Green Park to the tube station. Piccadilly or Victoria line to King's Cross St. Pancras. Try to rendezvous with the language students group, you should get less scrutiny. The leader is Madame Margaret Collins, she's French married to an Englishman. I can't go near the station so you're on your own. Leave your cell phone here, they'll track it. I'll keep them off the scent as long as I can. You're quite a performer, Sophia," said the driver.

She kissed her fingers and touched them to his cheek. She had her new passport and a Eurostar ticket to Paris. She was out of the car as it U-turned and headed back towards Buckingham Palace. Problem! She had no money to catch a tube or pay for a taxi in Paris, no purse or bank cards. And – she had no bloody spare underwear. She walked briskly in the cold grey December day. She risked a look over her shoulder. Blue lights and sirens to her left near Hyde Park Corner might be something to do with her but such sounds were the mood music of Metropolis. From now on it was freestyle.

She walked into the tube station. A big London Transport guy was guarding the barriers. She picked up a used ticket from the floor, strolled to the machine and pushed it into the slot. The barrier didn't respond. She retrieved the ticket and studied it. The big guy came over and used his pass card.

"Have a nice day, sugar," he said.

"You too, my hero."

He smiled.

"I'm here till 4:00. Might catch you on the way home or some other day."

She smiled internally. Any chance of any sniff of a woman and some guys were either shameless or helpless or both. Some days she rode a high horse. Some days she didn't mind at all. She rode the tube to the Eurostar high-speed train terminal at St. Pancras. She had less than an hour to clear security and both French and English border checks. Everywhere were armed police and soldiers, maybe alerted to her but more probably on routine anti-terrorist patrol. Her new passport looked good. They must have obtained her photo overnight from her police ID or from the passport she'd had at the Château Roche Courbon. She guessed Captain Côté had retrieved it after her escape. All that seemed like a lifetime ago. She had no time to find the language students or Madame Collins. One thing bothered her. The passport was French. Ahead of her the immigration officer was questioning all French citizens. IN FRENCH. Maybe she could blag her way through. Maybe not. The long black-bearded guy ahead was getting the third degree. She made a couple of haughty impatient sighs.

"*Mu syur. S'il vous plait. Pee pee,*" she said, crossing her legs and wincing.

The official looked up, reached for her passport over the guy's shoulder, saw the diplomatic title and waved her through. He could do without some female diplomat pissing on his patch. The train was already boarding. Her ticket was car 11 seat 33. A great chatter of students filled the air. A lady was already in the window seat.

"Madame Collins?" she asked.

"Sophia?"

"Yes. God, you made it. The police have detained Jean-Claude and my husband," she said.

"Your husband?"

"Yeah, he was your driver. We borrowed him for the day. Weekends he drives stock cars."

"What will they do with them? Where's the crime?"

"In theory you were in protective custody for your own safety. You could say they have obstructed the police. Your government has *at last* come off the fence and committed to Martine. All those who oppose her are now the enemy. Your prime minister will never give a decision until she is sure which choice will be in her own political interests. Until this morning everyone has been guessing and some trying to run with hares and hunt with hounds. Anna La Salle will get them released now we have some clarity," she said.

"And what about Caesar Roboris?"

"They are committed too. They have some support in the Patriotic Front, in the other political parties and in the military. Their believers and soldiers need absolute kings to reward them with new aristocracies. We can trust no one. The guys in Caesar Roboris don't even trust each other. Martine must survive at least until she can call elections and gain legitimate power. Once Charles is established on the throne no one will want or dare to destroy him," said Madame Collins.

"Why not?"

"He is so lovely, he has the teens, the mums and the grannies in his hand."

"He's a beautiful brave guy."

Madame Collins placed her hand on Sophia's arm.

"And he loves you so very, very, much. All the women of France can see it. The papers have uncovered many pictures of you together. They smile because there is love and cry because love is the helpless baby in every Frenchwoman's heart and their baby is crying."

"Are the French born to speak in poetry?"

"And to live it too. Never give up," said Madame Collins.

"You're not a language teacher are you?"

The woman smiled and shook her head.

"I'll make sure you get to your hotel and we'll talk there. For now let's relax and enjoy the ride."

CHAPTER 47

It was a mad world outside the Gare du Nord rail station in the heart of Paris. Seemingly gangs of young men surged around on cell phones, packages were exchanged, tourists were jostled. She walked directly to a taxi. Madame Collins gave the address of the hotel. It was a short ride to Pigalle. Through gaps between buildings Sophia glimpsed the almost magical white Basilique du Sacré Coeur, high above the city on the Butte de Montmartre. She was beginning to adore the beauty of Paris. In the taxi she didn't speak, better that no one gained any clue as to who she was. The hotel had a small entrance in a bustling street of small shops, unloading vans, swerving scooters, a corner café and the beep, beep of car horns. A man of North African appearance was at the desk. He recognized Madame Collins and handed her a key.

"*Trente minutes, Hakim,*" she said.

They took a small lift two floors. The small plain room looked out on La Rue Victor Massé.

"I'm Margaret Collins. After this chat you will never see me again. I am an agent of the DGSE, we call it La Boite, that's The Firm in English. We're the French CIA or your MI6. The guy downstairs is Hakim. He's been one of our special correspondents for years. He'll give you a simple cell phone. We can track you if we need to. The only person who will ever call you will be me. He will give you a weapon. It'll be the SIG Pro 2022, 12-shot. The Firm monitor all communications in France. We know who calls who and what they say. Clear so far?"

"Why do you need me?"

"You know the agent Bastian. That's vital."

"I know him, but very little about him."

"He's ex-Dutch Korps Commandotroepen. He's a mercenary working for Caesar Roboris with a bunch of pros as ruthless as he is. There's Seals, SAS, Foreign Legion, and French Special Forces. Their budget is infinite."

"So now he's a bad guy?" asked Sophia.

"Caesar Roboris wanted to support Martine in getting Charles onto the throne of France. Once she's done that, she's in the way. They see the new monarchy movement as a return to hard core rule by kings. Once a respected developed nation like France opens the door, all the would-be monarchs will crowd through it. We're talking about Russia, Turkey, Spain, Germany, Italy, Greece, Hungary, blah, blah, blah. The old EU has folded. Religious terrorism made nations build walls. People are anxious and looking for strong men, leaders to show the way."

"How can I change anything?"

"Charles is a decent guy. Once Martine is gone he's on his own and Caesar Roboris will force him to grab political power and then ratify all the other new kings or queens. If and when that pressure comes on, he will need you to give him strength," said Margaret.

"He'll have Nathalie as his bride," said Sophia.

"The poor kid was always a throwaway. She was never meant to win. Mason Trowel knew all about her Lolita footballer career, but she is lovely on the eyes. The plan was for Esmeralda to win but your ex-Prime Minister Cameron found out the problem with his Brexit referendum. You think the people are brainless sheep and you can push them however you want, with fear or with bribes."

"But the people rejected Esmeralda."

"Yes, people pay one euro to phone in but Trowel ignores the vote. Then a social media campaign and the T-shirts forced him to dump her. Martine needed a French winner and so Nathalie had to win."

"Where does all this leave me?"

"It leaves you as a massive social media subject. '*Chiennes Méchantes*' is a radical feminist group. They have been demonstrating against the *Rex Factor* show. They have seized on you as their icon. Prejudice against the older woman is hot," said Margaret.

"And what do they make of Martine?" asked Sophia.

"She's a woman and that's ninety percent of their politics."

"And what do you make of her?"

"The Firm accept her as president even though the Patriotic Front seized power illegally. A civil war would be a bloodbath. Behind the scenes she's promised proper elections after the monarchy circus is over," said Margaret.

"You're obviously an educated sophisticated person. I'm a street cop from a different culture. Tell me honestly what you think of this monarchy idea and Martine herself."

"As a woman I love her. She's strong but no less a woman. She has kindness in her and courage. She loves France. To be honest I would die for her."

"And the new king?"

"The fact is the plan has worked. Our country, like yours, was fragmenting into racist regional tribes, religions and age generations. Rich and poor were invisible to each other. The monarchy has focused all classes and groups into at least one fixed point of attention or even fascination. It was a daring idea and without political power it can do no harm, just like your British wedding and baby show," said Margaret.

"Would his bride have to be French?" asked Sophia.

"In my opinion no, far from it. She needs to speak good French but to me it is better if she's not from France."

"Why?"

"Because if she's from Paris, the people of the country don't trust her. If she is a country girl the Paris Intellos look down on her. If she is from the north the south says she only eats chips and drinks beer, if she is from the south they say she is lazy, slow talking, and so on," said Margaret.

"The Intellos are either locked up or hiding in holes. Can Martine ever convince them?"

"No, but the people can. Louis the Sixteenth and Marie Antoinette separated themselves from the people. The old European Union did the same and fell. The Intellos have the brains to read history. Charles must be a good and wise man. He will award honors and titles to those who fawn and grovel and also those with merit. Better an Intello be a marquis toady than a political journalist with a poison pen. Your British royals know this art extremely well," said Margaret.

There was a knock and Hakim entered with a rucksack in his hand. Margaret did the introductions.

"Keep that phone charged. I'll be at our HQ at Caserne de Tourelles. We need you to spot Bastian. We'll take him out, but if you're the last man standing it could be down to you," said Margaret.

Sophia hugged her and sat down on the bed to face Hakim.

"The main thing is that no one knows you're here. Bastian won't be looking for you," he said.

"Where is he now?" asked Sophia.

"No idea. We have no clue. The decision of your government is well known so effectively you are enemies," he replied.

"We were never friends but I came to respect him."

"Our guess is that he feels the same for you. That could be his one weak spot," he said with a smile.

"I'm a honey trap?"

"You're a sweet looking hornet," he said, pulling out a gun and three loaded clips.

"Can you handle one of these?"

"Simple answer—no."

"Thank God for that. I didn't want some cocky cowboy. I'll show you what you need to know."

He pulled out a phone and charger.

"You call no one, OK. Margaret will call you. You're going to be wherever Bastian shows up, we'll be there too. We need your eyes and maybe for you to hold him up, even for a couple of seconds," said Hakim.

"Will I be able to contact Charles?"

"I'm sorry but no. Let's go to the basement and fire off some rounds."

He led the way to a padded underground vault that seemed to extend out under the street. He fitted a silencer and showed her the single and double action of the gun. She fired off several clips until she was hitting full man size targets somewhere between head and feet at 30 yards.

"Beginner's luck," he said with a friendly smile.

He helped her fit the shoulder holster and store the gun.

A dull thud shook the building. Mortar fell from the curved brick ceiling. She'd heard this type of sound before at Anna's vineyard.

"Car bomb," said Hakim.

His cell phone was ringing. He listened and nodded, his face grim and serious.

"They got the bus. All dead and many passersby."

CHAPTER 48

Her heart leapt. All dead. The show was over.

"Where?"

"Boulevard de Magenta, close to La République, It's a couple of kilometers away."

"Oh my God, oh my God," she said.

Hakim was back on the phone. It was rolling a live Facebook video. Hakim translated:

People of France, you will be hearing there was an attempt on my life a few minutes ago in Paris. My heart is with all those who have lost their lives, the injured and all their families. My thanks to all the brave emergency services who are now at the scene. I had left the bus before the attack and brave police, gendarmes and soldiers were returning to their bases. The referendum result will be known tonight and you will have voted already or will vote according to your hearts and opinions. When we know the result, I will join you as king or fellow citizen in re-uniting our society. We will find the authors of this attack and apply to them the ruthlessness of our law. Vive la France!

"He's alive," she said.

"He was bloody lucky. It was a stupid Mason Trowel showbiz stunt. Something like this was so obvious. It was a Christmas present to the Intello terrorists," said Hakim.

"Powerless celebrity royalty is a showbiz stunt," said Sophia.

"That's straight out of the Caesar Roboris manual of politics," he replied.

"Dear Lord, why the fuck can't this world just rub along and deal with stuff like pollution and cancer?"

"Because you need power to fix those problems and power's an addiction. Addicts don't think of the wider problem. They think of the next fix."

"And that's straight out of the street cop's manual of politics."

He gave her a broad smile.

"I could really enjoy talking to you."

Sophia smiled back. A couple of weeks ago she hadn't even watched the news for half a year. She hadn't read a book or magazine. Her life had been her life, getting her daughter off to university, getting through her shift, cooking a curry to eat alone before her night duty in South London. Now she was in Paris chatting about the future of Europe or more with a secret agent. She wasn't watching the news. She was in it. She wasn't reading magazines, she was the front page. And all that was added to her Hollywood superstar daughter.

"I need to learn French and get some bloody education," she said.

"Let's start with an aperitif and a meal at the B9 Café. It's on the corner over there on Avenue Frochot. Martine will be giving the referendum result in an hour. It'll be on the screen," he said.

"You think no one will know me?"

"They'll think you're a tourist or a very expensive foreign working girl."

"What?"

"If we get the chance we'll stroll up to Place Pigalle, you'll see. This is the ooh-la-la part of Paris."

Sophia ordered in schoolgirl French. She had some powerful aniseed drink and hot buttered garlic snails followed by mysterious liver, chips, and salad. They shared a house Bordeaux wine. This was surreal. Probably she was in Paris to die yet never had she felt more alive.

"Once again I've got no fucking knickers," she semi-slurred at Hakim.

"Well, you didn't want to stand out in a crowd did you?"

She laughed. She was wound up inside to the limit of her spring and a bit woozy on alcohol.

"Let's hope you don't have to shoot anyone tonight, Sophia."

Hakim's eyes were on the screen. Images of France from the air were playing with fighter jets of La Patrouille de France display team screaming along the coastline trailing red, white, and blue smoke. The Arc de Triomphe, the Eiffel tower, Notre Dame, Sacré Coeur, La Defense morphed into forests, vineyards, châteaus, beaches, and mountains. Music played, soldiers marched, warships plunged through waves as a huge choir sang *La Marseillaise*. As the music continued the screen went to blue and then to the flag of France with the added *fleur-de-lys* royal logos in brilliant gold in the middle white band. Finally Martine La Plume in immaculate navy blue with white blouse and red scarf raised her head as if from prayer to address the nation. People in the bistro were already in tears and calling out to her.

"*Martine! La France! Vive Martine! Vive la France! Martine! Vive le roi, Vive Charles!*"

Everywhere the cars had stopped, the streets were deserted. Paris had taken a breath and was holding it. She glanced at Hakim. He was wiping his eyes.

"She has La Force you know. France is not her country, it is her faith and her pulse."

"Don't spoil it for yourself, Hakim. Just let me know the main points."

Patriots, all people of France, whatever your beliefs, whatever your race or color, whatever your politics, I reach out to you. If I could I would shake the hand or kiss the cheek of every citizen of France as my brother or sister in this historic moment. Let our church bells ring. Let us share this moment of joy together as a family at last at one table in a community of respect, friendship, and humanity.

A while ago we all started out together on a dangerous road to create a better chance for our beautiful nation. When I was tired, when there were setbacks, you, my patriots, carried me on. When enemies set upon us, brave patriots even on this day gave their lives for France. Each one of them will be remembered forever. This night I can tell you that the choir of the French nation has sung a single anthem of identity in harmony. Eight out of ten have voted for the creation of the constitutional monarchy of France. I propose that the coronation of Charles the Eleventh will be held the day after tomorrow. We must hasten because my friends, there are those who hold themselves above the will of the people, there are those who seek only the interests of their narrow elite class. These people are the soulless dictators of yesterday. I offer them a new soul, a soul of passion, love, and identity with all our people. Those who spit on our offered hand of forgiveness may expect our fist of vengeance.

Our new direction will be of this age, not some ancient tableau played out for foreign tourists with jesters and armored knights. The coronation will be at the grand arch of La Defense, the symbol of our modern supremacy. When Charles marries, the religious blessing will be at the Basilica of Sacré Coeur, a church unconnected with the monarchies of the past.

And now dear compatriots, my friends who have travelled with me along the road to this wonderful milestone, I leave you by placing my own heart in your hands. I know you will carry me onwards to our victory. Ring your bells, embrace your fellow patriots. Let no brother or sister of our nation family be ignored or alone this night. I feel the rhythm of your marching feet. We go forward in step together. Liberty. Identity. Fraternity. La France, I embrace you. I love you.

For a second, there was utter silence. So, this was how history was, a moment when everyone for the rest of their lives, would remember where they had been. Bells started to ring from churches, car horns sounded, everyone was embracing. For Sophia the moment was a single thought. She should be sharing this with Charles and maybe she would never even see him again. She was both happy and sad for Martine, a woman so alone and so full of love to give.

Fireworks were exploding, people were singing and dancing, every brand of music played from every bar and café. Hakim, gestured to her to step outside. He was carefully studying his cell phone.

"We've picked up a trace. A tablet device linked to one of Bastian's guys is active in Montparnasse. Do you know any of his men?"

"I met a guy who helped us escape from Roche Courbon in a post office van. He said his name was Sergeant Shawn Henning, medium build, strawberry blonde with blue eyes."

"Would you know him?"

She blew out her cheeks.

"I'm a cop, but only too human. I'd say yes."

"Let's go," he said.

They took the metro line-12 from Pigalle to Montparnasse Bienvenue. The green and white carriages of the train seemed so normal now as her heart raced in anticipation of something utterly abnormal. During the journey they didn't speak or give the impression of acquaintance. She was an innocent explorer in the cloak and dagger world of undercover agents. At Montparnasse Hakim led her to a line-4 train and took one stop to Denfert Rochereau.

"He's on McDonald's Wi-Fi," he said.

They emerged into the busy street. The great lion of Belfort statue caught her attention. What history lived the everyday life in this town? Hakim moved swiftly along the Avenue de Général Leclerc. He stopped about one hundred yards from the awning and glass conservatory that projected into the street.

"Looks like it's down to you and me. A team is coming but traffic is heavy. We don't go in together, we don't know each other. I'll go in, get a coffee and be somewhere near the door. You come in, get something, look around. He's still connected on their Wi-Fi. He may be with others. He'll be very surveillance-aware."

"It could be Bastian himself and he'll know me."

"But he won't know you're there for him. Hold him up, I'll do the rest," said Hakim. She walked with him to the door and kept walking as he went in. After two minutes she turned and went back. Her heart was pounding, her mouth dry. She caught sight of Hakim seated close to the door. She waited in line for a few seconds and ordered a cappuccino. She glanced around, a couple of young guys gave her the eye. French males just weren't correct. Then she saw her man, seated against the back wall. A tablet device was on the table in front of him. He was glancing up and down across the restaurant at Hakim, but as far as she could tell, hadn't spotted her. She didn't know this man but her detectors were crackling. Everything about this situation screamed imminent danger. If this shaven-headed stocky guy was sitting there with a tablet he may have known it could alert attention. Maybe they'd deliberately compromised a machine in order to use it as bait. And if he was inside, there would be someone outside. She took a seat and looked out of the window into the street. She could just keep the target in sight in the reflection from the corner of her eye. She'd learned a lot from Bastian. Hesitation was almost certain death. She glanced across at Hakim.

She knew that because of fear and lack of confidence she was waiting for the target to take the initiative. He was flexing his neck and shoulders. She knew French agents from La Boite were coming. They were two to one against this guy. There was a scattering of customers in the restaurant and she was a cop, not a killer.

She began to stand and swiped the coffee from the table onto the floor in the direction of the target.

"*Merde!*" she said.

She moved to pick it up, closing half the distance to his table. She pulled the gun and took a two handed aim, staying clear of his fighting arc. Hendon Metropolitan police training college day two: you can deflect a gun before the bandit can fire it.

The target almost went for a gun she could see in the inside pocket of his parka style hooded coat.

"*Bouge pas!*" said Hakim as he arrived, glancing a question at her with troubled eyes. There was a commotion at the door. Two guys in black motorcycle clothing and helmets strode in and came towards them. Hakim kept his gun focused on the target. Sophia turned to take aim.

"Don't shoot, these are our guys," said Hakim.

In seconds the guy was spread on the floor, searched and handcuffed.

Hakim spoke to the kitchen staff and signaled for them to use the rear exit. An unmarked dark Renault Trafic pulled up at the yard entrance with doors open. They slid in the prisoner face down and jumped up behind him. In the front passenger seats were two guys with French police issue M12 SD sub machine guns.

"*Putain!*" exclaimed Hakim.

"What?" she said.

"I was sitting there wondering what the fuck to do. And then you made the choice for us," said Hakim.

The van had moved off. Hakim put his finger to his lips.

"We'll talk later. Let's get our man to bed. He'll be tired," he said.

Still church bells were ringing. Groups of people were singing and drinking champagne from bottles, car horns were blaring. The van swerved through traffic. It looked as if there were blue emergency service lights in the front grille. The driver activated a two-tone siren. This was the familiar police life that Sophia knew so well. She felt a sudden surge of homesickness for her old life. The buzz from the action in the McDonald's had aroused her. Right now she wanted to take it out on a vigorous young man.

She had no idea where they were going and the van had no rear or side windows. She moved forward to check out the view.

"Boulevard Saint-Michel, we're just passing the Sorbonne University," said one of the officers, sensing her curiosity.

"We're heading for Ile de la Cité, police HQ close to Notre Dame," said Hakim.

A few minutes later they crossed the Seine and drove through guarded gates into an impressive cobbled courtyard. A number of uniformed and plain-clothed officers pulled the prisoner from the van and led him away. At last she could speak with Hakim.

"I thought it could be a trap. I could see he'd spotted you."

"We've got someone to question that's for sure. He's carrying a firearm so he's not getting out in a hurry. You handled that well. I knew he was suspicious of me, if he'd stood up I'd decided to draw a weapon. We've got specialist guys who'll get the whole story. At last we've got a place to start," said Hakim.

Sophia had little doubt that she didn't want to be around any of the special interviewers.

"So what now?" she asked.

Hakim looked at her as if evaluating her character.

"We mustn't risk Bastian finding out you're here. There's someone who wants to see you and this is a special day. I'm taking a chance on you on my account. Please, do not let me down."

She followed him to a parking area where there was a line of black Ovetto 125 motor scooters. She waited while he went through a door and reappeared with two helmets.

"Let's have a ride through Paris."

CHAPTER 49

Now this was what she called being alive. They crossed the Seine from Ile de la Cité and turned left along the river bank towards Place de la Concorde. The bells of Notre Dame were still ringing out. She clung to Hakim as he swerved and pushed his way through the traffic. How she had come to adore this city. At Concorde he took the Champs Elysées. The length of the cobbled iconic Avenue was sparkling with silver and white Christmas lamps in the trees. When they stopped at traffic lights, groups of Parisians and tourists singing and shouting crossed in front of them. A kid pulled a wheelie on a Vélib hire bike. This night Paris was a party and she was here alive, writing her own little postcard to the future from her desert oasis in the mirage of history. Neither Paris nor London could ever be safe from the horror of terrorism. Could Charles help unite this great nation? Could a young man so vulnerable survive without her?

Hakim did whatever Parisians do to circle the Arc de Triomphe and headed back down towards Concorde. He took a left into Avenue de Marigny and headed for the Elysée Palace. Soldiers checked Hakim's ID and waved him through into the courtyard of the Hotel de Marigny.

"This place is a fortress tonight but your Charles is here. There is still love in this world. The love of a woman is the bread and the wine on a Frenchman's table. If a man cannot love his woman and we live in fear like prisoners, then we may as well die. Our struggle is for this, the most ordinary and the most beautiful thing on this earth. I will show you the door of our new king's room. He loves you and he needs you, Sophia."

"I didn't know you knew him," she replied.

"Everyone knows love. You know it more if you don't have it. A good king needs a woman's love. If he has this, he has the insight of God."

"You guys are amazing."

"Life isn't just your Anglo-Saxon money, business, and technology. The dangerous man is the one left behind, not the man in front," he said.

She hugged him.

"Will you be in trouble for this?"

"I have a king to protect me."

They climbed the wide curving stair. Each room was guarded by armed soldiers. Hakim stopped at a grand carved door. Her heart was thumping.

"We'll call you if we need you. By morning our man will have told us all he knows. Be ready by 8:30. They sent you back to London to avoid the press. At all costs, no one must know you're here."

"Not even Anna La Salle. She's my boss."

"She is loyal and committed to Martine and Charles. She reports back truthfully to your government and we just can't be certain of everyone."

"And what about these soldiers?" she asked.

"These are hand-picked men of the new Royal Guard. We know everything of them and their families. They know we know where their sisters and mothers live."

Sophia stared at him. He was a sweet guy but she understood the steel menace behind his calm assurance. Could Charles ever accept or use the ruthlessness that underpins power?

Hakim turned the door handle and pushed it ajar. His open hand gestured her to enter,

"The king of France, madame. I'll see you at 8:30."

"Hakim, can you somehow get me some underwear? Any color. I don't know French sizes," she said.

He smiled.

"A hotel concierge knows such things," he said as he strolled away.

The room smelled of sandalwood, vanilla and maybe a trace of old-fashioned wax furniture polish. The theme was deep red and cream with ceiling-to-floor heavy curtains. Two long sofas were either side of a rich carpet. An elaborate gold and crystal chandelier glinted with an impossible opulence. There was no one in sight, but she could hear movement in an adjoining room. She squeezed the door shut and tiptoed to a sofa. If she lay down, she would be out of sight. She waited. At last he walked through, bare-chested, wearing black jeans and sat at a grand writing desk with his back to her.

"Charles," she whispered.

He looked left and right, but not behind.

"Charles," she whispered again.

He stood and turned. His torso was lithe, slim and hard with a decent tan. She watched his face as she sat up and smiled at him. He brought his hand up to his face and stared at her.

"Sophia. Sophia," he said.

She began to stand but suddenly he almost ran and knelt before her. He took her hands and kissed them, he pulled her to him and kissed her lips, he caressed her face time and time again. He was almost in tears. He kissed her hair, he hugged her legs and kissed her knees. All he could do was say her name and try to tumble in her essence.

"I love you so much. I thought you'd gone and I would go through all this without you."

She smiled at him and stroked his wavy dark hair. He would need a while before she focused him to her own desires with a slower style of kissing.

"How do you feel Charles? The people are celebrating out there. They want you."

"I feel ... I feel ... I *felt* so empty and afraid. Not now, my God, Sophia, stay with me now please?"

"I'll stay," she said.

"Will you?" he said, searching her eyes.

"I will."

"Why? Tell me why? "

"Because you're you. Because selfishly I want to keep you as mine, because I love you, because you're sexy and because my gorgeous King Charles, you make me feel like what I am in your eyes and not what I see from inside."

"Please don't just say you love me and that you'll stay if you don't mean it. I can't let myself believe it if it's not true."

"Let's see what you believe when we've made love," she said. "I want to feel you come inside me."

She kissed him gently, teasing his lips with her tongue. He responded, groaning a little and moving his hand to the side of her breast. His hand touched the shoulder holster of her firearm.

"Did you come to kill me?" he said with a surprised laugh.

"That depends on your stamina. I need a lot of loving sometimes."

He pulled up her T-shirt and kissed her belly. A trigger tightened in her hot groove. She wanted to keep him for later but needed him to touch her now. He was still kneeling facing her as she sat on the sofa. She undid the button of her jeans and slid down the zip, revealing her panties.

"I'm just letting myself get wet, I can't help it," she said.

She moved his hand to the fabric covering her clitoris. He'd remembered what she'd shown him and pressed gently. She pulled the fabric aside letting his fingers circle and caress her hood. He found her spot.

"Like that, like that," she said bringing his lips to hers. She held tight for one last joyous moment on the edge then let go, abandoned and wild as a wave falling helpless on the shore. She called out her surrender to nature onto his shoulder as she pulsed her hot little shaft against his touch.

"You're doing it to me, you're making me come," she said as she gripped his flesh in her teeth. He had stood and was undoing his jeans. In a second he was naked, his wet-tipped cock hard and pulsing with need. She wriggled out of her jeans and panties. He swung her legs onto the sofa and lay above her. There would be time for more finesse later. For now she was soaking and screaming with the void within her. He filled her, his hard cock so hot, hitting her entrance and her inner spot. She wanted to suck in his juice, feel the helpless rush and spurt of his release. He was filling her. She didn't care if she flooded the world with the mix of their bodies. She was starting to feel the blur and abandon of her own climax. She didn't care, she couldn't stop.

"Fuck me. Do it, come in my pussy, come in my pussy," she growled.

She watched his eyes lose focus as the contractions of her belly squeezed the cum from his spurting cock.

"Sophia."

"I love you," she said into his ear as he pumped his juice into the hot well of her desire. Her mind switched to her stored image of him shooting his jets of seed helpless with lust for her onto her breasts and belly.

"I want it, do it in me," she whispered.

Wave after wave of her own spasm matched the explosion of his release. Her legs were trembling, her belly bucking with jolts of bliss. He was grunting deep sounds from the oblivion of his sensations. Still he held himself at her peak, urging the pulses of his male juice to drench the woman flesh of her.

"You've made me more of a man's woman than I knew was possible."

He smiled at her, still semi-erect inside her.

"I look at your beautiful face and I can't believe I've got you."

She shuddered with an aftershock of release. What she'd said was true. His openness and need for her had slid under a door she'd slammed shut against the gaze and sense of entitlement of men. For sure he was a sexy guy, firm and beautiful with youth. And yet he came to her with unconditional love. He would love her anyway simply if she loved him. He would make no comparison of their ages even as her own body would hit the slope as he was still climbing to his peak. She had split with him because in her own conscience, she couldn't stand in his way. She understood now that she'd been wrong. To leave him would be to destroy him and deny him the chance to write the page of history that he had in his grasp.

"I'll stay to the very, very death of us," she said. "If I *have* to accept compromise I will."

"You might, but what kind of king is that? How can a king say he honestly loves his people when he cannot love honestly for himself."

"And where does that road take you?" she asked.

"It takes me back to the people who have called for me. When it comes to love, who else would you trust but the French nation?"

"And where does that lead you and me?"

"To the Basilica of Sacré Coeur, magical white gemstone high above this city. And there you'll be my wife, or there will be no king."

CHAPTER 50

They showered together. It had been quite a day for both of them. She soaped him as he soaped her, naked creatures in the expression of their mortal bodies. Then they lay together in the luxurious wide bed. He held her in his arms, her head against his chest.

"There can be no secrets between you and me," he said.

"So what do you know about the Caesar Roboris guys and what they plan?"

"I know they're pressuring me to declare myself as king in the name of God and rule as if I were Napoléon."

"Do you think they can make you do that?"

"No. I've told Bastian that my own path is that of love for my people. My job is to know them without the distorting lens of politics. The people will look into my life and I will look into theirs. I will speak for them in the name of God."

"So you believe that God shines a special light on those born in particular families with certain genes?"

"No, God shines many lights. What is the greatest instrument of music in the theatre? Is it the piano? The violin? The bass or the soprano?" he said.

"You can't choose."

"And you don't have to. The greatest instrument is the man or woman with no understanding of music. They feel the pulse and the emotion that comes from God without the complications of key or tempo. The true instrument of music is the heart of the innocent audience. The king has no special light upon him, he has the special duty to hear the music of his people and hum the tune of it to the world as their voice."

"Did you tell Bastian that?" she asked.

"He represents a new order of man; men who believe in ruthless personal leadership and strength. To be honest we've never agreed. He tells me that power will re-define me. I tell him that I will change the definition of power."

"Once you're on the throne Martine La Plume will have done her job. They'll kill her."

He sighed.

"I know you're right," he said. "She has enemies within her own party as well. She wants this monarchy as a focal point of the nation. The Patriotic Front is racist and I'm sure I'll clash with them sooner rather than later. I respect her daring and courage and don't want her to die."

"Then maybe Caesar Roboris makes sense. If you take more political power you can do it your way and keep her alive."

"Bastian's way? I don't think so," he replied.

"You know I'm here to spot him and maybe kill him," she said. "The sadness is that he's been an ally if not a friend until now."

"He's no danger to me at present. It's the Intello terrorists who want to kill me."

"I'm happy to kill them too," she replied, kissing his chest.

"Let's not kill anyone, Sophia! Let's live and rejoice in love."

"And on the subject of love, what's happened to your *Rex Factor* bride?"

"Poor, poor Nathalie. She's a bruised soul. She went on the show because she wanted fame, not because she wanted me. Martine's met with Mason Trowel and come to a deal. All the girls will be VIP guests at the coronation and there will be a final bonus show with a free phone-in to choose the bridesmaids for the royal wedding. All the others will be VIP guests. Many will get film and recording contracts. Some have been chosen as mistresses by Patriotic Front ministers with Trowel's lawyers getting their names on the deeds of apartments," he said.

"And Nathalie herself?"

"Vandervell's given her a big film deal for a Lolita re-make and Louis Zongalero has proposed marriage. She's refused to talk to police about her adolescent romp with him and other footballers. He's already installed her in his penthouse in Monaco. She's become a style and fashion journalist and one of the big TV channels wants her as a sports and music analyst," he said.

"Bit better than queen of France?" she said.

"Yeah, and no one's trying to kill her."

"And all these bridesmaids and VIP guests—whose wedding do they think it will be?

"There's been no announcement. Martine is happy to let the press go into a frenzy finding you and doing features about the last breakable taboo of the older woman. The scandal and celeb mags are selling out. The feminists are marching. I'm giving a press conference at noon tomorrow. I'm guessing there'll be a question or two."

"And what will you tell them?"

"The truth."

"But I haven't said yes," she said.

"Didn't you?"

"Let me see if you're the kind of man I need," she said, running her hand down his hard, taut stomach.

Hakim was right on time, equipped with motorcycle helmet and a pack of plain cotton panties. While she slipped them on she could hear their conversation.

"I do wish Martine had her husband here to share her achievement," said Charles.

"Martine's married to France and to...." Hakim hesitated.

"You were going to say power I think," said Charles.

"Yes, and as for her aim, well maybe none of us know that yet."

"Survival in the short term," said Sophia.

"Pinupskin's bankrolled her rise to power. He won't be taking a back seat. Our friend in McDonald's last night was an old KGB man like Pinupskin. He'd borrowed the tablet from one of the other guys to do some online gambling. It's banned in Russia and the guy's got addiction issues. He was like a kid in a sweetshop and just couldn't stop. That's how we tracked him."

"So what's his mission?"

"To link up with Bastian and his team."

"To do what?"

"Make sure Charles got his throne and that Martine understands her debt of loyalty to Pinupskin and the other Caesar Roboris guys," said Hakim.

"I can't see Martine accepting any hint of foreign control of France," said Sophia.

"Neither can Pinupskin," said Charles. "And I won't accept it either."

"Ronald Grump's not a would-be king of America I guess," said Sophia.

"No King Ronald that's for sure. We'd like to know a lot more about his strategy. So far he's washed his hands of Europe although he wanted Esmeralda as queen of France. It looks like he's letting Pinupskin play in his own backyard. As long as no one kicks a ball over the fence, Grump's just cutting his own lawn," said Hakim.

"He's the most powerful guy in the world. He may have closed the doors to America but he still needs to influence the rest of the planet," said Sophia.

Hakim shrugged. "You're an Anglo-Saxon, Sophia. You probably have more understanding than the French."

"So how do they intend to deal with Martine?" asked Charles.

"They have to achieve two things. They have to make the people turn against her and then they have to get rid of her. They could just kill her and blame the Intellos or the Muslims but you risk a civil war. If Martine has a drug issue and dies of an overdose, it's the perfect story," said Hakim.

"Is that the plan?" asked Sophia.

"According to our man from last night, that's exactly the plan. Remember these are the guys who've already taken out enemies with radioactive poison," said Hakim.

"And does she have a drug problem?" asked Sophia.

"Luckily no, but they'll simply plant an evidence trail. The Intello press would seize on it to smear her memory. She's had a couple of unusual relationships with women and it'll all boil up into a sex-and-drugs cloudy soup."

"And what's going to happen to our prisoner?"

"If he goes missing the rest will just go underground even further. We need them to come out and he gave us a couple of addresses. Our man is back out there with a story of a night of coronation celebration with a hooker. We've given him a little pocket money to help his gambling issues. And yeah, he's got a state of the art implanted tracker. With a bit of luck he'll lead us to Bastian," said Hakim.

"Where's Martine today?" asked Charles.

"She's got a meeting with the council of ministers this morning at the Élysée Palace. She'll be at your press conference in the Palace of Versailles and then she's going out to La Defense for a TV shoot at the coronation venue. Sophia and I won't be with her, but we'll be where she is."

"Let's saddle up," said Sophia, exhilarated at the prospect of a proper cop mission.

Charles hugged her.

"I want to be saying you don't need to be risking your life but I know your answer."

"You don't need to be risking yours either, Your Majesty," she said kissing his lips and then pulling on her helmet.

"We're just cruising around the Élysée. Keep your eyes open," said Hakim.

The morning was damp and misty. Police, gendarmes, and soldiers more or less lined the streets amongst the ghostly skeletons of winter trees. Convoys of limos and their escort vehicles swept in through the guarded gates. Hakim sped up and crossed La Place de La Concorde to a small park in front the Petit Palais. Police were taping off a crime scene. They parked the scooter and walked across. Hakim showed ID to a *sûreté* detective officer, spoke with him, and strolled back.

"He was under a bush, big incision in his chest and the tracking device in his mouth," said Hakim as they remounted the scooter.

CHAPTER 51

They pulled over outside a *tabac* in Rue Saint Honoré. Hakim got a pack of Marlboro and a copy of *Closer* magazine.

"Couldn't miss the front cover," he said, handing her the mag.

"*Amour Fou! Charles n'aime que son flic bi.*"

"Crazy love. Charles loves only his bisexual cop," he translated.

There was a still photo from the rooftop kiss video. The double page feature revealed her name and a lot of her personal history including her divorce and relationship to Izzy, the precocious sex queen of Hollywood.

"Bastian used to clean up this stuff with a quick hanging. Wish I smoked," she said to Hakim.

"There's not too many places they could have got this story. My guess is that he's their source."

"But why?"

"To get you under control. If you come out to fight then he can see you. If you go into hiding you're not looking for him. They want Charles as an innocent puppet with a bimbo bride. They fear you."

This was bad news. Izzy knew nothing of why she'd divorced. Poor Charles knew almost nothing of her history.

"When did this news hit the streets?"

"Just this minute. The guy was putting out the first copies."

A thousand thoughts were jangling in her mind.

"Charles has a press conference at noon. They're going to chuck this bucket of shit in his face," she said.

"I can't say you're wrong," said Hakim.

"Fuck! *Putain!* Shit! *Merde!*"

"You're bi-lingual with swearing. The rest of French grammar is easy," he said with a broad smile, lighting a second Marlboro.

"What can I do Hakim?"

He drew hard on the cigarette.

"Your problems are on two levels. You have your personal life with your daughter and with Charles. You have your professional duty to protect Martine and Charles as your own government and queen wishes. After the coronation tomorrow, all the Caesar Roboris guys including the closet members in the English royals will be showing their teeth and you're in that fight as a London cop," he said.

"So?"

"Who dares, wins. Bastian knows we're on to him and has sent us a message in the park back there. Let's send him a message and dare him to confront us. We need to think on our feet. Allah will provide."

"It's only an hour until the press conference. How is Charles going to handle the press when they ask him if his beautiful queen will be a middle-aged divorced dyke?"

"Sophia, you're a beautiful woman. Charles has put himself in the hands of his people. The old Intello class never wanted to hear their voice. He's re-writing the concept of democracy. There's something I want you to see and then we're heading for Versailles."

They climbed aboard the scooter and set out on a giddy swerving ride past the Opéra and onto La Place de La République. The square was blocked by a huge demonstration with people waving banners reading, "*Amour mon choix. Amour ma voix.*" Others were shrieking and banging drums. A woman with a loudhailer was calling out a slogan over and over.

"Drwah day fahm. *Droits des femmes.*"

Many protesters carried Sophia's picture on broomsticks. Others carried pictures of Martine.

"This is a huge new wave of feminism. The heroines are Martine and you. They reject boundaries of sex and age. It'd be a brave man to take on this lot. It's a new politics embracing liberal elites and downtrodden socially invisible women," said Hakim.

For a moment she watched in awe. A poor-looking African guy approached selling Martine and Sophia T-shirts. Sophia pulled off her helmet and looked at him.

"*Mon Dieu—c'est vous!*" he said.

She reached for some money in her jeans.

"*Non*—take! Give to you," he said. "Selfie, please, please."

Hakim parked the bike and offered to take the guy's phone. Sophia posed holding the T-shirt between her and the salesman. Hakim turned them to get the best shot of the crowd. He handed the phone back to him.

"That's an exclusive" he said. "Now you can make yourself some real money. Make sure you get credited copyright."

"Thank you, *merci, merci*," he said, making off into the crowd.

"That'll be viral and will send a lot of good messages. These guys are cute. That shot will be with every news agency in the world in ten minutes. Now let's head for that press conference."

Hakim beeped and swerved his way through Boulevard Haussman and around the Arc de Triomphe. They headed for Porte Dauphine and broke every speed limit through the Bois de Boulogne. The mist lingered like a furtive stranger darting and fading among the trees. The cold air chilled her body with its slap of reality. Bastian now knew she was in Paris. If you can't make yourself a target too small to see, make yourself a target that's too big to destroy. *This is it now. Sophia Castellana. This is the moment before Waterloo, the moment on the Olympic start line, the last try at the world record height, the zero of the rocket countdown. Go for it. All those stars, warriors and heroes are only human flesh. Go for it. Just do it!*

They removed helmets and firearms, cleared the security checks and crept into the back of the assembled press in the fabulous Hall of Mirrors. Crystal chandeliers seemed to merge in a perspective of ecstasy rejoicing and reflecting itself in an orgy of narcissism. The room wanted to make love only to itself over and over. Charles and Martine sat side by side on a raised stage. Countless microphones and cables cluttered the foreground. The new flags with the added *fleur-de-lys* draped behind them. Sophia kept her collar up and borrowed Hakim's scarf to obscure her face. So far no one had noticed them. She raked through her brain for every shred of the French language she'd ever learned. There was one phrase she'd learned during her one lesson in London. It would have to do. The conference was beginning. Every nation on Earth was represented and happily many spoke in English. A woman from CNN was directing questions at Martine.

"Could we call you a modern king-maker?"

"The king-makers are the patriots of France. Maybe I have opened a door for our king to make a role himself. He is a fine man who doesn't need a feeble woman like me," she said with a warm smile.

There was a murmur of laughter as Sophia watched her. She was so, so good. Just so good and there around her neck the crucifix Sophia had sent her.

Various questions poured in about the new constitution and her feelings about the Intellos. She smiled and cruised over every hurdle.

"You said you would release all the political prisoners?" said a BBC journalist.

"These are your words not mine. What species of politics is a bomb and thirty people dead? I will release and tag all those who have shown themselves to be against the love of patriots for their homeland," she said.

"You mean top professors, journalists, lawyers and scientists will have to wear criminal tags?"

"Their tags are criminal only if they choose murder instead of peace," she said. "Anyone not wanting a tag can stay in jail."

Charles was in the spotlight answering questions in French. He seemed calm but strained. Poor man, he must be dreading what's coming. Around her a few guys were looking at smart phones. It looked like her T-shirt photo had hit the wires.

A sharp-looking young American introduced himself as being from the Washington Post.

"I'm guessing some of my French colleagues don't want to raise the issue of your bride. How did you feel about the way our girl Esmeralda was treated?"

"For me she was the best candidate and a lovely girl. Your nation and her fantastic family should be very proud of her. It gave the whole world the chance to see her character and sheer spunk," said Charles.

The journalist looked a bit flat-footed. This was not what he expected. He needed a cop's take on questions. The room was almost completely still. Everyone knew what was coming.

"So will you marry any of the *Rex Factor* girls?" he asked.

"No, this has all been resolved with Mason Trowel. I suggest you ask him," said Charles.

"None of my French colleagues seem to want to interrupt me. I guess they're afraid of the jailhouse or the felon tag. Do you have a bride in mind, Your Majesty," said the reporter with utter sarcasm.

Charles glanced at Martine and then at some notes in front of him. This was the moment when the stalker shouts out an impediment from the back of the wedding ceremony.

"He sure does," she called out.

Every head snapped round. She began to walk confidently towards the stage, pulling off her scarf and shaking loose her hair. She fought to keep her breathing steady. She stopped at the end of the row of the questioner and motioned him forward. He advanced enough for her to shake his hand.

"*Je m'appelle Sophia Castellana,*" she said.

She walked on to the stage and seeing a chair, picked it up and placed it between Charles and Martine.

"What would you like to know?" she asked.

A second of silence was broken by a frenzy of noise and camera flashes. Questions were firing in.

Could she remember and perform this one phrase in French?

"*Mes amis, je ne suis qu'une étudiante de la belle langue française. Pardonnez moi,*" she said.

There was something like a roar from the floor. Martine and Charles turned to her in amazement. Someone started to applaud, many others joined in. As it stopped Charles pulled a microphone towards him and looked at the Washington post journalist.

"Hey fella, waddaya think of my girl?" he said in his best drawl.

"I can sure see why you chose her," he said.

A couple of colleagues patted him on the back. The mood in the room was almost joyous. The drilling poison pens had hit sugar.

"Do you find French grammar difficult?" came a question.

"*Je suis circonflexe,*" she said.

There came a cheer in response. The rest of the questions were about dresses, parties, bridesmaids and flowers. Finally everyone had the story they needed. Martine gave a closing statement.

"My good friends of the press, I want nothing but friendship with you. Let us never again look down on the patriots of our beautiful land. Many among you have been blessed with great talents but no more than the patriot who tends our corn as it pushes up in joy from the soil of our homeland. Such a man has the education of the heavens and the wisdom of the seasons. Tomorrow will be a great celebration as we crown our new king under the grand arch of La Defense. You know of our traditions of anointing our kings in the cathedral of Reims, this oil being delivered from God by a dove. Tomorrow our dove will be the humble sparrows and pigeons of our city as a reflection of our brother and sister patriots whom we encounter in our everyday streets. The ancient crown of Louis the Fifteenth, ancestor of Charles will be brought from the Louvre. I have chosen a very special person to place the crown on the head of the king. My friends, our road has been hard and there has been so much loss and sadness. Less than a day ago a cowardly terrorist outrage took the lives of many people. A young girl of ten years named Marianne was orphaned in that attack. My friends and patriots, this courageous child will crown our king in the spirit of togetherness and patriotic love of our undefeatable homeland. This innocent pleads to those who hold themselves to be wise above the toiling people for their compassion. Let anyone who defiles this day or would add to the misery of this child feel the heat and infinite force of our anger. My office will circulate her photograph. I ask you to respect her right to grieve. *Vive la France. Le roi est mort. Vive le roi!*"

Sophia felt a surge of emotion. Several reporters called out.

"*Vive la France. Vive le roi!*"

Martine was an artist, a brave and beautiful woman. She was also ruthless, devious, and a rhinestone ringmaster of requiem. She saw a few hardened hacks wipe away a tear. She could work the crowd and for now the people loved her. The Caesar Roboris guys would have been watching. She'd set out her stall. And those guys would not be buying.

CHAPTER 52

Gendarmes led them away to a side room while the press of the world made off with their spoils.

"I was hoping to stay undercover, but things moved out of my control," she said to Charles.

"You wouldn't believe how happy I was to see you," he said, taking both her hands as he faced her.

"There was stuff you didn't know."

"Yeah stuff, stuff, stuff. We'll have a stuff party. You tip out yours, I'll tip out mine. We'll build a bonfire with the trash and build our lives on the rest," he said with a smile.

"Bonfires aren't too eco."

"OK. We recycle the trash into an artwork, that's how your past should look. Like a beautiful fixed statue that isn't coming after you," he said.

"Martine, you were so wonderful out there," said Sophia unable to stop herself hugging her.

"And so were you. I'm going to get you the best teachers. You're going to be more French than the Cannes Film Festival. They loved you for speaking in our language."

"I'm learning from you guys."

"Vandervell's a genius. He's come up with all this pigeon and sparrow stuff. You know, echoes of Edith Piaf for the old timers. He's putting on one hell of a show for tomorrow," said Martine.

"And that poor orphan girl. Can she carry it through?"

"Sometimes you've got to hammer it home. I feel uneasy about using the child but I do believe it will prevent an attack. You're a sweet angel, Sophia. There were three kids in that blast. One of them lost both legs. I'm putting up a symbol. It's a cold calculating utterly cynical act of the purest love in my heart."

Sophia nodded and took her hand, as a tear ran helplessly down Martine's cheek.

"I can see that now. I'm sorry."

"I read your thoughts and you're right. I've asked the people to accept a lot of suffering to fulfill my dream, *yes my selfish dream* in the hope that I'm right. It's such a wonderful thing that I'm always right. So much sadness, so much sadness in this world."

"The terrorist Intellos are never going to go away," said Sophia.

"Neither are the people of France. The Intellos sneer at me for being what they call a populist. I am. I want the people to love me and come with me. They will love Charles too. Once that ball is rolling these guys will have to admit defeat. These next few days are crucial."

"I'd love to see your guest list for the coronation," said Sophia.

"Priority goes to the *Rex Factor* girls. The front rows will be filled with our wounded military veterans who will form the guard of honor and receive special medals from Charles. We've invited all the world heads of state but they will be behind. This is a people's coronation for the patriots of France, not the cozy Davos club of globalist puppet masters," said Martine.

"You're very special," said Sophia.

Martine La Plume, president of France smiled and hugged her.

"Stay close to us now. We're going to La Defense to check out the preparations. I'd love a moment or two to talk later," she said, her lovely eyes not wavering from Sophia's.

"Of course," she replied.

Charles was smiling. She took his offered arm and strolled with him the length of the Hall of Mirrors where Louis the Sixteenth as the Dauphin, had danced with Marie-Antoinette at a masked ball to celebrate their wedding in 1770. Could she really be here in this place with Charles the Eleventh of France as his queen-to-be? What kismet had made her take that radio call to Dulwich just a few weeks before? If she could turn back the clock to half an hour before her colleague Simon Westcott had died because of her decision, she would without hesitation.

She relaxed into the leather of the black Renault Espace. Gendarmerie motorcycle outriders cleared their path through traffic as they headed for the prestige office and hi-tech development at La Defense. She loved it for its sense of reaching up and its aching quest for light and modernity. She loathed it for its cold assertion of a global connectedness bigger, brighter and so, so much more powerful than the humble creatures at its feet.

"It's a 'Look, don't touch' place, 'Admire, not love' place," she said to Charles.

"It's a secular cathedral to the concept of a higher entity," he said.

"And what is that?"

"Wealth and the worship of it," he answered. "Wealth has angels, devils, messengers, prophets, omens and priests."

"And who are they?"

"Money lenders are angels and devils to those in need. Messengers are the markets and prophets are the investment experts. Superstitious omens are flash crash market panics and the priests are dealers, traders, brokers and the like. They have a Cosa Nostra money jargon as obscure as Vatican Latin."

"And your policy on such things, Your Majesty?"

"To talk of love first."

"And after that?"

"There is nothing after that. Love can't seize the wheel of the ship, but it may blow its warm wind to nudge its course. A king or queen is the mouth and lips of their people Sophia."

She sighed and squeezed his hand.

"I love you as my man and as my king."

He folded her hand between his.

"I need you to be with me. You came to me as an angel when all was lost. Whatever your beliefs I know that God sent you to me. Only God may take you away."

"You know I'm not a believer."

"You speak from your mind. God knows your heart. If you've ever loved or been loved then you know everything in the mind of God."

She kissed his cheek. She loved his mind and his gentleness but craved his sexual need for her. She'd be his groaning slut rather than his exulted angel. She cried out for the power of animal lust and disgusting wicked, even forbidden, pleasure. She wanted to submit to the selfish greed of a lover's grip on her. She wanted to be more woman than woman and draw passion in to her belly. She wanted the abandon and shameless performance of her desire. She wanted more than she could ever dare to name.

Surrounded by soldiers and police they walked up the steps towards the Grande Arche. The whole area in front of the building was being covered with a circus type big-top roof. There could only be one ringmaster who stood in the center of the huge space in his trademark mauve kaftan.

"Comrades!" bellowed Vandervell O'Brien. "This is the biggest unlikely fucking liftoff since the resurrection."

Martine laughed and kissed his cheeks.

"I'm looking at a genius," she said.

"Well, I'm pretty hard to miss," he replied, patting his very adequate abdomen. "I wasn't being irreligious, Your Majesty, back in those days they had to do miracles without CGI."

"Just a few donkeys and palm leaves," said Charles, shaking the great man's hand.

Looking back at the arch, a huge curtain was being raised to enclose the end.

"We're going to project a montage of all of the beauties of France and a roundup of French history. We're not featuring guillotines on health and safety advice. You've no idea how hard it is to get sexy shots of snails and swollen goose livers," he said. "During the show there'll just be the new flag with your old Boy Scout badges on it, Charles. Did you get your monarch patch?"

"With merit," said Charles.

"I knew you were a swot," said Sophia, sensing Charles's slight unease at Comrade O' Brien's revolutionary banter. He would always be a gentle boy and you can love a guy for that.

"So, since the old king is dead, the tradition of France makes you the king already. May I invite Your Majesties to my humble peasant caravan for an English working man's cheddar cheese and pickled onion luncheon. I'm afraid the bread is your French stuff."

"Can we make sure all these soldiers get a meal if they're waiting for us," said Charles.

"Good man," said Vandervell. "Spoken like a comrade and a king. I'll get food brought over from our canteen."

"Don't let them eat cakes," said Martine with a laugh.

The young soldier in front of Martine gave an involuntary cry as the bullet hit his chest. The sound of the gun followed.

"*À terre*! Sniper!" said another.

The young guy was down but alive. Charles took Sophia's arm and ran with her to the shelter of a big yellow mobile crane. All the others followed.

"Where's the sniper?" asked Charles.

"We won't know until he fires again," said a sergeant.

Sophia saw the young soldier sitting up. The others pulled off his top to reveal the damage to his bullet vest. He was bruised to hell but intact. The sound of the shot followed a while after the impact. Sophia figured the shooter was some distance away. A police chopper was overhead, heat seeking pod mounted underneath. If someone was there this wouldn't take too long. A burst of gunfire spat from the sky towards the rooftop of a building. Fire was returned and the chopper veered away. Soldiers were pouring into a big commercial shopping center, doubtless heading for the roof.

"That one was for you, Martine," panted Vandervell. "I'm going to have to pay these monkeys danger money now to get this show put on tomorrow."

"Whatever it takes and whatever it costs," she said.

"Do you feel human fear?" he asked.

Martine almost caressed the crucifix around her neck. "Sophia has shared her courage with me. If ever I get promoted to human I'll let you know," she said with a smile. "Now let's get back to my place."

CHAPTER 53

They gathered for a security briefing in Martine's office. Anna La Salle came over and hugged Sophia.

"Nice little body swerve on that car roof in London," she said with a raise of the eyebrow.

"I'm sorry, Anna. That woman Jean isn't fully on our side. She supports the Caesar Roboris version of hard core monarchy. I guess you knew that."

"Of course, but until Her Majesty's government chose a policy we were trying to play both sides of the net. Bastian has done a lot to get Charles to where he is. I always hoped he'd come over to us," said Anna.

"But Caesar Roboris hired him and he's got blood enough on his hands. Would you trust our government to support him if the heat came on from the Intello liberal media? They want to lock up old soldiers for what happened in war forty years ago just to look politically correct," said Sophia.

Anna sighed.

"You're right. You can't make omelettes without breaking eggs and the politicos would throw you to the vegan cannibals if it'd get them a vote."

Captain Côté had arrived with Hakim.

"The guy on the roof was a communist Intello," said the captain.

"So how the hell do we deal with this threat in the long run? I'm thinking out loud because in terms of lives, I'm running out fast," said Martine.

Captain Côté stood up.

"Madame, you're constantly giving these assassins the chance to attack you."

"I'm president, I can't hide. Well, I can hide but I can't hide and stay in power."

"If you permit me, I'll give you our overall situation. Ladies and gentlemen. We have a constant terrorist threat from this loose group of Intellos who are happy to kill anyone to prevent the reinstatement of the monarchy. They don't want Martine, Charles, or the Patriotic Front. We must expect attacks from these individuals for generations to come. The other threat is from the Caesar Roboris group who seek to re-create authoritarian monarchy wherever possible throughout the world. To some extent we have accepted their help and cooperation in defeating our own enemies. The patriots of France have voted for the return of the king, and the Caesar Roboris members want that king to rule by divine right. They identified Charles and brought him to France and offered him to Martine on the basis of his legitimate claim to the throne. Since Madame La Plume will not accept anything other than a politically powerless monarchy, we are in a state of war with a ruthless and powerful opponent."

"I keep asking, but who precisely is Caesar Roboris?" asked Sophia.

"Madame, it is a long list. Viktor Pinupskin of Russia, Ronald Grump of the USA, President Edamame of Turkey, Prince Fiscal Hessian of Arabia, Prince Richard of England, President Mc Nicol of Scotland, President Bhajimosa of India, President Dumerder of the Philippines, President Sarastro of Cuba. They have prepared pretenders to the thrones of Spain, Italy, and Germany. Kung Po Ginseng of China will follow if Pinupskin declares himself tsar. As a group they have the support of the World Bank. The fact is that most global corporate business is already run by stateless super-rich kings. Their politics is money and greed. Their land is the mortgaged world of the indebted poor. They back winners and enslave the losers. Caesar Roboris has infinite resources and an army of assassins," said Captain Côté.

"And what about the mass of people?" asked Charles.

"Irrelevant pawns, labor resource, and herded consumers," he said.

"I will never accept that definition," said Charles.

"You don't have to, Your Majesty, you have no political power. You can change nothing. You command no armies. You dress up and strut the stage," said the captain. "The likes of Pinupskin, Kung Po Ginseng, and Sarastro are already dictators who accept no compromise. To be frank, these are a different league of men."

"Different league but inferior character. Martine and Charles have brought peace and unity by offering pride and respect," said Sophia.

She was watching Martine. She was calm, thoughtful, and commanding.

"OK. I can't beat either group who is against us. I agree. And thanks, Sophia, for your words. You understand our aims and you are a special patriot. Captain Côté, I thank you for your frankness. It is good to have precise information," said Martine.

"There's a coronation tomorrow," said Anna La Salle, clearly ill at ease with the situation.

"Oh happy day," said Martine. "Two forces as much opposed to each other as they are to me. If I duck, they fire on the other and one side wins. I can never agree with Caesar Roboris and so I ally myself with the Intellos to defeat them. What are my weapons, ladies and gentlemen?"

"Honors, money, preference, châteaus, sex, blackmail," said Anna.

"Ah woman, not for nothing do we talk of Lady Macbeth, Madame Bovary, and Lucretia Borgia," said Martine with a warm smile. "Men aim the spears, women brew the poison for the tips," she said.

"You'll need to move quickly," said Anna.

"Hakim, identify the most influential and personally ambitious Intellos in the media clique. Let's go for TV, social media, and newsprint. Then we want a few singers, film and sports stars. I want toadies or at least people who would sell their mother for a scoop. Don't forget any slime balls with something to hide from their adoring fans. Find out where they are now even if they're in jail. See what you can do in an hour," said Martine.

"Are you about to throw a bucket of fish guts at the seagulls?" asked Sophia.

"Ah, you are a poet of the Eric Cantona School. You're turning French," said Martine with a chuckle. "Now we must talk privately, you and me. Let's go to my apartment. Let's regroup in forty-five minutes."

Martine poured two large glasses of scotch with ice and sat next to Sophia on the long red and cream sofa.

"How can any of us live with this constant menace of death from terrorism?" she asked with a long sigh. "What is the true nature of mankind? All I want is to bring unity and peace to the land I love."

"Everyone respects you for that," said Sophia, studying her weary, sad eyes.

"Sophia, it is a horrible thing to use someone, don't you think?"

"It can be. I guess it depends on your reasons."

"I want you to marry Charles tonight at the Hotel de Ville. Marriage in France is a civil affair, the religious stuff is merely a fancy dress party with holy Perrier. You'll get all that at Sacré Coeur. I've fixed an Elise Hameau dress, I hope you like my choice for you. It's gorgeous and we want some quality shots. A dressmaker is on hand to fit you. She'll also do a coronation robe overnight, maybe something velvet in French flag blue. I want to keep that young Bohemian style."

Sophia gulped. She had no time to fix anything.

"What about paperwork?"

"We can fix all that. I'm assuming you're OK with marrying him?"

"Yes, I've kind of agreed to that among all the bombs and bullets."

"He totally, totally adores you," said Martine.

"I love him too. He's beautiful, gentle, and will grow into a fine statesman I think."

"And you'll be there at his side."

"Of course."

"And I'll be by your side," said Martine.

Sophia turned to her. Whatever she did, nothing could block the pull of this woman.

"I'll need that strength," she said.

"This is our show to win, you and me. We are stronger. Charles would crumble without you. You know they have a plan for my death by drug overdose. A bullet, knife, car crash, or poison could find me any minute and we have come so far."

"I would die for you Martine, you know that," said Sophia, spontaneously taking her hand. Martine raised it to her lips and kissed the inside of her wrist. Sophia closed her eyes, not daring to give away the turmoil in her emotions.

"We know each other, Sophia, like the evening knows the kiss of sun and sea. You look out from the shore and you breathe the inescapable truth of it. Facing the power of human love, it's a wonderful thing to be so weak and small. Let it go and forgive your helplessness."

"I love Charles," she replied, scrambling for a handhold.

"I know your heart. There's something delicious in the tension of possibility don't you think?"

"Yes, yes there is. I've never thanked you for the perfume."

"I believe it was your gift that saved me today," said Martine, brushing her hand over the necklace, "And now to business. I want you to marry Charles tonight and become king and queen tomorrow. I'll invite the group of people I've asked Hakim to assemble. It will be the biggest scoop of their lives. They'll proclaim their support and I will heap them with the bangles and spangles of this world. You *are* a beautiful woman with a celebrity daughter. The Intello liberals will love to hint at your pan-sexual past. Your age difference adds that cougar spice. They dare not criticize you because their own class would turn on them. I need you to be free thinking, feminist, and liberal."

"I think I am," said Sophia.

"Exactly, the Intello class will *have* to love you. And to love you means to love the show. There'll be a few old frogs croaking on their diseased prostate lily pads but we can live with them and they'll draw fire from the weeping storm troopers of diversity," said Martine.

"And what about Charles?"

"You can explain it all to him. He'd marry you on a big dipper at Disneyland if that's what you wanted."

"Can I make so much difference?"

"I can give you the long answer in one word—Diana," said Martine.

"I'm not in that league," said Sophia.

"No, you're the naughty queen of France with attitude," said Martine.

CHAPTER 54

She had a couple of minutes with Charles before the meeting re-started.

"Martine wants us to marry tonight before the coronation," she said.

"So you'll be with me," he said, taking her in his arms.

"I told her I'd think about it."

"Think about what?"

"Big stuff like shall we have a cat or a dog and who empties the dishwasher."

Charles laughed.

"Whatever, as long as you're mine."

"So it's that simple. You take me how I am, whatever I've been."

"Naturally, how else would things be?"

"Complex, very often, like Romeo and Juliet," she said, kissing his lips.

"No one who ever pulls up on the cliff of love ends up by jumping. Their reasons for hesitation are complex, the fall is so, so simple," he said.

"And the rocks are hard."

"Firstly choose your cliff," he said.

"I love you Charles the Eleventh."

"And I adore and love you Queen Sophia. I can't tell you how happy I am."

"A true gentleman would at least try," said Anna as she entered. "Martine has filled me in. Brilliant!"

Hakim had prepared his list. Martine smiled with approval.

"I've created the grand order of Patriot Knight Chevalier. Recipients will be publicly awarded a sash of the new flag, a gold medal of the king and queen and a generous lifetime pension. They will sit on the national committee of patrimony and travel the world on expenses promoting our vision of identity. Others will address them as Chevalier Monsieur or Chevalière Madame. Let's see who will refuse," said Martine.

"A couple are being released from prison as we speak," said Hakim.

"I will assemble them all here and go to the marriage in limos. As soon as it's over Charles, Sophia, and I will present their honors. I want them to feast on food and wine wearing their baubles, and the videos up on every single channel and social media platform. Make sure that there are prison vans ready for any reluctant knights," said Martine.

"Quite a few of the other Intellos will hate them," said Anna.

"Divide and rule always broke the old working class, scabs against strikers while the bosses watched the sport. The globalists have set the poor of one land against the poor of their neighbor. The only thing on Earth that's new is what we've forgotten. Marie Antoinette said that," said Martine.

"We can smear most of the likely opponents," said Hakim.

"This is the happiest day of my life," said Sophia with a laugh.

"I know, politics takes the shine off romance," said Martine.

"But never love," said Charles.

"Can I get away to call my daughter?" asked Sophia.

"Go for it," said Martine.

She slipped out onto the stairs. It was so good to be away from the heady spin of conflict and intrigue. Izzy picked up.

"Hey Mum, you're just so famous. You're bigger than Hollywood."

"How are you? Do you need me to ask you if you're eating your greens and not getting VD?"

"Everything's cool on the VD and bowel movement front."

"Did you see any stories about me?"

"Nothing much, there was that bit of girl on girl stuff but hey? Selena wobbles on her axis quite a bit. I had a gay scene in a film about milkmaids last week. You know, longing looks among the udders."

"Was it a comedy?"

"No, it was real historical and arty with misty rivers, clanking atmospheric buckets and a girl singing out of tune."

"Sounds like a French film."

"I think it's aimed at the Cannes Festival."

"So you're good."

"Yeah, but I miss you, Mum."

"Miss you too. I'm getting married tonight and being crowned queen of France in the morning."

"Poor Mum. I love you. I wish I could be there."

Sophia sighed. She loved her but was so happy she was away from this cauldron of danger.

"Tonight is the legal ceremony. You'll be at the big church do at Sacré Coeur."

"I'm just so proud of you, Mum."

"Love you. Take care."

She sat with her head in her hands. From now on in her life a moment of solitary reflection would be a rare luxury. A few weeks ago she could have spent the evening with a romance story, a take-out fish and chips with a coke drunk out of the can. Martine was built for the life she was living but Sophia knew herself to be a different animal. She had the courage and love to go on, but the mind to go home. Since her humble south London flat was no longer hers, she would settle for the Palace of Versailles. She took a deep breath and focused on the path ahead.

The wedding dress was a fairy tale. The style was light and chic with elements of old days' gracefulness and new age Bohemia. Anna helped her with makeup. She knew she looked good as she stepped into the grand Salon des Ambassadeurs. Charles was there, impossibly handsome in a dark blue suit, white shirt, and red tie bearing the Bourbon family crest. An audible exclamation went up as the assembled people saw her. She smiled broadly and walked to Charles, framing his face in her hands and kissing his lips. Cameras fired off.

"*Encore*, Sophia," called out a snapper.

She smiled and obliged. She was shaking dozens of hands, received a couple of bows and curtsies, said a few "*Mercis*" and "*Plaisirs*." How easy it was to be rich, officially beautiful, and important. Champagne flowed as waiters worked to leave no need unfulfilled. Groomed sleek Intellos assured her of their loyalty and her exquisite beauty. A young woman in porn star specs hinted at her pan-sexual sisterhood and enthusiasm for Versailles. An old smoke-throated hack slurred his love for all things royal. An intense vegan professor of sociology begged her to visit his multi-cultural cow, goose, and pig sanctuary. She came, she saw, she conquered.

The half-drunk entourage piled into a train of black limos, the new national flag flying on each vehicle. Escort motorcyclists and police cars formed up around them. They set off towards Notre Dame and the Hotel de Ville for the scoop of the century and just maybe a private celebration of love.

The convoy followed the right bank of the Seine, turning the heads of Parisians and tourists. Sophia couldn't resist a few regal waves. The crowd of media and arty Intellos took themselves and their bonhomie into the Hotel de Ville while she waited with Charles. Then he left her with Martine to present himself at the table of the official who would perform the civil marriage.

Martine took her hand.

"I'll lead you in, then you just go and stand next to Charles. All you have to say is '*oui*.'"

"I'm terrified," said Sophia.

"You look so beautiful. I'm ridiculously jealous," said Martine.

"You're beautiful too, as well as all the other amazing things you are."

"Don't ever go away from me," said Martine with almost a tear in her kind, weary eyes.

"You know I won't. I promise."

Martine reached out and stroked her cheek. She leaned forward and left a light kiss on her lips.

"There's something I want to say to you so, so much Sophia," she said.

"I know. I know," said Sophia, nodding as she held her eyes.

"I'll keep those words here in my heart. They will always be there," she said pressing Sophia's hand to her breast.

"We're the strong ones, Martine. You told me that and I trust you with my life. You'd better look after that heart for me," she said.

"If you are not mine to give, tell me I'm wrong. I'm letting you go now, but I'm not setting you free," said Martine.

The bodyguards were waiting to surround them as they stepped from the Mercedes limo. Sophia took Martine's arm and walked with her into the Hotel de Ville.

"You're not wrong and you're not alone while I live," said Sophia.

The room was magnificent with a high ceiling covered in classical paintings. The rest was a blur of pillars, chandeliers, and archways. On either side of her were faces all turned to her. Among them she recognized actors, politicians, and faces she knew from TV. There was an air of wealth and confidence, a world and a lifetime away from everything she had lived or seen as a London street cop. At the far end of the hall was a table at which stood a youngish guy wearing a French flag sash with the new *fleur-de-lys* emblem. Charles was waiting, turning to smile as she approached. Someone called out.

"*Vive la reine Sophia. Vive les patriots.*"

She took one last look at Martine who seated herself in the front row. She stood at Charles's side while the official made a small relaxed speech and read out articles of French law. She understood the question that he put to her.

"*Sophia Castellana, consentez-vous de prendre pour époux Monsieur Charles Gonin?*"

"*Oui,*" she said.

"*Monsieur Charles Gonin, consentez-vous de prendre pour épouse Sophia Castellana?*"

"*Oui,*" he said

"*Au nom de la loi je déclare ... unis par le mariage.*"

She was in his arms, kissing as if to save her life. There was a wall of sound, applause, cries of Bravo! She'd done it. She'd bloody well married the king of France. Cameras were clicking. She was signing two sheets of paper. Charles was signing. A woman from the evening news show was signing as a witness, a guy she'd seen in films was signing, an old rock and roll singer, and a woman who led demonstrations about workers' rights was signing. She took a deep, deep breath, aware that a BFM TV news crew were interviewing Charles. A BBC reporter was like a wasp in her ear.

"Your Royal Highness, Your Royal Highness, Your Royal Highness, BBC, BBC."

"What?" she asked.

Charles was laughing.

"That's you, Sophia. Your Royal Highness. He means you."

She forced a smile and turned to the young guy.

"It's a proud moment for England for one of ours to be queen of France," he said.

"I hadn't thought about it. That isn't why I did it."

"Of course not, but how does this rate in your life?"

"It's like Crystal Palace winning the Champion's league, but not quite so miraculous," said Sophia with a laugh. She could get to enjoy this.

The young reporter was laughing.

"So, you're a Palace fan, Your Royal Highness?"

"Well, you've got to be when you're going to live at Versailles."

The reporter seemed stunned.

"That's kinda my idea of a royal joke," she added.

"Your Royal Highness, thanks so much," he said.

She gave him a big warm smile.

"Hope you're coming to the party at the Élysée?" she said.

She was becoming calmer and more aware. The more she smiled the more the cameras licked her face. She realized she had no idea of the time. There was a bloody coronation at noon maybe tomorrow? Maybe today? Poor Charles was trapped by armies of snappers and journalists. She pushed her way to his side.

"Gentlemen, are you ready?" she said.

The clamor ceased. She placed her hands on Charles's cheeks and kissed him passionately.

"*Mon mari, je t'aime,*" she said.

The mob cheered.

"*Encore!*" they cried.

"*Mon mari. Je t'aime take deux,*" she said. kissing him again.

The snappers had gone into a frenzy. There was a chant of "*Vive le roi. Vive Sophia.*"

Bodyguards were clearing their way to the door. She caught sight of Martine giving her a thumbs up sign. She was high on adrenalin and sheer relief. Oddly in this alien situation she had for a few moments re-found her old self. She was a bawdy London girl with a laugh in her heart and a wild freedom in her soul. She was learning fast that once everybody officially loves you, it so much easier to be officially loveable. Just maybe, if she ever booked on again for a night shift on a south London patrol car, she'd officially love the first angry no-hope kid and see what came back in the echo.

CHAPTER 55

The bells of Notre Dame were ringing out over Paris as they stepped out into the night of the great metropolis. She had come to adore this city of passionate restraint and arrogant shabbiness. She was queen of France and this metro accordion symphony in stone major was her home. Martine had joined them and hugged them both.

"You guys are stars. You are bringing real pride and prestige to our patriots."

"We love you," said Sophia.

"The same love is in my heart."

They settled into the limo.

"Your lives, my life will never be free again. You will breathe only the air that others have breathed out around you. Welcome inside the prison of fame. Charles and I have known this place for a while. Empty out your pockets Sophia and put on your velvet overalls," said Martine.

"I can do this gig, Martine. I can!"

"Yes, you can indeed but I offer you one last bite of the poisoned apple of anonymity. We're going to pull over at the river bus stop. There's an empty boat there with just one celeb snapper. It will take you up to Champs Élysées. We'll be waiting there. It's crazy but I don't think any terrorist or assassin will expect it," said Martine. "A spontaneous royal selfie with suitable background it would play big on social media. Terrorism has hit tourism."

She needed no encouragement as she held Charles's hand on the steps to the quay. As soon as they were aboard the boat set off. They stood together on the open deck. The flowing night ink of the great river Seine wrote their kisses into history and Facebook.

"It's not all advertising for show, Charles. I love you," she said.

"There's no showbiz in my love for you. You came to me as an angel."

"Then that's what I'll be unless you pull me down from heaven to ravish me."

He kissed her sensuously as she let herself melt into him. Around them the city trailed its fingers of light in the ever renewing tide.

"Does the river die at the sea or is that its birth?" she asked.

"The river loses its identity by re-finding its spirit. Nature loves a cycle," he answered.

She sighed.

"What will happen to us Charles?"

"We'll love each other and the rest will simply be."

Back in the Mercedes XLS 500, Charles handed the phone to an aide who flashed a royal river boat selfie kiss around the world. By the time he handed it back, the photo was retweeting from Beijing.

"What is place or identity anymore?" Charles asked into the void.

"You're Charles the Eleventh and this is the Élysée Palace. Don't think. Be king," said Martine.

An anthill of staff had balanced a miracle on top of a circus. The state dining room had been set out to feed everyone. Towers of Champagne glasses filled as waiters poured the wine in cascades. Once wine and aperitifs had been distributed, officials ushered the guests into the Salon des Ambassadeurs. Martine gave a short address.

"My wonderful friends and patriots. Welcome to my modest home and to a new age for our country. Thank you all for coming at such short notice. When we were attacked again today, Charles and Sophia came to me with their wish to be united in marriage against whatever dangers others with ill intent might bring to them. Our beautiful and courageous Sophia will be at Charles's side as his queen. Patriots of France have seen and shared the love there is between them. This is France where love and the human spirit will never again be mangled in the faceless gear wheels of globalist greed. Patriots, we are a beacon of the human soul to the world. Our new royal couple will proclaim our philosophy to all those nations still blinded by the grinding dust of meaningless toil. In a moment we will feast on the truth, love, and beauty of our cuisine. Others seek to turn an anonymous planet into a production line of plastic packaged brand-labeled swill. Patriots, we send a new sauce to the plates and kitchens of a world craving the flavor of identity.

And now, while our staff make their last touches to our banquet your king and queen will present the sashes and medals to our new Patriot Knight Chevaliers. I ask you all to come forward with us from this moment. Join us in offering a divided world the royal splendor that can bless the poorest home. The splendor of two people joined this night in our beautiful city of love."

Sophia studied her in awe. She was an artist, smiling as the throng of

Intellos applauded her. BFM, France 24 and TF1 had streamed her speech live. In a moment she herself would be playing to an audience of a couple of billion. The award recipients had formed in lines on either side of the room.

"We have to stay together because everyone wants to meet both of us, but mainly you," said Charles with a grin.

Officials followed them with silver trays loaded with folded sashes. They pinned on medals, draped the fabric, kissed cheeks, shook hands, received bows and curtsies. Camera lenses licked the lace from her dress and the light from her smile. By the time it was over she had facial RSI. It was 10:30 p.m. and there was the small matter of a coronation in the morning. Cops were paid by the hour, she'd never asked about queens.

The meal was sumptuous. She closed her eyes, swallowed and tried not to think about oysters. Foie gras spread into roasted lobster with black truffles. Artichoke soup flowed into caramelized quail. The wife of the American ambassador and an ex-mistress of the last president presented themselves with assurances of their attention and her beauty. Charles chatted to a cousin of Prince Fiscal Hessian who worked for Al Jazeera TV. Rafts of cheese and tropical islands of desserts dotted the vast ocean of consumption. She knew herself well enough to avoid the temptation of excess wine. Charles stood and gave a formal speech of thanks. A band started to play. A dance floor had been created in the adjoining *Jardin d'hiver*. Charles led her to the center and kissed her before leading her in the tradition of the first dance. The band struck up the Francis Cabrel song *Je l'aime à mourir*. The guests cheered and applauded.

"*Je t'aime, je t'aime*," he said as he held her to him.

"*Je t'aime à mourir,*" she answered, borrowing the words from the song.

"You're a good learner."

"I'm drunkenly fluent in love," she said.

The party flowed on towards dawn. Martine seemed never to tire.

"The coverage is fantastic. Everyone on Earth is following every word, every kiss, every glory of our nation. You're bigger than the British royals, Star Wars, Harry Potter, Facebook kittens, and even the Beckhams. These Intellos have sold their teeth for a title and a snout in the gravy bucket. You're too big and too beautiful to take down," she said.

"But what about the Caesar Roboris problem?" asked Charles.

"The good thing is that they want you, but not me. At least we know who the target will be," she said.

Sophia took her hand.

"They'd better understand that your life is our life too," she said.

"That's for sure," said Charles.

"If anything happens to me you must go on as patriots. The people would soon forget me. France now has an identity. A something is always going to defeat a nothing," she said.

Sophia studied her. There was an air of resignation in her manner. She knew the feelings that Martine held for her and yet she had propelled her into a marriage for the sake of France. And what did this magnificent clever brave woman have now except her success and her loneliness?

"We've come this far together, Martine. We're going to cross the line holding hands," said Charles.

An official bowed and spoke quietly to Martine. Sophia watched her nodding as she took in the news. Finally she raised her eyebrows and gave a faint smile.

"The Russian Duma has implored Viktor Pinupskin to accept the title of Tsar Viktor the First. He has told his people he won't accept the humiliation of attending the coronation in France as a peasant. He's just announced on state TV that he expects a royal welcome in Paris this morning. He is amending next year's Pinupskin calendar to show royal poses on every month. The Orthodox Church has sanctified his actions."

"Is this a good move or bad news?" said Charles.

"Vanity hath more blood than heart and doth of flatterers assassins make," said Sophia.

"Shakespeare?" asked Charles.

"Castellana," she said. "I helped my daughter with her school play lines. Crooks are vain, a lot of crime is more for kudos than for gain. The giant egosaurus is a broad target with a thin skin," she said.

"I think Tsar Viktor may find himself seated with the queen of France," said Martine. "In the meantime I will send him the best wishes of our proud nation."

"If you want a cop's view you're pretty safe from him today. Pinupskin's going to be posing and parading for his own gallery. He will not want any kind of counterpoint to his 1812 overture," said Sophia.

Charles shook his head with a smile.

"For a girl who's never followed politics you're a natural."

"Believe me police work is politics. Pinupskin was a KGB cop. We're kinda family."

"It's 4 a.m., guys. The party's thinning out," said Martine, kissing them both.

Sophia sighed into Charles's arms, proud she was sober at least.

"This should be a night of unbridled lust and debauchery," he said.

"How about a dawn of three hours sleep?" she said.

"That's a deal."

"Martine just has to realize the danger around her," she said.

"And where the hell is Bastian and who gives him his orders? Pinupskin's a big fish but he's only one. He's made his move and gone for broke but that may not play too well with all the others if they wanted a mass attack. His move alerts the opposition in all the other countries. These guys need me to declare myself king by divine right and take power."

"If I were one of the Caesar Roboris guys I'd be pissed off with Pinupskin. I'd be trying to sabotage the whole affair to stop him strutting on this stage. Remember he has no political opposition at home. Most of the others have to overcome experienced elected politicians who control the media," she said.

"And when will they act?"

"They know we're tired and probably not alert. This is the moment the police would go in, like right about now," she said.

CHAPTER 56

Charles showered while she pulled off her dress and collapsed gratefully onto the bed. So many times she'd charged at splintered doors in dawn police raids. How must that feel to the guy on the receiving end? This is when the bold attack. She knew it in her bones even though she was exhausted. She had to clean up and sleep. She wasn't a cop anymore. She hadn't even checked her bank to see if the Met' police was still paying her wages. This is when Bastian would attack. **This is when Bastian would attack**. She picked up Charles's iPhone to check world news, maybe in sheer vanity to see themselves. There was no Wi-Fi signal. This was the Élysée Palace and there was no fucking Internet! She looked out the window into the courtyard. A Citroën van was parked under the window. The doors were open and she could see trays of tools and rolls of cable. An Internet engineer was on some kind of job. She threw on her jeans, her trainers, and her leather biker's jacket over her bra. Charles was still in the shower. She was just being stupid. He would think she was paranoid and call the whole thing off. She stepped out of the room. Gendarmes and soldiers snapped to attention.

"I need to see Martine," she said.

A gendarme came with her along two corridors and around two corners. She tapped the door.

"Bastian, it's Sophia. I count you as a friend. If that means anything to you, let me come in. I won't lie to you and I'm not armed. I respect you as a pro far too much to try any tricks believe me. I'm alone here and I'm afraid. I've missed you. I'll always need a guy like you on my side," she said.

She motioned the gendarme to get out of sight and raise the alarm. The door swung open. Martine was seated naked on a chair with her mouth taped shut. Her eyes were calm and defiant. Sophia entered the room and turned as the door closed behind her. She swiveled to meet the cold-eyed stare of a man in I.T. Services overalls.

"Bastian, we're on the same side."

He motioned her with the barrel of an English army SA80 Heckler and Koch assault rifle to sit on a chair.

"Your government has changed sides. You're the last person I wanted to see."

"I don't mind seeing you, Bastian. We've been comrades in battle," she said. "What's your plan here?"

"They wanted me to kill Martine with a drug overdose. The stuff is there on the bed."

She noted a wrapped hypodermic syringe and a phial of liquid.

"But you didn't want to, did you?"

"No."

Now was the time to recall every last desperate suicide she'd tried to save, every exhausted armed crook driven into a corner, every terrified kid about to slam down the throttle of a stolen car. Metropolitan Police training school, day three. Every word out of the villain's mouth is one less punch in your face. And they say it's an unskilled job.

"I don't have to kill you," he said. "My bosses want a different type of world with clarity and decision. You're a cop for Christ's sake. Liberal shilly-shally shit has left everyone afraid of standing up for themselves. The scumbags and the slick lawyers sneer at law and order and take poor people's money to stuff their own pockets."

"No argument from me or Martine. Pinupskin's jumped the gun so where does that leave you, Bastian?"

He nodded thoughtfully. His respect for her and Martine was his weakness. Total fucking suicidal weakness. Remember to use his name, Sophia. Every time you use a killer's name you draw a little of his identity and anger into yourself. Castellana school of street survival.

"Shut the fuck up. Throw some clothes on Martine. We need a change of scene."

"OK Bastian, you're an old comrade," she said. "Who are we working for?"

"Caesar Roboris as always."

"But not Viktor the Tsar," she said.

"He was a player when it suited him but he only looks after himself," said Bastian.

"You don't want to kill us do you?" she repeated.

"I'm a soldier. I follow my orders. You and Martine've got guts. There's no need for you to die. All we need to do is slow down the bus, keep Pinupskin out of the driving seat, give my guys the chance to soften up their people. Once the world sees him posing bareback as a warrior tsar, the people will take fright and turn to democracy and all that fucking useless shit. We needed to move together."

"I can handle Pinupskin," she said.

"Too late. In a few hours he'll be posturing to the world while Esmeralda goes home as a loser. All I need to do is take Martine out of the picture and spoil the show. No celebrity endorsement, no sale," said Bastian.

"Do you have to keep her taped up?"

"Yes."

"How the hell are you going to get out of here? I've already raised the alarm. A couple of hundred troops and gendarmes know you're here."

"Maybe my only option is to kill Martine here."

"You'd have to kill me too and then none of your guys would get the nod of acceptance from the French royal family. Bastian, Charles and I would welcome and endorse Mickey Mouse as king of America if you wanted that."

He'd stopped responding. She could tell he'd gone into reptilian survival mode. He was too far away to reach and he knew every move in the book. He was going to kill Martine within the next few heartbeats. Bastian defined his life by the success of his mission. She had one last gambler's chance.

"I'll get you out of here," she said.

"Tell me how."

"I'll come with you. I trust and respect you, Bastian. Kidnap Martine to spoil Pinupskin's day and I'll tag along. No one is going to open fire and risk hitting either me or Martine. If I make a deal with you I'll stick to it."

Bastian's eyes fixed hers, calculating all the angles.

"I'll tape your mouth and hands. You walk behind me, Martine goes in front. Any hero stuff and I'll empty the gun into Martine. We're going back to my van in the courtyard. We're going to drive out and hit the Péripherique. I know half the French police and military will be following. We're going to enter the Belle Rive tunnel and block the road. We're going to get to an emergency exit which comes up at the edge of the Reuil Malmaison golf course. There's a chopper there ready to lift off. And we're all going to have a relaxing day, courtesy of…."

"Who? Come on, who?"

"You can't see it can you? Ronald Grump is the deal maker. Ron had a deal with Pinupskin and the fucking piece of shit double crossed him. He thought he could trust him. Ron likes deals but he wants himself big and the other guy small. If the world fragments into little states, Ron gets the deal he wants. If the big Russian bear stands up, all the little bunnies form alliances. If countries are independent businesses with one guy at the top, then you've got the recipe for deals. We're not talking Socrates or Thomas Paine here. We're talking business. Believe me, Esmeralda Grump should have been wearing that beautiful wedding dress. Sending her back as a loser was not in the script."

"Well, Grump can fuck right off."

"Let's go," said Bastian.

Sophia threw Martine some pajama bottoms and held them while she stepped in. She pulled off the bed cover to wrap her shoulders. For a second she looked into her eyes and kissed her forehead.

"Vive la France. Grump does deals and you've got one with me," said Sophia, holding out her wrists. Bastian wound them with tape, never dropping the machine gun.

It was time to go. Sophia knew that any young blade looking for his lifetime moment might fancy a head shot at Bastian. A high velocity large caliber bullet could take out all of them regardless which head it hit. He opened the door and motioned to Martine to step out. He followed her as Sophia made up the rear. Soldiers and gendarmes stood aside, guns pointed to the floor. He kept his weapon trained on Martine's spine. For a moment Sophia imagined a bullet splintering her bones. She nodded reassurance at the tense faces to either side. They descended a service stair and out into the courtyard. The van was a few paces away, the rear doors still open. He motioned for Martine to slide in between the racks of tools. He slammed the doors and pointed the gun at the passenger door for Sophia to get in the front. He kept the weapon trained on her as he went around the front of the vehicle.

Sophia caught some movement from the corner of her eye. A male figure in a black balaclava was crouched on the floor in front of the driver's seat and under the steering wheel. She had to guess he was a special forces agent. She thought it through. This guy had a chance as the door opened. Bastian was at the window, gun trained on her, the other hand reaching for the handle. Once the door opened she could throw herself across the seats. The door catch clicked. Bastian moved away slightly to allow the door to open. She heard the sound of his weapon against the metal of the vehicle. A gap was opening. His hand was reaching out for the steering wheel to pull himself in. The figure on the floor struck like a cobra. He sprang into the gap hitting Bastian in the chest and toppling him backwards. There were running feet. She scrambled across the seats. The agent was on top of Bastian, both hands on his wrist preventing him from firing. Police and soldiers arrived. The gun was kicked away. She heard the ratchet of handcuffs. The agent in the balaclava was brushing himself off.

"They would have killed you, Bastian. You're a mercenary but you've saved my life and been my friend. No one died here tonight and that will be our way forward," said a familiar male voice.

Sophia gasped. The figure was pulling off the black hood.

"Charles! What the fuck?" she said, jumping out of the van and embracing him.

"The gendarme alerted everyone. There was an ambush set up. I couldn't see him die."

"But you could have died,"

"And so could you. If I lost you there's no point in anything for me."

"How did they let you take that risk?"

"I'm the king for Christ's sake. I'm wearing a uniform today and I haven't had too many chances to show I deserve it."

Martine had been recovered from the back of the van. She was pulling the tape from her mouth as she joined them.

"You two are quite a team. I might have to offer you a job one day," she said with a smile.

Charles hugged her.

"You're a one off Martine," he said.

"Would he have killed us?" she asked, taking Sophia's hand.

"I don't believe he would. A warrior has bosses but his mission is to stand by his comrades. When he saw that, his loyalty was to us. Somewhere in the debris behind me I was a proud cop. Your value system starts to dress in uniform too."

"Fearless warrior, ruthless killer, freedom fighter, terrorist, anarchist, insurgent, partisan, rebel, patriot, and on and on. The victors pin the badges on the graves. We need a better way. We need to think beyond words and understand beyond labels," said Charles.

"Let's get some sleep," said Martine. "The band is playing and the house lights are fading. Today, the whole stage is a world," she said.

CHAPTER 57

Her dress fitting was at 8:30 a.m. Advisors and Martine had chosen a deep-blue fitted velvet full-length gown, the bodice embellished with a waterfall of crystals. A team of experts fixed her hair and makeup. She kept an eye on the TV coverage. The Pope had flown in and was holding a special mass at Notre Dame. Prince Richard was representing the queen of England. Viktor Pinupskin had arrived on the first ever flight of Russian Imperial Airways. His Ilyushin 96 stood on the tarmac at Paris Charles de Gaulle airport. A mass choir and an Orthodox Church bishop stood at the base of the steps. As he appeared, in the blue and gold full-dress uniform of a KGB Field Marshal, the band and choir belted out the Russian anthem. Ronald Grump had arrived earlier in Airforce One in a lounge suit and slouched into a Cadillac limo. The TV crews of the world were assembled at La Defense, detailing each expected guest. Chinese President Kung Po Ginseng was in town with an entourage of dragon dancers, putting on a free show under the Eiffel Tower.

"The dragon dance represents imperial power. It's a terrifying but benevolent beast. It also brings good luck and fertility. He's sending a coded message to his own people. Our intelligence guys say he'll declare himself emperor when he returns from the coronation. The embassy has sounded us out about receiving the Imperial Ambassador," said Martine as she breezed in.

"And will we?"

"Yeah, of course. We need a trade deal. There's a lot of Camembert virgins in China."

Footage of fighter jets and tanks caught her eye. The Americans were moving heavy armor into Poland. Russian Mig 29K aircraft were flying dummy attack missions at the USS Roosevelt in the Mediterranean. The F18 Hornets were simulating close attacks on the Russian carrier Admiral Kuznetsof.

"It's schoolyard trash, but it's dangerous," said Martine.

"We need some vodka, Scotch, and a secure, private room," said Sophia.

"I was thinking the same. You know those two boys have just got to learn to share their toys. Let's get our beautiful selves on TV and out there. We'll stun the world into peace."

"You're so much more than simply beautiful Martine," said Sophia, letting herself gaze at her.

"And you're stunning. I can't begin to tell you what I was feeling during that stuff last night. You were prepared to die just for me."

Sophia looked down, knowing this woman was waiting to meet her eyes as soon as she glanced up. And once she was held, her heart would lurch and her belly would feel a delicious warmth. She just had to hold herself away from it. Had to.

"Martine...."

Martine was kissing her, had raised her chin and was holding her lower lip with the softness of a petal.

"That can't have happened. I mustn't let myself believe that happened," said Sophia.

Martine was smiling.

"I do love Charles. I want to be faithful. I'd strayed in the past I know, but I was OK."

"I know. These days I know the value of longing and what a rich source it is for a woman. To know longing is to have a cathedral in your soul. The light through the windows, the reaching up, the choir, the organ. These things are longing, but not God. If I'd really kissed you I'd really have thought I'd touched heaven."

"I need to spend more time in church," said Sophia.

"I love you," said Martine.

Sophia sighed.

"I care so much about that, I don't want you not to. I'd feel desolate if I didn't have that in my heart. I'll never say to you that I don't have that feeling for you but please never make me say the words. I could never drink half a bottle of wine. Once the cork is out, you may as well go for it. I'm afraid of you and myself," she said.

"I'm a harmless middle-aged woman."

"You pull me, just pull me right through my ribs and into your heart or mind."

"And Charles feels that way for you."

"Yes he does and I value that so much too. He needs me to be at his side, the road ahead is going to be bumpy."

"You and I have a new type of society to create. I love my homeland. I love other nations because of what they are. Charles will be a voice for us, a gentle educated voice without ambition for himself. He's a brave and beautiful man. He has adoring fans who are ten years old now. They'll stay with him all their lives. But my dear Sophia, we wouldn't be here today in this situation if he'd not met you. That day you showed up we were in a very different story with a very different boy."

"Can you explain?" asked Sophia.

"Yes, in detail but not now.

"That's a cruel tease."

Martine smiled warmly.

"It is and you recognize it. Just think how terrible it is for an innocent man to love a woman."

"A lot of men are in love with you, Martine."

"Poor things, but maybe we can use it," she said with a laugh.

Sophia focused on the hours ahead.

"What the hell happens at coronations?"

"Whatever Vandervell has orchestrated. The queen of England has given us back the Stuart sapphire for you. It was brought to France when James the Second fled in 1688 and fell into the possession of George the Third of England by inheritance. Later it was put in the imperial crown of Queen Victoria. Cartier have made it the feature of a ruby, diamond, and sapphire crown for our new queen of France. A team has been working through the night."

"How the hell can I be worth all this?" said Sophia.

"Forget your value. Think of the value of the office of queen and what it means to our people. Let's go put on a show."

CHAPTER 58

Charles was in the dress uniform of the Colonel in Chief of the new National Patriotic Reserve. A dark blue tunic was crossed by a golden sash with red, white, and blue lanyards. The epaulettes carried two golden crowns and a *fleur-de-lys*. The trousers were also dark blue with a red stripe.

"Wow!" she said kissing his lips. "You're so handsome you could be a pop star fantasy."

"And you could be a cool regal queen."

"I love you, Your Majesty," she said.

She walked with him hand in hand to the black Citroen C6. She did love him, loved him for his love and need for her, for his beauty, for his kindness and courage. Few women had as much to love in a man. Martine was there, like a wrapped parcel in her life, the bow of the ribbon so beautiful. In her mind her hand stroked that ribbon and put it away in the back of a drawer.

They were sandwiched in a vast motorcade as they climbed the Champs Élysées. Paris wore its open smile of a perfect blue sky day. Through the center of the Arc de Triomphe she could see La Grande Arche of La Defense in perfect alignment. Crowds lined the route waving the new *fleur-de-lys* flags. Could this be her? Could this be happening? She sought the reassurance of Charles's hand. The vehicle drove onto the *Parvis*. The steps had been carpeted in red, white, and blue stripes. At the distant end of the Arche, projectors beamed huge images of Charles and her against a background of the beauties of France. A mass choir stood in an arc around an altar on a raised stage. As they stepped from the car a huge sound system played the massive chords of the Saint Saëns organ symphony. To left and right the great, the good, and the massive of the entire planet awaited them. Behind them crowds jammed the Esplanade de Charles de Gaulle. From them a huge sound arose, an exclamation of pride and power. Charles turned to them and waved. As she turned, the sound became a roar, a cry of joy. In one solid voice they called "So-fee-ah. Sophia. Sophia," as if in a football chant. She waved and blew a kiss. The crowd seized it and blew back a thousand.

"What's going on?" she said.

"They love you, that's all. They know the stories of your courage, you are Jeanne D'Arc and you are so, so beautiful," said Vandervell O' Brien.

She took in his smile and his full-dress tricolor kaftan with *fleur-de-lys* and gold cummerbund.

The music had changed to Handel's Coronation Anthems. Giant screens relayed the images to the crowds.

"Only three billion in the TV audience," said Vandervell.

"There's been no time for a rehearsal," she said.

"We'll give you the nod. Selena and Izzy are in there dressed as vestal virgins of the regal gusset. They'll nudge you along. It's up the steps and head for the Pope. He's the only other guy here with the panache to wear a kaftan. Just agree with whatever they say, do your stuff and sing *La Marseillaise*. Wouldn't mind a spontaneous sexy snog on the way out. I'll cue you in."

She hadn't even thought of her own daughter. Of course she would have flown in from Hollywood with Mason Trowel.

"Are you sure I won't have to say anything?" she asked.

"Only what's on the script."

"What script?

"I sent it over last night," said Vandervell.

"Things got confused last night with weddings and machine guns."

"That's no excuse," said Vandervell with a smile. "Red Flag of the Grimethorpe Zombies was unscripted—we got a golden asteroid or meteor for the screenplay. You're a cop Sophia. You know life's a freestyle."

She took Charles's arm and mounted the steps. She raked through everything she'd learned of French at school, Izzy's homework and from her lesson in London. She'd just have to go for it. Soldiers in dress uniform, swords drawn and pointed skyward escorted them. Everywhere she looked were heads of state, royalty and celebrities. As they approached the altar and two golden thrones, they reached the wounded soldiers who had been given the front seats. Charles stopped at the last row and turning to both left and right, saluted them. They returned his salute, many from wheelchairs, many with their sole injured arm. There was a deep exclamation from the people outside. It was theatre but how much could a man do with such power. This was a gentle man, but a man chosen to be king. She spotted Selena and Izzy in beautiful Galadriel Lord of the Rings-style dresses. Sundry gorgeous maidens chosen from the *Rex Factor* show carried Bibles, crucifixes, and trinkets. They advanced towards a raised plinth. Izzy motioned for her to kneel on a cushion next to Charles. The Pope sprinkled water from a chalice. The choir sang Ave Maria. Two girls approached with crowns on blue velvet cushions patterned with *fleur-de-lys*. The child Marianne appeared from behind the altar. Sophia felt a tear in her eye at the tragic innocence and fragility of this child, almost a seed of a nation blown in by chance to bloom a new beauty in the bloodied soil of sorrow past. Her dress was pure white with a sash of red, white, and blue. She stood in front of Charles and in her frail arms lifted the historic crown of Louis the Fifteenth and placed it on his head.

"*Au nom du peuple*," she said.

"*Je l'accepte à genoux devant un enfant de la France*," said Charles.

The child lifted the new Cartier crown with the Stuart sapphire and stood before Sophia, placing it on her head.

"*Au nom du peuple*," she said.

"*Au nom de la France et de l'amour, mon ange*." said Sophia, reaching out and taking the child's hands.

Charles glanced at her. Izzy's jaw had dropped. Behind her there was a stir, almost a sigh. The choir began to sing Fauré's Ave Verum Corpus. Charles stood and Sophia followed, and took their seats on the two thrones. *Rex Factor* maidens presented Charles with a Bible and Sophia with a jeweled bracelet of wisdom. In the distance Vandervell was signaling for them to stand and walk forward. Blizzards of red, white, blue, and gold *fleur-de-lys*-shaped paper petals fell from the top of the arch. The choir roared out *La Marseillaise*. She advanced with Charles to the open area beyond the arch, turned, took Charles's hand and turned him to kiss her. Vandervell was signaling to go for it. As she met his lips, the jet fighters of La Patrouille de France flew in low from the Arc de Triomphe, trailing their tricolor smoke before climbing vertically in a starburst. Cannons fired a salute. The fountains of La Defense shot skyward. Martine took a shot with her cell phone of the kiss and posted it on Twitter. The music changed to Zaz singing *Paris Sera Toujours Paris*. A big red Paris tour bus pulled up. Sophia boarded and climbed the stairs behind Charles. She knew it was a terrorist's dream of a target. Martine joined them with other ministers of the Patriotic Front.

"The queen of England has a golden carriage and she is the queen of her people. You are the people's queen," said Martine.

"We're probably not safe here," said Sophia.

"You're right. Sometimes you have to show you're not afraid. We always ask that of our people," said Charles.

"Kismet," said Martine.

"That's what Nelson said when the French killed him at Trafalgar," said Sophia.

"And he's your greatest immortal hero. What sort of job opportunity do you want?" said Martine.

Sophia laughed.

"You're right. What will be will be."

"Where did you get your words for the ceremony?" said Martine.

"I borrowed the first bit from what Marianne said and the other bit from some school homework I did for Izzy. I think I got eight out of ten."

Charles was quiet, waving to the crowds as the bus pulled away.

"You did it, Your Majesty," she said kissing his cheek.

"Yes, I believe we can make it worth it. Now we stand on the summit and I guess from here you can see all the steps you took to get here and all those who fell."

"Oh Charles—your sister."

"Yes, I always knew that I'd just buried all that, probably buried it under my own fear. It was my fault that it happened. She was just a kid at a friend's birthday party for Christ's sake. How she would have loved to have been a princess today."

They needed to explore his grief. But not now. Not yet. She had her own stuff to dig up.

"Don't twist the knife in your own wound, my man. It's not about us today. It's about what we can do for these men and women standing for hours just to see us go by. We've had no time alone. Let's do this and then level the field ready for the rest of our lives."

He smiled and took her in his arms.

"You're more a natural queen than ever I'll be a king."

"And just think, I always said I'd never take another job in uniform."

CHAPTER 59

The bus tour swept them around the closed roads of central Paris. Every pavement and every window was filled with waving flags and smiling faces. A military Aérospatiale Puma chopper was waiting on le Champ de Mars to hop them to the Palace of Versailles. As they landed, the first limousines of the world's élites were arriving. Musicians in regal uniforms started up a fanfare. Two white Citroen C4 Grand Picassos were making their way up the access road. Martine glanced at Sophia and motioned them to go inside.

"You guys need to be ready to meet and greet," she said.

Sophia glanced back at Martine. She was unusually tense. Something wasn't right. The white Citroens were close. It looked like the white dressed *Rex Factor* girls from the ceremony were the only passengers. Martine frowned and gave her a firm shooing gesture. Sophia had a light bulb moment. Maybe Esmeralda and Nathalie were among them. Just who the hell had planned this? It was a girl thing but she couldn't wait to find out what was going on. She was *not* looking for a beauty queen cat fight.

The rest was an endless hedgerow of faces, some thorny, some sweet, some in bloom, some withered. Ahead of her she saw Tsar Viktor Pinupskin in his gorgeous KGB Field Marshal uniform. She hoped he spoke some English. She gave a slight bow which he returned with a smile.

"You are very beautiful, Your Majesty."

"Thank you, your Imperial Majesty."

"Now it can be Viktor," he said. "Your dossier shows you and me have both been humble cops."

She noted the subtle menace in the mention of a KGB dossier.

"I didn't need a dossier on you Viktor, Charles got me your calendar."

Tsar Pinupskin drew himself up and pulled in his belly.

"And what did you think of it?"

"Not bad at all, Viktor. I go for the younger man myself but I know Martine's got her own secret copy. Could you join us with a few top people for a private drink later?"

"I will bring proper vodka," said Pinupskin with a broad grin.

She hardly ate. Her face hurt from smiling. The exhaustion from lack of sleep blended with the endless fatigue of trying to understand what people were saying. Now she knew how it must be for the deaf. If these last weeks had taught her anything it was that human experience is a crash course in compassion. Salvers of food came and went. Guests were throwing back the finest of wines and becoming loud and expansive. Dishes were being cleared and people were stretching their legs and mingling. Martine caught her eye, waving from a distance. Sophia gave Charles a kiss while he was in deep discussion with the president of the European commission. She went to join Martine.

"I'm exhausted," said Sophia.

"We need to talk."

Her manner was strained and not at all her normal calmness. Sophia's heart was beating hard. Something was coming. They walked to a grand side room and sat down opposite each other on beautifully embroidered Louis Sixteenth chairs.

"Sophia, I need you to understand how things were before you came into our lives. The Caesar Roboris guys had found and groomed Charles. They had approached me to help them create a new world of nations to fight this awful annihilation of our homelands by the globalists, the bankers and the grey controllers. They hired Mason Trowel and Vandervell O'Brien to turn the twisted face of politics into the flawless smile of show biz. They found this book by Oscar Sparrow buried on Amazon, they created the Boymondo band to get Charles famous. They made the TV series *Born to be King*. And it worked. Against all the odds it worked. France was fragmenting into regional groups and tribes. Your Great Britain had already split apart. The new monarchy pulled us together, whatever your faith or origins."

"Yeah, that's how it was. So?"

"So Charles crumbled. He saw the job and the weight of that bloody crown on his head. He was a kid, a kid dreaming of being a priest for Christ's sake. He freaked out and ran away home to find his mum and dad to tell them that the nasty world was being cruel to him," said Martine.

Sophia felt a surge of loyalty akin to anger.

"Come on Martine, be fair. Anyone would have run away from that if they'd had no experience in life."

"You're right, I shouldn't judge him like that. Since you came he's proved himself more than anyone could have asked. I'm sorry the way I said that."

"Oh Martine, I understand. I've had scared kids on my team in the police and I know the way you felt."

"In those early days there was a group planning a military coup, the Napoléon Brotherhood. You remember all that?"

"Yes, they lured Charles to London to kidnap him and then pin the blame on the Intellos to get you to lock them up. Once you did that they'd have deposed you in order to save democracy and the Intellos."

"Exactly. When some reckless cop planted a police van in the middle of their kidnap, one soldier panicked and opened fire. If they'd been arrested the whole plan would have crumbled. Here's the sad truth—they didn't know British cops weren't armed. The young guy expected a gun battle and that he had no choice."

"But they killed his sister," said Sophia.

Martine was in tears, shaking her head. Sophia kept her distance while she composed herself and took a deep breath.

"It's not your fault," said Sophia.

"You don't understand. You're going to hate me and I hate myself in some ways."

"Tell me!"

"OK, Bastian was working with us, even though he was hired by Caesar Roboris. He's a ruthless operator and you know how much he did for us. He wanted to bring Charles under control and convince him that our enemies would kill him anyway. He knew that the news of his sister's death would show him how reckless he'd been by running away."

"Bastian killed her?"

"No one killed her. She was in one of those white cars. She was at the coronation and she's here now. Charles's family have been under close guard, completely underground. I couldn't deny them the chance to be here today. Please forgive me," said Martine.

Sophia couldn't stop staring at her.

"And you knew the truth?"

"Yes. Mel knew and I knew. Mel was against it; completely against it. For once in my life I hesitated because I believed it would force Charles to behave. I was gambling everything on this scheme. I agreed to the deception and once I'd told the lie I couldn't go back. Then everything changed."

"How?"

"Charles came back from London a different man. He was devastated by the loss of his sister but he was also convinced that an angel had come to him. He knew your name and begged us to bring you over. You know he believes that God has called him."

Sophia was shaking her head. Desperately she was trying to think how she would have reacted to Bastian's cruel plan.

"Martine, I understand what you did and why. You've survived attacks, you've re-written the politics of the world. If you'd told him he would never have trusted you again and he wouldn't have had the maturity to see it through your eyes."

"Oh Sophia, thank you, thank you. I needed you to understand. We didn't know you would come and give him his strength."

"Strategic liar is just a slightly higher term for detective Martine and usually you don't have to care when the guy finds out," she said. "You've saved yourself and warmed my heart by bringing that girl here today. Weren't you worried he'd spot her?"

"She knows the situation and was given detailed instructions. Your daughter Izzy and Selena Fontesse have been on guard and they've done a great job. I was so worried about how you would take this. Can you hold me, just for a minute," said Martine, kneeling in the space between them.

"Of course," said Sophia, kneeling with her and holding her. "I'm so proud just to know you. I'll tell Charles in the morning."

"Will you really do that for me?"

"Yes, and I know he'll understand. He's stronger now than then."

"We're all stronger with an angel," said Martine.

"I wish angels never cried and that I'd never said I would never say I loved you."

CHAPTER 60

It was 2 a.m. when the Paris night swallowed the last tail lights of limousines and the navigation lights of choppers. Martine had danced the last slow dance to Julien Clerc's *Fais Moi Une Place* with Tsar Viktor Pinupskin. His eyes had never left hers and they had parted with a short kiss—but a kiss all the same. Even as the music ended she clung to Charles, never wanting to break the spell.

"Viktor and Ronald are staying on for an extra day. We're going to chat at the Élysée Palace tomorrow over aperitifs. Viktor's bringing special vodka and Ron's bringing Bourbon. Can you guys make it?" asked Martine.

"If I can wake up in the morning," said Sophia.

"I'll call you. We've got some stuff to fix up."

Sophia knew exactly what she meant.

"I'll call you when I'm on top of things."

Charles embraced them both. Martine had decided to return to the Élysée for an early meeting with her top ministers. At last they were alone, except for half a dozen bodyguards, a platoon of paratroopers and a range of valets, maids, and footmen. She knew that this was as alone as she would ever be in her life. At last just she and Charles closed the door on the bedroom of the royal suite.

"We're exhausted," she said.

"I'm OK to adore you as mine. You've been in my dreams every night so it won't matter if we fall asleep," he said.

She slipped out of her dress and showered with Charles, the beauty of his young lithe body beginning to arouse her. He was a good four inches taller, his dark wavy hair slicked by the water. He kissed her and brought his hand to her groin, teasing out a ping of pleasure. She closed her eyes and imagined the day washing away from her, leaving nothing but a growing warmth like sunlight lifting the mist in a landscape. Here there were no ranks of being, no pomp, no obligation, no lies. Here was merely a wordless creature focused on its own body. When he lay beside her he had become the lover, the student of foreplay, erecting the scaffolding around the structure of her orgasm. As his tongue and lips hit her sweet spot she was gripping his hair, growling her need for release. In her fatigue she let him control her, bring her off again, opening herself to the imperative of his possession. He filled her, his hot flesh pressing on some helpless spot that sought his seed. She needed him in turn to submit to her possession of him. She gripped his hard young body as he grunted out his climax, trembling and thrusting to the apex of her belly. She was the deep well of his need and ecstasy. He would long for the gift of woman she held out to him.

"You're quite a lover, Your Majesty and a good, gorgeous guy."

"I could never have thought of an angel as, you know, sexy."

"That's either because I'm not an angel or the books in the seminary are wrong about sex, angels, or both."

He lay back and sighed.

"I'm so, so happy, Sophia."

"Me too. We've not talked and we're so tired. You saw all that stuff in that magazine?" she said.

"Yes, and that's all I want to say. Just love me and be at my side. I'll make a deal with you. Don't ask what a mob of young guys go through in their struggle with celibacy. A king must understand this life, its imperfection, and the tidal pull of desire at the soul. Human love will find its expression somewhere. The weak spot in the pipe will leak, the grain will find the missed stitch in the sack."

"I know what you're saying and it's another reason to love you."

"I simply and utterly love you, Sophia. An element of that is sexual but there is so much more. I heard you once talking in England. You said that the big people in your life don't give you instructions, they give you permissions," he said.

"And you permit me to love your courageous gentle heart?"

"Please love what you see in me today and try to love me for the man I try to be."

"I love you Charles, without any conditions."

She slept in his arms. She loved the confident unhidden perfection of his unscarred, unblemished body. How careless she had been with her own youth, how little time she'd spent in the gallery of framed beauty that is the crumbling canvas of youth. She'd married at twenty, her man just a twenty-one- year-old gym-pumped cop with the heart of a lion and the rampant fertility of a bull. He'd been a sculpture in his own mind yet he'd wrapped her in his strength and ham-fisted adoration. It had been a joy to swim in that protected lagoon of his tireless beach patrol. And yet still she had sunk and drowned while he had paced the shore calling for her, calling for her in tears. The dream was fading. They had not drawn the curtains and the impatient schoolyard of light was crowding at the window. She got up naked and looked out at the view of fountains and manicured hedges. She realized that the room was warm and that she had no care as to the cost. A month ago she'd have been checking the credit on her card to see if she could heat her flat until payday. Charles was stirring.

"How the hell do we get a coffee or tea?"

"We drive to the town for a McBreakfast," he mumbled.

"Why don't we?" she said, quite thrilled by the idea.

"Because we'd cause endless shit for all the poor bastards who'd have to get up and guard us."

Sure, this was her life now. She went to a table and lifted a phone.

"Hi, this is Sophia, I'd love a nice strong cup of tea and a coffee for Charles, I expect."

"*J'arrive*," said a male voice.

She assumed she'd fixed it. She'd been glad to start the day with such trivia as if to re-make their contact on an everyday street. She looked at his fantasy pop star almost androgynous face. How many adolescent girls had fumbled the key into the lock of their ecstasy with his beautiful lips pressed to theirs? She remembered her own moment with—well, Madonna would never have to know. She'd gotten over it.

There was a knock. Sophia dived into bed as a nervous young maid in uniform brought in a tray. This life was surreal. Sophia poured tea and coffee.

"Charles, drink some coffee and then we've got to talk. There's something I've got to tell you. It's not bad at all but it's going to take the wisdom of a king to follow it."

"Not too many other kings in this room," he said.

She didn't want to tease around the subject, yet she wanted to prepare him.

"You'd never spoken about your sister until yesterday on the bus. You've never told me her name and I've never asked because her name wrapped your protected parcel of grief."

"Catherine."

"I wanted to know her name because I want to talk about her in this world, in this life. I want to talk about her as a living person," she said watching his face. She could see he wanted to stop her, not sell him a dream that he couldn't hold in the light of day. "Catherine is alive. She was at the coronation yesterday."

"Sophia—no, don't say something spiritual to soften the tragedy of it. Yes, her soul was there in my heart, I know you're trying to give me your words as a kindness because you love me and I love you for that."

"Charles, they lied to you. You escaped from Château Roche Courbon and got to London. Bastian wanted to make sure you didn't try a stunt like that again. He wanted you to feel you'd caused it by your stupidity. He wanted you to see that there were merciless killers outside the bubble of boy band fame and a TV show king. And Charles, we know he was right."

He was staring at her.

"I know you wouldn't say this to me if you didn't think you were right. Forgive me I just can't grip what you're saying."

"Catherine was one of the girls in the white dresses at La Defense. Martine knew what had happened and couldn't maintain the deceit. It was Bastian's plan and only Mel and Martine knew about it. Mel was against it but had to follow orders. Martine saw the pragmatic sense of it but loathed the cruelty. Once you start with a lie...."

"When did you know?"

"Last night, while you were talking to the chief of the European Commission. Martine told me and I agreed to tell you."

"Have you seen Catherine?"

"No, I guess I could have done but I didn't want to steal any of that moment from you."

He got up, hands clasped together and went to the window. She let him think uninterrupted. She called Martine.

"OK, it's good. Charles is fine."

"Get yourself decent and stay in your room. This shouldn't be a big production number in my view," said Martine.

"*Absolument d'accord,*" said Sophia deliberately trying to normalize events with a banal language sortie.

"About 20 minutes I guess, there'll be a knock."

CHAPTER 61

Some selfish devil in her held back news of the arrangement. She told herself he'd only be tense if he knew.

"Things are being organized. Martine will call me a bit later," she said. "Just think, Catherine will have a Hollywood star step-sister."

"You mean it, don't you? It's real isn't it?" he said, his eyes searching hers for the truth.

"It's real, we'd better get ready for when she calls."

"Where are we going?"

"Don't know yet. I also don't know anything about where your parents are."

Charles was pacing up and down, still naked.

"To be honest I ducked out of even trying to face them. They would have known everything was my fault and what excuse could I have?"

"You'll have no excuse for anything if you don't put on some clothes."

"Yes, Mum," he said with a laugh. "You know until a minute ago I wouldn't have been able to say any word like mum or dad because everything would have flooded back." She saw him wipe his cheek and went to hold him.

"Now you shouldn't do this with your mum," she said.

He dressed in a blue suit with a blue and gold *fleur-de-lys*-patterned tie. He looked a dish and a half. How the hell had she ended up married to this hunk? How the hell could she deserve him? She wore a classic Chanel knee-length cream dress with a jacket.

There was a knock at the door.

"They'll want the tea and coffee stuff," she said, moving deeper into the room to give him a clear view of the door.

"*Entrez*," he said.

A gap opened slowly, timidly. At last framed in the doorway, hand in hand were Izzy and a black-haired younger girl. She watched Charles's face as she ran at him.

"*Charles! T'es vraiment le roi,*" she said.

"I don't believe it. I don't believe it," he said.

Sophia held out her arms to Izzy who sprinted into a hug.

"Have you been the mother superior?" asked Sophia.

"No worries, Catherine's so cool. She didn't know that they'd lied to Charles. They just bundled her up with her mum and dad and hid them in some place called Fleetwood in the north of England."

"Fleetwood?"

"M.I.6 have got a safe house there," said Izzy.

"We didn't know about what they told Charles. The gunmen sent us all upstairs in that house in London and they waited for Charles. When he turned up everything happened and they took him away. Some agents took us to the north and told us not to contact him for the sake of everyone's safety," said Catherine.

"Dear Lord, then I rolled in to the story."

"You're very beautiful. The papers call you the queen of royals. You're so kind of noble."

"You mean I've got a big beak," said Sophia with a laugh and hugging her. "And where are your parents?"

"They fly in today," said Catherine.

"Martine was worried about their security. She still is," said Izzy.

"We mustn't get careless. Terrorism from some quarter is a fact of all our lives," said Charles.

"Can a queen get some tea and toast?"

"Let's explore," said Izzy.

They stepped out. Gendarmes escorted them.

"Izzy's kissed Liam Hemsworth," said Catherine to Charles.

"And I've kissed the queen of France. Just hold on to your kisses for a while yet, little sister. There's wolves in the forest."

Martine travelled out from Paris for what she described as a working lunch briefing. She plonked down a *saucisson sec*, a fresh baguette, and some apples. She addressed Charles head on.

"Whatever you could say to me, I accept because you have that right, Charles."

"You know, Martine, I'm tempted to say you're a heartless, ruthless bitch, and on one level you are. The psychology of a human is a high-rise building with stairs and several lifts stopping on several floors every second of life. You think for instance there's a floor for love and a floor for jealousy but it's one floor with many ways in," he said.

Martine nodded with a glance at Sophia.

"You should be a king."

"And you Madame Machiavelli should be president of France. If I search my own heart and don't spare myself the memory of my weakness before Sophia came, I know why you did it. I guess it worked. You've softened my feelings by your kindness in the end."

"And how do you feel about Bastian? You risked your own life just to stop the soldiers from killing him," said Sophia.

Charles sighed and looked to heaven.

"You remember the night we dragged Martine out of the World Bank to trick Major Barrois and the Napoléon Brotherhood?"

"Yes, you came back to save me."

"Bastian's fearlessness and the knowledge of what he would have expected of me was my courage that night. I was a trembling bloody kid. He's a mercenary and I accept this world creates such men. He needs either the love of a woman or a better master."

"I'm glad you see it that way Charles. I want a head of security and I want that man's first assignment to be care of your parents. I want Bastian absolutely on our side. Would you accept that?"

Charles smiled.

"He's ruthless and fearless. I wouldn't forgive myself for choosing anyone else."

"There's an armored limo outside with a driver and security staff. Maybe you'd like to meet your parents from their plane?"

"Of course. And Bastian is out there?"

"Yes."

"Then I have the courage of ten men," he said with a smile.

"Your courage the other night impressed him more than you can imagine. He respects you as a brother and a friend, Charles. He would never tell you that," said Martine.

"I'm so proud of you," said Sophia, going to Charles and hugging him.

"God, you bloody women are so soft," he said with a laugh.

"They're coming in on my presidential plane to Vélizy—Villacoublay. You'd better get going. If I may I'd like to chat to Sophia about our tête à tête with Pinupskin and Grump tonight and you'll have some private time with your folks."

Charles chuckled. "I'll gladly leave those guys to you girls. I think the tsar was hoping for an invitation upstairs last night, Martine."

"He'll have to import a few megatons of Brie and get the Russian nation onto brandy to get a sniff," she replied with a smile.

The two women stood at the enormous window as Charles went out to the Mercedes XLS 500 limo. Bastian stepped out in a dark suit and dark glasses looking every inch the agent. The men embraced.

"Brotherly love," commented Martine with a smile on her lips. "Let's grab some coffee and relax. I'll share everything I know. They'll be gone for an hour or so."

"You should make more time for yourself," said Sophia, reaching out and running her fingers back through Martine's hair.

Charles, his parents, Catherine, and Izzy stayed at Versailles while Martine and Sophia headed back to Paris in the limo for the informal Russian-American summit. Martine sighed softly.

"The queen and the lady president would be quite a story," she said.

"It is and will be quite a story," said Sophia leaning back and smiling warmly at her. "But will anyone believe it?"

"A world believes that Charles the First of England escaped the executioner and made a secret baby," said Martine.

"Belief is the messenger dove of love itself so who are we to argue?" said Sophia Castellana, queen of France.

EPILOGUE

Dawn climbing cobbled streets, a sparrow seeking croissant crumbs under coffee-scented café awnings. The scrape of *tables de terrasse*, the sound perspective of a distant motor scooter, the whack of wooden crates by gourmet bins at back-door kitchen footnotes to romance by cuisine. Monmartre, a spring morning bounding up steps in the tireless joy of youth to the basilica of Sacré Coeur, glinting in the horizon sun like a diamond ring raised on the finger of its bride—Paris.

Three months had passed. How much the wider world had changed. China had a new emperor, Germany a kaiser, India a mogul, Turkey a sultan, and on and on. A lonely warrior woman had raised a flag into the breeze of possibility and the sham of slick glass and concrete politics had fallen like ramshackle huts into the inevitability of a hurricane named Identity.

This Paris morning the new world order assembled at Sacré Coeur for the blessing by the Pope of the union of Charles the Eleventh of France and his English bride, Queen Sophia. Crowds lined the streets, a world had stopped to gasp. A queen in the ripe summer of her bloom on the same branch as the eager bud of her king stood together with him before God and their people. The royal princesses Catherine and Izzy sucked the frenzied lenses of the camerazzi to their faces and souls. On the steps, looking out on the vista of Paris, Sophia kissed her man as a framed picture for the world.

"Is it enough to say I love you?" he asked.

She smiled and drew his hand to rest beneath her breasts.

"No, I want you to say you love all three of me."

FIN

A Message From Emma

Hello,

Thank you for reading '*Crowns*' I hope you enjoyed it!

Please would you help me?

If you liked the book you've just read, I'd be forever grateful if you'd consider posting a short review. As an independent writer you guys really matter to me. It's very difficult for small authors to get visibility in the huge publishing machine, since we don't have the influence or advertising budgets of traditional publishers. Your review will give me a positive push and help other readers find a book they would enjoy.

Nothing long or complex is needed—just a sentence or two about what you enjoyed about the book.

Review Link: http://www.smarturl.it/CrownReview

Why not discover the stories behind both Anna La Salle and Shannon Aguerri in the first two novels: *Combat* and *Dynasty* too? Check out the next section for links to other books in the Passion Patrol Series as well as a **free book** if you join my mailing list.

Many thanks for your interest in my stories.
Emma x

A FREE book for you...

FREE DOWNLOAD

Meet the Passion Patrol Team

**Get this full-length
suspense romance novel**

FREE

**when you line up with
The Passion Patrol**

**...Join Emma Calin's
VIP Reader Club**

*"Emma Calin has written another
gripping romantic suspense
with plenty of both."*
P. Rees-Rohrbacker

Get My Free Book

If you enjoy my books, keep up to date with new releases, special offers and exclusive opportunities. As a valued reader, I'll send you a FREE e-book from my bookshelf. I email out a few newsletters each month with news snippets and background info to my stories, as well as sharing any bargains. Don't worry I will not bombard you! You may of course unsubscribe at any time.

Link: http://www.smarturl.it/LeadFromCrowns

Or scan the QR code:

Other titles by Emma Calin:
Passion Patrol Series Box Set 1

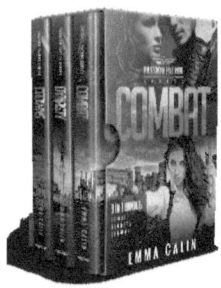

Grab the first three books in the *Passion Patrol Series* PLUS the companion cookbook to the second in the series in one **bargain** bundle. Titles included: *Combat, Dynasty, Seduction of Taste* and *Crowns*.

http://www.smarturl.it/webbox1

Or if you prefer to buy each ***Passion Patrol*** title individually…

Guilt, Combat, Crowns, Santa, Wealth, Power

Seduction of Taste

Seduction of Dynasty Plus (2-book bundle)

Coming in 2019: Desire

Combat

An early title in the *Passion Patrol Series.'*

Interpol cop, Anna Leyton, spirals down into a hopeless vortex of sexual and emotional passion as she fights to keep her professional cool. Who is deceiving whom in this fast-moving ride across continents? What motivates her art-loving prize bull of a lover, Freddie La Salle? The power of love and trust stands against greed and crime as conflicting forces grapple for that knockout punch.

A romance novel with a twist of suspense that will take you on a roller-coaster ride of passion, deception and love.

Link: http://www.smarturl.it/webcombat

Or scan QR code:

Dynasty

A sexy aristocrat. A wild-child inner city cop. A crime wave of passion.

(Previously published as *Passion Patrol 2 -Shannon's Law*)

http://www.smarturl.it/webdynasty

Blurb:

A steamy romance novel introducing a sassy female police officer who locks up criminals and always gets her man.

The second book in the *Seduction* series featuring hot cops, hot crime, and hot romance. Following the success of *Seduction of Combat,* the drama in this novel revolves around another feisty female cop—Shannon Aguerri.

Moved out from the city after one-too-many maverick missions, Shannon discovers there's more going on in the sleepy country village than meets the eye. The son of a local aristocrat arouses suspicion of drug crime activity... but his widower father arouses more animal instincts!

Could she really mix with the British Royal Family? Can she risk her heart and career on yet another high-risk unauthorized investigation? Can she get justice for an innocent boy? Dare a kid from the gutter dream of being a countess?

Wild child inner city cop Shannon Aguerri walks a dangerous line between her methods and justice. When the bosses lose their nerve, she is transferred to green pastures to play out the role of a routine village cop. In Fleetworth-Green she encounters signs of people and drug trafficking and homes-in on serious millionaire criminals. As a loner she has attracted men but nothing has stuck. When she meets Spencer, the hunky and widowed Earl of Bloxington, there is an immediate rapport between them. Their social differences mean nothing to their passion and need. Already in the mix is an upper-class female rival who has long plotted her way into the earl's bed. The jealousy is an evil shade of green and the anger is a violent scarlet.

Often inhibited by a sense of duty and honour, Spencer is slow to reveal his feelings. When Shannon confronts him with the need to choose between her word and that of her rival, he does not immediately support her. All the same, when they are forced together to carry out a desperate rescue mission, their love is stronger than everything ranged against them.

Please note: This book contains joyful sex between adults in a consenting relationship. There is also strong language in high-stress police confrontations with criminals.

http://smarturl.it/webdynasty

Seduction of Taste

Hot Cops. Hot Crime. Hot Romance..... Hot Food?

http://www.smarturl.it/CopsKitchen

Seduction of Taste is the companion cookbook to the hot romance novel that you've just read, *Seduction of Dynasty*.

A total of thirty-one recipes from appetizers and main courses to suggestions for sandwich fillings at a traditional afternoon tea. Late night suppers and romantic meals for two.

Food is the music of love. It sets the tone and the pace. It provides those moments when tastes and textures shared at the table form a metaphor for the physical appetites of love and lust.

As tough girl cop Shannon Aguerri abandons herself to love with a sexy aristocrat, many meals are shared. From the finest cuisine fit for royals, to the big power passion patrol fuel served in police canteens, *Seduction of Taste* gives you the recipes. You won't want to put the novel down. With the cookbook you can tickle your taste buds as Emma Calin's full on total romance tickles your mind. If it touches the lovers' lips in the story, you can experience that moment with a meal cooked for your own special lover, be they a cool cucumber or a passionate pepper.

Read the romance, feel the passion, taste the love!

Or, grab the bumper gourmet edition—with both the story and recipe books combined and linked – *Seduction of Dynasty Plus*

Santa

Santa – a Passion Patrol suspense romance from Emma Calin, his time with a holiday twist. I wonder what this naughty Santa has in his sack for our intrepid community cop, Paula?

http://www.smarturl.it/santa

Wealth

Masked gunmen strike an exclusive sports car.

Police pursuit interceptor Kaitlyn Thorn takes control.

She snaps the cuffs on the driver, gorgeous cocky Randolph Quinn, the world's richest banker. He doesn't make small talk but he wants to make love.

Sackman-Platinum bank launder the dirty sheets of the underworld. They know where the bodies are buried. As Kaitlyn throws off all sexual chains, she surrenders to pleasure, wealth and intrigue with Randolph.

Police chiefs let her run, encouraging her wild erotic passion for her man and money. In London, Paris, Milan and New York, Kaitlyn exposes herself to a wild trail of evil and greed.

Is everything what it seems?

Could lust, riches and sexual pleasure hide a simple heart in love?

http://www.smarturl.it/webwealth

Power

A thug pulls a knife on a mean London street. Police constable Olivia Johnston-Denny faces him down. A regular day. When irresistible American congressman Jackson T Paine intervenes, her life is changed forever. A spark of attraction starts an inferno of erotic heat.

In a world of bitter political division and deceit, this one man offers straightforward country-style honesty. Tipped as a future president, ruthless opponents plot his downfall, by smear or by death. Olivia and Jackson cannot risk involvement but forces of emotion and passion run out of control.

A merciless kidnap and gangster style international bankers fill Olivia's working days. Only in the shadows can she express her love for Jackson.

When her professional investigations lead to her lover's door she stands at a dark abyss. Is he everything he seems?

She has to know the truth as a cop and as a woman in love.

http://www.smarturl.it/webpower

Sub-Prime (#1 The Love in a Hopeless Place Collection)

Two powerless beings are swept together in a transient struggle for survival. Could the human spirit transcend the brutality and indifference of their brief experience before they are once again swept helplessly apart? Far more than a love story—this is a story about love

Sub-Prime: a short story of our times.

Available as an e-book (For Kindle and Kindle Apps for iPad, Android, PC MAC etc) at Amazon worldwide:

http://smarturl.it/Sub-Prime

The Chosen (#2 The Love in a Hopeless Place Collection)

A woman, a man, a van, and a plan. When the luck runs out; the lucky walk away. A short story set in the extremis of everyday.

Available as an e-book (For Kindle and Kindle Apps for iPad, Android, PC MAC etc) at Amazon worldwide on the following link:

https://www.emmacalin.com/ChosenThe

Escape to Love (#3 The Love in a Hopeless Place Collection)

A woman on the run from domestic violence with no one but her vulnerable autistic teenage child as a companion lives in isolation and fear. While her hand-to-mouth scenarios are played out in the shadow of a threatening suspense, a story of crime and love unfolds around her.

Angela (#4 The Love in a Hopeless Place Collection)

A mystery tale of a late-night taxi ride where the final passenger may not be all that she seems.

http://www.smarturl.it/shortAngela

Love in a Hopeless Place (#5 The Love in a Hopeless Place Collection)

A mature woman finds the truth of herself. She cannot go back even though physical and emotional violence erupt around her.

Dare she give in to love?

Will sexual passion and fear overwhelm her stable life?

Whom can she trust to love her for herself?

http://www.smarturl.it/LIAHP

The Love in a Hopeless Place Collection

Emma Calin's complete set of short stories and novelettes, available in one bargain "boxed set." This edition includes *Sub-Prime*, *The Chosen*, *Escape To Love*, *Love In A Hopeless Place* and short story: *Angela*. It is available as a paperback and e-book from Amazon Worldwide.

http://www.smarturl/it/LIAHPCollection

Children's Books by Emma Calin

The "Once Upon a NOW!" Series

The *"Once Upon a NOW!"* books form a series of illustrated, interactive children's stories, in the true fairy tale tradition with modern-day settings. Each is available in paperback, Kindle, and audio book formats. Digital versions come with clickable links to bonus video clips, photos, and drawings to color. The paperback has QR codes to scan and take you to the same bonus material to enrich the stories.

http://smarturl.it/OUANAmazon

Coming soon... The complete Box Set of all three books in the "***Once Upon a Now Series***" for Kindle. Grab this bargain bundle here:

http://www.smarturl.it/OUANBoxed

Alf The Workshop Dog

How could a scruffy dog in a bus depot, and the call of crows link back to another world of power and love? The ancient Kingdom of Zanubia and a stray dog looking for scraps in an inner-city repair garage, hold the secret. A wicked king, a beautiful girl, a young prince and the struggle between right and wrong maintain the fable tradition.

http://www.smarturl.it/Alf

Isabella's Pink Bicycle

There's something strange in the woodshed....

A poor little girl in a faraway land dreams of riding a pink bicycle. When she meets a strange animal, her dreams come true. Her happiness turns to sadness when a tragedy occurs in the town and her father doesn't come home. Maybe her new magic friend can find him?

http://www.smarturl.it/IsabellaPink

Kool Kid Kruncha and the High Trapeze

Charlie finds it tough when his parents divorce, but Auntie Kate helps him overcome his greatest fear.

When Charlie has to move from the country into the city, he leaves behind his home, his mates, and his beloved football team. He will need to make new friends. With his small size and red hair, some people aren't kind to him. He wonders if he can face another day at school.

A trip to the circus gives him the strength to see himself and others in a new way.

http://www.smarturl.it/Kruncha

About Emma Calin

Novelist, philosopher, blogger, poet, would be master chef. A woman pedaling between Peckham & Pigalle, in search of passion & enduring romance.

Emma Calin writes romance novels, gritty short stories and children's fiction about love and survival in the 21st century. She has published a number of digital, paperback, and audio books which are available from Amazon and other good bookstores worldwide.

She blogs about her dual life in St-Savinien sur Charente in Southwest France and Romsey, a market town in southern England. She feels extremely lucky to be able to experience the world and life through these two very different lenses. She spends any time she can, when not writing, on her tandem exploring the countryside.

Emma also records and produces audio books and plays the trombone (although not at the same time).

Find Emma Calin on the Internet:

Website: http://www.emmacalin.com

Blog: http://emmacalinblog.com/

Twitter: http://twitter.com/EmmaCalin

Facebook: http://www.facebook.com/emma.calin

Facebook Fan Page:
http://www.facebook.com/Knockout.Romance.Novel

Goodreads:
http://www.goodreads.com/author/show/4915751.Emma_Calin

Amazon Author Page: http://smarturl.it/EmmaAmazonWorldwide

Publisher

This book was published by Gallo-Romano Media. For details of other books and authors or if you would like to submit your book for publishing:

Email: contact@gallo-romano.co.uk

Web: http://www.gallo-romano.com

www.ingramcontent.com/pod-product-compliance
Lightning Source LLC
Chambersburg PA
CBHW020232260626
47156CB00002B/647